All Her Broken Pieces

THE BROKEN SERIES

MYA MORE

MORE LOVE ~ MORE SPICE ~ MORE HEAL

To all the black cats who wanted a good boy of their own.
Ethan's for you.

CONTENT WARNINGS

Mentions of anxiety and an on-page panic attack
Impact play (spanking)
Kink exploration
Mentions of cancer

Any scenes with kink depicted in this book are for entertainment purposes and are not intended to be educational or accurate depictions of a BDSM lifestyle. Please do your research before engaging in similar acts to make sure you are your partner(s) are informed and safe.

Please take this into consideration before reading. Your mental health matters.

Author's Note

This series contains a sex club named Pulse. I want to acknowledge that in 2016, a real nightclub named Pulse in Florida was the site of an unspeakable tragedy. While the Pulse in this story is entirely fictional and unrelated, I chose the name with care and intention. My hope is that this imagined space reflects the values the real Pulse came to represent: a place of safety, freedom, and inclusion. In this story, Pulse is a sanctuary where all people are welcome to explore their desires without fear, shame, or discrimination.

Dicktionary

For anyone wondering where the steamy scenes take place—
whether you're eager to dive right in or prefer to skip them
altogether—you'll find them in the following chapters:

Happy reading!

Next To Me—Nicotine Dolls
Out of My League—Fitz and The Tantrums
Can't Get You Out of My Head—Kylie Minogue
Certain Things—James Arthur
Broken Pieces Shine—Evanescence
Dangerous Hands—Austin Giorgio
I AM WOMAN—Emmy Meli
Adore You—Harry Styles
I Hope You're Happy—Blue October
I Can Do It With a Broken Heart—Taylor Swift
Hush—Angie Aparo
From Afar—Vance Joy
Voglia d'amare—Renato Zero
Wish You The Best—Lewis Capaldi
Say You Won't Let Go—James Arthur
We Can't Be Friends (wait for your love)—Ariana Grande
Broken Pieces (feat. Lacey)—Apocalyptica
Green Eyes—JOSEPH
No Such Thing—Sara Bareilles
Hands to Myself—Selena Gomez
Ordinary—Alex Warren

Contents

CHAPTER 1

Bridget

NUMBERS ARE EASY TO INTERPRET.

Numbers don't hide behind fancy words and pretty lies.

Numbers won't break my heart.

I treat men like a number. You, sir, are good for one night only. Good for two fingers of whiskey and a double orgasm. Ten inches is way too fucking many if I want to walk away with my cervix intact. I'll settle for a sixty-nine if he knows how to use his tongue.

Don't get me wrong, I enjoy the company of men—I just don't get emotions involved. I didn't get this far in life by letting feelings make my decisions. The right man can provide me with the release I need when my own hands and toys aren't enough, which is quite often lately. I might be open to the idea of a full-time fuck buddy, depending on his skills, but really, I just need something to get me through the next few weeks. Work is kicking my ass, causing my cortisol levels to fuck with my mood and sleep. As the CFO of a major supplement company, I'm responsible for making sure our finances are in order as we work to acquire a smaller brand.

Tonight, however, I'm only looking for a good time,

someone who will help me temporarily forget the weight on my shoulders. The pulsating bass reverberates through the club, each beat syncing with the erratic rhythm of colorful strobe lights. I sip my bourbon, the smoky flavor over-whelming my senses as Becka and I navigate through a throng of writhing young bodies on the dance floor. The air is thick with perfume, sweat, and anticipation, a heady mix that assaults my senses.

"Bridget, look at all these hot, young men!" Becka shouts over the music. "I think I have T-shirts older than most of the people in here."

"Damn, you need to get a new wardrobe if that's the case," I joke with a wink. Becka laughs, her eyes scanning the crowd as if searching for potential candidates for me. I know she's not looking for herself; I'm pretty sure her college sweetheart-turned-husband Robert would have a problem with that.

"Seriously, when did you become a cougar?"

"I'm just looking for a good time. I need to not think for a night, preferably while underneath a man who knows his way around the female anatomy," I admit, my words almost drowned out by the pounding beats.

"I'd bet a hundred bucks that most of this club has no clue what a cassette tape is, let alone how to use it, so good luck assuming they would know where the clit is. Why did I let you talk me into coming here? These aren't men, these are boys. Can we go somewhere else where I don't feel like the adultiest adult in the room?" Becka complains, her voice shouting above the music.

I'm so done with men my age. They're all either married, wanting to get married and start a family, divorced for good reason, or the weird leftovers you leave in your fridge for weeks and don't want to touch. "The younger they are, the longer the stamina."

"You're really committed to this whole 'no strings attached' thing, huh?"

I shoot her a defiant look as a man slides between us, grabbing my hips while pulling me into him to dance. "It's just a bit of fun. No complications, no heartbreak."

"What? I can barely hear you!" Becka cups her ear as the music swells in a crescendo.

"I need to get fucked!" I yell, and, of course, that's precisely when the DJ decides to change songs, allowing everyone around us to hear my candid admission, including the man grinding his pelvis on me. Becka shoots me a raised eyebrow, a mixture of concern and amusement in her eyes.

"I think I can help with that," the man croons into my ear as his fingers dig into my hips.

"Move along, Romeo!" Becka shoos my dance partner away and pulls me by the hand toward a booth in the back, away from the subwoofers and grinding bodies. She squeezes my hand, her concern evident. "Bridget, you deserve more than a temporary escape. I thought this was just a phase. You've never been in a serious relationship as long as I've known you, but I'm starting to think that you're deflecting a bigger issue."

"I'm fine," I say firmly, though the words feel hollow even to me. At this point, I'm not sure what it'll take to fix what's broken inside me.

Becka arches her eyebrow. "You're not, but I'll support you, even if it means navigating through a sea of boys who think Meat Loaf is just a dish their moms make them." She motions for me to lead the way back to the dance floor.

As we make our way through the pulsating crowd, my eyes stay fixed on the ground, watching my steps. I've had some near-misses in these heels before, and falling on my ass isn't an effective way to pick up a one-night stand.

"There's nowhere to fucking sit, bro. Wait, I think that booth is open." Those are the last words I hear before a hard body slams into me, knocking me sideways.

"Shit, Bridget!" Becka yelps as a strong arm encircles my

waist, catching me almost horizontally before righting me again.

"Careful there, Grace, we don't need you breaking anything." A pair of emerald eyes lock on mine as his lips pull into a crooked smile. His hand lingers on my waist, and my skin tingles on the spot before he lets me go, shoving his hands in his jeans pockets.

"My name isn't Grace," I snap back, my words sharper than intended. I pull at my dress, smoothing down the fabric.

"What, Grace isn't short for Graceful?"

I stare at him blankly.

"Sorry. It was my lame attempt at a joke." He runs his hand through his chestnut locks, pushing them back. A hint of something—embarrassment?—flushes his tan cheeks before the crooked smile returns, along with a single dimple.

"First, you knock me over, then you insult me with sarcastic nicknames. Your mom clearly raised a gentleman," I retort. Despite the irritation, I can't deny he's hot as fuck with that dimple, but I'll be damned if I let him know that. And I don't need rescuing, just a pair of shoes with a smaller heel.

His grin falters, and an emotion I can't quite place screws up his features briefly before the smile returns. "I didn't bump into you, that was my friend Alyx. He was in a rush to grab the booth behind you, but I apologize on his behalf. And I'm sorry for the joke. I was raised better, I promise. Can I buy you and your friend a drink to make it up to you?"

I glance at Alyx, happily planted in the booth. Hell, Alyx is cute too, with brown eyes, dark brown hair, and tawny-colored skin covered in tattoos. He flashes a panty-dropping smile before turning to flag down a server.

"I'm Ethan, by the way. Since we've established that you aren't Grace, do I get the pleasure of learning your actual name?"

"Her name's Bridget, and I'm Becka, and we'd love a drink," my traitorous friend pipes up. Great, now I need to add *find a new best friend* to my ever-growing to-do list. It's a shame. It took me years to break this one in.

"I have a good feeling about him," she whispers in my ear.

"It's nice to meet you both." Ethan smiles again, and that damn dimple makes another appearance. His smile is as smooth as his skin. He's got to be in his twenties, but it's hard to tell if it's early twenties or late because of the lighting in the club.

Becka turns toward the circular booth and slides in next to Alyx as I follow behind her. Ethan sits beside me, his arm resting on the back of the booth behind me. His clean scent fills my nostrils, and there's something familiar about it that I can't place.

The server comes by, and Ethan hands over his card to open a tab. Clearly, he's old enough to drink, so I'll call that a win. "What would you ladies like? It's on me."

"I'll take a gin and tonic, and Bridget will take a bourbon neat," Becka says.

"Put it on my tab," Alyx says to the server as he hands Ethan back his card. "It's the least I can do since I'm the ass who bumped into you and your pretty friend."

"Sorry to burst your bubble, but her pretty friend is only the wing-woman." Becka points at her wedding band.

"My bad. Can't blame me for trying, though," he says, batting his lashes.

"If this is your game, I have to admit it's not bad." I point at Alyx. "You bump into the target so your friend here can catch them as they fall and swoop in like Prince Charming."

"Shit, sorry. We've been circling like vultures all night, trying to find a table. My bad." His eyes look so sincere, and it's hard to believe either of them did anything intentional.

"Your game must be off if you're going to clubs only to sit down all night. We can get away with it because of our fashionable footwear choices. What's your excuse?" I ask.

"Feisty! I like it." Alyx flashes that grin again. "I've been trying to get my man Ethan here to come out with me, but it's like trying to bathe a stray cat who fights you at every turn."

Ethan and Alyx exchange glances, and I can tell they are having a telepathic conversation before Ethan chuckles and turns to me. "Alyx exaggerates. This isn't really my scene. I just prefer a quiet night in most nights."

"Or every night," Alyx mutters right as the server drops off our drinks.

I raise an eyebrow at Ethan. "A quiet night in, huh?"

"I find it hard to make a real connection in places like this," he confesses. "Everyone's too caught up in the chaos to appreciate the quiet moments."

I take a sip of bourbon, the liquid burning down my throat. The contrast between Ethan's preference for quiet nights and my intentional plunge into chaos isn't lost on me. He's the calm sea sailors crave while I'm the tempest stirring up wreckage in my wake.

"We're here to celebrate her birthday," Becka tells them. I groan internally. *Be cool, girl, don't scare them off too soon.*

Actually, this is good. If he's scared of my age, this won't work out anyway.

"Happy birthday," Ethan and Alyx chime in together, most likely out of obligation.

"Thanks. It was two days ago, but who goes out on a Wednesday night?" I swirl the remaining liquid in my glass.

"How many candles are we blowing out?" Alyx inquires. "Ouch!" He whines after Ethan kicks him under the table.

"It's not cool to ask people that, bro," Ethan mutters.

"It's fine. I turned thirty-eight."

"So other than a birthday, what brings you to the club tonight?" Ethan asks, inching closer to me so our thighs touch.

Giving him a once-over, I take a sip of my drink. "I'm interested in making a connection," I reply, lowering my eyelashes.

"They look pretty connected." Alyx points at a couple a

few booths over behind Ethan who are practically dry humping.

Ethan turns to look and then drops his head against his chest. "I don't think that's what she meant. What even is happening right now?"

"Well, when a man loves a woman…" Becka starts.

Alyx and I burst out laughing as Ethan's head shoots up.

"I knew you were our people." Alyx wipes tears from the corners of his eyes.

"So you did bump into me on purpose!" I accuse, as a grin forms on my lips.

"I really didn't, but I'm glad I ran into you, and I'm pretty sure he's glad I did too." He winks at Ethan and then turns to Becka. "As a fellow wing-person, would you do me the honor of accompanying me on the dance floor so our friends can make a 'better connection'?" He wiggles his eyebrows.

"Jesus, can you stop?" Ethan begs. Alyx is clearly the fuckboy while Ethan appears to have more of a quiet charm.

Alyx and Becka continue bantering as if we aren't here. "I'll dance with you if you keep your hands where I can see them and act as my buffer. I'm not here on the prowl."

"It would be an honor," Alyx says while extending his hand, though I swear I catch a hint of disappointment cross his face briefly. "Actually, you can be my wing-woman if you want."

"I think this could be the start of a very entertaining friendship," Becka tells him as they walk to the dance floor.

"Should I be worried about that? He'll keep his hands to himself, right?" I ask Ethan.

"Yeah, he's all flirt, but he's a good guy. He understands that no means no and will brother her."

"Brother her?"

"Act like a brother, watch out for her, not let anyone touch her."

"Ah, so he friend-zoned himself, just like that?"

"Just like that. He's honestly one of the best guys I know. His moms raised him to respect women. Trust me, they'd be mortified to know he knocked you over like that. It's not a scam we run, I promise."

"Mm-hmm. Is that why he left you so we could 'make a connection'?" I ask, using finger quotes to emphasize my point.

Realization dawns on his face as he looks back at the couple sucking face a few booths over. "That's not... What I mean is... Shit. I don't want to assume..."

Laughing, I place my hand on his muscular forearm. "I'm just teasing you."

"Sorry. I haven't really been in a good headspace lately, and Alyx's been begging me to come out for a while, but I'm not a fan of his aggressive meddling." He laughs nervously. "Let's try this again. So, Bridget, what brings you to a place like this tonight?" His gaze focused on me as the lighting casts a subtle glow on his features. He really is handsome.

"You're so bad at this." I lean back against the circular booth. "What if I'm just looking for the next shiny thing to distract me?" My words are light, casual, and deliberately vague as my hand runs up the corded muscle of his arm. There's no point getting attached. I don't let that happen.

His gaze meets mine, a subtle challenge lingering in his emerald eyes, and I can't ignore the eager look I find there. "I can think of many ways I could...distract you."

"How old are you?" I ask. Is he even old enough to ride this ride?

"Age is just a number."

"Oh, I'm really good at numbers."

Yeah, this is happening. I've read enough romance books to understand what's going on here. This man has serious Golden Retriever vibes, like he's eager to please. This pup may be just what I need tonight.

Ethan

"Do you wanna dance?" I ask as offer Bridget my hand. The heated look in her eyes as she takes it makes my cock twitch in my jeans. I've never gotten a semi from just a single look before. Damn. This girl may be trouble, but I'm here for it.

As she slides out of the booth, my eyes rake over the tight, black dress that accentuates all her curves. It hits mid-thigh, and her heels make her legs look like they go on for days. But it's the confidence with which she moves that I find most attractive. This woman knows what she wants, and I find strong women sexy as fuck.

Alyx assured me this was the most popular club in Columbus when he convinced me to come out tonight. He knows I've been in a funk for the past year since my Nonna died, and has been doing everything in his power to raise my spirits. This is more Alyx's scene than mine, though, and I'm tired of following him to clubs only to be ditched while he fucks his way through half the city. I usually prefer relation-ships over casual hookups, and while I've made a few connec-tions with women this past year, none have held my interest until tonight.

The dance floor is full of bodies, and we stay off to the side. Gripping her hips, I pull Bridget close to me. "Is this okay?" I whisper in her ear.

Her head falls back onto my shoulder. "Yes, but you can get closer, you know. I don't bite unless you want me to." She grinds her perfect ass into me, her brown hair falling in waves around her shoulders. That semi is at full mast now. If her words didn't do it, her sweet ass against me completed the job. She's confident, taking what she wants from me, then wrig-gling out of my hold as though our connection is fleeting.

We continue this game, her body pressed against mine, giving me just enough before moving, causing me to chase after her, desperate for a chance to hold on to her. After a while, I'm able to get her against a wall, boxing her in with my arms. She's all over me, running her hands up and down the muscles on my abs and chest, then she turns her back to me and straddles my leg while grinding on my thigh, pushing her ass against my erection as she snakes her hands around my neck. I cannot get enough of her body flush against mine. Never in my life have I wanted a woman more.

Bridget escapes my hold once again, and I spin to follow her, grabbing on to her waist to pull her against me as she twerks into my crotch while holding her knees. I lose control, digging my fingertips into her hips as my back hits the wall and then I spin us, so now her back is against the wall.

"You like that, Pup, don't you? I can feel how hard you are," she says peering up at me through her lashes.

Not sure why she's calling me pup, but I roll with it and place my hands on either side of her head as my hips move against her. "Know a quiet place we can go to—"

"Make a better connection?" she finishes my thought, and I briefly wonder if she's flirting or teasing. My earlier nerves are gone, my confidence growing as big as my erection.

"It's really not a line I use. You're just really fucking hot, and I'm finding it hard to keep my hands to myself when I'm around you." I need to kiss her more than I need my next breath.

"Then don't," she challenges, running her hands up my pecs and hooking a leg around my thigh. I stare down at her, pinning her to the wall with my hips. "Fucking kiss me already, Pup."

I grab her jaw and crash my lips down on hers. She opens for me, tangling her tongue with mine. She tastes sweet like berries and spicy like the bourbon she was drinking. Her hands continue to roam my body as she climbs me like a tree, wrapping her legs around my waist as if she can't get close enough to me.

I pull back, trying to catch my breath. "Fuck, Bridge. I knew you'd taste good."

She rears back suddenly, and her blue eyes burn holes into me. "Don't call me that. I don't do nicknames. Especially not that one."

"Okay," I drawl, feeling like I am corralling a skittish mare. "What do you want me to call you then?" I move my lips closer to her ear and run my tongue along the shell before nibbling on her lobe. "Sweetheart?"

"Fine. Just don't get too attached, Pup." She pants for breath and writhes against my boner as I lick down the column of her neck. "This is only for tonight."

"Got it." I suck and nip across her collarbone as she lets out a low moan.

"I mean it. I don't do complicated, and in my experience, more than once gets complicated."

"The only complications between us are the positions I want to put you in while you scream my name," I groan before sealing my mouth over hers again in a bruising kiss. I swear she's trying to show me that she's in control with the acrobatics of her tongue alone.

There's a tap on my shoulder, and I reluctantly pull my mouth from hers to see Alyx and Becka next to us, mouths agape.

"Damn, girl, you two are worse than that couple in the booth," Becka teases as Bridget shimmies down my body and returns to stand on her own. "You gonna be okay if I head out?"

"Yeah, I'm good. I think Ethan and I are going to head back to my place. Want to share a ride?"

Fuck yeah. Something about this woman intrigues me, and I want to spend more time getting to know her. And if I get a chance to find out how she sounds when she comes, even better.

"I'm headed out too, bro. I want to check out that new club

across town. Don't wait up for me." Alyx winks before side-hugging me with a slap on my back. "I already closed out our tab. Catch up tomorrow?"

"Sure thing, man. Be safe," I tell Alyx before pulling Bridget into my side and guiding us toward the exit with Becka close behind.

CHAPTER 2
Ethan

"LIKE I SAID EARLIER, this is only for tonight. No complications," she says as she unlocks the door to her apartment and lets me in. It's obvious from the interior that she does well for herself.

Floor-to-ceiling windows provide an amazing view of the city, but I barely have time to take in more before she shoves me against the wall and pulls my lips to hers. I'm groping her hips while licking along the spot on her collarbone that made her moan earlier and whispering, "It doesn't have to be complicated. Give me a chance to prove to you that you can trust me with your pleasure for more than one night."

The car ride over gave me some time to think and breathe. The pull I feel to this woman is unlike anything I've ever experienced. I couldn't keep my hands off her in the club, and I thought that would calm down with the car ride here. Even with Becka as our buffer, I couldn't stop touching her, stroking her arm, squeezing her thigh. I haven't felt this alive in years. She's awakened something in me, and if I'm certain of anything in my life, it's that one night with Bridget won't be enough.

"You talk a big game, but I rarely do repeats."

13

"Rarely isn't never, and I want more than one night with you. You're so fucking beautiful, sweetheart. I won't be able to walk away after one night."

She reaches for the hem of my shirt before pulling it up, and I help her take it off.

"Holy fuck, it's like somebody drew you. Do you live in a gym?"

"Not quite, but I do spend a good bit of time there."

As her eyes continue to peruse me, I reach for her waist, gliding up to the zipper on the back of her dress before tugging it down. It pools around her feet as my eyes rake up her body.

Long, toned legs with thick thighs.

Rounded hips that slope in to a smaller waist. So many soft curves, and I want to lick every inch of them.

The most incredible tits I've ever seen. More than a handful.

The perfect hourglass figure with enough curves to grab on to. This is the kind of body that has truly lived life, and I want to explore all of it.

"Goddamn, sweetheart, every inch of you is exquisite."

"Bedroom, now," she purrs. "Down the hall, on the left."

Her lips continue their assault on my neck as I lift her up and walk us down the hallway to the bedroom. I deposit her onto the cream-colored comforter, the air charged with sexual tension. She unhooks her bra and tosses it aside, then falls back onto the king-sized mattress.

I make quick work of removing my own clothing, leaving my black boxer briefs on as I kiss my way down her stomach. Hooking my fingers into the sides of her thong, I pull it off in one swift movement.

"Wow, I've never had someone remove my underwear so efficiently."

"I aim to please," I growl as I move down her pubic bone to her warm heat. I push her legs open a little wider.

14

"Yes, please," she whispers as her hips wriggle.

"Four words. That's all I need. Faster, slower, harder, or softer." My lips continue pressing kisses on her inner thighs as I slowly inch my way up. "Tell me what you need, sweetheart. I want to learn what makes you scream my name the loudest."

"Four is a good… ahhh… round number." Her breaths become shallower as I run my tongue along the crease where her inner thigh meets her torso.

I finally bury my face between her legs. Fuck. She tastes so fucking sweet, and I start making slow, light circles, barely grazing her clit.

"Harder," she pleads, her hands gliding up her body to cup her breasts.

Yes, ma'am. Pressing harder with my tongue, I increase the pressure on her clit slowly until I feel her hips bucking up to meet me.

"Ethan, yes, faster!" she moans as her delicate fingers pinch her nipples.

Her hips keep rocking as I move my tongue faster against her clit. I snake my arm up to her stomach and press down, holding her in place as I move my other hand to her entrance and press a finger inside. Fuck, she's so tight.

"Yes! Shit, that feels amazing, but I need more."

Pulling her clit into my mouth, I alternate between sucking and flicking it with my tongue. I apply more pressure to her abdomen with my palm, while adding a second finger into her pussy, hooking my fingers up to stroke her G-spot.

Her breathing stills as she grinds her heat against my face, her hands moving down to tug at my hair as her thighs squeeze me tighter.

"Ethan, fuck, I'm gonna…" She lets out a feral moan as she squirts, coating my face. I continue licking up every drop as she comes down from her orgasm.

After several moments, she props up on her elbows and looks down at me in astonishment. "Holy fuck, did I squirt on you? I've never squirted before. This is so embarrassing." Her hands fly up to her face, covering her eyes as she tries to roll away from me.

"You did squirt, and it was so fucking hot." I crawl up her body until my face is inches away from hers. "Taste how sweet you are," I say as I thrust my tongue into her mouth. She opens for me and matches my hunger, our tongues dancing back and forth as she licks every drop of herself off me. "I need to be inside you," I growl between kisses.

She pushes me off, flipping me over so she's straddling me, and leans to open her nightstand.

I look over to see she's holding a condom in her hand. "I can't use that kind," I admit.

Her nose scrunches in the cutest way. "What, latex? Do you have an allergy?"

"No, latex is fine. I prefer a different size. I have some magnums in my wallet if you want to grab one."

"Oh. Oh shit! Should I do some stretches first?" The look on her face makes my cock ache in my briefs.

Chuckling, I reassure her, "Why do you think I'm so good at eating pussy? I've got to make sure you're ready to handle this cock." I thrust my hips up into her, and her head drops back as her hips match my thrusts. After a few minutes of dry humping me through my underwear, I ask, "Condom?"

There's reluctance on her face as she climbs off the bed, walks over to my discarded pants, and pulls out my wallet. Damn, that look does something for my ego. I haven't even fucked her yet, and already I want more with this woman. Shucking off my boxer briefs, I lay back on the bed, stroking my length, ready to be inside her.

"Holy shit," she whispers. I assume she's shocked at the size of my cock. But when I look over, I see her holding my wallet up to her face as if she's trying to get a closer look at something. "You're twenty-two?"

"Last I checked. Is that a problem?" She looks up at me,

concern in her blue eyes quickly morphing to desire as her eyes settle on my cock. "See something you like?"

"One night. We said one night," she mutters and drops the wallet.

"Who are you trying to convince, sweetheart? I didn't agree to those terms. Now get the fuck over here so I can feel that sweet pussy squeeze my cock."

Condom in hand, she saunters back to the bed, ripping the foil packet open and sliding the condom down my shaft before I can exhale the breath I didn't realize I was holding.

Straddling me, she begins rubbing her slick center along the shaft of my cock, never letting me penetrate her entrance. My hands grip her hips, aiding her rhythm. "That's it, treat me like your personal fuck toy. Use my cock. Take what you need."

"Fuck, yes. Oh fuck, yes." She screams as her legs shake and her orgasm takes over, vibrating through her entire body.

"That's a good girl, getting this cock nice and wet." I pull her up my chest and grip the bottom of my shaft, positioning the tip of my cock at her entrance. "Now be a good fucking girl and ride my cock. I want you dripping all over it."

"I don't think I can. I think you might be too big." She winces as I push my crown into her hot, tight cunt. "Oh *fuck*."

"You can take it. Just breathe, sweetheart. Relax those muscles. I'm going to make you feel so good," I say as I move one hand between us and rub circles on her clit. Slowly, I feel her relax, and I push another inch into her. "That's it, fuck, you're so tight."

I need to give her time to adjust, but fuck, I'm fighting every urge to bury myself fully inside her. As if she's reading my thoughts, Bridget gingerly pushes up with her arms on my chest and slides another few inches down my cock. "So full," she moans.

"You're taking me so well," I say as I push the last of my cock into her, seating myself to the hilt. "Fuck, this pussy is perfect." It feels like she was made for me, and I fight the urge to say it, knowing it'd scare her off.

"I need a minute. Fuck, you're so big."

"Can't hear that enough, sweetheart." I smile as I pull her against me and pepper her neck with kisses. Her body tastes so good, I can't help licking and sucking on every inch of her.

"Seriously, the perfect length, but damn, the girth is more than I'm used to." She takes a deep breath and begins rocking her hips, slowly at first, until she gets more comfortable.

Fuck, I'm going to blow quick, she feels so good, so tight. I've never experienced something so intense with someone this quickly. Or at all, really. I need more than just a single night with this woman.

Getting more comfortable with my size, she lets loose, arching her back and resting her hands on my thighs behind her as she grinds along my shaft, giving me the perfect view of her gorgeous tits as they bounce with her every thrust. "Ethan, fuck, you feel so good, oh fuck!" Her body shudders as her walls squeeze my shaft.

Think about baseball stats. Cooking meals with Nonna. Helping my siblings with their homework. Anything but how good this fucking woman feels coming apart on my cock.

I let her ride through the last bit of her orgasm before I lift her off me, flip her over, and grab her hips from behind before slamming all the way into her in one quick movement.

"Fuck, sweetheart. Could stay buried in your sweet cunt all night."

"Yes, please! Harder, oh fuck, harder." She fists the sheets in front of her while arching back into me, matching me thrust for thrust.

Her moans and the sounds of our bodies slapping together fill the room as I slam into her. My balls tighten and spots cloud my vision as her pussy spasms around my cock like a vise, another orgasm consuming her. I fall over the edge too this time.

She melts against me as I wrap an arm around her waist and grind out the last of my orgasm. We roll onto the bed, her little spoon to my big, staying connected as we lay there panting.

After what feels like hours, but is probably only minutes, she finally speaks. "If you need to go clean up, the en suite has washcloths in the linen closet."

"Trying to get rid of me so soon?" I smile as I pull out of her and shuffle to the bathroom, where I take care of the condom and clean myself off.

"I, uh… have an early morning tomorrow," she shouts from the bedroom.

"Bullshit. Tomorrow is Saturday," I call back, walking toward her with a warm washcloth.

"I do. There's the… uh… farmer's market, and I… need to stop by the bank…" she says unconvincingly, trailing off as I approach. I grab her by the ankle, pulling her to the side of the bed. "What are you doing?"

"I'm cleaning you up. I told you my momma raised me right," I say as I press the warm cloth against her skin, taking care to clean her.

She arches a brow at me. "You're educated about the importance of cleaning up a woman after sex? You expect me to believe your mom taught you all about aftercare?"

"It was my stepmom, actually, and no, while she may not have given me detailed instructions on aftercare, she did emphasize the importance of taking care of your woman at all times."

"Let's get this straight right now: I'm not *your* woman. This is one night only."

"One night for now, sweetheart. But you *are* my woman, at least for tonight. You became my woman the moment you came all over my face." I toss the washcloth aside, drop to my knees, and lower my head between her legs.

"Wh-what are you doing?" She gasps as my tongue parts

her folds, and I lick up her seam before sucking her clit into my mouth again.

"I'm convincing you that I'm worth more than one night." I wink before returning to flick her clit with my tongue. After a few minutes of playing with her clit and bringing her close to the edge, I get up and climb onto the bed, moving the pillows and lying back near the headboard.

"Why did you stop? I was close," she whines.

"Because I want you to sit on my face and ride me until you come again," I command, grabbing her hand and pulling her to me.

"Like sit on it? I'll crush you."

"I'll be fine, I promise. Now get that sweet pussy over here and let me feast on you."

Nervously, she climbs up my body until her pussy is hovering over me. "I said sit, not hover," I growl as I pull her thighs down, and she finally relaxes. I resume licking and push my tongue into her tight pussy as I use my hands to rock her body, encouraging her to move. Slowly she gains confidence and grinds her clit against my nose while I flick my tongue along her opening. Adding a finger, I push against her G-spot until I feel her walls clamp down and her slickness coats my face as her muffled cries fill the air.

She crumples over, falling onto the bed next to me as she continues trying to catch her breath while I do the same.

"No one's ever—"

"Let you ride their face? Made you squirt? Given you that many orgasms in one night? How many was that so far? I know you kept count given how much you like numbers."

"Five," she whispers. She lies still briefly before her head pops up. "Wait, 'so far'? What do you mean so far? I don't think I have any more in me."

"I did mention more complicated positions, and we've only just begun."

"You twentysomethings and your stamina. I'm going to

need a minute." Dropping her head back to the mattress, she drapes her arms over her face, giving me a delectable view of her heavy breasts.

"How about we make a deal? I'll give you a break if you give me another night. I've at least earned that, don't you think?" Shifting onto my side, I rope an arm over her torso as I pull her into me.

"My, my, you're cocky."

"I know what I'm worth. And I'm pretty sure I know your worth too. You deflect with humor, thinking you can hide it, but I see it, see you," I murmur, kissing up her stomach to her perfect breasts. "You're a fucking queen, Bridget, and I'd happily fall to my knees and worship at your throne." Fuck, I'm going to scare her off with my declarations, so I pull one of her nipples into my mouth, distracting her so she can't unpack the way I'm wearing my heart on my sleeve.

"Fuck, that feels good," she pants as she writhes underneath me.

"Let me show you how a queen deserves to be treated." I continue, nibbling on her nipple as I hover over her, grinding my cock through her wet heat as I pulse my crown against her clit. After a few minutes of lavishing attention to both of her breasts and thrusting against her, she tenses beneath me as she lets out a throaty moan. Blinking, she looks up at me with a look of shock on her face.

"How did you... that came out of nowhere...Jesus. I... Fuck, I can't form a coherent thought."

Chuckling, I press a kiss to her lips before pushing off the bed. "Let's go," I urge before grabbing her arm and pulling her off the bed.

"Where? I'm not sure if my legs are working at the moment."

"I got you," I say before picking her up and moving toward the en suite. Using my foot, I push the door open so we can enter, then grab the handle to the shower, opening it and depositing her onto the bench seat on the tile. I turn on the water, hissing as the cold water hits my back.

"What are you doing?"

"I'm shielding you from the spray until it warms up."

"That's... that's so..."

"Considerate?" I finish her thought.

"No one's ever made this much fuss over me. I'm not sure I like it," she says, shifting uncomfortably on the tiled seat.

Who the fuck has she been with that failed to see her for the queen she is? Failed to worship her and treat her right?

"I don't know why. A queen deserves to be pampered, and that's what I intend to do." Slowly, the water heats, and I pull her up against me. A shiver passes through her as I move her into the warm water. "I know you have a routine in here. What do you normally start with? Shampoo?"

"What? Um, yeah, I shampoo first."

"Tilt your head back."

"Why?"

"I'm going to wash your hair."

CHAPTER 3

Bridget

NO ONE'S ever washed my hair for me—well, not outside of a salon. Certainly, none of my previous hookups. It's intimate, and I don't do intimate.

"I can do it myself. I'm a big girl." I laugh nervously, pushing at Ethan's chest.

He grabs my wrists and holds me flush with his hard, naked body.

"I know you're fully capable, but I'd like to do this for you," he pleads as he flashes me that dimple. Releasing me, he snakes his hands up my back and into my hair. Applying pressure to my scalp, he makes small circles with his fingertips as the tension slowly eases out of my muscles.

"I'll let you do anything you want if you keep doing that," I moan. Fuck that dimple and its magical powers.

He reaches over and grabs my shampoo, squirting a generous dollop into his palm. He turns me around so my back is against his chest and rubs his hands together before massaging the suds into my scalp. Fuck, that feels so good. I melt into his chest. My shower has a massage head, and he removes it from the holder as he begins to play with the nozzle.

"What are you doing?" I ask, confused.

"Finding the right pressure. Too hard, and it'll splash into your eyes. Too soft, and it'll take too long to rinse out."

"Are you the Goldilocks of washing hair? All the women you sleep with must love this."

Chuckling, he uses his hand to shield my eyes from the soapy water that runs down my face as I tilt my head further back. "Close your eyes," he says, ignoring my jabs.

After a few minutes of the most amazingly intimate experience of my life, he continues, "You keep making light of this experience, but I'm serious about wanting more than one night with you. I'm not going to scare off that easily. I have five younger sisters, and they will confirm that I'm great at washing hair. My mom—well, technically stepmom—needed my help with bathtime so we could get through it faster since my dad was always working, and I helped wash hair for as long as it was appropriate for an older brother to do so with younger sisters. And to address your other comment, all the women you speak of are few and far between. I don't have a lot of random hookups, and I've never done this with anyone."

That is equal parts endearing and terrifying. I can picture him kneeling on the floor next to his mom as little girls splash water in the tub. As an only child, I didn't grow up in that kind of chaos, and I'm not sure it's something I'd like to participate in. And the thought that a man like this has not only done it, but probably wants to experience it with children of his own one day, is the reality check I need to cut this off before it goes any further. I cannot give him the future he craves.

"Where's that beautiful head of yours at, sweetheart? I spent five minutes massaging the stress out of you only for you to go rigid in my arms."

"Thank you for washing my hair. But I need to remind you that this is just for tonight."

"I'm not asking for a lifetime. Just one more night, and then we'll see where it goes from there."

"That's the thing. It's not going anywhere else. I don't do relationships, just sex."

"If you think what we did tonight was just sex—"

"Nope, I'm going to stop you there," I cut him off before he can finish that thought. "It was great sex, but nothing more." The last thing I need is a puppy following me around thinking he's found his new home.

"If I only get one night, then I get the *whole* night."

"I didn't agree to those terms," I say, throwing his earlier words back at him.

"Well, I didn't agree to only one night. So, if we're going to compromise, I get the whole night."

"Fine," I acquiesce. I'll kick him out in the morning. "But don't expect breakfast." The more you feed a stray, the more likely it is to return. My time in Cougar Town will only be for the night. I won't be taking home any pets, no matter how cute this pup is.

I add conditioner to my hair, letting it sit as I scrub my body with body wash. Ethan takes the bottle from my hand, squirts some soap into his hand, and glides it over his well-defined pecs and chiseled abs as my eyes track the movement. "You're drooling, sweetheart."

Flustered, I roll my eyes in annoyance. How does he keep doing that? Seeing through my armor? Or am I not good enough at hiding from him?

"I'm not drooling. Can you turn around? You're distracting me, and I need to wash all my parts without feeling like I'm a cat bathing myself in front of an audience."

Flashing me that dimple, he smiles as he turns toward the wall. "Now I'm picturing all the positions I can bend your body into in order to lick you clean."

"Behave. I'm almost done," I chide as I finish washing my

intimate parts. My eyes drift down to his backside. His perfectly round ass is held up by some tree trunk-looking thighs. Fuck, he looks like one of those rugby players in those videos Becka keeps sending me. He slowly bends, running the soap over his thick thighs.

As if he can feel my eyes boring holes into his backside, he stands and turns before stalking toward me, backing me up against the shower wall. He leans back as the water cascades down his body, tiny soap bubbles sluicing over his muscles. My hand moves up his abs, my finger dipping and tracing every divot along the way up to his nipple before tweaking it and rolling it between my fingers.

"Fuck, sweetheart, do you feel that energy when we touch? I've never felt that with anyone."

He opens the shower door and leans out, and I momentarily feel the loss as he reaches toward the counter to grab another condom he'd brought into the bathroom. With the foil packet gripped between two fingers, he grabs my hips and grinds his cock against my pelvis. I pluck the condom from his hand and drop to my knees as I lick the drop of pre-cum off his tip.

Sucking in a breath, he hisses his appreciation as I take his thick cock into my mouth—or as much of it as I can take. I'm going to need some practice with a dick this size if I ever plan to deep-throat him.

What the fuck. Just tonight, only tonight. This is not happening again.

I continue pulling him in as far as I can, hollowing my cheeks to create the perfect amount of suction.

After a few minutes of bobbing, he grabs my hair and starts thrusting into my mouth, fucking my face. I can only take so much of him at a time, but slowly, my throat relaxes, allowing me to take more of him.

"Condom!" he barks through gritted teeth.

"I don't mind if you come in my mouth," I purr, holding up

the condom between my fingers while swirling my tongue around the sensitive part of his head.

"Fuuuck, that mouth is perfection, but I want to come inside your tight little cunt, sweetheart."

He pulls away long enough to roll the condom down his length before reaching up to angle the water toward the tiled wall of the shower. "Stand up and bend over. Spread your legs and grab your ankles."

Who said yoga would never come in handy? I get into position and feel him push inside me. He grabs on to my hips and sets a steady rhythm, the slapping of our bodies creating a chorus of echoes off the shower tiles.

Like earlier in the bedroom, my orgasm builds quickly, coiling in my center as he rubs my G-spot in just the right way. Fuck me, this is a magical dick.

"Again, can't hear that enough."

Shit, did I say that out loud?

"Fuck, Ethan, right there. Yes....ahhhgnnn."

"That's it, sweetheart. Such a good girl, taking"—*thrust*—"me" —*thrust*— "so"—*thrust*—"well."

I let go of my ankles and brace my hands against the shower wall so the momentum of his pounding doesn't knock me over. Before I can adjust to the change in angle, Ethan ropes an arm around my stomach and lifts me up against him. I hook my ankles behind his knees as he carries me over to the tile bench, fully seated inside me the whole time.

He lowers us onto the bench, and I slide my feet to the floor, sitting in between his massive thighs.

"Grind on me. Ahhh, fuuuck, that's it. Just like that. You're doing so well, taking all this cock into your tight little pussy."

I swear I can feel him getting harder inside me. I swivel my hips in circles, grinding on his lap, pretending we're in the champagne room and I'm giving him the lap dance of his life as my hands press against both walls of the shower. His hands alternate between my hips and ass, grabbing handfuls as he presses his fingers into my flesh. I don't even care if I have bruises tomorrow because of it. Worth it.

"Open your legs," he commands.

As I prop one leg over his quad, his hand moves to my clit. He snakes his other hand down and, in one quick motion, picks my other leg up and places it over his other thigh so I'm open wide, straddling his lap.

I continue circling my hips, though it's difficult with my feet dangling over his thighs as I can't get enough traction. I try to shift myself when Ethan shoots his hips up in a powerful thrust. Now that I'm spread between his thighs, he has full access to my clit and uses his fingers to continue his ministrations, applying the exact pressure I like as his hips push up into me. Talk about multitasking.

"Holy fuck, I'm going to come again," I moan right as the most powerful orgasm of my life slams into me. Despite being in the shower, the spray is angled away from us, so I know the wetness running down his length and thighs is from me as he continues pumping up into me from beneath.

"FUUUCKKK," he roars. His movements get erratic and sloppy as his orgasm overtakes him.

My walls are still pulsing as the last bits of my orgasm consume me, I drop my head back on his shoulder as I pant for breath.

"You sat on this throne like a motherfucking queen," he pants into my ear as his arms band around my waist, holding me in place.

"Fuck. I've never squirted before, and you made it happen twice in one night," I say, dumbfounded as I gasp for breath.

"I'm happy to serve you anytime, my queen."

We dry off after the shower, and I pull on a pajama set out of my dresser and go through my nighttime skincare routine. I walk into the bedroom expecting him to be gone and instead find him climbing into my bed.

"What are you doing?" I ask suspiciously as he pulls back

the covers, patting the mattress to get me to join him. "You're not sleeping over."

"Oh, I am, sweetheart. I get the whole night, remember?"

Fuck, I think I did agree to that in my post-orgasm bliss. "Fine, but you better not snore." I climb into bed, keeping my back to him, and plug my phone in beside me. I feel him moving around behind me. "And don't even think about cuddling."

"Wouldn't even dream of it," he says as he drapes his arm over my torso. I tense beneath him as his warm breath tickles the shell of my ear. "This isn't cuddling, just so you know. I need to prop my arm up to help me sleep."

"You're pushing it," I warn.

After a minute of silence, I hear his soft, deep voice rumble against my back. "I need to see you again. Tell me I can see you again."

"I'll think about it," I counter. His arms squeeze me tighter and he pulls me closer.

"What are you doing tomorrow?"

"I told you. I have plans," I say, hoping he'll take the hint, but he flips me to my back and hovers over me.

"What about the day after?" I swear his eyes get bigger as he starts to pout.

I roll away from him, pushing my head into the pillow to hide my smile. "So eager."

"For you? Yes. There's something here, Bridget. You can deny it, but I can't."

Relenting, I turn over under his arm. Our faces are inches apart as our breaths mingle. "Tell you what. If I wake up tomorrow morning and you're gone, I'll think about another night."

"Seems like a trap."

"I told you, I don't do repeats, and I don't do complicated. Keep pushing me and see what happens."

His arm reaches up and playfully shoves my shoulder.

"Did you just push me?" I scoff.

"I wanted to see what would happen." He flashes me his entire smile, his dimple on full display.

Fuck. I'm screwed.

———————

When the morning sunlight warms my bed, several hours later, I'm alone. A brief feeling of disappointment washes over me as I reach for my phone on the nightstand. I notice an AirDrop message on my lock screen where Ethan sent me his contact info. Unlocking my phone with my passcode—because it never recognizes my early morning face—I open the message, debating whether I should save his contact info. Looking over at the nightstand, I see a scrap of paper with his name and number scribbled on it, too.

I did tell this man I'd give him another night if he left, and he kept his end of the deal. I'm nothing if not for my word. After saving his contact info in my phone, I send him a quick text.

Morning, Pup.

Three dots appear instantly. This was a bad idea.

PUP

Morning, queen. I meant to ask, what's with you calling me pup?

You followed me around the club. What else was I supposed to call you?

That's fair.

Not going to deny it?

Not even a little. I'd follow you anywhere.

Especially now that I've feasted on you.

Jesus

When do I get to see you again?

I said I'd think about it 😉

I should give him an honest answer, but that seems like a complication and like tomorrow's problem.

My phone pings again, but this time it's a text from Becka.

BECKA

So...

Did you enjoy your visit to Cougar Town?

Fuck you

No thanks. We still on for coffee?

8 am at our usual spot

Can't wait to hear all the details!

It's 7:55 when I walk into The Daily Grind, our favorite local coffee shop. The smell of vanilla and coffee calms me as I step up to the counter and order our usuals, an Americano for me and a flat white for Becka. My dark to her light.

At 8:10, I see her smiling face rush in as she scurries to my table. I stand and extend the cup to her, repeating our regular greeting for our coffee dates. "The first rule of fight club..."

"We don't talk about fight club."

"Not even to Robert," I admonish as she pulls me into a hug.

"You act like this is the first time we've met to discuss one of your hookups." She rolls her eyes at me as she takes a seat. "This isn't amateur hour."

I wince as I sit back down in my chair. Damn, it's been a while since I've been thoroughly fucked like this.

"It hurts to sit, doesn't it? Was he good in bed? Tell me he's good in bed, and that face is an it-hurts-to-sit-because-the-sex-is-so-good face!"

"Yes and no." Pushing my palm into my abdomen, I blow out a breath as the sharp pain in my torso slowly eases.

She looks at me confused, and then recognition stretches across her face. "Oh shit, it's getting worse, isn't it?"

"While it is true that Ethan is the reason sitting hurts right now, the cramps are getting worse."

"Are you getting it checked out?"

"Yeah, I have my yearly checkup next week. It's probably nothing."

"Text me after, yeah?"

"I will. Anyway, where were we?"

"The dick. You were telling me all about the dicking you got from Ethan."

Laughing, I take a sip of my Americano, letting the bitter flavors swirl over my tongue.

"I don't know how you can drink that without cream or sugar." She makes a gagging face as she empties three sugar packets into her cup while humming "A Spoonful of Sugar" and swirling the drink with a stirrer.

"And I don't know how you can drink that swill."

"We like what we like, I guess." She flashes a grin at me as though my barbs do nothing to her. And they don't. Her armor is impenetrable to my thorns. That's why we've been friends for so long.

Becka and I have known each other since college. She's the yin to my yang. The extrovert who adopted this introvert kicking and screaming. She's light, bubbly, and happy, an eternal optimist. I, on the other hand, don't like people. I tried to resist her, but she somehow worked her way into my heart, and I wouldn't have it any other way.

"Anyway, you were saying?" She flutters her lashes at me.

"He was… quite unexpected." I can feel my cheeks heat as images of the previous evening flood my mind. "Becka, the mouth on this man. At first I thought he was shy, or annoyed with his friend, but there was an entirely different side to him once we were alone. I swear there was one time when I was rubbing up on him, and his words alone made me come. And his dick! I've been with well-endowed men before, but this was different. He actually knew how to use it. I've been railed by a guy or two who thought having a big dick was enough and jackhammering me into the mattress with it was acceptable. Zero out of ten stars, do not recommend. But Ethan? He had the right length and more than enough girth."

"So, he had BDE and knew how to use it? You found the unicorn. Please tell me you're going to see him again."

"I don't know. He texted me, but he's so young, and I don't need any complications right now. It was just mind-blowing sex."

"And how often do you have sex like that?"

"Good sex? Often enough. Great sex? Sometimes. Mind-blowing? That was a first. I sat on the man's face, Becka—like, actually *sat* on it. I tried to hover, and he growled and pulled me down."

"Unreal. I have to tell the book club about this. I've only ever read that in a book."

"Don't you dare tell your mom friends about my sex life! The first rule of fight club…"

"I'm just kidding… maybe." She giggles, but I know my secret's safe with her. "Seriously, I'm living vicariously through you. Robert and I have been together for so long that we have a routine down, and it's nothing like what you experienced."

I examine her more closely. I see more than envy in her

green eyes; there's a hint of sadness there too. "Is everything okay with you and Robert?"

She takes a sip of her coffee before twisting her wrist in the air to brush me off. "Yeah, I think we're just in a rut. It's fine. I'm fine."

"You don't seem fine."

"Oh no, you don't. You don't get to reverse this on me. I'm glad you met someone who gave you an amazing night, but you're still deflecting a bigger issue here."

I thought I played that off better. "I really am fine."

"No woman who says they're fine is honestly fine, me included. I'm not ready to talk about me and Robert. Are you ready to talk about what's bothering you?"

I sigh. "Work is a lot lately. I'm under a lot of pressure because of the acquisition, and I'm extremely stressed. Sex helps me relieve that stress."

"I get that, but maybe it's time for more?"

"Why do I need a man when I have you? Your friendship means more to me than you know. And men? They're fun to play with. I'm not interested in a relationship or starting a family. I'm thirty-eight now. I'm pretty sure that window is almost closed, and I'm totally fine with that."

"Are you? You know I'll support you in anything you choose whether you want to have a family or not."

"I'm not sure I want marriage, but I know I don't want kids. You're my family. I don't feel any kind of internal clock urging me to reproduce. I already have what I need. You. And work. And a great apartment."

"Bridget, you'll always be my family, but as long as I've known you, you've never been in a relationship. I've never seen you have a boyfriend. I'm not even sure I've ever heard you mention other friends."

I start to open my mouth to protest, but she stops me.

"Coworkers don't count."

"Fine. It's true, you're my longest relationship. So?"

"And it took me years to annoy my way into your life. I mean, I love that journey for us, but why is that? Why don't you let more people in?"

I steel myself for this conversation. "Do you remember how I told you that when I was younger, someone broke my heart?"

"Breadcrumbs, Bridget, you're giving me breadcrumbs." I give her a look to let her know that I'm serious, and she bites her lips and nods for me to continue. "Sorry. I remember that shithead you dated briefly in college, and I think I remember you saying you dated an asshole in high school, but you've never shared more than that with me, just that men suck and that's why you don't date."

I huff, peeling at the label on my coffee cup. "I was cheated on and publicly humiliated. After that I swore I'd never give another man that kind of power over my emotions."

She squeezes my hand. "Naturally. I'm so sorry that happened to you."

"I'm not. I learned young that men cannot be trusted and that relationships are a waste of time. I nearly let that guy in high school derail my entire future. And why?" My voice is louder than I intend, and I look around the coffee shop in case I'm causing a scene.

Becka leans in. "Because you loved him, right? And he betrayed you. I know you don't let a lot of people in, and I am grateful you trust me. But you do know that not all men are like that, right? Despite our rut, Robert is a great man. There are good ones out there. And if a relationship is something you decide you want one day, I'll support you. I just don't want to see you end up alone unless that's your choice. But I also don't want to see you overlook someone who could be good for you just because someone else hurt you."

"I'm not alone, I have you. And I can get on an app and have anything I want delivered. I can get a ride anywhere I want at the push of a button. And if I get desperate, I can find someone for a night. I'm fine."

"Fine. But promise me you'll give Ethan a chance."

"Where is this coming from? Did you not just hear my speech? I don't need a man, I have apps," I say, wiggling my phone in my hands.

"It's cute that you think that, but I think he could be good for you. Try with him, please? Worst case, it doesn't work out and you go back to your apps. Best case? You get more mind-blowing sex and maybe he turns into a worthwhile companion. You can always break it off if it's not for you. Just try, that's all I'm asking."

"Why are you pushing this?"

"Because I've never seen you... *glow* about a guy before. You've shared a lot of your sexcapades with me and never have you been this excited about it. And you've shared *a lot* of details. So many details. But also, I know how hard it was to become part of your life. I spent years knocking through your walls like the Kool-Aid Man. I bet there are dozens of Becka-shaped holes in all those walls you keep around you. And Ethan..." She pauses and takes a sip of her drink. She does this to me all the time. Hooks me in with some epiphany and then makes me wait for the rest of her thought. "He seems like someone who'd smash through your walls too. And I love the idea of you having someone else in your corner."

"I admit the sex was amazing. Fuck, it was the best sex I've ever had. What if I never have sex like that again with anyone else? What if it's all downhill from here?"

"And that's exactly why you should keep seeing him. Keep having more amazing sex with him and see where it goes. There must be a reason you two are so compatible sexually."

"He listened to me, Becka," I confess quietly. "All of me. Not just my words, but my entire body. It's like he was tuned in to every word, every little movement I made and learned what I needed and gave it to me. If I told him to go slower, he did. Speed up? He did. You know how some guys rush through everything? Ethan took his time. I came so many times I lost count."

"*You* lost count? Miss Queen of Numbers? Damn, girl, if that's not enough to convince you, I don't know what is."

"But that's exactly why I can't see him again."

Becka looks confused. "I'm not following."

"I lost count. I *never* lose count. Numbers are my safe space, and he pulled me out of it. He's exactly the kind of guy that I could get attached to, but when I get attached, I get hurt."

"Sometimes it's okay to let go. And sometimes the scary things are the most worthwhile. Pursuing them isn't easy, but the payoff is worth it. You gave him control of your body, and maybe you could try giving up control over other areas of your life. Get uncomfortable. I dare you."

"There's nothing about that man's body that's uncomfortable. Trust me."

"Except his heart. And what he might do to yours."

"Damn, Becka. Way to make it real."

"Thanks for coming to my TED talk." She tips her coffee up to mine. "Seriously, though, I really do like him for you."

"But what else could we possibly have in common? He's twenty-two."

"Just get to know him. I bet you have more in common than orgasms."

I sigh. "I hate when you make sense. It doesn't mean I'm agreeing, however."

"Again, I'm the adultiest adult in the room."

"Truth. But don't think I won't be circling back to that comment about you and Robert being in a rut. I have an idea that could help. I read in a book once about a group of friends who all texted their men asking to sit on their faces. Each man's response was more unhinged than the last. You should try it."

"I'll make you a deal. I'll text Robert asking to sit on his face if you see Ethan again."

"Ugh," I groan, annoyed with myself for falling for her traps. They come from a place of love, but I hate how she knows all the ways to make me confront things that I find uncomfortable. "Why do you do shit like this to me?"

"Because I love you," she singsongs as she finishes the last of her coffee.

CHAPTER 4

Bridget

I LEAVE the office a little early on Monday afternoon so I can make it to my doctor's appointment on time.

Dr. Francis enters the room with the nurse following behind her. "Hello, Bridget. So, we're performing your yearly exam today."

My eyes lock on a spot on the ceiling as I shift uncomfortably on the table. "Correct."

"How is everything? Do you have any changes in your medical history? Any concerns?"

"Yeah, I've had some pain on my right side, and my periods have been more painful than normal."

"I see. Can you describe the pain?"

"Most of the time it's dull, but sometimes I get a sharp stabbing pain. More so on my right side."

"Is it constant or intermittent? Does it happen during sex? During your cycle?"

"It comes and goes. I haven't noticed it during sex, but it does seem to be stronger during my period."

"Understood." Dr. Francis pulls the stirrups out of the table, and I continue inching my body to the edge until nearly my entire ass is hanging off, then ease my legs into the stirrups. Despite the way the stirrups' position holds me open, I still try closing my legs, as though this medieval contraption would allow that. Is everyone like this at the gynecologist, or is it just me?

I stare at the same spot on the ceiling as I hear the nurse preparing the tools for the scraping and prodding that will inevitably ensue. The rolling stool shuffles around me as I feel cold, gloved fingers on my inner thighs. "Ahhh," I groan as goosebumps prickle my skin.

"Sorry, but you know what they say, 'cold hands,'" Dr. Francis begins.

"Warm heart," the nurse finishes, not even pretending to be amused. How many times a week must she finish that line for her? Here's an idea: Buy the woman some hand warmers so she isn't making uncomfortable women more uncomfortable.

Why am I like this? Why can't I do pleasantries like normal people? Laugh at a doctor's awkward small talk and interact with people like everyone else?

The exam progresses like usual except for what feels like a lot of extra prodding once the doctor begins the *I'm going to see how far I can shove my arm inside of you* part. I don't remember this much examining in my normal yearly visits, and anxiety niggles the back of my brain.

"Ow," I hiss when her fingers hit a tender spot on my right side.

She performs the rest of the pelvic exam without incident before moving on to the breast exam, then allowing me to sit up. And of course, I feel the thin paper beneath me disintegrate as my ass rubs all over the table underneath. Ugh.

"Your breast exam is clear, but it would be wise to schedule a mammogram in the next year or so. We usually start at forty, but given the family history in your chart, it might be worth starting sooner. We should have the results of your Pap back in a few days, but I'm going to send you over to radiology for an ultrasound. I was able to feel what might be a cyst on your right ovary, and I'd like to take some blood and run some tests to rule out a few things."

"Like cancer?"

"Yes, like cancer, but until we know for certain, there's no cause for concern. Ovarian cysts can be somewhat common, and not all are cancerous. Many can be removed laparoscopically, but not all benign cysts need to be removed, depending on the amount of pain they cause."

"Okay."

Fuck.

She smiles at me and places a hand on my knee. I can't help but recoil at her touch. I don't mean to, but I'm not in a place emotionally to receive physical touch.

"Do you have any questions?"

"No. But I'm sure I will once we have more answers." I give her a smile I pray looks sincere and less murderous than I feel.

Dr. Francis and her nurse leave, and I rise and move toward my clothes. I dig my underwear out of its hiding place and stand balancing on one leg at a time as I pull them on. Running a hand over my ass, I feel the thin strips of paper from the exam table that have congealed to my sweaty butt cheeks. Gross. I shuffle across the room with my panties around my knees until I close in on the trashcan. Its opening stands taller than ass-level so I tip it, angling it against me as I attempt to wipe the thin wet shreds of paper off me and into the mouth of the receptacle. I vow to invent a better covering for OB/GYNs to use on their exam tables.

After pulling myself together and putting on the rest of my clothes, I exit the exam room and meet the eyes of the impatient nurse. "This way," she says as I follow her quick steps down the hallway to the ultrasound room.

The rest of the afternoon continues in a blur as the ultrasound confirms that I do indeed have a cyst but will need to wait for the results of my blood test before I find out if it's benign or not.

By the time I get home, I'm exhausted and decide to take a quick shower before changing for bed. I realize that I haven't even checked my phone since leaving work and retrieve it from my purse, plugging it in on my nightstand. Looking at the screen, I see a ton of messages from Becka. Shit.

BECKA

How did today go?

What did the doctor say?

Seriously, are you ok?

I can see you haven't read my messages yet

CHARGE YOUR PHONE

I'm not freaking out

Ok, maybe I'm picnicking

Picnic

Panic

Ducking autocorrect

Fucking

Ughhhhhh answer me

You said you'd text me after your appt

I'm fine

Sorry, haven't looked at my phone all day

Appt was fine but they had to run some extra tests

My phone lights up with a call from Becka, and I swipe to answer the call. Her panicked voice doesn't even say hello before she peppers me with questions. "Extra tests? Did they find something? Is it cancer? What did the doctor say?"

I run a hand through my hair and blow out a long breath. "Becka, stop. I'm fine."

"I swear if you say 'I'm fine' one more time!"

"There's nothing to worry about. Dr. Francis said I have a cyst on one of my ovaries and they ran some tests to see if it is cancerous or not. I should have the results in a few days. There's nothing to worry about yet."

"Damn, girl. Okay, we'll get through this. Let's get coffee soon and we can talk about everything when you know more."

"Deal. Now go spend some time with your husband."

Hanging up the call, I turn off the light and lie back on my bed staring up at my ceiling. Seconds later, my phone buzzes and I roll over to see what Becka wants. Only, it's not Becka.

PUP

It's been 3 days. I'm dying to know what you're thinking.

I'm thinking about a lot of things—thoughts I haven't shared with anyone, not even Becka—but after being faced with what could potentially be my own mortality today, I decide to give the pup a chance. He was excellent at so many things the other night, and I could use a distraction right now.

Want to know what I'm thinking about?

You

I can't stop thinking about you

Hypothetically, if this were to happen again, what are your plans?

I wanna take you out on a real date

The thought of going out in public with him gives me anxiety. What if people think I'm his mother? Fuck, I *am* technically old enough to be his mother. I know we met in a club, but this is different. This is not a club full of drunk people looking to hook up. What if we're out at a nice restaurant and someone I know sees us? What would people think? This is a bad idea.

Or we could stay in. I could cook for you

It's as though he can sense my hesitation. Maybe this could work. I said one more night, and a night in would be perfect.

What would you make?

What do you like?

Are you implying you can actually cook?

I'm not implying anything. I can, and I will.

What would you like me to make?

Surprise me

CHAPTER 5
Ethan

TUESDAY CANNOT COME FAST ENOUGH. When Bridget asked if I could cook, I realized that we'd never talked about what we do for a living. And she has no idea that I'm a sous chef at Mangia Bene. Actually, I have no idea what she does.

I want to know everything there is to know about Bridget. Ever since our night together, I haven't been able to stop thinking about her. Her crystal-blue eyes. That electricity that hummed between us every time we touched. The way she gave up control of her pleasure to me. I don't think that's something she does with anyone.

Our date is in about thirty minutes, and I'm putting the finishing touches on our meal at the restaurant. Since I'm off tonight and it's not busy, Alyx let me in. Mangia Bene has three sous chefs, and Alyx and I are two of them. We work for two of the best head chefs in the world, Alyx's moms. While most restaurants would only have one head chef and one sous chef, Mina and Dre work well together and created their restaurant to allow all of us a better work-life balance. Any of the five of us can run a dinner service, allowing everyone flexibility with our schedules. It's been an incredible training

45

ground that's allowed me to experiment with my culinary skills.

"Smells good, bro. So you finally convinced Bridget to see you again?" Alyx asks.

"I did, actually. Sorry to cook and run, but I need to plate this and head over there."

"No worries. I can clean your station and then prep for service tonight." Alyx starts moving around me, stacking up pans and carrying them to the dishwasher.

"Thanks, I owe you," I shout at his retreating back as I pack up the last of the meal I created. "Oh, and tell Mina to take the wine out of my next check," I say, holding up the bottle for him to see.

Bridget lives just a few blocks from the restaurant, which was a pleasant surprise to learn the other night. I'm knocking on her door when my phone buzzes in my pocket. I juggle the bags to retrieve my phone.

BRIDGET
I can't do tonight.

Shoving my phone back into my pocket, I knock harder on the door. "Bridget, open up!" The distinct noise of her moving around her apartment is obvious as I stand in her hallway.

"Why are you so early? It's only four-thirty," she calls through the door.

"I'd love to tell you if you open the door."

"I can't. Let's reschedule."

"We can do that, but I still have food for you. If you open the door, I can set it up and then take off, if you want."

The door cracks open, and I see one gorgeous blue eye emerge under the chain in the door. "I'm not prepared for company. I'm not wearing makeup, nor am I dressed. I can't, I'm sorry."

She's flustered, and I can tell something is wrong. "I really don't care what you're wearing, and I meant what I said. I can

46

drop this food and go, but please let me in. Unless you want your neighbors to hear our conversation?" I flash her a smile. The door closes, and I hear her mutter something about a dimple while she fumbles with the chain before it opens again, and I step inside.

Standing behind the door, she gestures to her right. "Kitchen's over there."

She's in black sweats and a cream-colored tank top. It must have a built-in bra because her puckered nipples are peeking through the fabric, taunting me. I'm honestly not sure why she's worried about no makeup when we've showered together and I already know she looks great without it. "Hey, sweetheart, you look beautiful," I whisper before giving her a quick peck on the cheek.

I walk over to the kitchen and begin unpacking the bags as she closes the door and saunters over.

"Look, I'm not feeling well, and I...did you get food from Mangia Bene? I thought you said you were cooking. That's cheating." She reaches for the bag and pulls out one of the containers. "Ugh, this smells so good. How did you know it's my favorite restaurant? They make this tortellini dish with brown butter and sage that's to die for. It's not on the normal menu, so I have to call and ask for the specials to see when they have it."

"Sorry about that. It's my signature dish, and we only offer it when I'm leading service."

The look on her face is priceless. Her eyes are huge, and her mouth is hanging open in shock. "Are you telling me that you're a chef at my favorite restaurant and you're responsible for my favorite meal?"

"It appears so." I smile as I pull the tortellini out of the bag and place it in front of her. "You can't tell me this doesn't mean something."

Her eyebrows furrow. "It's just a coincidence. It's not a big deal..." she starts before grabbing her abdomen and wincing.

47

"Are you okay?" I move over to her, unsure of what she needs but feeling distraught over the pain flashing across her face.

After several deep breaths, she straightens. "It's nothing, I'm just not feeling well."

"Where does it hurt? You're holding your abdomen. Could it be appendicitis?"

"It's not appendicitis. I'm fine." Her hand moves from her abdomen to her lower back before my brain fills in the blanks.

"Have you taken anything for the pain? Where's your heating pad? Point me in the direction of what you need, and I'll take care of it. Go sit on the couch."

The little huffing noises she's making are cute. I move toward the cupboards, about to look for painkillers, before she relents with a huge sigh. "Aleve is in the cabinet next to the fridge, and my heating pad is on my bed. How did you—"

"I have five sisters." She walks down the hall while I grab the Aleve and get her a glass of water. After I finish plating the food, I carry it into the living room and set it down on the table with the water and pills. She disappeared into her bedroom, so I knock before entering. I don't see her inside. But I spot the heating pad, grab it, and head back to the living room. There's an outlet near her pile of blankets, and I plug it in and turn it on as she enters the room.

"Were you trying to cancel our date because you got your period?"

Her cheeks redden. "Ugh, this is so embarrassing."

I walk over and grab her hand. "Sweetheart, there's nothing to be embarrassed about. I grew up in a house with six women, and not all of their cycles synced up. It was always someone's time of the month, and I'm a protective older brother. I got good at helping take care of everyone. Aleve and water are next to your food, and I plugged the heating pad in so it should be warmed up soon."

She looks down at the table, and I swear I see disappointment cross her delicate features. It guts me, and I'd do anything to prevent that look. "I'll stay if you want. Or I can come back another day. It's up to you." I let go of her hand and glide my hands up her arms. *Don't look at her nipples.* Fuck, it's so hard not to when they're right there, begging to be touched.

"Are you avoiding looking at my breasts?" She laughs, and the sound is music to my ears.

"What gave it away?"

"The way your eyes keep darting around. You keep looking at me in the face, then your eyes drift down, and then all around the room like you're avoiding something. Can't say I blame you when this top leaves little to the imagination." She shifts and crosses her arms over her chest.

Message received. I drop my hands, shoving them in my pockets. "Sorry, I'll put away the rest of the food and get out of your hair."

I quickly move toward the kitchen when the sound of her voice freezes me in my tracks.

"Actually…" she trails off as I slowly turn to stare at her.

"Actually, what?" I cross my arms to mirror her position, feeling cocky.

"Nothing."

"Nuh-uh. I'm going to need to hear you say it."

"Jesus, you're infuriating," she huffs. "Yukinst," she mumbles with her chin down toward her chest, eyes on the floor.

"I'm sorry, what was that? I didn't quite catch it."

"You can stay," she says clearly, rolling her eyes while kicking at nothing on the floor with her toe.

"I can what?" I ask as I carefully cross over to her.

"Stay!" she shouts. "Jesus."

My arms reach out, grabbing her and pulling her into me. I can't touch her fast enough. Can't get her close enough. "That's what I thought you said." I breathe into her, our lips millimeters apart. Our eyes lock, and it feels like hundreds of words pass between us, paragraphs and essays full of declarations. "Sweetheart, I—"

Before I can finish, her lips crash into mine, frantic and full of bite. She tastes like vanilla and desperation, moving against me with fervor. We're licking, biting, and sucking as she pulls on my lower lip while wrapping her arms around my waist. I'm not even trying to hide my hard-on as I thrust it into her pelvis. Her lips pull away, but my hand around the back of her head keeps her face close as I kiss my way along her jaw and down her neck.

"I can't. My period," she moans but doesn't pull away.

"Sweetheart, you're wrong if you think a little blood will scare me away," I whisper between kissing and sucking on her neck.

"It's not just... I... oh shit, that feels so good... I can't," she whines while I kiss her before abruptly pushing me away.

"It's okay," I breathe out as she backs away from me. "We can just eat and talk, but I'm going to need a minute before I sit with you." She looks at the bulge in my pants and laughs. Fucking *laughs*.

Once back in the kitchen, I make myself a plate of food while I wait for my erection to calm down. Opening a drawer in her kitchen island, I find the bottle opener on the first try and grab the bottle of wine. Turning, I open a cabinet, and the wine glasses are exactly where I'd expect them to be.

Bridget has a suspicious look on her face. "Um, how do you know where everything is in my kitchen?"

"Honestly, I'm not sure, but everything is exactly where I'd put it. Great minds think alike?"

"It's kind of creepy."

"Or it's another sign that there's something here worth exploring." I flash her another grin, and she rolls her eyes. "Keep rolling your eyes, and I'll spank that ass so hard it'll take your mind off those period cramps." Her eyes meet mine, and I don't see annoyance or disgust there. There's only longing and desire as a small blush creeps across her cheeks. "You'd like that, wouldn't you?"

"You keep talking like you're going to see me again after tonight," she says with a hint of challenge in her tone.

"I do know where you live. And I make your favorite meal. Don't think this is going to be over after tonight," I say cheekily.

"So Mangia Bene, huh? Are you the head chef there?" Deflecting is her MO, so I'm not surprised by the sudden change of topic.

"I'm a sous chef along with Alyx and his sister Nyomi. You remember him from the other night, right?" She nods, and I continue. "His moms own the restaurant and are the head chefs."

"Dre and Mina are Alyx's moms?" she asks with a look of surprise on her face. "What a small world."

"I'm surprised we haven't met before."

"I mostly do takeout after work. I don't dine in a lot." So she's a workaholic. Makes sense. She's probably poured herself into her career since she clearly views relationships as distractions. "But I've met Dre and Mina several times when I pick up my food. Dre is so sweet, and Mina is hilarious."

"Please don't say she's told you the pickle story." I groan, dropping my head into my hands.

"She hasn't, but now I must hear it. Tell me, Pup."

"Oh no. No, no, no. I'm not telling you that story." Fuck, I'll never live it down if she hears it. "Anyway, you know what I do and know way too much about my place of employment, apparently. Tell me more about you and what you do."

"It's your turn to deflect, eh? I'll bite. I'm the CFO for a supplement brand, and right now, I'm in the middle of a major acquisition."

"So, numbers are literally your job?" Of course she loves numbers. It's all making sense now. Everything in her life has

MYA MORE

a place. She craves order, structure, control. Totally left-brained, driven by logic and data.

Realizing she's probably not going to give me any more details, I relent, and we eat in silence for several minutes. "How is it?" I ask, gesturing to the almost empty plate in front of her.

"Delicious," she groans between mouthfuls. Seeing her satisfaction while eating my food does something to me. My cock twitches in my jeans as my eyes focus on the way her throat bobs as she swallows another bite. I've enjoyed cooking since my Nonna taught me, and I thrive on the sense of purpose it gives me. But there is something innately sexy about this woman enjoying my creation.

Her phone buzzes on the couch, and a look of concern falls over her face as she gets up. "Sorry, I need to take this." She walks over to the kitchen, and I try not to listen to her conversation, but I hear bits and pieces as I finish my meal.

"You did?... What does that mean?... Can you spell that?... When do I need to... Oh, that's soon... Okay... Yeah, I can make that work. I need to move some things around..."

When she hangs up, the silence in the room is deafening. "How much of that did you hear?" she asks with a tremble in her voice.

It takes a few strides to reach her and I pull her into my arms. I'm not sure what she was discussing on the call, but given the shift in her demeanor, it wasn't good news. "I heard parts, but I promise to only remember the parts you want to share with me," I assure her while kissing her hairline.

"Fuck." I squeeze her tighter and stroke my hand up and down her spine. The tension in her muscles slowly relaxes as she blows out several deep breaths. "You have the worst timing. Or I do. Or my doctor does. Ugh, why did I say that? It's like I can't shut up around you."

With my hand under her chin, I tilt her face so her eyes meet mine. "Maybe it's good that I'm here. I'm not sure what's happening, but I get the feeling you shouldn't be alone right now."

Bridget pulls away from me and starts frantically tapping at her phone, muttering curses under her breath. She's rattled, and frustration mars her features. "Fuck, it's Becka and Robert's anniversary, and he's surprising her with a trip, and my parents are on a Mediterranean cruise that week. Shit, and the acquisition. I have so much to do before then."

"I can help," I offer before I can think it through. She needs someone, and it's a chance for me to prove that I can be what she needs. Maybe at the end of this, she'll see how good I can be for her.

Her eyes flick up to mine, and the anger that sears me is feral like a hellcat about to unleash. Throwing my hands up between us, I try to calm her ire. "I'm happy to help. I'm not sure what's going on, but it sounds like the people you normally lean on are occupied, and you might need someone. Tell me what's going on."

"Why would you do that? We fucked once, and you think you know me?" she spits out.

Hurt people hurt people. I repeat the mantra my mom ingrained in me. Something bad just happened to Bridget, and she's taking her anger out on me.

"I'm not sure what that call was about, but I can tell that you received some upsetting news—"

"Don't do that. Don't psychoanalyze me and act like you know me. You don't know me or anything about me. I knew this was a mistake." As she turns to leave the kitchen, I catch her hand, and she stands there for a few seconds frozen with her phone in one hand and her other captured in mine. "I can't do this," she says quietly. "You're a complication I can't afford."

"It's only complicated if we make it. Let me help you. Please."

"You can't help me. You don't even know me. I barely know you. I'll figure something out. I always do."

My heart breaks at her words. How many people have let her down? How many times has she been hurt to the point where she won't let anyone in? There's something comforting in knowing that we have more in common than she realizes.

We stand there, half in her kitchen and half in her living room. I thread her fingers through mine and squeeze her hand a little tighter as she stands there with her back to me, refusing to let me in, refusing to let me see her.

"It was my doctor's office," she starts in a voice so small I almost don't hear her. "I found out on Monday that there's a cyst on one of my ovaries, and they ran some additional tests..." she trails off, and I let her sit in the silence, rubbing my thumb on the back of her hand to let her know that I'm still here. "It's not cancer, but there's a family history of the BRCA-2 gene, so they want to remove the cyst and my ovary since I have a thirty percent chance of developing ovarian cancer. I can't even believe I'm telling you this." She pauses, and my thumb continues moving in soothing circles. "Anyway, they want to do something called a... fuck, I wrote it down."

"You need surgery, I take it? And they want to do the procedure soon, but your emergency contacts all have conflicts?"

"They do, but I'll figure it out." She withdraws her hand from mine, and I feel the loss of her warmth immediately.

"I can help."

"No, absolutely not."

"My Nonna died of cancer last year, and I was her primary caretaker. I spent months as her nurse, so a few weeks helping you would be easy."

It broke me seeing the strong, feisty woman I loved slowly lose that strength as she succumbed to her illness. This must be the reason the universe put Bridget in my path. I need a do-over. And I can prove to her that I can be helpful and worth her time and affection, and maybe one day her love.

"I'm not asking you to do that."

"No, I'm offering. Are you worried I'll have to change your diapers? Because I have experience with that too," I joke, attempting to lighten her mood.

"Jesus," she groans, unamused, but I see her turn slightly to hide her smile before she straightens and addresses me. "Look, you're a nice young man—"

"Nope, I'm going to stop you right there. You keep throwing my age at me like it's a weapon. I'm not here begging for more dates with you because of your age or mine. I'm not here offering you help because of age." I pull her into me before flashing her my dimple, which I've figured out is her kryptonite. "And my desire to fuck you has nothing to do with age. I like you as a person, not a number. Please let me do this for you."

"That fucking dimple." She drops her head against my chest. "I'm not saying yes. I will keep you as an option, but not if you mention diapers again."

"Fair enough. That's all I'm asking for." For now.

CHAPTER 6

Bridget

ETHAN STAYED through dinner before I cut him free with a short kiss at the door. For the life of me, I cannot figure out what he possibly sees in me, and I cannot let him continue chasing me. It's a waste of both of our time. Especially now with my cyst. While it's unlikely, and I'm basing most of my information on Google because I couldn't ask the nurse any questions in front of Ethan, I've found out that while this procedure may not make me infertile, the likelihood of me having children will significantly decrease. If my age hasn't already impacted that.

There's a sadness that lingers in the back of my brain about it. I've never wanted children. But knowing now with certainty that the odds really are against me brings out a melancholy in me I didn't know existed. Not sadness over not having children, but over the loss of the choice. I've felt good about my decision not to have them, but now the choice might not even be mine. And I feel guilty over that when there are women out there who are heartbroken over not conceiving, and I'm heartbroken over the lack of a choice. What is wrong with me?

And then there's Becka. She's going to start pestering me with questions about my test results, and if I tell her the truth, she'll want to stay and take care of me, especially since she already knows that my parents can't help. And she doesn't know about the surprise anniversary trip yet. She'll try to bail on that to help me, and Robert's worked hard planning this for her. I'm going to have to tell partial truths and find someone who's not Ethan to help me.

Like clockwork, my phone lights up with a text.

BECKA

Any word from the doctor yet?

Are we drinking coffee or wine?

Does coffee mean everything's fine, and wine means it's gone to shit?

You get it.

Coffee

Seriously?

Yup, not cancer.

Also, go ahead and prepare that text for Robert.

You're going to be sitting on his face in the near future.

Wait, does this mean you're seeing Ethan again?

I saw him earlier tonight.

Then why are you talking to me?

He left a little bit ago. No sleepovers tonight. Early meeting in the morning.

For real this time.

Can we grab coffee tomorrow before?

Sure, if it's quick.

Are you texting Robert?

He's in the bathroom right now.

It's one of those "I'm pooping, but I'm really watching videos" situations.

Not the best timing. I'll do it during coffee tomorrow morning.

7:30 at our spot.

The next morning, I oversleep for the first time in over twenty years. I could blame it on my period and the pain I was in. Or I could chalk it up to the bad news the nurse shared with me. But I'm pretty sure the anomaly could be pinpointed back to Ethan. Every time I closed my eyes, I saw his deep green ones. And that dimple. That fucking dimple. It haunts me. What is so alluring about it?

I walk into The Daily Grind feeling sweaty and flustered and spot Becka immediately.

"You're late." There is a hint of awe in her voice as a Cheshire Cat-like grin stretches across her face. She thrusts an Americano into my hand as I pull out my chair and sit.

"What's with the creepy smile?"

"Did Ethan come back for round two?"

I nearly spit out my coffee. "What? No. I went to bed after we texted."

"But you're never late. You practically worship numbers, and last I checked, telling time is like, all numbers."

"I'm here to help you get your mojo back with Robert." I

texted him after I was done with Becka last night. He'd needed me to keep her distracted this morning so he could pack some of her items for their secret trip. They need some time away together without their daughter, and I'm happy to help. I didn't tell him about my bargain with Becka, but I'm sure he'll appreciate it.

I thrust my hand across the table, gesturing for her to give me her phone. She snatches it away quickly and holds it against her chest. "Nope, I want to hear about this date first."

Sucking in a deep breath, I let everything out in one breath. "It's not a big deal. I tried to cancel, but he knocked on my door at the same time I sent the text. I'd started my period and my cramps were brutal, but he said he understood because he has five sisters, and he helped and brought me tortellini from Mangia Bene. Turns out he's a sous chef there, and we ate and talked for a little bit, and there was no sex, and it was fine and then he left. Happy?"

"That's a lot of information in a short amount of time. I'm honestly kinda impressed."

"I'm nothing if not efficient, and I have a meeting soon." *And I'm trying to avoid talking about my doctor's visit, so I'm distracting you.* "Now, text your husband."

"Fine! I already have it drafted." She slides her phone over to me, and I nod my approval.

"Send it." I grin into my cup as I take a sip.

She taps her phone a few times and relaxes into her chair. "It's sent." Seconds later, her phone buzzes on the table, and she looks at it with wide eyes.

"Is that Robert already? What'd he say?"

Becka's face turns a deep crimson as her eyes meet mine. "He said, 'Fuck yeah, babe, suffocate me with that sweet pussy.'" She whispers the last part, her eyes darting around as though she's worried someone might hear.

"This is going to be so good for you! I have a feeling your rut is ending soon."

"I don't get it, though. That's not at all what I expected him to say. He sounds excited."

I had no idea it had gotten this bad between them. "Why wouldn't he be excited? How often does he do that kind of stuff to you?"

"Um, like, never lately. Ever since we had Hallie, we basically have to schedule our sexy times, and even then, we rush through it with little foreplay, afraid she might wake up or interrupt us. She normally sleeps in our bed, so when we want to have adult time, it's usually not long before Hallie wanders into our room, wanting to snuggle with us. She doesn't seem to sleep as well in her bed."

"And that's another reason why I don't want kids," I say.

"Wait, Hallie is four. Are you telling me you've had boring sex for the past four years?"

"I wouldn't say boring, just… routine. It's been a while since we've mixed things up."

"Do you ever ask for what you want? Boss him around or even push his head down there?"

"Oh, hell no. Even texting him something like that was a first. That's why I made that bargain with you. I didn't think you'd hold up your end. It's hard for me to ask for what I want in the bedroom, especially that. I always feel so awkward because I'm too much of a people pleaser. I wish I were one of those women who own their sexuality, like the ones I read about in romance books."

"You shouldn't feel bad or nervous about asking for what you want. I do it all the time. In the office and in the bedroom. It's always a no if you don't ask. And from the looks of that text, it seems like Robert isn't upset you did. And the whole point of our bargain was to push each other out of our comfort zones. Right?"

"I didn't even think about that, but you're right. Are you going to see Ethan again?"

"I might not have a choice," I mutter under my breath.

"Come again? Always with the breadcrumbs."

"Well, he does make my favorite dish at my favorite restaurant so I'm sure we'll see each other." I leave out the part that I might have to let him take me to and from my surgery.

———————

Over the next few days, I think about asking a handful of different coworkers for help. Think about it, but don't act on it. It takes very little small talk with each person to figure out that I don't actually know or trust any of them well enough to ask for that kind of favor. Fuck, Becka is right. I need more friends.

I love my life and the limited people I allow in it, but when you are as fiercely independent as I am and suddenly find yourself needing to depend on outside help, you start rethinking your choices to keep everyone at arm's length.

"Bridget, can I see you in my office?" our CEO Mark asks from my office door, pulling me out of my thoughts.

"Sure," I say curiously, following him down the hall. I take the seat across from him as he taps at his computer, not giving me his full attention.

"I want to make sure all of the reports are up to date before you take off on your little vacation."

"I'm having surgery, not going on a vacation," I snap. I know this man didn't bring me to his office to talk about something that could've been an email.

"Ah, that's right. What's this for again?"

"Respectfully, Mark, you're not allowed to ask me that, but it's fine. I'm having a cyst and ovary removed." The rules don't apply to men like this. He has enough money to make any problem disappear, so I opt for honesty.

"Trying to become one of the guys?" He laughs, proud of his joke as I swallow down the retort I really want to make at his blatant misogyny.

"I still have more balls than half the assholes you have working around here," I shoot back.

"That you do. How long till you're back up and running?"

"I'll be off for a couple weeks, but working remotely for a month after that, so six weeks out of the office." I need him to see me as irreplaceable.

"Sounds good," he says, still looking at his computer as he waves me off.

During the walk back to my office, it becomes painfully clear that I may need to consider Ethan's offer for help. The quicker my recovery, the sooner I can get back to work, where I belong.

CHAPTER 7

Ethan

"YOU HEAR FROM BRIDGET YET? It's been like, what, a week?" Alyx asks me while we're preparing for dinner service.

"Yup," I say, popping the "p" and taking a deep breath while I dice up vegetables. "But who's counting?"

"I've never seen you this hung up on a girl."

"I think you should go for it. She seems sweet," Dre says as she passes my station on her way to the walk-in cooler.

Mina stands with her arms folded over her chest next to me. "If you don't make a move, I'm gonna tell her the pickle story the next time she comes to pick up food."

I set my knife down in horror. "You wouldn't dare."

"Try me." She grins before popping a piece of diced pepper in her mouth.

"I want something more with her, but I'm not the obstacle here," I say, hoping to silence all my critics within earshot. "I think she's fucking awesome, but she's not really open to a relationship."

"Ethan, baby, we've got dinner service covered tonight. Alyx can finish prep. Why don't you see if she's free tonight? If anyone can break through her shell, it's you." Dre wraps an arm around my shoulder. "I appreciate how much you help around here, but it sounds like she needs your help more than we do right now."

Looking her in the eyes, I see hope, but I'm not feeling it. It's been a week since I've seen Bridget and a few days since the last "Good morning" text I sent went unanswered. "I can try," I concede while untying my apron and removing it.

"Go ahead and head out. You could use a night off anyway. We got you covered." Dre comforts me while patting my back.

"Thanks. Mind if I grab some food for the road?"

Dre smiles at me, her warm brown skin wrinkling around her eyes. "You better feed that girl. I haven't seen her pick up takeout in a while."

"Actually, can I talk to you about something?"

"Anything, baby, you know you're like a son to me." Dre tugs me into her office, closing the door so we have some privacy.

"Do you think I could take some time off?"

"Absolutely, how much were you thinking?"

"I dunno, a few weeks?" I suggest hesitantly.

"Done."

"It's...wait, what? Really?"

"Really. You're a good man, Ethan. I've seen how you take care of your sisters, how you cared for your Nonna, and how you look out for Alyx. Anyone lucky enough to have your attention is important to me. And Bridget? I've seen her come in and out of my restaurant for a couple years now. Always alone. Ordering food for only herself. She seems like she needs someone in her corner, and I can't think of a better person for that job than you."

"You don't care that she's..."

"Older than you? Hell no. Mina is eight years older than me, but our age difference isn't our biggest battle. We are a biracial lesbian couple in this country. You think age is our biggest concern?"

"I guess not," I say sheepishly, tugging at my neck.

"Do you want to know a secret? I was never truly happy with who I was, never truly secure in any relationship, until I stopped caring more about what other people thought, and focused on what Mina thought, what made her happy. You can't control what other people say or think about you or her, baby boy. You can only control the way you react to it. Don't worry about how people on the outside perceive your relationship. Focus on her. I have a good feeling about you two." She winks at me before walking off.

I pull my phone from my pocket and send Bridget a text.

Leaving the restaurant

Might have made too much tortellini.

Know anyone who'd take it off my hands?

Also, my offer still stands.

Packing up a carryout bag and making my way out of the restaurant, I head toward Bridget's apartment. The slight breeze is a pleasant caress, the heat of the summer still a month or more away. As I round the corner near her building, someone bumps into me, head buried in their phone. The scent of berries and vanilla hits me as I look down and see Bridget flailing one arm, the other clutching her phone tightly to her chest.

Balancing the food in one hand, I reach out for her arm and jerk her up and into me, preventing her from falling back onto the pavement. "We've got to stop meeting this way."

"Ethan." A look of embarrassment stains her cheeks. My eyes follow hers as they focus on my lips.

Fuck, it's good to see her again.

"I was just on my way to your place. You weren't in a hurry to avoid me, were you?" I tease.

The red in her cheeks darkens, and her eyes shift around

nervously. Shit, she *was* avoiding me. I let go of her arm, not even realizing I was still holding it.

"Ethan, I..." she trails off, her eyes evading mine.

"Dre mentioned that she hadn't seen you at the restaurant in a little while, and I figured I'd bring you some food," I explain. The bag feels like a lead weight in my hand as I extend it to her.

"Thank you." A ghost of a smile crosses her lips as she takes the food. The sun gives her face a warm glow and the few freckles that dot her cheeks stand out. Fuck, she's beautiful.

I reach out and brush the back of my hand along her forearm before she finally speaks. "I don't know how to do this."

"Do what?" I've learned not to make assumptions with her. She doles out information in small doses, never giving me enough to make me feel secure.

"I'm not good at accepting help. I have three and a half people in my life that I trust."

I huff out a laugh. "A half?"

"My mom, dad, and Becka are the three people I trust. Becka's husband Robert is the half," she says. "And I only trust him because of Becka."

"Makes sense." My hand continues stroking her arm, and goosebumps form in her skin. I know she feels this energy between us, even if she won't admit it. "I'd like to join that circle of trust if you'd allow me. I can take time off from the restaurant, and I can be at your disposal while you recover from your surgery."

"Why? Why would you do that?"

"Why wouldn't I?"

"You're very sweet, and we had a great time the other night. But I don't want a relationship. I've made that clear," she says firmly.

"You don't feel it?" I ask, gesturing between us with my

free hand. "This thing between us is unlike anything I've ever felt. I can't walk away from this without knowing I've done everything in my power to explore it."

"Ethan," she warns.

"Please let me help you. As a friend, if that makes you more comfortable. I want to help. I need to help. Don't make me pull the dead grandma card."

Her eyes flicker to mine as she sucks in a deep breath. *Please let her see how good this can be between us.* I know we could be amazing together.

"Okay, you can help," she relents as she pulls her arm away from mine. "But as a *friend*," she emphasizes, "which means the touching has to stop."

"You got it." Warmth spreads in my chest as I smile down at her.

"And that." She points at my cheek. "Stop it with that dimple."

"I can't make any promises. It has a mind of its own."

"Thank you for doing this for me. I'll text you the details," she says as she turns back in the direction of her apartment. I pump my fist in the air as I watch her walk away from me determined not to squander this opportunity she's giving me.

Bridget

What the actual fuck am I doing? I must have lost my mind. That's the only logical explanation for why I agreed to let Ethan help me.

The feel of his hand on my arm was...well, it was something. I've noticed that he does that a lot when I'm around him. Little touches here and there.

It's hard to deny the attraction I feel for him, but that's never been my problem. I don't do well with intimacy. What Ethan and I experienced wasn't just sex, and that's what scares me. It was intimate, but it came naturally. I'm not sure what it is about him that makes me open up. I've shared things with him that I never would with any other man, confessing feelings that I'd rather keep to myself.

Letting Ethan help me makes me uncomfortable. I don't depend on anyone for anything. My life is built around having independence. I'm not even sure I'd enjoy being tied to one person, and I certainly wouldn't make a good partner to anyone. Not with all the baggage I have.

I'll let Ethan drive me to and from the surgery. He can help me get settled in my apartment, and then I'll send him on his way. I'm sure he has plenty of other things he would rather be doing. He's young and has his whole life ahead of him. He certainly doesn't need to be tied to me, stuck out of polite obligation just because we shared a great night of sex.

What could he possibly get out of this? I'm going to be recovering from surgery so it's not like there's going to be any sex happening. Just friendship. That's all there can be between us.

CHAPTER 8

Ethan

I'VE DONE a lot of research on oophorectomies since Bridget agreed to let me help. According to experiences women have shared on Reddit, the recovery could be more than Bridget is expecting it to be. But she's tough and fiercely independent, so she may not need—or want—much help.

Bridget and I sit in the waiting room at the hospital. She wrinkles her nose as she fills out the form. It's not clear if she's annoyed or confused, but it makes me want to kiss the creases on her face until they relax.

"Need any help?" I offer.

"I need an emergency contact for the procedure. I haven't told Becka or my parents about this, and I don't want them to get a call and find out that way."

"Use me."

Her eyes flit up to mine. "What?"

"Use me as your emergency contact."

She hesitates for several seconds, her head down, eyes glued to the form as her pen sits poised to write. I look over to see what question has her stumped and notice that she's written my first name but not my last. "Black. My last name is Black."

"Jesus Christ. This is a mistake," she grits out of the side of her mouth, her lips barely moving, her volume almost a whisper. "I don't even know your last name. You're a fucking one-night stand whose full name I don't know."

"My full name is Ethan Joseph Black. Now you know. And you saw my license that night, if I recall."

"I wasn't looking at your name, I was too distracted by your birth year. Mine starts with a nineteen and yours doesn't."

"I'm well aware of my birthday. What other information do you need from me?" I don't give two fucks about our age gap or one-night stand. I'm not going anywhere.

Reluctantly, she writes down my name, and I recite my contact information so she can add it to the form. Her free hand rests on the arm of the chair, and I grab it. "Thank you for letting me be here for you."

She doesn't acknowledge me, but she doesn't remove her hand from mine either as she continues filling out the form.

Once she finishes, I grab the clipboard from her hand and return it to the desk.

"I could've done that myself."

"But you shouldn't have to. It's okay to let me help. I won't bite."

We wait in silence for a few minutes before a nurse emerges from a door. "Bridget Connors?" she calls.

I follow closely behind as we walk through the hallway and into a room. The nurse hands Bridget a gown while giving instructions for what she can expect during the procedure. She disappears into the bathroom and reemerges in the hospital gown, holding her clothes in a neatly folded pile.

She walks through the room, balancing her clothes in one hand while her other hand holds the gown closed. Shuffling by me, she sets her clothing down before sitting on the bed, being careful not to let me see her backside. It's quite comical considering I've already seen and enjoyed every inch of her amazing body. But I push those thoughts away as this isn't the time or place to pop a boner.

Another nurse walks in and approaches Bridget as I take a seat in the chair next to her clothing.

"Good morning, my name is Maggie, and I'm the nurse on duty this morning. Do you have any questions before we get started today?" Bridget shakes her head before Maggie continues. "Great. We have you scheduled for a unilateral salpingo-oophorectomy today to remove your right ovary and the accompanying cyst. The plan is to remove it laparoscopically through a small cut in your abdomen. The surgeon will insert a small camera with a light on it. Once the ovary is removed, the surgeon will make sure the surrounding tissue is healthy. If no early-stage cancer is detected, we can close you up and send you home to recover.

"As long as everything looks good, this is the plan, but there's a small risk that the surgeon may begin the procedure laparoscopically but change to an open procedure once they see what's happening inside. If we do find cancer present, they'll want to remove any cancerous cells. There's nothing to indicate that this may happen, but things can change on the operating table, and it's important to know the risks."

Studying Bridget's face, I can see the worry crossing her brows. Not over the thought that a more invasive surgery may be necessary. She's most likely worried that if that does occur, she'll need to depend on me for longer.

Maggie continues to speak, laying out all the steps they will take before beginning the procedure. Her eyes cut to me. "Once we take you back, your son can take your personal belongings and wait for you in the waiting area."

"He's not my son. I don't have any children," Bridget spits at the nurse with a look of disgust on her face.

"I'm her boyfriend," I say brightly, smirking at Bridget.

The look in her eyes is murderous. "He's a friend," she corrects through gritted teeth.

"Oh gosh," Nurse Maggie starts, her face flush with embarrassment. "I'm so sorry. Your friend can wait for you in the family waiting area. The procedure shouldn't take more than an hour and a half, barring any complications. I'm going to give you two a minute. They should be wheeling you back to surgery soon. If you need anything in the meantime, press the call button."

As Nurse Maggie leaves the room, Bridget sits up taller in the bed and wraps her arms around her waist. The air feels like it's been sucked from the room now that we're alone. I give no fucks that someone assumed that I'm Bridget's adult son. I mean, I don't think she looks that much older than I do. But it definitely bothers Bridget. If she could compress herself into a smaller ball, she looks like she would. Her legs are now folded up against her chest as she wraps her arms around them.

"I can't do this," she whispers against her knees, pressing her eyes closed.

I stand and cross to the bed, placing a hand on her shoulder. "It's okay. The procedure should be over quickly, and the nurse did say that it wasn't likely to be cancer," I reassure her.

Blowing out a deep breath, she continues speaking into her knees, eyes closed. "I'm not talking about the procedure."

Fuck. That nurse spooked her. What little progress I'd made with her feels like dandelion seeds fluttering away in a spring breeze, so close you think you can grab hold but far enough out of reach to tease you with its presence. If that's not Bridget in a nutshell, I don't know what is.

"If you think that's going to scare me off, think again, sweetheart. The only place I'm going is out to the waiting room. I'll see you after surgery," I promise, planting a kiss on her hairline. I pull back, and she squeezes her eyes closed. Turning toward the chair, I swipe her personal effects and start toward the door.

"Thank you," she says in a voice so small and weak I almost can't believe it's coming from this powerful woman.

The minute my feet cross the threshold out of her room and into the hallway, a cold emptiness settles over me. It's the same feeling I get when she lets go of my hand or leans away from my touch. In a few short weeks, Bridget has managed to find a place in my life and my heart, and I'll be damned if I let anyone take that away from me, including her.

CHAPTER 9

Bridget

THE WHIRRING and beeping of machines nudge my brain back into consciousness. My hands fly up to my eyes, like a bug zapper collecting mosquitos on a hot summer night. "Lights," I croak, my throat dry and scratchy.

"Hey, beautiful." Ethan's soothing voice comes from his chair across the room. I hear a switch being flipped, but the brightness behind my eyes is still intense.

"More lights off," I whisper. I feel a slight headache coming on and a dull ache in my abdomen.

"I can't turn the sun off, sweetheart, but lemme see if closing these blinds helps."

His sneakers make small squeaks on the polished hospital floor as he moves around the windows. At least, that's what it sounds like is happening. The brightness behind my closed eyes lessens, but the ache persists. "Need anything else? Are you thirsty?"

"Water, please," I croak, unable to hide the desperation in my voice.

I can hear him filling up a cup with water, but my eyes are still sensitive as I rub my fingers over them, pushing into the sockets.

"Here." I feel Styrofoam against my lower lip as Ethan holds the cup up to my mouth.

"I can do it myself," I scold as I feel for the cup with my fingers.

"There's my favorite hellcat." Even though my eyes are closed, I can feel that dimple with every word he says, his smile evident in his teasing words.

"Fuck you."

"There won't be any of that until the doctor says it's okay." I can feel his breath near the shell of my ear before his lips press against my cheek. "But you don't have to do everything for yourself. I'm happy to help."

I can feel the heat of his skin, but I refuse to open my eyes. This feels too intimate, too close. This is not the kind of encounter I should be having with someone I just met.

"Hello, Bridget. It's Nurse Maggie. How are you feeling?"

Slowly, my eyes blink open and the nurse's face comes into focus.

"I'm fine."

"Honey, you just had surgery. You're not fine, and that's okay."

"Really, I'm fine. My eyes are super sensitive to light, and I feel a headache developing, but it's nothing I can't handle."

She walks around my bed, checking my IV and my vitals. "Any pain in your abdomen? Or anywhere else? On a scale of one to ten, how is your pain?"

"I'm a little sore, but my pain is probably a two or three."

"That may change as the anesthesia wears off. You should be able to go home in the next hour or two. Do you have someone that can take you home and stay with you?" she asks, glancing at Ethan.

"She does. I'll be there to help. Is there anything we need to know?" Ethan asks, leaning forward in his chair.

"You'll receive post-op instructions upon discharge, but we can go over the highlights," she says as she pulls a rolling stool over to my bed. "No showers for the next twenty-four to seventy-two hours, and no baths for at least two weeks. Once you do shower, be sure to gently pat dry your incision areas. No scrubbing them with a towel or washcloth. You can leave the tape on for about a week or whenever it falls off on its own."

"What about sponge baths?" Ethan asks, standing and taking a step closer to the bed.

If he thinks I'm going to let him give me a sponge bath, he's delusional. I shoot him a glare, expecting to find that smirk on his face. Instead, his face is sincere, concern etched in his brow as he looks at Nurse Maggie.

It's unnerving. I expected him to be jovial, cracking jokes about getting in my pants. I can handle that guy. What I can't handle is this man I barely know showing genuine concern for me. What's his angle? What does he get out of this?

"Sponge baths are okay as long as you keep the incision site dry for the first seventy-two hours," Nurse Maggie replies. "You may have a moderate amount of pain for the first three to five days. We've called in a prescription to your pharmacy for Percocet, but you can switch to ibuprofen when that runs out."

"I'd prefer not to use narcotics, if possible."

"It's up to you, but the prescription is there if you want to fill it, just in case. You may change your mind about that as the anesthesia wears off. Also, it's common to have soreness in your belly and/or shoulder, cramping, and even pain around your incisions for the first few days following surgery."

"Her shoulder?" Placing his hand on mine, his thumb rubs small circles on the back of my palm.

"Yes, during the procedure, the surgeon used gas to inflate the belly so they can see the organs better. This can cause shoulder or back pain for a few days after. She'll need to take it easy, but she should try to walk and be moderately active every day. Try to build up your endurance and walk a little more each day. This can help with blood flow and can get stuff moving, if you know what I mean."

"I'm not sure I do," I say. Actually, I'm very sure I do, but this is not the kind of conversation I want to have in front of Ethan.

"It can help you pass gas and also prevent constipation."

"That's enough of that." I shoot a look at Nurse Maggie, silently pleading with her to stop talking about this.

A crooked grin appears on Ethan's face as he squeezes my hand in his. "Everyone farts and poops, Bridget. They're normal bodily functions."

"Your boyfriend is correct," the traitorous nurse agrees.

"He's *not* my boyfriend," I correct her again with a deep sigh and groan. Suddenly, a sharp pain slices through my abdomen, and I release Ethan's hand and clutch my belly. "Shit. Shit. Shit." The pain is overwhelming as I squeeze my eyes closed to fight back any tears that are thinking about making an appearance.

Nurse Traitor quickly slides her stool over to the bed, pulls back the sheet, and starts lifting my gown to remove the tape and inspect my incision sites. "Be careful there, honey. Your incisions look okay, but you'll want to take caution when coughing, laughing, or taking deep breaths like that. It'll help to hold a pillow against your abdomen."

Ethan's fingers caress my bicep, making featherlight strokes up and down. His mouth is close to my ear, and I can feel the heat of his breath on me as he whispers, "Shhh." When did he get so close?

After a few minutes of his soothing, I turn to Nurse Maggie who has returned to her computer, most likely to type up the aftercare instructions for when I'm discharged. "How soon can I return to work?"

Her stern eyes connect with mine. "Probably not as quickly as you want to. Listen, Bridget, it's important that you take it easy, okay? The best thing you can do is to go home, rest, and let your boyfriend here take care of you," she says, gesturing at Ethan.

The nerve of this woman. "Excuse me? I asked you a simple question. I didn't ask to be judged. I don't need anyone to take care of me." Ethan's hand glides up my arm and along my neck before gently pushing the hair out of my face and tucking it behind my ear. His touch is relaxing, equal parts soothing and infuriating. What is happening to me?

Nurse Maggie looks remorseful, her soft brown eyes crinkling as a soft smile crosses her lips. "You're right, you did ask me a question. The answer is two to six weeks. That's how much time you should spend resting before going back to work. But something tells me that you aren't going to do that. And if that's the case, you're going to end up right back here. You've just had surgery. That's a big deal. You're lucky it wasn't a bilateral oophorectomy, or we'd be discussing all the additional complications, like early menopause. You have one working ovary left. That ovary has the sole responsibility of handling your fertility and hormone production."

Rage courses through me, lighting up my blood in waves of molten lava. Who the fuck does this nurse think she is? "I'm going to stop you right there, *honey*," I spit the last word, sarcasm dripping off the sentiment. "I'm aware of what ovaries do and how many I have left. I didn't ask for a lecture or a patronizing speech about what my body is capable of. It's capable of whatever I choose. I don't appreciate the assumption that I need to rest my body so my remaining ovary can relax before pumping out eggs for me to turn into babies. Not everyone wants to have kids, and you shouldn't assume they do."

"I'm sorry, that was not my intention. But regardless of your choices, you do still need to rest. I'll be at the nurse's station. Hit the call button if you need anything." She smiles and then turns and leaves.

"Fuck." I take deep, slow breaths, careful not to cause any more shooting pain in my abdomen. I can feel the flush on my cheeks darken as my brain registers that I had that exchange in front of Ethan. I'm not sure why I feel embarrassed. It's better that he finds out now that I don't want kids. Maybe that will cure his need for me.

CHAPTER 10

Bridget

I FEEL LIKE SHIT. It's been two hours since I left the hospital, and my pain meds are starting to wear off. Why do I feel like I can do everything? I'm clearly not impervious to pain. It's obvious I may need to expand my inner circle to avoid situations like this with Ethan.

My puppy dog has followed me around all day. To the pharmacy to pick up my pain meds. To my apartment to take care of me. Around the block when I went for my mandatory daily doctor-prescribed walk. I literally felt like I was taking him for a walk like a damn puppy. He's always nearby, and it's unnerving.

When we first met, he told me he prefers a quiet night in. At first, I thought he was fucking with me because what young guy in his twenties doesn't like going out to clubs and partying? But he's spent the entire day in waiting rooms, hospital rooms, and now he's sitting in my living room, offering me quiet support on the loveseat across from where I'm lying. I thought he'd get bored or annoyed by now and leave, but I'm beginning to think he was telling the truth.

I've been alone most of my life. Growing up as an only child, I didn't have many friends to play with. My parents were decent parents. They supported me. My needs were always met, and I never went without. But I never felt like I was their priority, more like an addition to their relationship, a welcome one most of the time. But it still felt like it was them against the world. Even now they're on a cruise together while someone who's practically a stranger takes care of their bedridden daughter. And if he weren't here, I probably would've used an app to find someone to run errands for me.

I had a few friends in school, but I preferred to keep my head down and get lost in a book. Escaping into another world was fun. Safe. I could experience the drama without it being a part of my life. And if things ever got too intense, I could put the book down and come back to it.

Friendships aren't like that. If you walk away from someone's drama, it's considered rude. And in my experience, teenage girls are drama. Listening to story after story of who did what to who was exhausting. I'd had to perfect my resting listening face. If I feigned enough interest, it would appease most people. There was a formula to figuring people out and then giving them what they needed. Some wanted you to listen to their drama. Some wanted you to solve their problems. Once I figured out what each friend required, I could follow that formula and maintain that friendship.

That was until the end of tenth grade when everything went to shit. When my high school boyfriend cheated on me, I didn't find out from him. I was standing at my locker when I overheard the gossip that he'd gotten someone pregnant. I never found out who it was. Did it matter? The one person that I'd trusted with my true friendship, my love, my virginity, had betrayed me. And to make matters worse, all my so-called friends sided with him.

"But, Bridget, they're having a baby. What do you expect? He's not going to leave his baby for you!"

"Don't you think it's kind of selfish to expect him to choose you over her? They're having a baby together."

Like having a baby warrants someone's loyalty over all else. It just means you didn't practice safe sex. I couldn't imagine ever choosing anyone else's happiness at the sacrifice of my own. I couldn't imagine loving anyone else more than myself. All those years I spent making, maintaining, and perfecting those friendships. Gone in the blink of an eye. Gone in the few minutes it takes to take a pregnancy test. And how dare I expect him to choose me? How dare I expect any of those friends to choose me? I listened to all their drama, and the one time I got caught up in the drama that wasn't even my own making, those friends immediately abandoned me.

Because that's what people do—they choose other people over you. My parents did. My friends did. My first boyfriend did. I didn't understand people or friendships like I'd thought. Clearly, there were unknown variables that could affect the outcome. Like drama. And babies.

Becka is the only real friendship I've ever maintained. She was an anomaly I couldn't figure out, and eventually I stopped trying. I could ignore her for days, but she never seemed mad at me about it. Maybe our friendship worked because I hadn't treated it like I did in my youth. I didn't try to figure out the formula to her happiness or the formula to our friendship. I simply let it be. And she accepted me for who I was. She's the only person on this planet who loves me for me.

"Penny for your thoughts?" Ethan asks from across the couch. Like hell am I sharing any of my thoughts with him.

Wincing, I try to sit up. "Christ, I feel like shit."

Ethan stands and crosses to the kitchen. I hear him moving around, opening cupboards, filling a glass with water. He returns with my Percocet and a glass of ice water. "Here, take this. I know you said you didn't want to take any narcotics, but this will help. You can take half the dose if you like, or I can help you wean off them."

"I won't need your help after today."

"I'm not sure that's true."

"It is. I'm fine."

"You're not fine. You're in pain. I can see it in your face and in the stiffness in your body."

"I'll be okay."

"I get the feeling that you're not used to having someone take care of you. But I want to help you."

"And what do you get out of this?"

A pained look crosses his face as his brows pinch. "I'm not doing this because I want something out of it. I'm doing it because I genuinely like you and want to spend time with you."

Well, fuck. That's… nice. But there's still a motive here. In my experience, people don't do things out of the kindness of their hearts without expecting something in return. I've seen it in business time and time again. It's why I'm so successful. I figure out what people want and leverage it to get what I want.

"We aren't sleeping together again."

"Not for the next four to six weeks," he agrees easily. "I'm going to go run over to my place and pack an overnight bag. I'll stay on your couch, if that's okay. In case you need anything during the night. And I can grab you anything you need while I'm out. You're almost out of ice, and it doesn't look like your ice maker is working. And I know you like your water cold."

Dumbfounded, I stare at him. How did he know that? We've shared one meal together. "It's been low on the priority list."

"I can look at it. Tell me, what kind of ice do you like? Big chunks? Little pellets?"

Blinking up at him, I'm at a complete loss for words. "I've never really thought about it before," I reply, unsure of where he's going with this.

"Cool. It looks like you're low on coffee too, and I didn't see any creamer in there." He strides toward the door.

"I don't take creamer in my coffee."

"I do." He turns back to me and asks, "Is there anything you'd like me to cook for you this week? I can grab some ingredients while I'm out."

"Week? I'll give you the night, Pup. You're not staying a whole week."

He taps his knuckles twice on the doorframe. "We'll see about that." With that, he leaves my apartment before I can offer a retort.

Grabbing for the water, I swallow two pills and lie back on the couch, waiting for them to take effect and usher me into a painless sleep.

———

The smell of something delicious tickles my nose and brings me back to consciousness. I can hear Ethan moving around in the kitchen. "How long was I out?"

"About four hours," his sexy voice calls back. "It's dinner time."

"That smells delicious," I say, gingerly attempting to prop myself up on my elbows.

Ethan comes rushing over from the kitchen. "Here, let me help you. Your discharge papers mentioned that you may need help sitting up for the next couple days."

"I'm fin—" A sharp pain stabs at one of the incisions on my right side as I try to sit all the way up.

"Careful, Hellcat. I kind of want you in one piece," he croons, flashing me a boyish smile. "How's your pain?" He gently places his hands around my back and shoulders as he helps guide me to sit up.

"It was better after I took my pain pills, but I think I tweaked something," I admit.

"Do you think you can walk to the dining table, or would you like dinner here?"

"I can walk, you don't have to baby me. I'm a grown woman."

I hear his soft chuckle as I cross toward the kitchen, and I freeze when I see an assortment of ice cube trays on the kitchen island. He places his hands on my shoulders as he comes up behind me and whispers in my ear. "I thought we could figure out which ice you prefer. I borrowed a bunch of different ice cube trays from the bar at the restaurant. You have tons of options. Giant round spheres and cubes like what we use for whiskey. Long cylindrical cubes for a water bottle. Little tiny pellet cubes. I've got round ice, square ice, big ice, small ice. I'm the Dr. Fucking Seuss of ice."

I laugh, then clutch my side as pain lances it. "Don't make me laugh, it hurts."

"Sorry," he says as he runs his hands from my shoulders down my arms, squeezing lightly. "Since I wasn't sure how hungry you'd be and your discharge papers mentioned starting with a simple diet, I grilled you some chicken with rice. Admittedly, it's not my best dish since I only seasoned it with a little bit of salt, but I promise to add more spice as you heal." He crosses around the island and begins putting food on plates for us.

"Are you flirting with me?"

"Maybe. Is it working?"

"No." I laugh lightly, pushing a palm to my side to ease the pain.

"Brutal." He smiles. "Did you decide which ice to try in your water?"

I didn't tell him earlier, but I know exactly what kind of ice I like in every possible scenario. But I'll throw him a bone since he put in some effort to get this right for me. I just can't figure out why he's doing it. I get that he's smitten and our chemistry is intense, but what does he *want* from me? People aren't this nice for no reason. There's always an ulterior motive. Give me time, and I'll figure out his.

Shit, what am I saying? This has already gone on long enough. I'm not giving him any more time, if I do, he'll get attached and then there's bound to be drama when it ends.

And it will end, because I'm old enough to be his mom.

Because I don't want kids, and he probably does.

Because people will judge us like Nurse Maggie did.

Because I've worked too fucking hard all my life to be reduced to a fucking stereotypical label like "cougar."

And because, like every other relationship in my life, this will end, and it'll be messy when it happens. I can tell.

"Earth to Bridget."

"What? Oh, you asked about ice. Um… the normal-sized cubes are fine with dinner," I say, not willing to go into my whole speech about what ice should be used in what scenario.

He gathers up all the other ice trays and puts them back in the freezer before fixing me a glass of water with the ice I requested. After he hands me a plate, he offers me two more pain pills. "It's been long enough that you can take two more, but I know you mentioned not wanting to rely on them. Is your pain better after your nap?"

"It's manageable right now, as long as you don't keep making me laugh."

"In that case, I'll save the pickle story for another night."

"Asshole. You're such a tease."

Shooting me a flirty look, he pulls out the chair next to me and begins eating his dinner. This motherfucker chows down like he didn't just tease me. I'm not even sure why I want to know so bad.

Breaking the silence, he offers, "I'll tell you when you're ready to hear it."

"On second thought, I don't want to hear it."

"Liar." He smirks as he stares ahead, never making eye contact while scooping another bite into his mouth.

We finish our meal in silence. Picking up my plate, I start to move toward the sink before Ethan's large hand reaches out to grab my dish. The veins pop on the corded muscle of his forearm as he steals the plate out of my hand. "Let me. I can clean up in here while you relax."

I don't think anyone has ever said sexier words to me. Settling back into my spot on the couch, I turn on the TV to binge some mindless entertainment on one of my streaming services.

Ethan moves around in the kitchen, the clatter of pans in the sink producing a cacophony of background noises. It feels very... domesticated. I need some space. Gingerly, I rise from the couch and move toward the hallway toward my bedroom. I don't want him to feel at home here. I already agreed to let him stay tonight, but that's it; this isn't becoming a thing.

"Are you headed to bed?" he calls out after me.

"No, uh... going to my room."

"Have you pooped yet?"

That's it. I pause in the hallway, one hand resting on the wall. I'm not talking to this man about my bowel movements.

"I read that painkillers can sometimes slow down your bowels. Your paperwork recommends adding a stool softener and laxative if you haven't pooped within a few days after surgery."

My back still to him, I take a deep breath, counting to ten before I release it. "I'm not talking to you about that," I grit out before walking into my room and closing the door behind me. Leaning back against it, I don't relax again until I hear the clanking of dishes resuming in the kitchen.

I can't do this. This is too hard. Recovering from surgery would've been awkward but manageable if Becka or my parents were here. But Ethan? Navigating this with him feels reckless. One of us is bound to get hurt, and I pray it's him because I'm not sure I could survive it.

CHAPTER 11
Ethan

"FUCKING STUPID," I mutter under my breath as I move around the kitchen putting away the leftovers and cleaning up the last of the dishes. Why would I ask her about pooping? *Because I'm supposed to be her friend and nurse.* While she slept, I googled everything I could about her procedure and what she could expect during recovery. Now it's all I can think about.

Is she getting enough rest? Should I have made her stay in bed today while the pain and risk of tearing her incisions is the highest? What would she have done if I wasn't here?

It's what I've always been, the caretaker. With five younger sisters, I fell into the role naturally. Hell, I should count my father in my list of people I take care of. He's always been immature and wild, often needing to be corralled by either my stepmom Ashley or me. Doing bedtime with him is a nightmare. He gets all the girls wound up, chasing them and tickling them while Mom and I calm them down after his antics. He's a great father to them. And to me. But sometimes, it feels as though I raised him.

I can only imagine how wild he must have been before he met my stepmom. She seems to have tamed him, and having her and all us kids has given him a greater sense of purpose.

88

But raising six children isn't cheap, and he's often at work, picking up extra jobs to help make ends meet.

Thankfully his impulsiveness skipped me. I can see it manifesting in a couple of my sisters, though. My parents will have their hands full with them now that I've moved out, but after Nonna died, I needed to get out of that house. Since Alyx and I work together, it made sense for us to share an apartment. Alyx and his younger sister Nyomi and his moms are like a second family to me. Where my house was loud and chaotic growing up, his family is chill and has always been welcoming. Mina always jokes that I'm her favorite stray.

It hits me how fortunate I am to have two amazing families that love and support me. Hell, the rest of the staff at Mangia Bene is like an extended family as well. The only person I'm not close to is my bio mom Monica. But Bridget? She only has three people in her life that she's let in. Three people that she can count on—and now, when she needs someone the most, she doesn't include them. I know she said they were busy, but I wonder if she even asked them. I wonder if she's even told them she's had surgery.

Soft footsteps pad down the hallway. Turning, I lock eyes with Bridget. Her brilliant blue eyes hold my gaze. She's changed into a tiny little pajama set for bed. Fuck me, she's not wearing a bra, and her nipples have puckered, the points pressing against the fabric of her shirt. Does she know how beautiful she is? Would she believe me if I told her?

She arches an eyebrow. "Eyes up here, big boy."

"S-sorry," I stutter. "Do you need anything, or are you headed for bed?"

"I forgot to take my pills with dinner, and getting changed for bed was more difficult than I thought it would be." I can tell she's trying to hide it, but I can see the pain she can't mask in her face and notice how she's pressing her hand against the right side of her abdomen.

"I could've helped you." She rolls her eyes at me. "I

would've been a gentleman. You're recovering from surgery. I wouldn't start something I couldn't finish." I give her a genuine smile. Nothing too flirty, but fuck if my cock doesn't twitch in my pants at the thought of finishing her off.

"Right, well, I did it all by myself. I might need to take something for the pain now, but I'll be fine. In fact, you probably don't need to spend the night. Thank you for your help, but I've got it from here."

"Bullshit."

"Excuse me?"

"You're holding your side and wincing. Let me check your incisions to see if you did anything."

"I know you think it's fun to play nurse, but you aren't actually a nurse. I can follow up with the doctor in the morning if there are any issues."

I cross to her in three steps and drop to my knees, lifting up her shirt. "Wh-what are you doing?" she asks, her breath picking up.

"I'm looking to see if you popped a stitch, or if there's any redness or swelling on your incision sites." I gently peel back the tape holding her dressings in place and examine each of the small incisions on her abdomen. Goosebumps prickle her flesh everywhere my fingers graze. Once I'm satisfied that she hasn't done any damage, I drop her shirt and stand. "Everything looks okay. I can tuck you in, but I'm staying here. I'll crash on the couch."

"I don't need your help. You can head out. Thanks for everything."

"I'm not leaving, sweetheart. I don't scare that easily. Like I said, I've taken care of my sisters and Nonna, and believe it or not, a few of them put up a bigger fight than you," I double down. She's running away from me. Emotionally, at least. I wonder if it was the poop comment or the taking care of her. Or both.

"Fuck, you're infuriating," she yells.

"Can you stop being—"

"What? Stop being what? A bitch?" she spits out.

"I'd never call you that," I say, taking a step closer, hoping she sees the sincerity in my eyes.

"Then what were you going to say?"

"Difficult. Can you stop being so difficult and let me help you?" Her brows knit as her blue eyes stay locked on mine. "I told you, you don't have to do this alone. Let me help."

She heaves out a huge sigh and turns, heading back down the hallway. I grab her two pain pills and get her a glass of water, adding the ice cubes she used at dinner. When I reach the doorway to her bedroom, I pause briefly, taking in the sight of her. "You forgot these," I start, stretching out my hand to her. She takes the medication and glass from my hands. I watch her throat bob as she takes a large pull of the cool liquid. Fuck me.

"Thanks." Her mouth opens and closes as she looks at the glass of water. She looks like she wants to say something but can't form the words.

"Is it okay? Did I not use the right ice? It's what you asked for earlier."

"It's fine. It's just… I like the big ice at bed. I normally use one of my insulated tumblers and put more ice than water in it. That way, it stays cold and there's still ice in it in the morning."

"That's kind of brilliant, actually. So, when you said you didn't know what kind of ice you liked, you lied. You just didn't want to weird me out with your ice fetish, huh?"

"It's not a *fetish*. Different types of ice have different purposes. And I like different types of ice depending on the situation. It's not a big deal. I just didn't want to be a pain."

"I want to know everything about you, sweetheart," I say, tipping her chin up so she's looking at me. "You're not a pain. Why do you think I brought so many ice trays? I wanted to give you options."

Her gaze drops as her lashes flutter. "I appreciate every-thing you did for me today. You're a good person. A good friend."

"Well, fuck, if that's not what every guy wants to hear from a beautiful woman," I tease. "I'll try to be your friend if that's what you want." I lean down and press a kiss to the top of her head. "Can I snag a pillow and blanket for the couch before I go?"

"Yeah, they're in the closet, next to the en suite."

After I grab what I need from her closet, I head to the living room. I use the half bathroom to do my bedtime routine. Right as I finish brushing my teeth, I hear Bridget curse from her bedroom.

"Shit!"

"Everything okay in there?" I call out, pausing at the door before entering.

"Yeah, I just forgot to wash my face."

I push the door open to see her struggling to sit up in her bed. "You really shouldn't be doing that right after surgery. Here, let me help," I offer as I slide a hand under her legs and back and lift her, carrying her toward the en suite.

"Put me down," she protests. "I don't need to be carried."

I set her down on the counter in the bathroom and stand in between her open thighs.

"What are you doing?" she asks, a slight blush creeping across her chest.

"I'm going to help you wash your face. What do you start with?" She stares at me, a look of defiance in her fiery eyes, the pupils dilated so much that the rings of blue in her irises are barely visible. "I mean, I could guess and start digging around in here." I point to a basket full of neatly organized products.

After several seconds enduring her death glare, she surprises me when she relents. "Fucking A," she mutters. "I don't normally let people see me with no makeup on."

"I've already seen you without it, and you had surgery today. Are you telling me you wore it during that?"

"I didn't, but I put some on earlier after you left. I'm not comfortable going bare."

"Are you forgetting that I saw every inch of you bare and dripping wet in your shower a couple of weeks ago?"

She covers her face as she speaks through her hands. "Grab a washcloth from the linen closet over there," she says as I grab two. "And everything else I need is in that basket over there." She gestures to the basket on the countertop with eight different vials and bottles of varying concoctions, none of which look familiar to me.

"First, I start with the moisturizing cleanser. If you hand it to me, I can do it."

"Nuh-uh. I don't want you bending and twisting. Let me do this for you." I squeeze a dollop of cleanser into my hand.

"That's too much!" she says as I spread the cleanser onto her face.

"Not a problem." I wipe the excess off her before dabbing it on my cheeks.

She laughs as she takes over, rubbing the product into her skin. "You missed some spots," she chuckles as she reaches up to my face, working the soap into a lather. Her fingers light a spark everywhere they land, and I lean into her touch. "Soak the cloth in some warm water to wipe it off."

Before I can wipe her face, she grabs the cloth from my hand and cleans off her face. I look into the mirror behind her and do the same.

"Next is the hydrating face wash."

"Didn't we already clean our faces?"

"Double cleansing is where it's at, though. You can probably skip this step since you're still young."

"So are you," I say back immediately, flashing her a heated look. It's important that she stops seeing me as just my age, just a number. With a little more force than I intend, I pump the face wash into my hand. She reaches out to stop me, and the feeling of her skin on mine soothes the anger I feel. Rubbing the liquid between my hands, I massage it into her face, using what's left to wash mine. If she's going to use it, so will I.

I rinse out her washcloth, and she wipes the face wash off as I repeat her actions. Taking her washcloth, I rinse them out again, ready for her instruction.

"After we double cleanse, we apply toner," she explains as I reach for the next bottle in the basket.

I squeeze some into her hand, and instead of applying it to her face, she reaches up and smooths it over my cheeks. "Are you blushing?" she teases me while rubbing it in.

"Am I? I can't help it if your touch lights me up inside." I smile back at her. With full dimple. And now she's blushing. I rub the toner into my hands and work it into her skin, repeating the actions she took on my face. "And now we wash it off?" I ask, reaching for the cloth.

"Nope. Now we apply moisturizer, and we leave that on too."

Replacing the used items back in the basket, I reach for the moisturizer and open the lid.

"You probably could skip this or use only a little if you have oily skin. I tend to have dry skin, so this is an important step for me," she explains as she dips her fingers into the tub and scoops out the cream. My skin isn't super oily, so I take a little and apply it to the parts of my face that I think might need it.

We are several steps in, and she's already looking more relaxed.

"Next, I apply SPF."

I look at her confused. "You do that before going to bed? Isn't that to protect you from the sun?"

"Yeah, but it's something I've always done. My mom did it,

and so do I. I dunno, it's just part of my routine," she murmurs, dropping her chin to her chest.

"Then we'll do it if it's part of your routine." I grab the SPF and hand it to her. She squeezes some on her hand and reaches up to rub it into my skin. I close my eyes at her touch and think non-arousing thoughts to quell the boner tightening my pants.

After she finishes my face, she applies the SPF to hers. "I don't use a lot, but I figure it can't hurt if my mom's been doing this all her life. And she looks great for her age."

It hits me that she does this whole routine to fight off aging. I don't know why that didn't click for me until now, and I get why it's so important to her. It's not because of our age gap, but because she's probably been told by society, the media, and even her own mother that it's necessary for someone her age.

"You're really fucking gorgeous, you know that?" I cup the back of her neck, pressing my forehead and nose to hers. She inhales a sharp breath but doesn't say anything.

Breaking the tension, I continue rubbing my nose against hers before dragging it all over her cheeks, teasing her. "Sorry, I thought I saw some extra on there. Gotta be sure we rub it all in." Smooshing my face against hers, I rub our faces together like a dog nosing around in someone's crotch.

"Ethan, stop." She laughs, and I continue rubbing my face against hers. "This is not how you're supposed to apply the product."

I pull back, still cupping her neck with both hands, and pull her mouth against mine. It's a quick kiss, but I nip at her bottom lip as I pull back.

"Fuck," she breathes. "Just friends."

"What's next?" I ask, bringing her attention back to me. The effect that kiss had on her makes my heart and my cock swell.

"Um, we do the hyaluronic acid serum next."

"Acid?" I wince at the thought of putting acid on my face.

She chuckles. "It doesn't burn. It helps moisturize."

I lean down and press my lips to hers again. Her taste is sweet and subtle with a hint of mint from when she brushed her teeth earlier. When I pull back this time, she's captured my lower lip between her teeth, tugging on it as we part.

"Not just friends," I whisper against her ear before pecking her cheek.

I hand her the acid that somehow moisturizes, and she dabs it on her face and neck and hands it to me, so I follow her actions.

"I finish with a retinol cream and some eye cream."

I reach for the creams and place them on the counter beside her. "Should I use them too?"

"You can if you want." She shrugs, her tone suddenly less playful than it had been. Maybe I pushed too much with my "not just friends" comment. Sometimes the banter between us is fun and playful. Other times, it strikes a chord in her I didn't know existed, and she's throwing walls up around herself, pushing me out.

We finish the last two steps, and I follow her instructions precisely. I neatly return all the items to the basket in their proper order and pick her up off the counter before depositing her gently in the bed.

Leaning down, I kiss her forehead. "Good night, sweetheart. I'll be on the couch if you need me."

———

The sound of retching wakes me from a restless sleep. I look at my phone and see it's around two in the morning. I hurry back to her room, not knocking or waiting to be invited in. When I find her in the bathroom, she's hunched over the toilet, emptying the contents of her stomach in a violent manner.

"It's okay, I'm here," I say softly as I run a hand up her back and gather the hair she was holding for herself, taking it out of her hand. She'd probably fight me on this or tell me to leave if she wasn't so sick.

I snake one hand up to her forehead, brushing back the hair that sticks to her sweat-coated face. Her skin feels clammy but cool, no signs of a fever.

Moving my hand to her back, I rub small circles against her exposed skin while blowing out cool breaths against her.

"You should—" Bridget starts but is interrupted by another heaving tremor. I can hear liquid hitting the water, but looking over her shoulder, it appears to be mostly clear at this point. How long was she vomiting before I woke?

"It's okay. Try not to talk," I soothe. The sounds of her groans and retching calm down as I continue rubbing her back, lowering myself to the floor next to her, still holding her hair in my other hand. "I know you like numbers, so let me share some with you, and maybe that will help take your mind off things.

"Thirty. That's the percentage of people that experience nausea and vomiting after undergoing general anesthesia."

She groans into the bowl, and I keep lightly trailing my hand along her back as I continue.

"Four. That's the number of months my youngest sister, Evelyn, experienced projectile vomiting during her infancy. It was like *The Exorcist*. I'd be holding her on my shoulder in the kitchen and hear a random splash of liquid hit the floor three feet behind me while warm liquid dripped down my back. I had no clue how her little body could launch vomit so far. It was impressive, actually. And terrifying. I was seventeen. Taking care of her was the ultimate form of birth control for me.

"Five. That's how old Evelyn is now. She hasn't thrown up on me since.

"Twelve. That's how old my sister Ella was when she had

97

her tonsils removed. I was helping my mom take care of her, and being the budding chef that I was, I offered to make her something she could eat that wouldn't hurt her throat. I didn't know then that anesthesia could make some people sick after surgery. I mashed up some fresh peaches in the blender and added some vanilla ice cream. It lasted twenty minutes in her stomach before it came back up. She ran into me on her way to the bathroom and covered me in peach ice cream-flavored barf.

"Sixteen. That's how old Ella is now. I plan to share that story with her prom date, in case he thinks about trying something."

I feel Bridget's back shake with a small laugh, and she stills, still hunched over the toilet.

"Twenty. That's how old I was when Alyx and I attended culinary school in Italy together. We'd lived there a few months, and I'd saved all my money and splurged on a nice pair of Italian leather loafers. They were the only nice thing I owned. Alyx saved up his money and splurged on a huge bottle of Limoncello, which he downed in its entirety in a single night. I was getting in from a night out with some friends, and I was about to slip my shoes off when Alyx came running toward me. He missed the bathroom mere feet from me and vomited all over my new shoes.

"Three. That's the number of people that have thrown up on me. Ella, Evelyn, and Alyx. I get that I'm the last person you want to be vulnerable in front of right now. But I promise, you're safe in my care. Though, if you wanted to keep your aim in the bowl, I wouldn't object."

She sits back on her legs, still kneeling on the tiled floor, while swiping the back of her hand along her mouth. "I'm glad you stayed. I shouldn't have tried to make you leave." She must feel bad if she's willing to give up that nugget of truth. Hope springs in my chest at the thought that I might finally be scaling one of her walls.

CHAPTER 12
Bridget

THE SMELL of coffee draws me out of my room like a moth to a flame. Ethan's back is to me at the counter. The sound of a girl giggling comes from his phone.

"Are you watching porn?" I ask as I try to look over his shoulder.

"Jesus Christ!" he yelps as he fumbles with his phone, nearly dropping it before turning it off and putting it face down on the counter.

"You are, aren't you?"

"It's not porn," he insists but offers nothing else. Someone woke up on the wrong side of the bed this morning. "I made coffee. I take it you like yours black?"

"Black, like my heart." Ethan's smile falls as though my words wound him. "Becka always laughs at that one," I say with an edge to my tone.

He clears his throat as I move past him to reach for a mug from the upper cabinet.

"Let me. You should be taking it easy. I can bring it to you."

Hands on my hips, I pin him with my best "Are you fucking serious?" look. "I can make my own damn coffee. It's not exactly heavy lifting." When it's clear that he's not budging, I throw up my hands in defeat and sulk over to the couch. My fuse is always shorter than normal before I've had coffee.

I'm momentarily stunned when I notice that he's neatly folded his blanket and pillow.

It's no secret that I like neatness and order, and his small gesture isn't lost on me. *Nope, don't go all soft on him now. We are not keeping him.* This is temporary. Just for another day. Or two.

Ethan hands me a mug, and I bring it to my lips, savoring the bitter flavor and aroma. "This is delicious," I moan into my mug, the words escaping me before I can stop them.

"It's an Italian coffee we carry at the restaurant. It was my favorite back in culinary school. We import it straight from Italy." He sips the light brown liquid in his mug from his spot next to me on the couch.

"That's a lot of cream you have in your coffee," I point out, twisting my face in disgust.

"I like it sweet," he says.

"Is that how you drank it in Italy?"

"Actually, I love a good cappuccino. If you had an espresso machine, I'd make you one."

"I do have an espresso maker. It's in the lower cupboard under the island. I don't keep it out since it takes up so much space on the counter."

His face lights up as he sets his mug down and all but races to the kitchen. He locates it in the cupboard and flashes a playful, dimple-filled grin at me. He has entirely too much twentysomething energy this early in the morning. "Tomorrow, I'm making you something special. I need to stop by the restaurant and grab some espresso powder and a few other things. Maybe we can swing by there on our walk later today."

Fuck, he's already planning another day here. "We'll see how today goes," I warn as I continue sipping my nectar of life. Every swallow makes me feel more human. Though I'm interested to see what he can whip up. *Nope. Tamp that thought down right now.*

Eager to change the subject, I ask, "So what were you watching when I came in?"

"Do you promise not to tease me?"

"I can make no such promise."

He lets out a deep breath before turning on his phone and handing it to me, sitting beside me on the couch. The girlish giggling continues as the woman on the screen says, "The uglier you go to bed, the hotter you'll be when you wake up!" She gestures wildly, moving her hands back and forth to show off the products in front of her.

"Are you watching get unready with me videos?" I can't hide the shock in my voice. Why would he do this? How long has he been up watching these?

"Yup. They're actually interesting. Until you showed me your routine last night, I didn't know this was a thing. I had so many questions after you went to bed, that I ended up lying out here on the couch, falling down a rabbit hole." He rests his hand on my leg as his thumb swipes back and forth over my bare skin. A shiver briefly runs through me at the touch. "And then this morning, I honestly felt a difference in my skin, so I wanted to keep learning more about it... and you were sleeping. I figured you needed your rest."

"Are you fucking with me right now?" I ask incredulously.

"What do you mean?" His brows knit in confusion.

"This doesn't make sense to me." I wave a hand over his body to make my point. "I don't understand why you're doing this. Make it make sense."

"It's important to you. I wanted to learn everything I could about it." He pauses but I don't give him a reaction. "Isn't that what you do for the people you care about?"

"No one's ever done this for me."

"Then you need better friends," he chides, nudging his shoulder into mine. He must see the anger flash in my eyes, so he adds, "Or maybe they've done this for you, and you never noticed."

I must look like a fish the way my mouth hangs open as I stare into his emerald eyes. This is dangerous. The way he's looking at me, and not just with his eyes. As though he truly sees me. I have barriers in place to prevent this. How did he get past them?

He starts speaking before I can form a thought. "When you shared your routine with me last night, it got me thinking. You'd mentioned that you did parts of it because it's what you were taught. I like knowing the why behind things. I thought it was kind of strange putting on SPF before bed, so I wanted to know if there was a reason behind it."

"And what did you find out?" I ask, partly interested in what he may have learned but equally annoyed that it feels like he might be questioning my methods and reasoning.

"According to several influencers, it's not necessary and can clog your pores. Apparently, there are varying schools of thought around eye cream too. Some think it's necessary, and others say you don't need a special cream for one part of your face when you can use an all-over moisturizer, which you do.

"I also saw that there's this stone you can use to rub your products in called a gua sha. And I know I'm pronouncing that right because I watched multiple videos where it was mentioned. It's actually not recommended that you use a washcloth, so you might want to switch to a microfiber cloth for drying your face and a silicone body mitt for scrubbing. Oh, and there are these LED face and neck massagers that look cool, like rubbing a lightsaber on your face."

I look at him dumbstruck. He looks so proud of himself, and it pisses me off more.

"You know what a gua sha is, right?" he asks.

"You're not mansplaining skincare to me right now, are you?"

Embarrassment lights up his face as he realizes that he was doing exactly that. "Shit, I didn't mean to. I tend to go down an information rabbit hole when I research and get really excited about what I learn. My mom's a teacher and always says that the best way to retain information is by teaching it to others. When I learn something, I end up giving someone an info dump of that knowledge. It drives Alyx crazy when I do it at the restaurant."

"It's driving me crazy. I know what a gua sha is. I just never found it effective. Maybe I wasn't using it consistently enough, though."

"That's fair. Have you tried one of those LED face and neck massagers though? Now I'm wondering if they actually work or if I've fallen victim to viral marketing. Damn influencers making me drink their Kool-Aid." He laughs, and I can't help how charming I find it.

"I haven't tried one of those. But I've wondered the same thing," I admit. "Those Korean collagen masks too."

He flashes me a genuine smile, and I can't help but release the tension I'd been holding in my clenched hands. It's kind of sweet that he spent the night learning about this, as long as he doesn't try to tell me what to do. I know what's best for me and my skin. I know what's best for everything in my life.

"One of my sisters is on the autism spectrum, and she tends to obsess over different things. I end up researching everything I can about the things that pique her interest, and that habit shows up in other areas of my life. With other…" he trails off, clearing his throat. "Uh… friends." It sounds like the word feels bitter on his tongue, but at least it's starting to sink in for him. We are just friends.

"What kind of stuff is your sister into?" I ask hesitantly, not sure I want to learn more about him and his life but honestly curious after everything he shared about his barfing sisters last night.

"Right now, she's in her friendship bracelet era, like any other thirteen-year-old girl, courtesy of Miss Swift," he says, holding up his wrist to show off a bracelet I hadn't noticed before. It's understated, adorned in black and gray beads with some letters that spell something I can't make out. "She made me this one last week. She made me promise not to take it off."

It's sweet, and it's clear his sister is talented as it looks like something he might have purchased at a store.

"What does it say?"

"Master bro chef. She thought it sounded like Joseph, which is my middle name."

"That's adorable." I grab his wrist to examine it closer. "She did an excellent job. She could sell these on Etsy." As my fingers connect with the skin on his wrist, a wave of electricity emanates from the point of contact, and he locks eyes with me as if to see if I feel it too. I feel it every time we touch, but I refuse to acknowledge it.

"I'll tell her you said that. It would make her day. She's always been creative, and once she got into beads and bracelets, I researched all the best places to gather supplies for her projects. I wanted to know which beads would be the best value and would hold up. It was also important to Lizzy to try and source her supplies responsibly, so she tends to use more glass and clay beads than plastic ones, but most letter beads are plastic. She has some lava beads that are cool too. Not all the recycled material beads are pretty, so she tends to mix it up, mostly opting for sustainability unless the aesthetic is off."

"You're a good big brother to her. To all of them, it sounds like." A pang of jealousy washes over me when I think about the childhood his sisters have had with someone like him looking out for them. Meanwhile, I have to get a one-night stand to take care of me after surgery.

He must do stuff like this for them all the time. I realize that the research he described doing for Lizzy is exactly what he's been doing for me. Reading every word of my discharge papers to know what symptoms I might have. To know what to cook for me. Looking up more about skincare to help understand and improve my routine.

If I don't break this off soon, this could get messy, the more emotions start getting involved. Plus, given how good he is with his sisters, it seems like he's going to make a great dad someday, and that life is definitely not in my future.

I pull my legs up onto the couch, keeping them tight against my body so I can rest my chin on my knees. The pressure eases some of the pain in my torso, and I blow out a deep breath of relief. Looking out the large window in front of me, I keep my eyes trained ahead as I feel his eyes boring holes into me.

"Are you feeling better? You kind of scared me last night."

"About that." I clear my throat. "While I'm mortified that you had to witness the exorcism, I appreciate what you did for me." I shift awkwardly in my seat to wrap my arms around my legs while balancing my coffee in one hand. A twinge of pain flashes through my abdomen and I close my eyes as it passes.

"Did you get any sleep?"

"Not really," I confess, raising my mug to my lips and taking a big pull. "Hence this," I say, holding my empty mug up to him for a refill. "After all the vomiting, I didn't want to take any more pain meds. I wasn't sure what I'd expelled and what was still in my system. My mouth was so dry, and my throat burned too, but I was afraid to drink too much water. It was hard to sleep after that."

He takes the cup and heads to the kitchen. "Can I get you anything? Do you want to take anything for the pain now?"

"Maybe some ibuprofen? I want to start weaning myself off the harder stuff. Maybe save one for after our walk," I offer.

"What kind of ice do you require post-coffee?"

"I knew I shouldn't have said anything."

"I'm only teasing. I think it's cute, and I want to get it right. If the perfect ice in your drink will bring you a little joy, then I'm happy to help."

"Could you fill my cup up with the pellet ice? I haven't

been hungry since the demon vacated my body last night. Crunching on some ice might help."

"Coming right up." He opens the freezer and begins preparing my water. After refilling the trays and putting them back, he strides over to me with two ibuprofen and the perfect glass of water in his hands.

If he's going to wait on me hand and foot, maybe I could get used to this.

Shit.

CHAPTER 13
Bridget

THE SOUND of metal clanking rouses me. I didn't even realize that I'd dozed off. It's been two days since my surgery, and he's still here. Sleep has been difficult with the amount of pain I've been in, so naps have become the norm, but I hadn't intended to take one, and there's a pillow under my head propping me up while the blanket that Ethan's been using is strewn across me. Did he do this? Looking over to the kitchen, I see Ethan, and holy *fuck*.

His shirt is off, and sweat trickles down the defined muscles of his back while his head is hidden in the freezer. Wait, why is he shirtless?

I notice that most of my freezer's contents are spread out on the island, and the fridge has been pulled away from the wall.

"Are you fixing my ice maker?" I croak, my throat froggy with sleep.

"I was attempting to, but it looks like this could be caused by a bigger issue with your water line. Your ice maker isn't making ice because the water line isn't getting enough water to the unit. I'm pretty handy, but you might need a plumber to check this out." He turns toward me and leans over the island, wiping his brow with his forearm.

Fuck me. What is it about a shirtless man in a backwards ball cap? And why does it make me feral? The way the veins of his forearm pop along the corded muscles is sexy as fuck.

"That doesn't explain why you're all sweaty and shirtless when half of your body is in my freezer."

"I run hot?" he suggests with a crooked smile, the hint of his dimple appearing. "You need a plumber. Want me to call one for you? I know a pretty good one."

"You do?"

"Yeah, my dad. I wouldn't let him charge you, though."

"That's okay. I'll call someone to deal with it eventually," I say as he puts everything back in the freezer and moves the fridge back to its place.

The last thing I need is his father or any of his family in my apartment. What would they even think about me dating their son? Would they think I'm too old for him? That I'm his sugar mama or a cougar?

"I need to hit the shower, you mind?" Ethan asks, pulling me from my thoughts.

"Help yourself," I say, making a sweeping motion with my arm in the direction of my bedroom.

"Thanks. Let me know if you want that sponge bath after." He winks at me as he passes.

After a ten-minute standoff, I reluctantly agree to go for a walk around the block with Ethan. I was hoping to get a little time on my own. He's incredibly sweet and respectful of my space, but I'm an introvert of the worst kind sometimes. My social battery is drained, and I need time to recharge.

It's not that I was looking forward to this surgery, but the prospect of working remotely was appealing to me. Not having to go into the office and make small talk as I get my morning coffee in the break room? Sign me up.

But it was clear my pup had a bone he wouldn't let go of, hence our circling the block, headed toward Mangia Bene. I usually frequent this restaurant once a week, yet going there with Ethan today feels different.

"Penny for your thoughts?"

Several minutes pass as I ignore his question, thoughts swirling in my head like a snow globe that's been given a good shake by a rowdy child.

"Why are you so curious what I'm thinking? Can't I enjoy a walk in silence?" I finally snap. I catch myself. "Shit, that was mean. What I meant was, you're really nice…" I trail off, hoping he'll take the hint.

"But? It sounds like there's a but."

"But I don't think this is going to work out. I appreciate your help the past two days."

"It's about that time, isn't it?" He grabs my hand, threading his fingers through mine and anchoring me so I can't let go despite my attempts to tug free.

"What are you talking about?"

"For you to run or push me away. At least a couple times a day you attempt some variation of this speech. While I understand that you're a fiercely independent introvert, you just had a pretty significant operation and need someone to help you while you recover."

"Becka gets back soon. I can call her to help."

"What I can't figure out is what set you off this time. I'm not pushing you for more. I didn't ask about your bowel movements—"

"Jesus."

"You don't seem particularly vulnerable right now, and it's not the first time we've been out in public together."

"Remember what happened last time we were around people? Nurse Maggie thought you were my son."

Ethan stops on the sidewalk and gently tugs on our linked hands, pulling me back to him. For a fleeting moment, I hope that he'll touch me, lean into me. Then I realize how close we are to the restaurant, and anxiety creeps in, making me worry that someone will see us. I'm too exposed right now, too raw. I don't think I could hear one piece of negativity or criticism without feeling like I'll collapse like a house of cards. So I opt for honesty.

"I feel like shit right now. It feels like someone has punched my insides out. Walking hurts. I still can't get out of bed without your help or going extremely slow because of the pain. I can't do any of my normal routines, and now I'm out in public in little makeup with someone who's been mistaken for my child."

He lets go of my hand and slides his palm up my arm, grabbing my shoulder to get my full attention. This feels less intimate than the hand-holding, and I'm grateful for the reprieve.

"I think you're fucking beautiful, Bridget. Just like this. But more importantly, you have a beautiful soul. You don't take shit from people. You know what you want and who you are, and you don't apologize for going after what you want. I want to be around that kind of energy. I'm proud to be seen with you. If people don't understand our friendship, fuck 'em."

"Fuck 'em," I repeat with a hollow laugh. "I wish I had your ability to not care about what others think."

"I'll get it out of you," he promises. "But if you're worried, you can wait out here, and I'll grab what we need from the restaurant."

I let out a deep breath. What will it hurt? This is the lowest-risk scenario, right? Anyone in there already knows me as a customer and thinks of him as part of the family. If anyone would accept this friendship, it'd be the people in that restaurant. "It's fine, I'll go. Maybe don't hold my hand. I don't want to give anyone the wrong idea."

"Friends can hold hands."

"Do you and Alyx?"

He rolls his eyes. "I suppose you have a point there."

He opens the door for me as we approach the entrance. The aroma of garlic and cheese hits me as we cross the threshold and Mina greets us at the hostess stand.

"Pickle! We weren't expecting you today," Mina exclaims.

"I just need to grab a few things from the kitchen if you don't mind."

"Help yourself!" Dre calls out from near the bar as she joins us, planting a kiss on Mina's cheek. "The prodigal son has returned. How's the patient?" she asks, turning her attention on me. Seeing the embarrassment on my cheeks, she continues, "Ethan never asks for time off. He said he was helping a friend recover from surgery." Relief washes over me as I realize that he hasn't told them everything.

"I'm good, thanks. Just wiped out," I say through a tight smile, forcing my face to look polite. I'm too tired to fake pleasantries with people right now, despite how kind Mina and Dre are.

"If you need anything, let us know. Or Ethan. He's always a huge help to us here. He's a good person to have in your corner." Dre winks at me before kissing Mina's cheek again and loudly whispering "Behave" in her ear.

"Uh, we're standing right here, can you not?" Ethan says to Mina as Dre retreats to the kitchen.

"Oh, that wasn't flirting. It was a warning for her," Dre explains, pointing at Mina as she walks backward toward the kitchen.

Mina crosses her arms over her chest and raises her chin to Ethan. "I warned you what would happen if you didn't..." Her eyes cut to me and then back to Ethan. A silent conversation passing between them before Ethan pulls my body flush into his side, dropping a kiss on my head.

"Satisfied?" he says through gritted teeth. A hint of a smile and desperation in his eyes. I wonder what that's about.

"That'll do for now, Pickle." She smiles before grabbing a rag from under the hostess stand and stalking to the bar to wipe it down.

"What was that about, *Pickle*?" I ask as I look up at Ethan still plastered against my side.

"Later," he promises as his hand tips my chin up.

Once we get back to the apartment, my cell vibrates in my pocket. "It's Dr. Francis's office," I explain as I excuse myself, walking toward my room.

"Hi, Bridget. This is Dr. Francis's nurse calling to check in on you and see how you're doing."

"I'm fine," I grumble.

"That's good to hear. We got a call at the office yesterday morning. Your boyfriend was concerned. He said you experienced some vomiting the night you came home."

"That's correct. That I vomited, not the other part. He's not my boyfriend." I continue down the hall, walking into my room and pulling the door closed behind me, not wanting Ethan to hear my conversation.

Choosing to ignore my awkwardness, the nurse continues, "How are your incision sites healing? Any redness or swelling?"

"Nope, they look good. Will I be able to shower soon?"

"You should wait at least seventy-two hours, so maybe tomorrow evening. Have you been able to pass gas and have a bowel movement?"

"Um, yeah, I've been able to pass gas," I start, thinking about the handful of times I left Ethan alone in a room to sneak off to my bathroom. "But I haven't had the urge to do more than that."

"That's okay, honey. Your body's still adjusting. But if you don't have a bowel movement in the next three days, give us a call. In the meantime, I can call in a stool softener and laxative for you."

"No, that's okay. I have some over-the-counter stuff I can try if I need to," I reply, glancing toward my bathroom, where I keep most of my medications.

"Perfect. How's your pain been on a scale from one to ten?"

"Without medication, it's been a five or six. But it's not constant. The Percocet obviously helps, but I've been swapping it for ibuprofen. So maybe a two or three once it kicks in? My shoulder's been sore too."

"That'll happen. You could continue with the Percocet and add the ibuprofen in instead of swapping it out."

"I'll think about it. I'm not sure that I want to continue with the harder stuff. I don't want to grow dependent on it, but it mainly knocks me out, leaving me feeling vulnerable and sleepy. Plus, I think it's messing with my sleep cycle." I know Ethan would never take advantage of me in that state, but the thought of being vulnerable like that around anyone makes me uncomfortable.

"Fair enough. Do you have someone you can count on as a caretaker? You'll need someone to get groceries for you. You shouldn't be lifting heavy bags."

"It's fine. I use an app for grocery deliveries."

"Do they bring it in and put it away for you? Because the last thing you want is to hurt yourself lifting a gallon of milk."

"Not typically, but it'll be fine. I don't drink much milk anyway, so I don't buy it by the gallon."

"It's not just milk. Anything heavy like that can do damage right now, even carrying a laundry basket. You should avoid any moderate or heavy lifting for the next six weeks. It can be hard for a lot of women, especially those with kids or pets—"

"Then it's a good thing I have neither," I retort with a bit of bite in my tone.

"Well, okay," she stutters. "Please don't hesitate to reach out if you have any questions or need anything."

Ending the call, I toss my phone down on the bed. I think about Becka. She and Robert will get back in a few days, and I'm going to have to tell her about my surgery, especially if I'm going to enlist her help instead of Ethan's.

But if Becka comes, she'll probably need to bring her daughter Hallie with her, and while she's adorable, the thought of a four-year-old running through my apartment and getting things sticky when I should be resting—well, it doesn't sound relaxing.

It's much later in the day as Ethan begins prepping dinner in the kitchen, while I sit on the loveseat in the living room watching him, my show forgotten in the background. He's oblivious to my blatant staring as he opens drawers and cabinets to pull out various items he needs: a cutting board, a few different knives I own but clearly don't know all the different uses for, and several pots and pans with matching lids. I track his body as he dances around, organizing his workspace. Oh, to be in my early twenties again and have that kind of energy —though Ethan has far less worries and a hell of a lot more optimism than I ever had at that age.

His forearms flex and pop as he skillfully angles the knife up and down, chopping carrots and celery. After several minutes of chopping, he stills, wiping the blade on the edge of his apron.

"Where did you get an apron?" I ask with confusion. I don't own any, and I don't remember him putting one on. Maybe he did it while I was watching TV. I mean, I haven't been staring at him this whole time. Have I?

"From my bag."

"You bring aprons with you when you pack an overnight bag?"

He chuckles as he sets the now-clean knife down. "I knew I'd be doing a good bit of cooking for you, and I like wearing one when I cook."

"That tracks, I guess."

"You always gonna bust my balls this hard?"

"Maybe," I shoot back.

"Good, I like it. Keeps me on my toes." He smiles, showing off his perfectly straight teeth and adjacent dimple.

He turns his back to me and opens the fridge, gathering various items in his arms. I'm grateful for the break in his attention as my cheeks flush. I might be starting to like our back and forth.

"I'll get you in here with me one day," he promises as he lines up items on the counter and begins filling a pot with water. "Once you're healed, I'll teach you some things. But for now, just enjoy the show, beautiful."

"You sound pretty sure about that. Didn't realize you were so cocky."

"Only when it comes to you, sweetheart." He turns to put the pot on the stove. "I make your favorite meal, after all."

"You could teach me how to make it."

"And have you stop coming into the restaurant? Then what would you need me for? I wasn't born yesterday."

"It may not have been yesterday, but it wasn't that long ago."

His brows furrow, and a line appears between them. "Don't do that."

"What?"

"Make jokes about my age. You keep using it as an excuse to push me away. I've already told you, it's not going to scare me off." His eyes darken and roam up and down my body.

I shift awkwardly in my seat, the heat of his gaze lighting up my insides as I taunt, "What are you going to do about it?"

He leans forward, bracing his hands on the island in front of him. The move makes his muscles strain against the fabric of his shirt, stirring something deep in my core. And even though he's in the kitchen and I'm in the living room, it feels like we are inches apart. "Once you get the green light, I'm going to punish that perfect little ass of yours. Either with my hand, my tongue, or my cock. So I suggest you stop mentioning our ages, or you pick a safe word. It's your choice."

I can feel my arousal soaking my panties. The goddamn mouth on this man. It's not often I'm rendered speechless. Witty comebacks are my thing. Part of my armor. Equally part of my charm and downfall. I've picked up a lot of things working in the corporate world, and being able to give it back to men verbally is a skill I've honed. It's surprising how easily men trust you when you can take a joke and snap one back. It's part of what helped me move up at my company. Men like working with women who don't create drama and have a good sense of humor. And I've put up with a lot of good ole boys in my career. But no one's ever spoken to me like Ethan.

However, at this moment, not a single word comes to mind. Not a single thought enters my head other than the thought of Ethan doing all those things to me.

Several tortuous moments pass, and Ethan returns his focus to our meal, but I can't stop picturing all the ways he'll punish my body. Careful not to make any sudden movements, I use my arms to push myself off the couch.

"I'm going to take a shower," I announce, not sure why I'm doing so. Maybe because I want him to picture me naked the way I'm picturing him right now. I turn and begin heading down the hall to my bedroom.

"No, you're not." His deep voice booms across the apartment. "You have to wait seventy-two hours, remember?"

Even though I haven't been very active since I came home

—aside from our walks—I'm starting to feel like I want to bathe, even if it might hurt to bend and reach all my places.

"That'll be tomorrow. Close enough," I call out, keeping my back to him.

Before I have a chance to register what's happening, his hands are holding my biceps, pulling me back to him. I wince at the pain that lances my shoulder from the movement.

"Shit, sorry. Did I hurt you?"

"No, my shoulder's been hurting since last night."

"The nurse said that could happen. Need anything for the pain?" he asks, gently turning me to face him.

"I might take something with dinner," I acquiesce. Suddenly, I'm aware of how close we are standing. His body is mere inches from mine as the energy sparks between us.

"I've got soup simmering on the stove, and it should be ready in the next thirty minutes. Then I can help you with a sponge bath, and we can get a heating pad on your shoulder while you relax on the couch. That sound like a plan?"

"Y-yeah," I breathe as the heat from the closeness of his body sends a shiver through me.

Noticing the tremor, he shoves his hands in his pockets as he leans in close to my ear and asks, "Are you cold?"

"No, I…"

My words trail off as he leans in closer. "I know you feel this, Bridget. If you need to call it a friendship, I'll play along. For now. But I really fucking like you. Your spark. Your wit. Your bite. Your body. You're the whole goddamn package, and I'd be a fool to let you push me away. I know you don't let a lot of people in, but I'll knock on your door every fucking day for the chance to spend even a minute with you."

An appliance beeps in the kitchen, causing him to back away slowly, his hands still in his pockets.

We finish dinner, but Ethan's plea from earlier keeps swirling around in my head. Thoughts of his plan for me after dinner send a thrill of delight through me.

Letting him give me a sponge bath should scare me. It's an incredibly intimate act. But this man has shown me that he's not afraid of intimacy even if my hesitancy is obvious. He's always offered me an out, knowing I need it, but still pushing me for more. We've already showered together, and he washed my hair. This is just like that, right?

I couldn't imagine letting anyone else in my inner circle do this for me. The thought of Ethan doing it excites me, and for once I don't have an urge to push him away. Huh. When did that happen?

Ethan removes our dishes from the table, loading up the dishwasher and letting the pots and pans he used to prepare our meal soak in the sink. "I can help with that," I offer.

"Nope. No lifting things, remember?"

"It's kind of ridiculous to expect me not to carry anything at all for six weeks. When the nurse called earlier, she scolded me not to lift any laundry or groceries. She also said something about not lifting kids or pets. I told her I didn't have either and that she could fuck off."

"Why doesn't that surprise me?"

"Ok, maybe I didn't actually tell her to fuck off, but it was implied."

"After I finish cleaning these dishes, I'll clean you," he says over his shoulder, winking at me before turning back to the sink.

"You're ridiculous."

With his back still to me, he says, "Why is it that I can feel that eye roll without even seeing your face?"

"I'm going to head to the bathroom and wash my face," I say, slowly rising from my chair.

He drops a dish into the sink, fumbling with his soapy hands before he grabs a towel and starts drying them. "Don't," he starts, a look of sincerity crossing his handsome features. "I'd like to help you with that again. I got you something earlier."

"You did? When? I was with you the whole time."

Crossing to his overnight bag near the couch, he pulls out a small brown paper bag and hands it to me. "I asked Dre to grab it for me. She handed it to me before we left the restaurant."

Reaching into the bag, I pull out a vial of vitamin C serum and two collagen face masks.

"I told her about all the videos I was watching and about your routine. She said these were the secret to her youthful look."

"Thank you, this is so thoughtful of her. I'll have to thank her the next time I see her."

"You ready for that sponge bath now?" He waggles his eyebrows in a suggestive manner.

"Not if you're going to act like a teenager who's just seen his first set of boobs."

"I was sixteen. A late bloomer."

"Don't you have dishes to finish?"

"I'm not letting you push me away again, remember?"

I turn and head toward the bathroom, new skincare products in hand. Ethan helps me with my skincare routine and repeats every step on himself like he did the night before. Standing next to him in my bathroom feels natural, like he's meant to be here and not an unwelcome visitor.

A pang of nerves hits me at the thought of him bathing me, but I swallow it and slowly start removing my clothes, giving him an awkward silent striptease free of eye contact. I've removed my shirt and bra when I notice him staring at me.

"Uh… w-what're you d-doing?" He stutters out as I watch his reflection in the mirror. His eyes rake over me as he reaches down and adjusts himself in his pants.

"I assume I'm going to need to be naked for this sponge bath?"

"Right, uh, I didn't think about that part when I offered," he says as his breathing picks up and a light sheen of sweat breaks out along his hairline.

"Don't get shy on me now, Pup."

"It's not that. I just didn't expect you to actually let me, let alone try to strip all the way down. I'm not sure my dick can take it."

"If you need to go rub one out, you can use the other bathroom. I'll wait," I challenge him with a fire in my eyes.

"Jesus," he mutters, running a hand down his face. "It's fine. You're just really fucking gorgeous. This body. These tits."

"I can see this is going to be"—my eyes move down to his crotch—"hard for you. I can do it if you're not up for the job, *friend*."

"Fuck that," he says as he crosses to the linen closet and pulls out a washcloth and a towel. After turning on the faucet and adjusting it to the right temperature, he soaks the cloth and rings out the extra moisture as he turns to me, his eyes roaming up and down my body as though he's a starved man and I'm something he plans to devour.

Feeling a little embarrassed like I'm being examined under a microscope, I slowly turn and offer him my back to start. "I think I've earned the pickle story now," I proclaim, proud of myself for the baby steps I'm taking with this man.

"Okay," he breathes out. "But it's really embarrassing. Promise you won't make fun of me."

"I make no such promise."

He carefully cleans my back, lightly scrubbing me with the warm soapy cloth before patting me dry with the towel. He moves on to my arms and shoulders, being careful not to aggravate the pain in my shoulder as he washes.

Just when I think I've pushed him too far with the teasing, he turns my body to face his and our eyes connect. Looking down at me, he slowly moves from my shoulders down my chest, and I suck in a deep breath as warmth pools in my core. His deep voice is low when he starts speaking.

"I had to lead service one night, and I hadn't done laundry in a while and all my chef pants were dirty. Alyx gave me a pair to borrow, but they were a little tighter than I was used to. I wasn't too worried about it since my apron would cover me."

"Why is it kind of hot picturing you dressed as a chef?"

"Behave," he warns as his cloth massages my breasts, cleaning in small circles before he wipes away the moisture with the towel.

"Do you wear the little hat and everything?" I question through shallow breaths trying to focus on his words and not the feelings he's awakening in my body.

"I have a chef hat that I earned from culinary school in Italy, but I don't usually wear it. I normally wear a black Aussie chef box hat if I'm leading service. Otherwise, I wear a ball cap." His hands move beneath my breasts as he cleans the area right above my incisions. "You're missing the point. The important part of the story is my pants, not my hat."

"Just painting a mental picture of what you look like in uniform." I chuckle as he kneels and begins his focus on my feet, moving up my legs as he continues.

"Anyway, I was leading service, and a guest asked to speak with the chef. It'd been a busy night, and I'd forgotten about my pants. I walked over to the table and had lifted my apron to wipe my hands off so I could shake the guest's hands when a little girl at the table loudly declared, 'Look at him, mama, he has a pickle in his pants!' She said it loud enough for the entire restaurant to hear. I was mortified."

"Wait, I thought you said this was embarrassing? Aren't most guys proud of having a big dick?" I ask as he finishes the front of my legs and grabs my hips to spin me to face away from him.

"Well, the little girl didn't mention the size of the pickle, so the kitchen staff got creative. Now, when I run a dinner service, the staff will refer to me as Pickle. Instead of 'yes, Chef,' it's 'yes, Pickle.' I can't tell you how many times they refer to my 'little gherkin.' And it's not like I'm going to whip my dick out and correct them. So now my unofficial nickname is Pickle. Every time we get an order for extra pickles, the wait staff will toss some at me like I'm a stripper. It's humiliating."

"I don't see what the big dill is."

He groans. "Fuck, not you too. I knew this was a bad idea."

"Pickle puns must be your bread and butter."

He playfully smacks my ass before palming it in his hand and squeezing it through the fabric of my shorts. "Jesus Christ, why aren't you wearing any panties?" he grits out through clenched teeth.

"The extra fabric on my waist kept rubbing on my dressings, so I took them off."

"If I pull these down—"

"I don't know if it's a good idea to finish that sentence, *friend*," I say, half-warning, half-teasing. We can't do anything about these feelings right now anyway.

"Got it," he says, pushing up to stand. He gestures to the towels. "I'm going to go start a load of laundry for these and my apron. Do you have anything else I could throw in for you?"

"Sure, there's a little bit in the hamper by the door."

Gripping the edge of the counter for support, I let out a breath. The air in the room feels colder now that he's gone, and my brain doesn't know how to process that information. The temperature wouldn't actually lower enough for my body to notice a difference just because there's one less body in here. But it's not my brain that's registering these changes right now. It's my heart.

This man. Fuck.

CHAPTER 14
Ethan

WITH EACH DAY that Bridget doesn't kick me out, I feel one step closer to scaling her walls. Granted, these are most likely little hurdles, the kind used in track meets. I imagine the walls only get higher and stronger—fortified with brick and mortar—the further she lets me in.

I'm determined to show her how good we could be together. Last night's sponge bath was a huge step for her. Although I had to give up the pickle story and endure her teasing me with the title too, it's worth it if it brings her amusement. I have a feeling she needs more light moments like that in her life, and I want to be the one to give them to her.

The fact that I'm still here after three days is monumental. At this point, with the way she's been avoiding her texts, I don't think she would've let even Becka stay longer than this. I don't know a lot about her relationship with her parents, but it doesn't sound like they're super close either. If I wasn't here, she probably would've tried to do it all herself, and that's why she doesn't appreciate anyone telling her she needs a man or a family. She doesn't need anyone, but fuck, if a woman like her wanted me, chose me, I'd have everything I wanted in life.

I pull out the espresso machine as I move around the kitchen, careful to make as little noise as possible. Bridget had mentioned that she likes Americanos, so hopefully she'll enjoy what I make her. Nothing beats an authentic Italian espresso. If I can master her favorite meal and her favorite drink, maybe she'll want me to stay and help with her full recovery.

After several minutes of me clearly not being as quiet as I thought I was, Bridget emerges from her room, padding down the hallway into the kitchen before delicately reaching for a stool at the counter. I catch her wince as she starts to pull out the chair with her right hand, before switching to using her left. Her shoulder must still be bothering her.

I reach for her pain meds and drink, handing her the Americano as I set her meds on the counter and flash her a smile. Her hair is a little disheveled and her face is bare, and she looks so beautiful. Small button nose. High cheekbones and a sharp jawline. Plump lips with a Cupid's bow and the tiniest laugh lines that only appear when she shares a genuine smile —which will be more often if I have anything to do with it. The most stunning blue eyes I've ever seen with the faintest of crow's lines that crinkle when she laughs. Fucking stunning.

She doesn't say anything as she reaches for the cup, but her eyes widen the moment the warm liquid reaches her taste buds. I've seen it countless times as a chef, the moment a guest tastes my creation, the light in their eyes, the way their eyebrows rise in surprise as a smile slowly takes over their features. It gives me life, and even more so because it's Bridget enjoying what I made. I'd spend the rest of my life serving her if it meant I could give her that joy.

"This is delicious," she groans into her cup.

"How'd you sleep?"

"Not great." Surprised at her sudden honesty, I keep my mouth shut, waiting for her to continue, hoping this is a wall she's letting me peek over. "My shoulder's making it difficult to sleep."

"Did you take anything for it?" I question, glancing at the two bottles of pain pills I set in front of her, one over-the-counter, and one prescription.

"No, I don't want to depend on anything for the pain."

"Or anyone?" I offer, unsure why I'm poking the bear who has clearly not had enough coffee yet.

"Excuse me?" Her eyes shoot up to mine as she gives me a once-over, and not the kind I like.

"You heard me. You don't like depending on anything or anyone. And while it's one of the things that I admire most about you, I'm literally here to help, so let me." I say, sliding the pill bottle toward her.

She's quiet for several minutes, sipping her coffee while she maintains her death stare with me. I contemplate how quickly I'm going to need to pack when she throws me out, before her eyes unexpectedly soften.

"My first full sentence was 'I do it.' Apparently, I've been self-sufficient from birth, which suited my parents fine since they always seemed more occupied with each other than me. And it was fine. I didn't need a lot of doting on anyway. I've always known what's best for me, and I've never been afraid to ask for it. I kind of raised myself. My parents were great, don't get me wrong, but they were never in tune with my needs. I always told them what I needed, and they provided it for me."

Understanding washes over me. She's never had anyone truly take care of her, not even as a child. Being provided for and being nurtured are entirely different things. No wonder she never asks for help. It's almost as though she doesn't ask for help not only because she doesn't know how, but also because her brain has convinced her that she can't. The fact that I'm here being allowed to help her is a bigger deal than I realized.

"I'm not used to people wanting to help me," she starts softly, her gaze cast down into her mug, as if it's painful to look at me while she shares this truth. "You being here is hard for me. Having anyone see me like this, weak and fragile…" She trails off as her voice wobbles. Her eyes won't meet mine, but I can feel the pain in them to the depths of my soul. I reach across the kitchen island and place my hand against hers as she holds her mug.

"You're so goddamn strong. There's nothing fragile about you, Bridget. You just had surgery. Some things aren't meant to be done alone. It doesn't make you weak."

"But I should be able to do this!" She raises her voice, not quite yelling, but full of frustration. "My whole life, I've taken care of everything myself. I studied, I got good grades, I got into college and graduated with honors. I passed the GMAT and got my MBA. I landed a great job at a great company and worked my way up to the C-suite before I turned thirty-three. I gave up all distractions to accomplish what I wanted."

It's hard to ignore the number of times she said "I," and it breaks my heart to think of all she had to do on her own. "What kind of distractions?" I question, though I fear I already know the answer.

"Relationships. They're messy and steal focus from every-thing I've tried to accomplish for myself. I knew enough about how to fit in, what I needed to do to get the right people to like me, respect me, want to promote me. But I keep my head down and do my work. I produce results, and my numbers speak for themselves. And I'm good at it. Fucking great at it." Her head is still down, eyes staring into her coffee.

"But at what cost? You can have a career and friendships, Bridget. You don't have to sacrifice real human connection to succeed."

"I have to. I can't…" She stops herself as her nervous energy manifests. The fingers not covered by my hand tap against her cup as her leg bounces against her stool making a small squeaking noise as it moves. Her head tilts side to side, her eyes still avoiding mine, as she tries to stretch her neck while I continue speaking.

"Why can't you? What happened that made you have these feelings? Was there some shitty asshole who made you feel this way about yourself?"

Her whole body stills, her little fidgety movements ceasing as it's clear I've struck a nerve. She pulls her hand away from mine as she brings her cup to her lips and takes a sip while she avoids answering my questions for several minutes. I watch as she opens the pill bottle and takes one, following the bob of her throat as she swallows.

"I don't want to talk about that." There's a finality in her tone that makes me hesitant to press further, yet I'm grateful for the walls she let me climb just now.

CHAPTER 15

Bridget

THE NEXT MORNING, I emerge from my bedroom like a zombie looking for fresh brains in the form of caffeine. I had trouble sleeping for more than two hours at a time between my shoulder pain, my abdominal pain, and my racing thoughts. I probably should've taken my pain medication, but I only want to use them when necessary. I will not become dependent on anything or anyone.

Ethan has the espresso machine on the counter again and is fiddling with the knobs and parts. And he's shirtless *again*. Did this man not pack any T-shirts? As I get closer to the kitchen, I notice that Ethan is not only shirtless, he's wearing a towel slung low over his hips, the deep V of his muscles drawing my attention down to the bulge I see hiding behind the white cotton.

"Morning. I was excited to play with this beauty again. I made you something new."

"Did you take a shower in my bathroom?" I ask. When had he been in my room? Maybe I did get more sleep than I thought. Walking into the kitchen, I set my phone on the island and lean back against the counter as sports highlights fill the muted TV screen.

"That is the only place to shower in your apartment." He looks concerned. "I didn't wake you, did I? You looked zonked when I snuck in."

"It's fine. Just put some clothes on. Didn't you do laundry recently?" My tone comes out more annoyed than I intend, but the sight of him nearly naked is a little more than I can take this early in the morning. *Be strong, Bridget.*

He saunters to his overnight bag and grabs a pair of athletic shorts, dropping the towel and revealing his entire backside as he pulls the shorts up his hips. Fuck, I forgot about his rugby thighs and perfect ass. Clearing my throat, I try to pull myself together. "You could've done that in the bathroom," I huff as he crosses to the laundry closet off the kitchen and tosses the towel into the washing machine.

"Do you normally check out your *friends'* asses?" he shoots back.

Touché. I scrub a hand down my face, hoping to hide the heat I feel in my cheeks as I move around the island.

"Let me know what you think about this." He hands me an espresso mug.

Bringing the mug to my mouth I savor the rich aroma before taking a sip. My taste buds explode the second the coffee touches my tongue. "Is this an Americano? It's better than the one you made yesterday, if that's even possible."

He smiles. "It's a doppio espresso. It's basically a double espresso. Americanos are diluted with water. A doppio has a stronger, richer flavor."

Damn, he sounds sexy when he speaks in Italian. "Your Italian accent's not too bad," I say. "Did you pick up a lot of Italian when you lived in Italy?"

"A little. And trust me, my accent is shit. If you hear a native speaker, you'll realize I sound like a cheap knockoff."

"Why does your espresso taste better than mine?" I breathe in the earthy aroma.

"I did go to culinary school, you know," he teases, leaning

back against the island as I pull up a stool next to him. "But it's probably the espresso powder I used. The restaurant imports it."

"Do you know how to say anything else in Italian?" I try not to blush, but I can feel the heat seeping into my cheeks.

"You like when I speak Italian, eh?" He leans over, placing one hand behind my neck while cupping my cheek with the other. "Voglio che siamo più che amici."

The breath whooshes from my lungs as I pant for air. My kitchen suddenly feels one hundred degrees hotter. "What did you say?" I ask, my voice sounding breathier than normal before my brain overrides my libido. "Did you just mention my puking?"

He chuckles softly, his lips moving millimeters from my forehead. "No. It means that... I'm... uh... I'm glad we are friends." His soft breaths warm my skin before he presses his lips to my forehead, hovering longer than he should.

"Oh," I breathe out as his green eyes lock on mine. I couldn't care less what it means as he slowly inches forward and pulls our faces closer.

I can't deny this energy I feel any longer. It crackles between us as our chests heave, and we pant warm breaths against each other's mouths. I can smell the hint of his coffee on his breath, the sickly-sweet aroma surprisingly enticing.

"Voglio di più," he pleads against my mouth. Just as I feel the brushing of his lips over mine, my phone buzzes on the counter, breaking our bubble and sending me back to reality.

He reaches across the island to grab it, handing it to me. As several more texts come through, I look at the screen and see that it's Becka.

BECKA

It's beautiful here

[picture of sand and clear blue water]

I miss you

Have you seen Ethan again?

I blow out a frustrated breath. I'm not sure what I want from Ethan, and I'm not ready to explain my feelings to Becka yet. And I'll have to come clean about my surgery if I want her to take over for Ethan. But despite my threat to replace him with Becka, I'm not sure if she could drop everything to come help me so quickly, especially once she finds out I hid this from her.

Not ready to deal with all of that, I set my phone face down on the counter.

"Bad news?" he questions with a concerned look still standing next to my stool, leaning back against the island as he sips his coffee.

"It's just Becka. She'll be getting back in a few days and I'm nervous about telling her about all of this," I say, waving a hand in a back-and-forth motion between the two of us. "She gets excited easily, and I'm still so worn out."

"Embarrassed of me?" He pushes out his lower lip while making sad puppy dog eyes.

"Not embarrassed. Just lacking the energy to deal with her... zeal. I love Becka, but as you may have discovered, I live a quiet life, and she's a rather loud part of mine."

"Yeah, I've been meaning to ask you about that. I swear I remember you telling me that you were looking for chaos when we first met at the club, while I was there against my will, since Alyx forced me out of our place."

"That was different. I was blowing off steam. I wasn't looking for a real connection." I wince, looking at him as I wonder if my words hit a nerve. "I didn't mean..."

"It's okay, you were looking for a hookup. And even though I normally prefer quiet nights in, I'm the one who bull-dozed my way into your life. You weren't looking for more than sex that night, but there was something about you that I couldn't walk away from, and I'd give up all my quiet nights to spend more time in your chaos," he says sincerely.

It feels as though all the air in my lungs has been punched out, each of his words landing a precise blow. I throw back the remnants of my coffee and push my stool back from the counter, needing to get some space before I do something I might regret. *Still. Just. Friends.* "I'm going to go take a shower."

"Okay."

"That's it? You aren't going to offer to help me? Make a dirty joke? Or try to stop me?"

"Do you want me to? Kinda seemed like one of those times you didn't want me to chase you."

"I… I…" Fuck. How does he do that? It is so unnerving the way he can read me.

"Your paperwork mentioned leaving the bandages on until they fall off on their own and patting things dry. No scrubbing."

I nod and turn toward my room, secretly grateful that someone memorized my post-op aftercare instructions so that it's one less thing I have to worry about.

CHAPTER 16

Ethan

MY FEET SLAP the sidewalk as my thighs propel me forward. I'm usually very active, hitting the gym at least every other day, but I've put that on hold for the past five days to take care of Bridget. Although I've been able to sneak out for a run every morning before she wakes up. From what I can tell, she's normally an early riser, but she hasn't been since I've been staying with her. Most nights, I can hear her from my bed on the couch. She groans every time she rolls over or gets up, and from what it sounds like, she's up every couple of hours. Taking her pain meds would probably help her get more rest, but I understand her desire to avoid them.

Part of me worries she's too hard on herself. I know she wants to be self-sufficient as quickly as possible, but if she pushes too hard too soon, she'll regret it later.

I know how hard it is for her to allow me into her space, and after her confession the other night, I'm more determined to break through her walls and show her how good we could be together. It's obvious she's attracted to me, but I want more than just a physical relationship with her, and helping her recover from surgery has been the perfect opportunity to get to know her better. I like everything about her. Her laugh. Her snark. Her drive. We're both focused on our careers, have similar values, laugh at the same jokes, and I admire how she's unapologetically gone after what she's wanted. She defines success on her terms, and it's hot as fuck. I've always been attracted to strong women, and Bridget is a fucking queen.

Rounding the corner near her building, I spot Bridget leaving her apartment.

"Bridget!" I call, and as she turns toward me, I take in her beautiful face and the gentle arch of her eyebrows as they furrow slightly on her forehead.

"I wondered where you went so early."

"Were you hoping I'd left?" I flash her a lopsided grin, the one that makes her blush.

"I figured you didn't since your bag was still in the living room."

"You're up early. Going for a walk already?"

"Yeah, I wanted to get a head start." Her eyes refuse to meet mine.

Sensing her need to be alone, I start my cool-down stretches as she shifts awkwardly on her feet. "Go ahead without me," I tell her. "I'm going to grab a shower and get your coffee ready for you."

"Oh... um... okay." A small smirk crosses her lips as she turns and walks away from me, her perfect ass swaying with each pop of her hips.

I head inside and get to work preparing her a doppio. I'm determined to get her to relax today.

I can't control this overwhelming desire to know everything about Bridget, but she only hands bits of herself out in pieces. It's up to me to collect them, put them together, and make her whole. It's clear that no one's ever tried to do this, to truly understand her. I'm getting pieces she hasn't shared with anyone—not Becka, and probably not even herself.

She can try to keep me out, but I'm slowly chipping away at her walls. If she's never been shown what a healthy relationship looks like, it'll take longer to get through to her, but I'm undeterred.

After Bridget returned from her walk, I gave her some space, running errands to pick up ingredients for this evening's meal.

We are now sitting in the living room while the TV plays in the background after we ate and I cleaned up the kitchen. I sensed she needed some time to herself today, so I've backed off my nursing efforts and have been letting her try to get around on her own. The less she needs my help, the more panic claws my throat at the thought of my time ending here. I hope I've done enough to convince her to keep seeing me, only nothing is easy with Bridget. But anything easy isn't worth having, is it? I like her challenge. I love it.

She shifts in place on the loveseat, brushing a lock of her gorgeous chestnut hair behind her ear. She's wearing it in loose curls today. It's the first time she's styled her hair since her surgery, and I take it as a good sign that she's starting to feel more like herself again.

"I can't believe I'm going to say this, but I'm bored. There's nothing to watch on here. I feel like I'm going crazy being so cooped up."

"We can play truth or dare?"

"We're not playing truth or dare."

"Scared you'll lose?"

She sighs loudly. "Fine. Who starts?"

"Hold up, we need to go over the rules first."

"It's truth or dare, you pick one and do it. What do we need to go over?"

"Sure, that's the basic version. For every dare you successfully complete, you get one point. For every truth you tell, you get two points. First to ten points wins."

"Why aren't dares worth more?"

"Because sharing truths seems to be more difficult for you."

"What if there's a dare I can't complete?"

"Then you have to tell a truth. You get one pass that you can use on a truth with no consequences. Everything else you must answer or complete a dare instead."

"What do I get if I win?"

"What do you want?" I cringe internally because I'm worried that her answer will involve me leaving or pushing me away.

"If I win, you have to go back to sleeping at your place."

There it is. She's sitting on the loveseat across from me, a stern look on her face, letting me know that she means business. "Fine. If I win, you let me stay for the whole six weeks," I counter.

She crosses her arms in challenge, an invisible wall already going up. "Truth or dare."

"Truth."

"Why are you here?"

"Are you seriously wasting your truth on that question?" I ask incredulously. How does she not know the answer to that by now?

"Scared?"

"Not in the slightest. I'm an open book when it comes to you, but I'm hurt you even had to ask that. I'm here because I like you."

"You just like helping people, and I'm your latest project."

This is new. Deflecting with humor is easy to handle, but this hurt is harder to hurdle. "Helping is in my nature. It gives me a sense of purpose. I may not be good at a lot of things, but I can be helpful. With my sisters, my parents."

"Your Nonna," she adds hesitantly.

"Yeah. I needed to help her, to feel like I was doing everything in my power to repay her for everything she'd given me. But it wasn't enough. When she passed a little over a year ago, it broke me. That's why Alyx dragged me out the night we met. He was tired of me bumming him out."

"Or he was worried about you," she suggests.

"Maybe. But honestly, I offered to help you because a selfish part of me wanted a do-over. That maybe this time I could help someone and the outcome would be better."

"You need to be needed," she says knowingly.

"Trust me, I know you don't need me, but I promise, you're not a project to me, and I hope that one day you'll want more than just my help. Truth or dare?" I tack on the question quickly, not giving her a chance to throw up more walls.

She hesitates for a moment, chewing on her lip before she looks at me and declares, "Dare."

Several ideas pop in my head before I land on something that will allow me to touch her. "Sit on my lap for the rest of the game."

She rolls her eyes and stands, crossing to me before sitting on my legs like a child would sit on Santa's lap. Nothing is intimate about the gesture, so I clarify. "Nope, you have to straddle me, one leg on either side of my thighs.

"That's not what you said. You said to sit on your lap, and I am. You didn't say how to sit."

Well, she has me there.

"This is already uncomfortable. I thought your rugby thighs would be more comfortable than this," she bemoans, shifting her ass to get comfortable.

"Rugby thighs?" I laugh, confused. "I mean, I don't skip leg day, if that's what you're implying."

She doesn't clarify the rugby thighs comment and instead redirects us back to the game. "Your turn, truth or dare?"

"Dare," I say confidently.

"I dare you to unlock your phone and let me go through it for five minutes."

I pull out my phone and hand it to her. "The passcode is 'lizzyb' spelled out in numbers, and you can spend as much time as you want going through it," I tell her. I have nothing to hide.

"Starting to think you might have a favorite sister," she jokes.

"Nah, she uses my phone a lot, and it's easy for her to remember my code when it's her name."

Her fingers fly furiously across the screen, opening up my photos and scrolling through them.

"Wow, that's a lot of food pics. I figured you'd have more nudes in here."

Huffing out a laugh, I lean closer to her as I watch her scroll through pic after pic. "What can I say, I'm a chef. Food porn is my favorite."

"Are these all meals you've cooked?"

"Not all of them. I like seeing how other chefs plate dishes. Sometimes it gives me inspiration for new recipes or creative ways to plate my food."

"Are these your sisters?"

I look over her shoulder before confirming. "Yup." She keeps scrolling through pictures of me and my sisters before I spot a photo I don't want her to see. "Actually, I changed my mind, I'll take that now." I reach for the phone, but she's faster, shifting her weight and turning away from me as she clutches the phone against her chest and bends over to protect it from my reach.

"Now I have to see what you're trying to hide from me."

My hands wrap around her as I try to grab for the phone from both sides.

"That tickles!" My hands wiggle their way closer to her chest, reaching for the phone. "If you make me fall off your lap, I still get the points," she declares between fits of laughter. Her pain pills must have kicked in, and I'm careful not to jostle her too much.

With one hand, she lifts the phone up and away from me as she scrolls one-handed to the exact photo I didn't want her to see. "Who is this lovely lady? One of your sisters?"

I drop my arms and lean back against the couch, draping my hands over my face. "I think you know exactly who that is."

Her soft laughter wraps around my chest, squeezing it tight. "This is amazing."

I groan. "I forgot to delete those."

"Do you wear makeup often? You look very pretty in this," she declares, holding up my phone for me to see.

"I was babysitting my four youngest sisters, and they wanted to see who could do the best makeup. To make it fair, they decided that they would all use me as their canvas." I gesture to the picture she's holding up on the screen. "That one was Erin's. She's nine."

"Wait, there's more?" She keeps scrolling through as she peruses all the looks my sisters gave me. "Sweet baby Jesus, this one is really good. The contouring is fantastic."

I glance at the screen to see which look she's referencing, "That one was Ella's. The whole thing was her idea. She's obsessed with makeup and hair. She's thinking of cosmetology school, but I'm not sure my dad is going to go for that. He wants her to go to college."

"I hope he changes his mind. She has real talent. I'd let her do my makeup." Studying my photos a little longer, she leans into me and asks, "Any other photos you don't want me to see?"

"Nope."

"Good, now let's look at your browser history."

I look at her unblinking, not the least bit fazed. "Have at it. Just don't close out any open tabs. I don't want to lose anything."

"Damn, there are like a hundred open tabs in here. Don't you organize this shit? You know you can make folders and categorize all this, don't you?" She scrolls through my open tabs before getting bored and opening a new one as she types in "pornhu" before I stop her.

"Whoa, Hellcat, don't type any more letters, please. I told you Lizzy uses my phone, remember?"

"I figured a certain website would come up if I started typing that, but it didn't."

'Yeah, I don't look at that on my phone."

"But you do look at it?"

"You'll have to use your next truth on that one," I taunt with a wink.

Her eyebrows furrow briefly before she hands me back my phone. I can't stand to see the hurt look on her face, and it's clear that my teasing jab didn't land like I intended.

I cover her hand in mine, holding it briefly, as I take the phone from her. "I do watch it from time to time, but not on my phone. I have a computer the girls don't have access to, so I use that."

"Oh. Why did you tell me that?"

"I saw the look on your face when I didn't offer it up initially, and I didn't want to give you a reason to doubt me. I was trying to be playful. Sorry if it didn't come across that way."

"It's fine. You don't owe me anything."

"Anything else you want to know about my extracurriculars?"

She hesitates briefly before asking, "What kind do you watch?"

"I'm not picky, usually whatever is trending. I'm extremely visual, so just seeing it does it for me."

Her cheeks flush as a pink hue creeps up her neck. If she keeps shifting on my lap, I'm going to have a problem. "Might want to stop all that wiggling unless you want me to get hard, sweetheart."

She shoves my chest. "You're ridiculous."

"Your turn, gorgeous, truth or dare?"

"Truth." She spits the word like venom. Deciding to start out her first truth with an easy one, I ask, "Do you prefer books or movies?"

A genuine smile crosses her lips, and I've clearly touched on a topic she's passionate about. "Books will always be better than movies. In books, you get all the inner dialogue. You get to know everything that character thinks and feels without relying on a mediocre actor only known for their looks to convey all that subtext. And you get to decide what all the places look like. And those can change the second time you read it. In movies, you only get to rely on the words that are said and any body language used for subtext."

"Not everyone picks up on nonverbal cues."

"Exactly." She's animated as she continues speaking, her ass wiggling on my legs as her hands gesture wildly making her point. "There's no guessing how a character feels when you're in their point of view, their inner monologue shares everything. And some books give you multiple points of view so you can relive the same scene through each character's viewpoint. But when that scene is translated onto film, it's as though you're piecing it together at the same time."

"And different people read body language differently, so what comes across as annoyed to one person may read as angry to someone else."

"Yeah…" she starts, raising an eyebrow at me. Her eyes bore holes into me, as if seeing me for the first time. "It's like you're in my head."

I lift the back of my hand to stroke her thigh, my other hand fisting at my side, eager to grab hold of her, but I restrain myself.

"I don't like it," she mutters.

My hand stills on her leg. "You don't like me touching you or that I'm in your head?"

"All of it," she spits. I can see the tension creeping into her muscles as her legs clench on my lap. "It's like you know what I'm thinking before I verbalize it."

"Maybe your body language gives you away? Or maybe I'm good at reading you."

Her head turns, and we lock eyes, distrust written all over her features. "My sister," I supply as the crease between her brows softens and a breath escapes her lips.

"Oh. I'm an asshole."

"You're really not. I've had a lot of practice helping Lizzy. She also likes to read, and I think it's for the very reason you mentioned. The books she seems to gravitate toward have characters sharing all their innermost thoughts on the page, so she understands what they're dealing with. She doesn't have to pick up on social cues or body language when it's all laid out on the page. Plus, with a book, if she gets overwhelmed, she can put it down. Sometimes movies overstimulate her sensory issues even after I've turned it off."

"I'm not used to people paying close enough attention to me to be able to read me the way you do. That kind of attention makes me uncomfortable."

"Why does it make you uncomfortable? Are you telling me that no one you've dated has ever paid attention to you?"

"That's another question. I already answered your truth."

She shifts on my lap. I'd give anything to dig deeper into her past. She doesn't strike me as the kind of person who'd put up with shitty men, but it's clear she has. It's unlikely that I'll make any progress on that front tonight, so I decide to let it go for now.

My hands are balled up into fists at my side, itching to touch her but needing her to give me the go-ahead after the way she shut down. "Is this okay?" I question after I decide to rub my hand up along her spine tentatively.

She takes a deep breath and holds it as I trail my fingers down her spine in light languid strokes. In the past, my touch has seemed to calm her, and I want her grounded to me if we are going to make any progress. "Yeah, it feels good," she whispers as her head drops to her chest, her eyes hidden from me. "Truth or dare?"

"Truth." I'm willing to give her every piece of me in exchange for whatever she'll give me.

"Have you ever had a girlfriend?"

"I've had a few, a couple in high school, and then I dated a girl during culinary school. That lasted about six months before she got tired of my schedule cockblocking us."

"Charming."

"What can I say? I was young, on my own in a foreign country, and horny. There was a lot of passion, but unfortunately most of it was outside of the bedroom. She couldn't handle my long hours. When I wasn't in the kitchen or classes, I was babysitting Alyx's ass in a club. We roomed together in a tiny studio apartment. I was on the top bunk, which made alone time difficult. Alyx didn't have a hard time, though. I swear, that man hooked up with anything with two legs."

"I'm sure that's an exaggeration."

"Alyx is a lover of all types—men, women, all sizes, ages, and colors. I've walked in on him in all kinds of compromising positions with multiple partners, often at the same time. It wouldn't have been so bad if we didn't share a studio apartment with a bunk bed." I roll my eyes. "Okay, enough about Alyx's exploits, truth or dare?"

She blows out a breath. "Truth."

"What are three things you would look for in a partner?"

"I'm not looking for a partner. I told you, I don't do relationships."

"You don't get points for that."

"Bullshit. I answered the question."

"The question wasn't what you'd look for in a partner if you wanted a relationship. It's what you would look for in a partner."

Her eyes lock with mine in a standoff. Crossing my arms

over my chest, I give her a slight nod with my chin to let her know that I'm not backing down.

"Fine." Her fingers fidget in her lap as she picks at her nails, carefully weighing out her answer before she continues. "Trust is huge for me. Nothing else matters if I don't have that."

"Got it. Trust," I parrot back to her. Clearly, there's something or someone in her past that has created trust issues for her.

"To be honest, I don't have enough experience to really tell you what else I'd look for in a partner. I could tell you more about what I look for in a fuck," she deflects as she continues picking at her nails.

"Nice try, Hellcat. If you were going to let someone into your life, besides trust, what else would they need to give you for you to feel safe? To feel cherished?"

She picks up her thigh, readjusting her weight as she blows out a breath. "I, uh... I think it would be nice to have someone who likes spending quality time with me, just being present when we're together. I didn't get a lot of that growing up."

A small smile curves my lips as I think about the amount of quality time we've spent together over the past week. "What else?" I coax.

"Maybe someone who's optimistic. I tend to let my anxiety take over, and someone encouraging could make me laugh and get out of my head."

Her eyes stay trained on her lap, so I reach out and gently tilt her face toward mine. "You act as though spending time with you is a chore."

"Isn't it? I didn't have a lot of friends growing up. No siblings. I have Becka, and I push even her away at times. There aren't a lot of people clamoring to spend time with me."

"I am." I cup her cheek, forcing her to hold my gaze. "I'm desperate to spend time with you, as much as you'll let me. I know you feel this energy between us, and I know it's scary, but I want to be here, getting to know you."

I have to physically force myself to stop speaking before I scare her off, but hearing her basically describe me in what she wants in a partner makes me want to scream from the hilltops about how good we could be together if she would stop pushing me away.

For once, her eyes remain locked on mine, my hand still on her cheek as she asks, "Truth or dare, Pup?"

"You know the answer. Truth. I'll tell you anything you want to know."

"You've talked about your sisters as though you're their primary caretaker. Are you not close to your parents?"

"That's a little complicated."

"We've got time. It's not like you're letting me leave this apartment any time soon."

"You aren't a prisoner, you're recovering from surgery. And I get the feeling that you'll do whatever you want, despite what your doctor, nurse, or I might say."

"True."

"So if you're letting me stay here and play nurse with you, it's your choice."

"I didn't have much of a choice in the first days after. I tried to get rid of you, but you kept taking care of me."

"And it's a good thing I did. It's okay to let people in and accept help."

She shifts again on my lap. "Are you uncomfortable? You could get up," I offer.

"And lose my points? Nice try."

"Straddling me might be more comfortable," I hint with a wink.

"Just answer my question. Are you close to your parents?"

"My bio mom and I are not close. To be honest, I don't know where she lives now or even if she's still alive. I haven't spoken to her in years. She and my dad never married, and they had a pretty rocky relationship after she became addicted to opiates. My dad tried to get her help, but he had a hard time juggling being a single parent and sole income provider. My paternal grandparents weren't supportive of their relationship and cut us out of their lives. I never heard anything about my grandparents on her side. I was three when she left. I have some memories of her, but most of what I know is from stories my dad has shared about her."

"What kind of mother walks away from her own child?"

"The kind that's too selfish to put someone else's needs over her own." The words feel bitter coming out of my mouth as I ball up my free hand, pushing it into the fabric of the couch. Bridget must sense my anger, and she shifts in my lap, straddling me. The movement puts her face almost at eye level, and she rests her hands on my shoulders, her eyes locked on mine, letting me know it's okay to continue. "I love my biological mother as a person. I wish her well and hope she finds happiness, but it isn't with me and I'm okay with that. It wasn't until my dad married my stepmom, Ashley, that I truly understood what motherly love was. She was born to be a mom. She's the kindest person I know. She tamed my dad and grounded him in a way no one else ever could."

"But you're close to your dad?"

"Again, that's a bit complicated. My parents were young when they had me, and I grew up feeling like a burden. I don't have many memories from that time, but they all involved yelling. It's probably where my need to help came from. If I was helpful enough, maybe they'd stop fighting, maybe my dad would be around more, maybe my mom wouldn't have left."

"Oh, Ethan, that's not on you. You were just a kid."

"I know, but I didn't understand that back then. My dad barely finished high school and went to trade school with me in tow most of the time. And when he started working, he picked up as many jobs as he could to pay the bills, and I ended up staying with neighbors. I grew up thinking that adults always left." My voice cracks as my throat clogs with emotion. Fuck, I'm not about to cry in front of her. Not because I'm embarrassed, I have no problem expressing my emotions, including crying. My concern is that she'll assume it's a tactic to manipulate her.

Bridget doesn't say anything, just moves her hands from my shoulders to encircle my neck as she leans in to hug me, her chest flush against mine as our breathing synchronizes. Her sweet scent surrounds me, calms me.

"I think I've been angry at him for most of my life. He works hard to provide for our family, and I get that now, but as a kid, I wanted to spend time with him. Nothing I did was ever helpful enough until my sisters were born. Then I poured myself into helping my stepmom raise them."

"You surrounded yourself with people who needed you."

"Yeah, I guess I did. I never really felt like my dad needed me, but my stepmom and sisters needed me, so I focused my attention there. Dad was more involved with all my sisters too, so I felt like… like…" I struggle to find the right words before Bridget speaks.

"Like you had to prove yourself to earn his love?"

"Yeah, now who's in whose head?"

She lets out a huff of a laugh as she leans back and looks in my eyes, her arms still wrapped around my neck. "I know a lot about having to prove myself."

"No one should have to earn love from another person," I say, careful to hold her gaze so she understands that regardless of the men she's been with, I'm someone who will love her freely should she choose to accept it. "You alone are worthy of love and respect. There's nothing that you'd have to do to earn that from me."

"I… uh…" She drops her head and arms, crossing them over her body. "Just friends," she mutters under her breath.

"To be clear, I'm not saying I'm in love with you." *Yet*, I think to myself because fuck, I could see myself falling in love with her. My hand lifts her chin, forcing her to look at me. "I believe that if you love someone—a friend, sibling, parent, whomever—you should tell that person you love them and often. You never know who hears it enough, and everyone should know they are loved by the people in their lives."

"That's beautiful, but not everyone can put themselves out there and share their emotions so easily," she says bitterly.

"Then I'll do it for those who can't. I'd rather people know that they matter to someone. That they matter to me. It can make a difference for some. I've seen how shitty people can be, and I never want my people to think that they don't matter in this world." I think about all the shitty things I've overheard people call Lizzy when they thought I was out of earshot, and I'd die before I let any of those words take root in her head.

I can feel the tension in her body as she takes in my words. Not wanting her to feel any more uncomfortable, I ask, "Truth or dare?"

"Well, if I'm going to catch up to you, I'm going to have to start sharing some more truths, as much as it pains me."

"Tell me about a relationship you've had and what you would have done differently."

Still straddling my lap, she takes a deep breath and clearly thinks through what she wants to share with me. "I dated this guy in college named Brad. He was nice, but I always felt like he was with me for my study guides."

"Study guides?"

"I'm extremely detail-oriented, and I organized all my notes into these study guides that I used to prepare for tests, quizzes, midterms, and finals. It kind of became the thing I was known for, and I had people asking me to sell them at one point. Brad and I weren't together long, but we never really went out on dates. At first, I didn't think anything of it. We'd stay in, watch movies, order takeout. We were poor college kids, so it didn't raise any red flags. We had a few classes together, so we'd study a lot. I'd share my notes with him, but I didn't share my study guides. They were important to me. I wasn't going to just give them away."

"Shit, did he take your study guides?"

"He tried. It was the week before finals, and I couldn't sleep. Brad was spending the night, and I rolled over and couldn't find him. When I walked out to the living room, I caught him taking photos with a digital camera."

"Of the study guides?"

"Yup. Is it sad that I walked out there hoping he was taking pictures of my underwear or something equally creepy? Like that would've been better than the way he went behind my back and stole the one thing I hadn't given him."

"Please tell me you kicked Brad in the balls." I try to ease the tension as her words feel like they hold a double meaning. I hope that the only thing he took from her was her study guides.

"I confronted the motherfucker and made him hand over his camera. He argued with me before caving and giving it to me. I destroyed the SD card and dumped his ass so fast. I should've known better. We started dating before midterms, and this incident took place before finals. He was just using me. And that was the last time I let a man take advantage of me."

"What's an SD card?" I ask, hoping to ease the tension.

"Fuck off," she says teasingly.

"Why do I get the feeling that Brad's not the only one that used you like that?"

"Fuck, you're nosy. I already answered your truth and your follow-up questions," she gripes as she shifts nervously in her seat. "I feel like you owe me extra points."

"No extra points," I say. "But that's shitty that he did that to you."

She lets out a resounding sigh. "It is what it is."

"I think it's important to be straightforward and lay everything out. What you see is what you get with me. I'm someone who wears their heart on their sleeve. You'll always know where you stand with me, Bridget."

"Good to know, *friend*."

The way she emphasizes the word "friend" is like a punch in the gut. I've been inside this woman—there's no way in hell I'm going to stay in this friend zone.

"So, Ethan, truth or dare?"

Doing the math in my head, I know we're tied at seven points, so I opt for truth, knowing I can end it with a dare and pull out a victory.

"If you could only eat one food for the rest of your life, what would it be? And don't be that guy who says they'd eat pussy."

"I'd happily feast on your sweet cunt every day if you'd let me, but since I can't say that, I'd say apples. There are so many different varieties, and they go well in so many dishes. They can be sweet or tart, and they're incredibly healthy. I've actually been playing around with a twist on your favorite dish that incorporates apples."

"The tortellini with brown butter?"

"Yep, except it's ravioli, and I add apples to the cheese. It's savory and sweet, but I still use the brown butter and sage."

"Fuck, I'd like to try that."

"I'll keep experimenting with the recipe here. I'm still trying to find the perfect cheese and protein to pair with it." Although she's looking straight ahead, I see the corner of her lips lift in a small smile and I know what I'll be spending the next week doing in her kitchen. "Truth or dare?"

"Truth," she declares confidently, and I love that she's getting more comfortable sharing her truths with me.

"Where in the world would you want to go on vacation if money and time off were not factors?"

"Anywhere. I have so much PTO saved up that I've never used. This is the longest I've gone without working. But honestly, I don't care where I go. Europe. South America. Somewhere with books and beaches. And good coffee. Where I can go to relax and unplug, and I don't have to be someone for everyone else. I can just be me."

"I love that." My mind wanders with all the places I could take her and enjoy quality time with her.

"Truth or dare? And make it good because we're tied nine to nine."

I flash her my dimple, smirking. "In that case, I'll do a dare if I only need one point to win." Her blue eyes blink rapidly as her mind races with ideas. "Make it challenging, because if I win, you know what I want."

"I dare you to make me come without touching me," she says, her arms propped on her knees, her legs still straddling my thighs.

"Easy." I sit up so I can get closer to her. The sweet scent of vanilla and berries hits me again, and it has my dick twitching to life like Pavlov's dog comes running for food at the sound of a bell.

"You really think you can, Pup?" she questions as she rubs her palms up and down her thighs. My mind races with the possibilities of what we can do with the extra time we'll have with my extended stay if I win.

"I saw how wet you got from my words alone. I'm pretty sure you have a praise kink, probably from all the people-pleasing you do. When someone finally praises you for being the good girl you are, it makes you wet, doesn't it?"

One of her slender eyebrows rises. "Oh, are you starting now? It's going to take more than that."

Challenge accepted. "I know how much you like numbers. Should I start counting all the things I like about you?"

"That's not necessary, and frankly, it's insulting. You think merely counting in front of me is going to give me an actual orgasm?" She huffs, crossing her arms under her breasts, the movement pushing them up, making them look tantalizing as my cock jumps in my joggers.

"You know what I like the most about you?"

"This should be good. My tits?"

"They're great tits, but that's not it," I praise as my eyes rake over them. "I like how responsive you are. The little noises you make. How you get so fucking wet. I felt it that night we spent together. Christ, I'll never forget that night as long as I live. No other experience will ever compare to what we shared. You made me come so fucking hard in your shower that I almost blacked out. Your cunt was gripping me so tight as you rode me, your perfect ass slapping against my stomach. I've never seen a more delicious sight."

"Should I take that as a compliment since you're a chef?"

Trailing my hand down my chest, I trace the outline of my pecs and abs as her eyes track the movement, her tongue peeking out to wet her bottom lip. The definition of my cock is clearly visible through my pants, and I catch her looking at it. Pushing up from leaning back on the couch, I move my face as close to hers as I can get, my breath hot against her ear. "We both know I'm the only man to make you squirt. Twice."

She has nothing to say, no witty retort. My erection presses against my joggers as I glide my palm over it, running it up the seam before I grab the waistband of my pants with one hand and lean back, tugging it down, careful to keep her balanced on my legs. My cock springs free, stretching up toward my stomach as her eyes follow the movement.

"That's cheating." She gets distracted as her gaze fixes on my cock, and she licks her lips.

I wrap my hand around the shaft and fist it, pumping up and down as I tilt my head back against the couch. "You said I couldn't touch you. You didn't say I couldn't touch myself," I assert between pumps as my breathing picks up. "Fuck, Bridget, I'm imagining this is your tight cunt squeezing me as you ride my length, your gorgeous tits bouncing in my face with every thrust."

Her legs squeeze mine as she shifts on my lap.

"I want to fuck that pretty mouth of yours and smear that perfect lipstick. You take me so well, your hot mouth sucking as you try to swallow my length." Holding out my hand to her mouth, I order her, "Spit."

"What? You can't be s–"

"I'm fucking serious. If I can't have that smart mouth or that perfect cunt, then my hand will have to do for now. Spit."

It's clear no one's ever asked her to do this before, and her first attempt is underwhelming.

"I'm going to need more than that, sweetheart. You see how big this dick is. I want to cover it in you. Give me more." Her second attempt is more productive, and I use her spit to wet my dick as I give it hard, slow pumps. "Fuck, it feels so good being coated in you," I rasp out between strokes. "I'm going to pretend my hand is your tight little pussy. You squeeze me so good."

Bridget shifts on my lap until her pussy is resting on one of my thighs as she sits at a slight angle. I continue fucking my hand, pretending it's her tight cunt as her hips start making small movements against me.

"That's it, be a good girl and rub that pretty pussy all over my leg. Make a mess. Fuck. I'd do anything to taste your sweet cunt again," I plead as my hand moves faster, pumping my length.

Her hair cascades over her shoulders, framing her beautiful face as she continues making small movements with her hips over my thigh while biting on her lower lip. "I want to suck that lip into my mouth and kiss the fuck out of you."

"No one's ever kissed me the way you did that night. I couldn't think about anything but what you were doing to me."

Stunned by her confession, I pause my strokes, holding on to the base of my cock. "Eyes on me, Bridget."

Her arms are still crossed, and her head is tilted down. Her eyes are closed as she slowly shakes her head.

"Look at me," I demand.

I'm not sure if it's my words or my tone, but her head snaps up, those gorgeous blue eyes fixed on mine.

"That's my good little hellcat. No one's ever kissed me with the passion you did that night. What you felt wasn't one-sided." I continue stroking. "And no one's ever made me this hard. See this?" I watch her gaze fall to where I'm fisting my cock. "This is what you do to me. You make me so goddamn desperate for you. I want you so fucking bad that I'm willing to do whatever it takes. Scale any wall you need me to, just to get close to you."

As her eyelashes flutter and her brow furrows, she continues seeking friction on my leg. Her movements are subtle, and I'm unsure if she's in pain from her surgery or if she's trying to fight the urge to come.

"You feel so fucking good, I wish it was you squeezing my cock, I... fuuuck." A jolt of pleasure surges through me as she continues staring in my eyes. I slow my movement down, determined not to be the first to come.

"Oh, fuck. I can't... Ethan... fuck, I'm coming... I'm... Ahhh," she moans, trying to maintain eye contact with me before dropping her head back, a guttural moan escaping her throat. Her hands grab my shoulders as she steadies herself, her hips stilling their movements. I squeeze my shaft, tugging it hard as I follow behind her as jets of warm cum spill onto my hand and down my shaft.

"I've never done anything like that before. Why was that so hot?" The vulnerability I see in her face is overwhelming, and I reach up to grab her jaw with my free hand. I press our foreheads together as our breaths mingle. I want to kiss her so bad, and as I tilt my head to take her lips, she speaks as she pulls back.

"I'll go get a towel to clean you up."

Still holding her jaw in my hand, I grab my shirt I'd taken off earlier and wipe myself clean. "There, I'm clean," I tell her with a bit of a bite. For every step forward we take, she seems to push me two steps back. The last time I made her come, she did everything in her power to get rid of me before the next morning, and I'll be damned if I let her do that again. I see her eyes flick to the shirt. "I'll do a load of laundry soon, don't worry."

"That's not what I..." Her words trail off, and I wonder if I've been too harsh with my tone.

"I'm sorry, it felt like you were pushing me away, and like I said, I wear my heart on my sleeve."

"You actually made me come without touching me," she breathes, her words barely audible, and her response is not what I was expecting.

"I did, but you rubbing on my thigh might've helped."

A small smile crosses her lips, and I run my thumb over it. She winces briefly, and my thumb stills.

"Did I hurt you?"

"No, I think my pain meds are wearing off, and I may have overdone it a little with all the gyrating. But I'm a big girl. Nothing I can't handle." She stands from my lap, her words seeming to hold another meaning.

Before I can overthink my actions, my hand clasps her wrist. "Please don't pull away, please don't shut me out. Let me be here for you."

"Okay." Her voice is small, and her eyes won't meet mine, but it's a start.

"I'll grab your ibuprofen. Why don't you head back to your bedroom and lie down?"

"Does this mean you're going to stay the whole six weeks?"

"I did complete the dare, didn't I?"

"Good" is all she says as she turns down the hallway toward her bedroom. I can't help the smile that stretches across my face.

CHAPTER 17
Bridget

OVER THE NEXT FEW DAYS, Ethan stays no matter how hard I try to kick him out. And I try. Nothing deters this man, and I can't decide if it's annoying or endearing. He's constantly underfoot. I've never felt like my apartment was small before, but now he's everywhere I turn, his presence larger than life. It's like I can't escape him or his twenty-two-year-old energy. Seriously, how does he have so much energy all the time? I must have been high off that orgasm when I agreed to let him stay.

I've never lived with anyone aside from my parents and a roommate my freshman year of college, and even then I spent so much time in the library and in study groups around campus, I never really felt like I lived with anyone. Hell, I don't even remember her name. As soon as possible, I moved off-campus into an apartment on my own and have lived that way ever since.

So, having Ethan here every day for the past week has been… a lot. I mean, it hasn't been terrible having someone take care of my laundry and heavy lifting, while handing me coffee every morning. And he has my ice idiosyncrasies down pat.

It's harder to remain Ethan's friend when, for the first time in my adult life, I think I want more from a man. But I'm not sure if it's actually him that I want, or if it's the forced proximity that's making him seem more attractive. I'm not saying I want to be in a serious relationship with him today, but if I'm going to do more than fuck someone for the first time in over eighteen years, he could be a good candidate. Letting someone in is scary, though. But carrying all this baggage is so fucking exhausting too.

We're compatible physically, but is he someone I can trust with my heart? And does he want the same things I do? I'm not about to let someone in only to find out they want different things out of life. It's a risk I'm not willing to take. I need to look out for myself, because if there's one thing I've learned, it's that no one will ever put me first, so I have to.

But isn't that exactly what Ethan's been doing for the past week? Putting me first? It seems to come naturally to him. How long will it really last? Sure, we're in a post-op bubble now, but once we go back to our normal lives, he's sure to move on.

To someone younger.

To someone with more free time.

To someone who can give him more than I can.

It's early evening, we're watching something mindless and bingeable on a streaming service. I'm reclining on the couch, propped up by pillows, while he sits across from me on the loveseat.

"You mentioned something to Nurse Maggie that surprised me, and I wanted to know more about it."

"Okaaay," I draw out, confused about what he could be referring to since it's been a week since I've had surgery, and his question seems to come out of nowhere.

"Did you mean what you said before you were discharged? About not wanting to have kids?"

He's been sitting on this for a week? Unsure where he's

going with this, I look into his emerald-green eyes. Is he disappointed? Do I want him to be? Does he think I'll change my mind? Regardless of his answer now, will he change his mind?

"I meant it. Having kids isn't something I've pictured in my future. Especially now that I only have one working ovary. I'm thirty-eight years old. If I wanted kids, I should've started before now. I don't know if you've noticed, but I don't have a lot of people in my life. No support system to help me raise a family. And I'm not sure I'm capable of taking care of another person when some days I feel like I'm barely holding it together. But I think it's good for us to get this out in the open now so you can move on from this and find someone that wants to make a family with you."

"You make a lot of assumptions about me based on my age. You know that?"

"You'll want kids, Ethan. You're young. You have so many years ahead of you to find someone your age that can give you the family you're going to want. Even if you don't want it now, there's plenty of time for you to change your mind."

"Did *you* change your mind?"

My brows knit together as the realization hits that my argument is falling apart. "No, I didn't."

"For someone who recently went off on a nurse for assuming she'd want kids, you sure are doing the same thing to me because of my age."

I open my mouth to speak and close it again when I realize he's right. Fuck.

"I came from a big, blended family. My dad and bio mom had me when they were young. Dad wanted lots of kids, which wasn't in the cards for them. He met Ashley when I was four. She'd escaped an abusive marriage with her one-year-old daughter, Emma. After they married, they had four more girls: Ella, Elizabeth, Erin, and Evie. They thought it was a sign that both of their kids had E names, so they kept the trend for all of us," he says, rolling his eyes.

"So you don't want kids?"

"Nope. I grew up in a house full of kids. I'm okay never having my own." His eyes meet mine. "Truly, I am. Most of my sisters are still kids. The youngest is five. I'd be happy being the fun uncle. Our house was loud and chaotic. There are so many other things I want to do with my life, and having kids would complicate that."

"But you could change your mind. You're young." I'm grasping at straws here, unsure how to convince him and not sure why I'm trying so hard.

Ethan moves to sit next to me. I pull my legs closer to me as he reaches out and clasps my hands in his, looking directly into my eyes when he speaks.

"I'm twenty-two, and I know what I want out of life. Kids aren't part of that. I've seen how my parents struggled to make ends meet. My dad works so much he's hardly around. Plumbers make decent money, and yet he still picks up extra work where he can. I see how it wears him out, and money is still tight for them. That's not the kind of life I want."

"What do you want?"

"Would it be cheesy to say I want you?"

I drop my head so I can avoid that perfect fucking dimple and its magical powers. One of his hands cups my cheek and lifts my face up, forcing our eyes to connect. His eyes darken, and the look he gives me is penetrating, as though he wants me to understand his truth.

"I'm not really sure what I want to do with my life, but I do know this. I want to get to know you in whatever way you'll let me. I want you to be part of my life moving forward. I've never felt this way about someone, and I cannot ignore all the signs the universe is giving me when it comes to you. Something is drawing us together. Can you honestly say you don't feel it?"

I hesitate, dropping my eyes briefly. "I... I don't think..." My words trail off, and all rational thought leaves my brain as he leans into me and pulls my face close to his, resting his forehead against mine. Our lips are a whisper apart. All I'd have to do is push them out in a pucker and we'd be kissing.

"Don't think. Be in the moment with me." His lips graze mine as he speaks. The air between us feels charged. I've never felt this kind of energy with anyone before. It's just sexual chemistry, though, right?

Short, warm breaths heat my skin as his breathing picks up. My heart feels like it's going to beat out of my chest. Arousal pools deep in my core, awakening part of my body that only he seems to control lately. His fingertips pull on the back of my neck as his thumb makes slow swipes along my cheekbone.

"Bridget, I want you so fucking bad it hurts." His words are a desperate plea against my skin that matches the desire gathering in my core. How does he have this effect on me? The tip of his nose rubs against mine as his words continue to pierce my shell. "I'll do anything you ask. I've never wanted anything more in my life."

The words tumble out of my mouth without thought. "Kiss me."

Before I can take my next breath, his lips are on mine, nipping and teasing. "Fuck, you taste so good," he mumbles between kisses. His other hand lets go of mine and slowly glides up my arm until it's on my neck, fingers threading in my hair, holding me firmly in place. As if there is anywhere else I'd want to be right now. Something about the press of his lips on mine just feels right. There's no urge to run—in fact, I need him closer. I reach for him, unfolding my legs from against my body and laying them over his lap as he smooths my arms up his chest before wrapping them around his neck as he leans into me. The little moans that escape my throat should be embarrassing, but I can't be bothered to care.

Our tongues tangle together, desire building between us as our hands grope and grip each other tighter. It's intoxicating, casting a spell over my senses. Right when I think I can't take one more minute without him inside me, he pulls back, pressing his forehead against mine. A few seconds pass as his touch continues lighting up my skin, our breaths mingling as we come down from the high.

"Why did you stop?" The plea is out before I can contain it.

"I'd love nothing more than to lay you out and feast on every inch of your delicious body." A moan bubbles in my throat at the thought of his tongue against my clit. No one's ever commanded my body like he has. "But I'm pretty sure your paperwork mentioned no sex for four to six weeks. You might feel great now, but if yesterday was any indication, that pain pill will wear off here in a couple of hours, and you'll need to rest."

"Fuck the paperwork. I thought you said you'd do anything I ask?"

"Not if it means hurting you." His green eyes bore into mine. "I'll do anything, but I won't hurt you. I promise." Placing a gentle kiss on my lips, he hoists me into his lap, and I wrap my legs around his waist as he stands and walks us back to the bedroom. "But I'll take care of you tonight."

He gently deposits me on the bed, standing between my legs as I sit on the edge. "Arms up." His tone is firm—a command, not a request. I lift my arms, and he carefully drags my shirt up without tugging too hard on my shoulders. His eyes drop to my chest as his gaze lingers on my puckered nipples. "Dammit, Bridget. You're making this really hard."

Chuckling, I lean back on my arms and wrap my legs around his waist, pulling him flush with my hips. I should feel self-conscious about the bandages covering my incisions. I should kick him out before things get messier than they already are. But right now, I'm pulled to him like a magnet. "Kiss me," I plead again, but there's a challenge in my tone, testing his word and resolve.

"Fuuuck." He drags out the word as his head lowers to my chest. He places gentle kisses on my breasts, nipping and sucking the fleshy parts without giving me the pressure I need in the areas I crave it. His eyes flick up to mine, and a pained look crosses his brow. "We should stop before this goes too far because if I pull one of these nipples into my mouth, I won't be able to stop until you're coming on my tongue."

I can see the outline of his cock pressing into the seam of his pants as he backs away from me and walks to my dresser. A few seconds later, he's crossing the room with a fresh pair of pajamas in hand. He takes his time putting the silky camisole on me before dropping to his knees. "Stand up and place your hands on my shoulders so I can put the bottoms on for you."

"O-okay." There's a hitch in my breath as I stand and grip his shoulders. A surge of heat courses through me and his muscles flex under my touch as he slowly lowers my leggings and panties to the floor.

"Fuck, you're dripping for me, sweetheart." His eyes rake over my pussy, bare and exposed to him. The heat of his stare becomes too much as I move a hand to cover myself.

His eyes flick up to mine. "Don't you dare hide this from me. You are beautiful, and if all I can do is look right now, I want to bask in every glorious fucking inch of you." He reaches out, placing my hand back on his shoulder as he continues his perusal of my body. I can feel his mouth only inches from my skin.

Every minute that his eyes are on me, I feel more aroused yet also self-conscious. Anxiety picks away at me, causing me to worry that he's looking too closely at each wrinkle, scar, and dimple on my body.

The stretch marks that plague my hips and belly.

The cellulite that pocks my thighs and ass.

The errant hair that I inevitably missed while shaving.

I've never been insecure about my body, but it's hard not to be when someone is inches away from it, examining the most intimate parts with laser focus.

Shifting on my legs, I rub my thighs together and drop my

hands from his shoulders, unable to bear the weight of his gaze any longer. "Please stop looking at me like that. I can feel your eyes hovering over every imperfection. My body has been through a lot over the years, more so in the past week, and I—"

"Your body is a fucking work of art." His eyes darken, and a look of hunger crosses his features as he speaks. "Every mark on this beautiful skin tells me more about who you are and the life you've lived. There isn't an inch of you that I'd change. There isn't an inch of you that I don't want to put my mouth on. What you see as imperfections, I see as an autobiography of your life. Each mark a word on the page of who you are. Together, they tell a story. Without them, that story wouldn't be as interesting, nor would it be complete. And when you're healed, I can't wait to leave my own marks on you. I'm not here for just a chapter, Bridget. I want to fucking own the rest of your story."

He holds out my panties so I can step into them and then shimmies them up my legs. The silky sleep shorts are next, and he makes quick work of helping me into them as well. That was a hell of a lot easier than doing it on my own.

After I'm dressed, he guides me to the bathroom so I can brush my teeth, holding back my hair for me as I spit in the sink. I'm starting to crave the feel of his hands on me, the little ways he touches me.

I follow him back into the bedroom, holding his hand as I trail behind him. "Stay with me tonight."

He turns and looks at me over his shoulder, his brown hair whipping against his forehead. The look in his eyes is adorable. "In here? Are you sure?"

A flash of rejection washes over me. Does he not want to stay? Casting my eyes to the floor, I drop his hand.

"I'm just surprised you aren't still trying to kick me out," he quickly reassures me. "I'm used to begging you to let me stay, not the other way around."

"I wasn't begging," I snap. When our eyes connect again, his smirk appears, and that dimple taunts me. "Fuck you."

"That's better. I was starting to wonder where my hellcat was hiding."

"Get in the fucking bed before I change my mind." I turn off the bedside lamp and climb in, pulling the covers back for him. The soft light from the moon dimly illuminates the room as he lies down, threading his arms behind his head. Inching closer to him, I lay on my side and drape an arm over his torso as I hook my thigh over his.

I never thought I'd see the day I'd willingly cuddle a man, but something about him soothes my nerves. His touch has become a balm for my soul.

The screen on my phone lights up the room briefly.

"Do you need me to hand you that?" he asks.

"That's probably Becka," I say into his chest. She and Robert are probably home by now, and I still haven't replied to any of her texts or calls yet. "She's going to freak out when she finds out I had surgery. And I don't have the energy to explain everything to her right now."

"You didn't tell her?" he asks, not a hint of judgment in this tone.

"I didn't want to worry her. She needed time away with Robert. If I'd told her, she would've tried to cut the vacation short, and Robert put a lot of time and thought into that surprise for her. Besides, she worries, and it can be exhausting to deal with a worried Becka."

"Are you going to tell her?" I can feel his muscles tighten and I wonder what has him so tense.

"I will, but I don't have it in me right now."

"I can do it. So you don't have to." His hand strokes my back as I consider his offer. "I'll only share what you're comfortable with."

"Why would you do that?" I shift to look up at him, my cheek still pressed against his chest.

"Because I want to take care of you. You need your rest, and it seems like this conversation might drain your emotional battery more than you're willing to admit."

How does he do that? At times, it feels as though he's reading my thoughts, understanding who I am better than I understand myself, anticipating my needs before I've even made a mental checklist of what to do first.

"Okay. You can tell her everything. I may ghost her at times, but when I reemerge, I'm an open book with her. And I don't want her to worry. She's nothing if not persistent. I give her twenty-four hours before she's over here unannounced." Honestly, it'll probably be less than that if I know Becka.

"I'll call her for you tomorrow," he offers, threading a hand through my hair.

My fingers move in lines up and down his stomach, pausing to examine each little groove and divot. A soft groan escapes his lips as his breathing picks up.

"You should stop," he whispers as my fingers travel down to the waistband of his boxer briefs. My fingers graze the hard head of his cock as it stretches up his abdomen. He hisses and reaches for my hand, stilling my movements. "Bridget," he warns in a low voice.

"I like it when you say my name like that," I purr seductively, pulling my hand free and reaching into his boxers to stroke his hard length.

"You can't—"

"*I* can't have sex for six weeks," I correct him. "But you can."

"Fuck," he groans as I grip his cock, collecting the pre-cum from his head before sliding it up and down his shaft. "I don't want you to hurt yourself."

"I know you have a big dick, but it doesn't weigh ten pounds, so it isn't considered heavy lifting." I continue moving my hand up and down.

"Christ, that feels good," he groans. I try to sit up a little so

I can angle toward him more, but I feel a twinge of pain in my stomach and freeze. Ethan looks up at me as I close my eyes and let out a deep breath.

"What happened?" I can hear the concern in his voice as he shifts to his side.

"Nothing. I think my pain meds are wearing off. I'll be fine." I let out a few more deep breaths as the pain lessens and reach for his waistband again.

"Bridget, stop. You shouldn't be twisting your torso like that."

"Fine." I lay back down, facing him, still on my side. "I have an idea."

"I'm listening," he says, shifting to his side and staring into my eyes.

"I have some lube in the nightstand. Hand it to me, please?"

"We can't—"

"It's not for me. It's for you. If I lie still like this," I say as I extend my hand toward him, "and hold my hand like this"—I make a circle to show him—"you can fuck my hand, and I don't have to move."

"Fucking hell," he moans as he grabs the bottle of lube and hands it to me.

I pop the cap open and squirt a generous amount on my palm before setting it on the bed between us. He shifts onto his back and pulls his boxer briefs off before rolling over and facing me again. My hand connects with his cock, and I spread the lube up and down his length as a low groan escapes his lips.

"Fuck my hand like you want to fuck my mouth," I say as he pushes his thick cock into my hand and slowly pumps in and out.

"Holy fuck, this feels amazing," he growls as his movements quicken, his thrusts becoming hard and sloppy. When he finds a good rhythm, I start twisting my hand while he thrusts in and out. "Yes, just like that. Such a good fucking girl."

"Look at you, fucking this hand like a needy little slut. You'll take anything I give you, won't you?"

"Yes, fuck, yes," he moans as he turns his head into his pillow, his teeth biting into it as his muffled groans get louder and his breathing picks up. I keep pumping his cock with the same twisting motion as he grinds up into it. He pulls his face out of the pillow and looks directly in my eyes. "Non siamo solo amici," he croaks through gritted teeth, a pleading look on his face.

I have no idea what he said, but I can see the desperation on his face. "You look so fucking good when you beg."

"Please, fuck, you feel so good. Please don't stop, please make me come."

It's so fucking sexy watching this man lose control and come apart for me. It makes me feel like I can do anything, like I really am a queen commanding my subject.

"You have a little praise and degradation kink too, I see," I say as I squeeze harder on each thrust. "Are you going to be a good boy and come for me?"

"Yes, Jesus, fuck." He thrusts into my hand a few more times before he stills with my hand gripped at the root of his cock. He shifts onto his back as he comes with a roar. "Fuck, Bridget." Thick ropes of cum spill out of his cock, painting his chest and abdomen.

We lie there for several minutes as I lean into him, pressing kisses onto his boulder of a bicep.

"I don't think I've ever come that hard before," he says, his deep voice rough and raspy as though he just woke up. His arm snakes down off the bed, grabbing his boxers as he uses them to wipe off his stomach. "I'll go throw these in the wash and grab something to clean you up with." He picks the lube up off the bed, stowing it back in the drawer before leaving the room.

Fuck, that was intense. No one's ever brought out this side of me before. I don't usually talk this much during sex. I've never been afraid to ask for what I want, give directions, or moan, but this is different.

He's slowly chipping away at my defenses, and the odd thing is that I don't feel as scared as I did or as worried as I probably should. Maybe I should give him a chance. In the past few days, he's proven that he cares, making more of an effort than any guy I've ever been with.

My phone lights up the dimly lit room, and I roll over to grab it with my hand that's not covered in lube. Scrolling through all Becka's messages, it's clear that I'm going to have to reach out to her soon.

BECKA

I can see you've read these so I assume you're alive.

Robert and I are getting home in a few hours. We need to talk.

I check the timestamp on her last message. Shit, that was several hours ago.

Why aren't you responding to me?

Oh shit, did something happen?

You ok?

ANSWER ME!

I swear if you're ghosting me again...

I need to know you're ok.

Also...

Something happened while on our trip, and I need to talk to you about it.

I hear him enter the room before I see him, his presence

looming over me as he stands at the edge of the bed. Using the cloth, he carefully wipes my hand as I continue reading one-handed.

"I want to return the favor, but I think you need some rest."

I stop scrolling and look up at him through bleary eyes. "I do, but I think something is going on with Becka and Robert," I say, tilting the phone to him.

After placing the cloth on the nightstand, he hands me two ibuprofen and a glass of water as he bends to look at my phone. The exchange feels oddly domestic, as though we've gone through this routine hundreds of times, and it hits me that I've never felt this comfortable with another person.

"That's a lot of messages. Are you going to answer her?"

"Tomorrow," I reply through a yawn.

"What do you think happened?"

"There's no telling with Becka." I chuckle. "She has the most hilarious stories and tells them in the most dramatic way. It's probably something like that." I roll over and plug my phone in. Ethan moves around the room, slipping into the bathroom. I hear the toilet flush and the faucet run as he washes his hands and brushes his teeth.

"Mind if I use some of your products on my face?" he asks, popping his head out of the bathroom.

The light shines in my eyes as I cover it and squint up at him. Is he fucking with me, or is he serious? I know we went through my skincare routine after the sponge bath, but I haven't seen him do all that again. And he hasn't asked me. "What?"

"I liked the way my skin felt after we went through your nighttime routine. And I wanted to make sure you were cool with me using some of your products."

"Shit. I totally forgot to do all that tonight." What is happening to me? I feel like every time I'm near this man, he throws me off-balance. I move to sit up too quickly and wince as pain lances my abdomen. "Fuck."

He rushes to my side, "Shit, you okay?"

Tears well in my eyes as I squeeze them shut, determined not to show any more weakness in front of this man. "Fine," I grit out.

"Not buying that, but let's take it easy, okay? We can skip the skin care tonight. You just focus on resting. You've been pretty active today, twisting more than normal, and your muscles need to rest."

"Fuck it, it's not like I put on any makeup today. I guess it's okay to go without washing my face for one night. I just need this ibuprofen to kick in," I whine as I lie back against my pillow.

"I'll help you with it in the morning," he promises as he shuts off the bathroom light and crawls into bed beside me, pulling me against him.

CHAPTER 18

Ethan

WHEN I REALIZED that Bridget hadn't told Becka about her surgery, I felt honored that she had trusted me to be her person through it. My thoughts quickly shifted as I realized that Becka's return could mean that my days of playing caretaker to Bridget may be over sooner than I had hoped. She said I could stay the whole six weeks, but who knows if she'll change her mind. We've been living in our own little bubble the past week, and I'm not ready to give that up yet—not when I feel like I'm slowly making progress with her.

Bridget dozed off quickly, falling asleep on her back before shifting to get comfortable, but her sleep was fitful. She ended up wrapped around me, arm draped over my torso, a thigh thrown over mine.

I, on the other hand, have been awake for a couple of hours. At first, the fact that I was sleeping in her bed next to her made me more excited than a child the night before Christmas. My heart was beating wildly out of my chest. And then she ended up cuddling on top of me. She'd been restless in her sleep for about forty-five minutes. Once she curled up against me, her breathing evened out, and she became as still as a sleeping kitten. I was afraid to move for fear she'd wake.

172

All I want is for her to get some peace and rest. If lying here next to her, practically holding my breath, affords her some comfort, then I'll gladly serve my queen.

There's a loud and persistent knock at the door. I slowly extricate myself from Bridget's embrace, careful not to rouse her.

Unsure of who it could be at this hour, I pull on a pair of joggers and a shirt and move quickly down the hallway toward the door.

"Bridget! Bridget, open up!" a female voice wails from the other side.

"Shhh," I soothe Becka as I open the door. I should've known. Bridget warned me this could happen.

"Ethan? What are you doing here? Are you guys hooking up again? I'm so sorry to interrupt." Becka nervously looks around behind me.

"Not exactly. Why don't you come in? I've been expecting you, though not at eleven at night." I take a step back, allowing Becka to enter the apartment. She tentatively walks in with a look of confusion on her face.

"Sorry, I know it's late, but if you aren't hooking up, what are you doing here?"

"Why don't you take a seat?"

"Is everything okay? You're scaring me. Robert and I got back this afternoon, but I haven't heard from Bridget at all. We normally text daily."

"Bridget's okay. She's recovering from a procedure. She told you about her cyst, right?"

"Before I left. The doctor told her it was fine, though."

"It was, it is. There's no cancer from what they can tell, but because of her family history, they wanted to remove the cyst and the ovary it was attached to as soon as possible."

"And I wasn't here." There's a pained look on her face before clarity sets in. "She let you take care of her? What about her parents?"

"They're in Europe on a cruise. I offered to help because–"

"She was going to take a rideshare to and from surgery, wasn't she?"

"It's hilarious how well you know her."

"Fucking Bridget." She chuckles softly. "She let you in. She let you help. She never lets anyone help."

"I'm learning that. Trust me, it wasn't easy. She only agreed to a friendship during her recovery. It was the only way she would let me help."

"But you don't want just a friendship."

"Not even close."

Her smile is warm, and it feels like I've found an ally in her. "I really like you for her. Please don't give up on her. She needs someone else in her corner. I can't be there for her all the time, and I worry about her. She may come across as uncaring or cold, but she has the biggest heart. She just doesn't like people to know."

"Any advice?"

"Be consistent and show up for her. It's the only way to build trust with her. She'll try to push you away, but don't let her. It took me years to break through her shell, but you'll never find someone more loyal once you do. And tell her to call me."

"I will." After Becka leaves, I glance at my watch and walk to the kitchen to get a glass of ice water and a couple of pain pills, knowing she'll need them soon. I select an insulated tumbler from the cupboard and pick two large ice cubes to fill the cup first. I then fill it with smaller cubes before adding the water, ensuring her water stays cold throughout the night. I head back toward her bedroom and crawl in beside her.

Her back is to me, and I scoot in close to her, careful about how I drape my arm over her torso. The room is silent, save for her small, even breaths. A warmth fills my chest when her body heat envelops me as I mold myself around her.

A small moan escapes her, and I kiss her shoulder in response. "It hurts."

Shit, maybe our activity earlier was a bit too much for her. "What hurts?"

"My lower abdomen. I think I was a little over-eager earlier. Can you check to see if I'm bleeding?" I reach the nightstand and turn on a lamp as she rolls over onto her back, lifting her shirt. Peeling back the gauze that covers her incisions, I smooth my fingers around them, careful not to touch the small gashes in her skin. She makes a small moan at my movements, and I still my fingers, afraid I've exacerbated her pain.

"Everything looks good," I assure her as I carefully reapply the coverings over her incisions.

"Is it almost time for my pain medication?"

"You've got another couple of hours before you can take an ibuprofen, but you can take a Percocet. I know you've been avoiding using them, but maybe half of one will take the edge off so you can get some rest?"

"That's fine, I just need it to stop," she moans as she drags her hands down her face.

I hand her half a Percocet and the water, and she gingerly takes them both. "I'll check on you in a couple of hours. If that doesn't help, we can do more ibuprofen then," I promise as I set the cup on the nightstand and stand.

Her hand reaches out, holding me in place. "Don't go." Her plea is barely audible, as if she's insecure about voicing it. Half-kneeling on the bed, my other foot on the floor, I freeze. I had every intention of sleeping in her bed tonight, but I thought I'd watch TV for a little bit, giving her some space while her meds kick in.

"What do you need, sweetheart?" I ask, peeling back the covers and crawling in next to her.

"This is going to sound weird—"

"I promise you, it's not."

She blows out a breath. "It felt so good the way your fingers were tracing around my incisions. Can you tickle my stomach like that?"

That was a moan of pleasure earlier, not pain. I grin to myself, deciding to tease her a little. "Are you asking me to scratch your tummy, Hellcat? Last time I tried that, the cat hissed at me, and I got scratched."

Even though the room is dark, I can feel her rolling her eyes.

Chuckling, I reach for her shirt. "I'm just teasing. I've got you." My hand lightly grazes the skin around her bandages as she relaxes into the mattress. "Becka stopped by a little bit ago, I'm surprised she didn't wake you with the way she was pounding on the door."

"I was afraid that would happen. I'm sorry. How did she take the news?"

"Surprisingly well, but she wants you to call her."

There's no response, and when I look over, she's fast asleep.

CHAPTER 19
Bridget

IT'S UNNERVING how quickly Ethan's made himself comfortable in my apartment and in my daily life. Twice in the last week, he ended up sleeping in my bed, and each time I took more solace in his presence than I'm comfortable doing.

He's the only man I've ever let spend the night. Most of my one-night stands leave right after. A handful have stayed long enough for round two but still leave after the fun is over. Ethan is the only man I've ever fucked that I've also slept with, and that realization is terrifying. And he's spent more nights since then snuggled up next to me. And I like it. Fuck.

It's getting harder to concentrate on my recovery when I keep getting texts and emails from work colleagues asking for important financial information ahead of the merger. My anxiety is through the roof. I girl-bossed too hard, and now I'm saddled with responsibilities only I can handle. And while I have the job I've always wanted, it wasn't until recently, when life hit me hard, that I realized how much I've truly sacrificed of myself to get where I am in my career.

The constant pressure to do everything looms over me like a storm cloud, threatening to unleash its fury at any minute. For Christ's sake, I'm on medical leave, and somehow, I'm still the only one who can handle certain responsibilities for this merger. God forbid anything happened to me. How could this company function?

I need to recover from surgery, from a procedure I had done because part of my body couldn't keep up anymore, which makes me feel like less of a woman, in a way.

I have to balance it all at work, but unlike my male counterparts, I worry about how I look doing it. It's not like I can just throw on a suit and do my job. No, if I wear an outfit that's too tight, then I'm accused of using my body to get ahead or called any slew of derogatory names. If I wear an outfit that's too loose, I'm a slob who doesn't care about her appearance. Not once in my career have I ever heard a man be criticized for his attire in the same manner, but I can't go a single day without hearing at least one comment being made about a woman's body from one of the men in my office.

I have to be assertive to get what I want, but not too much. I can't call out any double standards or bad behavior without being labeled a bitch or difficult. If I speak up, I'm too bossy, but if I don't speak up then I'm walked all over. Putting up with the good ole boy club is a constant struggle, as is dealing with its stepchild, bro culture. The kind of misogynistic bullshit these men spew daily makes my eye twitch and my gut boil every single fucking time I hear it. But I plaster on a smile and roll with the punches so I can be likable and "one of the guys." Inside, my inner feminist is screaming that I'm a fraud, that I should speak up and defend the sisterhood. Though, what good would that do? I wouldn't have the career I want, the life I've worked so hard to achieve. And now that I can feel the top of the glass ceiling caress the crown of my head, the small bit of hope left in me prays that it wasn't in vain and that I'm paving the way for those behind me, so they don't have to endure what I did to get here.

I've tolerated a lot to get where I am, and the worry that it could be stripped away in four to six weeks because one of my female reproductive organs stopped working reminds me that nothing I do as a woman will ever be enough. So I double down, desperate to prove myself. To prove my worth. To show others that I matter. To use my independence as a strength—despite the weakness it seems to have become lately. It's something I've been doing my entire life, but the thought that I'll have to continue at this pace fills me with dread, as though I'm a hamster on a never-ending wheel making no progress at all toward my own happiness and freedom.

All these thoughts fill my head, making it difficult to concentrate on anything. The only thing that's ever seemed to quiet the voices in my head telling me that I'm not enough and too much at the same time is a night of mindless fucking, where I can focus solely on pleasure and touch.

I haven't worried much about work these past few weeks, and I'm starting to wonder if it's because of Ethan. I can recall countless times since I met him when my brain has been over-whelmed with paralyzing thoughts and how his touch quieted the tempest churning in my head. In fact, the night we met was the quietest my brain had ever been.

Admitting that to him feels too raw, as if my entire soul is bare and on display. Knowledge is power, and I'll be damned if I give anyone that kind of power over my heart.

Sitting on the bed, I push down my swirling thoughts, hover over my laptop, and resume going through emails. It's early afternoon, and I don't have much time left before Ethan gets home.

I mean, gets back. Not home. This is *my* home.

Ethan's running the lunch service today, having only agreed to go back to work after I assured him I'd be fine working from home on my own. It took him three days of hovering while I sat on the bed stuck in random work Zoom calls about the merger before he relented and started picking up shifts at the restaurant. However, this is my first full day back at work and sitting here for most of the day has been more exhausting than I expected it to be.

Thanks to his truth or dare win, I've had to come to terms with our living arrangement. Having lived alone most of my life, I'm not used to sharing a living space, and it's taken some getting used to. I only have a few more weeks before I get my apartment to myself again and can settle back into my usual routine. Although, it has been nice to wake up to a cup of the most delicious coffee I've ever tasted. And having my own personal chef hasn't exactly been a hardship. I've even incorporated some of the tricks Ethan picked up in his research into my nighttime skincare routine.

When I really think about it, dating someone like Ethan wouldn't be so bad if perks like these were part of it.

I hear the apartment door open, and Ethan's heavy footsteps echo down the hall.

"Hi, sweetheart. How'd it go today? Have you even left this spot? You're exactly where I left you."

"I still have a couple of hours of work to get done before I can call it quits. No rest for the wicked," I say, my eyes never leaving the computer as my fingers fly across the keys. The *tap tap tap* from my pecking fills the silence between us as I feel Ethan's gaze on me.

"I got you something."

"What?" I say, half-listening as I finish typing a formula into the cell of my spreadsheet. Looking up, I notice a small gift bag in his hand and an eager smile on his lips.

"This is for you."

I take it from his hand, holding out the bag in front of me like it's an animal that's going to bite me. "What's this for?"

"Open it."

Pulling out the tissue paper, I notice several animal-themed face masks, a gift card for a food delivery app, and a bag of sour gummy candy. Looking up at him, he holds out a bottle of white sparkling grape juice he'd been concealing behind his back, and I can't contain the laugh that slips out as I dump the contents of the gift bag onto the bed. "What's all this?"

Grinning, he sits on the bed. "It's a care package. I Face-timed with my sister Erin yesterday, and she suggested it. I saw her before work, and she helped me pick out everything. I know you've been frustrated being cooped up here, so I got you a de-stress kit."

"I…" I trail off when one of the animal masks catches my attention, and I get lost reading the back of it.

"The grape juice is because you still shouldn't have alcohol, and this way, we can drink bubbles while we wear face masks. I noticed you were almost out of candy in your pantry, and you seem to go through sour gummies when you're stressed. You can use the gift card to order lunch when I can't be here to cook for you. And when I told Erin about your love of skin-care, she picked out the masks. I figure we can put them on tonight and watch a movie."

"But the animals?"

"She's nine. She thought they were cute."

Holding them up, I declare, "I get to be the cheetah. Do you want to be the kitty, panda, or puppy?"

"Surprise me." He beams and flashes me the dimple, seeming pleased that I'm going along with his plans for the evening.

"What's on the menu tonight, chef?" I ask absentmindedly as I put the masks in the bag and turn back to the screen, determined to finish this spreadsheet before dinner.

"Fuck, it's kind of hot when you call me that."

"Doesn't an entire kitchen staff call you that when you lead service?"

"Yeah, but I don't want to fuck them."

I can feel the blush painting my cheeks as I ignore his comment. It's getting harder and harder to convince myself that I only want to be this man's friend.

When I emerge from my room several hours later, Ethan has dinner ready.

It's like he knows my taste buds better than I do. Everything this man has cooked has been like heaven in my mouth. Tonight, he made pecan-crusted salmon and a light salad in a raspberry vinaigrette. While I'm not normally big on fish or seafood, I gobble up every crumb on my plate.

Ethan clears the table, puts our plates in the dishwasher, and starts the machine before putting the leftovers away. "There's an extra filet if you want that for lunch tomorrow. I picked up a shift at the restaurant. Mina and Dre are out this week, and Alyx asked me to cover for him."

I can feel the disappointment instantly; it tastes bitter as I swallow and attempt to clear it. "Oh" is all I can squeak out.

"Set the oven to two hundred and seventy-five degrees and pop it in there for about ten to fifteen minutes. You'll want to put it on a baking sheet lined with parchment paper. Think you can handle that?"

"Yeah, I can handle it. I'm not completely inept in the kitchen," I snap back.

"Whoa, Hellcat, I didn't mean it like that. I'm used to walking my sisters through instructions several times and…"

"It's fine." It's not fine. I don't know why I'm suddenly snapping at him. I know he didn't mean to imply I couldn't reheat something. His tone was fine, he just… Fuck. I think I'm starting to like him being around, and finding out he won't be here tomorrow has me spiraling.

"I have five sisters. I know when a woman says something is fine, it most definitely is not fine."

Deciding to put it out there—because what can it hurt—I take a deep breath and admit, "I was just counting on you being around tomorrow, and I guess I'm annoyed."

He grins. "I'm growing on you, am I?"

"Maybe."

"Was that so hard?"

Yes. Yes, it was fucking hard. I don't let people in. I don't tell them how I feel, and I just told him how his absence affected me. My chest feels warm and tight at the same time, and I clutch at it, pushing my palm to it in hopes of easing the ache.

"Thank you," I rasp out, still holding my chest.

"For what, sweetheart?"

"For my gift. For dinner. For your help, even when I insisted I didn't need it. You've made this recovery easier on me, and you deserve to know that I appreciate it."

"I'm happy to help. Now, excuse me while I slip into something more comfortable and put my mask on."

In a less than a month's time, Ethan has quickly become one of my closest friends. I enjoy spending time with him. He makes me laugh and he calls me out, holding me accountable. His personality balances mine in ways I never expected. And the way he reads me is equally unnerving and exhilarating at the same time. I like that I don't have to be someone I'm not around him. I don't have to hide the parts of myself that the world deems unpalatable. And all that scares me. But I'm starting to think that only being friends isn't possible. Maybe we could be more.

Just as my revelation reignites that ache in my chest, Ethan emerges with the puppy mask on his face and a huge smile.

"Of course you'd pick that one, Pup. I should've known."

He laughs as he settles onto the couch next to me, wrapping an arm around my shoulders. "Can't disappoint my hellcat."

CHAPTER 20

Bridget

EACH DAY, the pain in my abdomen lessens, and I start to feel more and more like my pre-surgery self. Working from home has been an adjustment; I'm back to my normal workload, but I feel more productive without all the interruptions that come from working in an office.

Ethan and I have settled into a comfortable cadence. At this point, he spends more nights in my bed than on the couch, and his stuff is slowly infiltrating my space and closet. I felt bad that he was still living out of his overnight bag, so I figured if I'd agreed to let him stay the whole six weeks, the least I could do is let him unpack.

The utensils and gadgets he's added to my kitchen are foreign to me, but I'm not complaining if they help him prepare the gourmet meals he's been making. He's still mostly doing lunch shifts, but he's picked up a few dinner services, and that means that tonight I have my place to myself.

Well, not entirely to myself. Becka is joining me. We've texted a bit since she got back in town a few weeks ago. While it wasn't my intention to keep anything from her, I realized how my lie of omission hurt her, and I've been trying to work back into her good graces. Tonight is a chance to make things right and show her how much she means to me.

I've ordered pizza for us, so when there's a knock on the door, I'm expecting it to be the delivery person, but Becka is there, pizza in hand.

"The delivery guy followed me up here, so I told him I'd take it. I tipped him well, so you're welcome." She walks past me and into the kitchen.

"Becka, I ordered online. I already pre-tipped in the app."

"No wonder he was so thrilled to let me take it off his hands." She opens the box and takes a big bite, the stringy cheese in her mouth still connected to the slice.

I grab two plates, hand her one, and add some slices to mine. We eat at the counter in silence for several minutes, savoring the cheesy goodness. Well, I am. Becka has already inhaled two pieces as I chew on the crust of my first slice.

"Fuck, Becka, you training to beat Joey Chestnut in next year's hotdog eating contest?"

She lets out a burp. "I forgot how amazing it is to eat without a child interrupting me every five seconds. If I don't inhale my food, I don't eat warm food," she explains. "So, we gonna talk about what's happening with you and Ethan?"

I knew this was coming. She's been careful not to talk about him too much, only casually asking about him here or there in a text.

"There's not much to talk about. He's just a friend who's been helping me with my recovery."

"You and I both know that's a load of horseshit. That man is crazy about you. And what help do you even need at this point? You seem to be getting along just fine now. I'm pretty sure you'd have kicked him out if you wanted to."

"Yeah, I can't."

"Because you like him as more than a friend?"

"Because we played truth or dare one night, and he won. He picked staying the whole six weeks as his prize."

"Ooh, that's kind of clever of him. But you didn't deny that you like him. The Bridget I know wouldn't let anyone stay in her apartment for that long unless there was something more going on."

"We... might have had a moment a few weeks ago," I admit.

"And?"

"We kissed, and I gave him a hand job, but the angle I was in when I did it pulled something in my stomach, so it's been hands-off since then. I don't want to reinjure myself, and I don't want to rely on someone again for that much help. That first week was really hard for me."

"I'm sorry I couldn't be here for you, but it sounds like Ethan stepped up."

"He really did. Becka, he held my hair as I vomited into the toilet. It was extremely uncomfortable being that vulnerable and dependent on another person. I'd have felt equally as unbearable depending on you."

"Gee, thanks."

"You know what I mean. I've lived most of my life on my own. I don't need anyone to open my jars or change a lightbulb for me. And letting someone see me at my most vulnerable felt exposing in a way I'll never be comfortable with."

"But you let him," she says leadingly.

I give her a look. "You obviously have an opinion about this. Spit it out."

"He's perfect for you, and I'm worried you're going to push him away because getting attached to people scares you. It's clear that he likes you. He might be falling in love with you."

"And that's also why I stopped the physical stuff. I cannot fall in love with him."

"With him or with anyone?"

"Did I piss you off or something? Why are you coming at me so hard about him?"

"I was pissed at you when you didn't tell me about your surgery. I get that you did it so Robert and I could get some time away, and I'm grateful, but you needed someone. And when I came over and saw Ethan, it was all over his face, his concern for you, how much he cares about you. I knew then you made the right decision, and I was thrilled you let someone else into your bubble. We weren't meant to do life alone, and here is this man who wants to be part of your world. Why are you keeping him in the friend zone?"

It takes a minute to force out an answer as I try not to cry. I never thought I'd find myself in this situation again, letting another person take up residence in my heart, consuming my thoughts. What if he betrays me like every other man I've let in? A pain stabs at my chest, and I press my palm against my sternum to ease the ache.

"Because I don't think I'd recover if it didn't work out." I hold back the sob that wants to escape, but my voice cracks on the last word, and I bury my head in my hands.

"Oh, honey, you can't think like that. What if it did work out, and you missed out because you didn't give him a chance?"

I let her words linger in my mind, searching for a response, but I come up short. An adult would ponder this more, weighing out options and feelings before deciding. Fuck that shit. Deflecting is my go-to.

"Hey, so you mentioned that something happened with Robert on your trip, but you never told me what it was."

"Nope, I know what you're doing, and it won't work. We'll talk about that later. I may have made it into a bigger deal anyway since you weren't texting me back as quickly as I wanted."

Well, fuck. How else can I get out of this conversation?

"Why don't we make a list?" Becka offers. "You love lists, and this might help you process how you feel. I think you'll be surprised how many pros are in his favor, and maybe it'll help you stop fixating on the cons."

I sigh, knowing I can't derail her now. "There's a notepad in the junk drawer on the end, pens too." She retrieves them and joins me on a stool at the island.

"Which should we do first?"

I shoot her a look. As if she really needs to ask me that.

"Cons it is."

She writes out "Pros" and "Cons" on the top of the paper, adding a line down the middle.

I think for a few seconds. "He's only twenty-two."

"Got it. What else?"

My fingers tap in a rhythm against the granite countertop as my brain tries to find more reasons. "He... uh... Actually, let's do some pros. I'm sure I'll come up with more cons as I think through things."

"Sure." There's a hint of disbelief in her tone as she draws out the word.

"Okay, pros. He's amazing in bed."

She holds up the paper pointing to the dick she's already doodled in the pro column. "The Goldilocks penis. Not too small, not too long, just right."

There's a fit of cackles between us before I continue. "He's an amazing cook. And he's incredibly sweet and thoughtful. Oh, he doesn't want kids."

"He doesn't?"

"Nope, that's what led to the hand job."

"Breadcrumbs, Bridget. I feel like you're leaving out important details."

"He has sisters that he's had to help raise so he doesn't want kids of his own."

Becka puts the pen down and focuses on me. If I look at her, I'll crack. "Don't say it, I know what you're thinking."

"That he's made for—"

"Stop. We're doing this so I can decide. You only need to take notes and remain impartial."

"I didn't agree to that last part but continue." She picks up the pen again.

"Oh, I've got a con!" I exclaim. "His dimple."

"I thought you liked his dimple?"

"I do, but I swear it makes me do things I wouldn't normally do."

"Forces you out of your comfort zone, pro," she says as she writes.

It takes a while to come up with the next con. "Oh, I know, he can read my mind. He's so in tune with me sometimes. It's like he's in my head. I can't hide what I'm feeling."

"Are you hearing yourself? I'd love to have Robert be able to read me like that. The key is if he does anything with that information. Like, does he read you and then give you what you need without asking? Because that sounds like the dream."

"Kind of? Sometimes, he asks if I'm feeling a certain way, but he's always spot-on. It just feels intrusive, like I'm being called out."

"Honey, that sounds like he is perfectly in tune with your needs. I'm adding that to the pros."

I pause again, thinking. "He's always *here*," I complain. "In the beginning, every time I'd turn around, he'd be there. And even now, when he's not at work, he's here all the time. Sometimes I need my space."

"I can see how you'd think that's a con, but does he give you your space when you ask for it?"

"Yeah…"

"You're an introvert and you need your time alone to recharge, but that doesn't mean you should always be alone, and as long as he respects your need for space when you ask, it's a pro."

I think again, an even longer pause this time. "I got it.

People judge us. If I went out with a man my age, I wouldn't get the same kind of looks from people that I do when I'm out with Ethan. That's a con."

"That sounds like a you problem, not a con. It's not his fault, or yours, if people stare or judge you."

"Well, it fucking sucks. I get enough judgment in my career; I don't want to deal with more in my personal life too. Put it under cons."

"Honey, all the things you think are cons can be pros. You tend to focus on the negative and what could go wrong, even if things are great."

"That's the definition of a pessimist," I concur, my tone biting, not liking where this is headed.

"You need someone to balance out that little rain cloud. He does that for you."

"Read them back to me."

She looks down at the pad of paper, picking it up as she reads, "Pros: that dick, cooks, sweet, thoughtful—"

"I said sweet *and* thoughtful. Those don't count separately."

"They mean different things. We aren't arguing semantics," she asserts before continuing, "DINK—"

"What the fuck does that mean?"

"Dual income, no kids. It's what you guys would be. Think of the life you would live. Going out to eat, vacations, hobbies. You guys have more in common than just sex, right?"

I nod.

"Like?"

"We both enjoy cooking, reading, and we like the same hockey team. But you're forgetting the part about not wanting to be seen out with him."

"I wish we had another income. Having a kid really changes your budgeting. I love Hallie, don't get me wrong, but I miss the financial freedom we had pre-child," she laments.

"So, in your case, DINK is a pro. Continuing on... the dimple, in tune with you, supportive."

"I feel like you twisted some of my words there. Read out the cons," I say, frustrated.

"Cons: younger."

"That's it? I swear there were more."

"The only other con was 'people judging,' but that goes with the age thing and shouldn't count against him."

"There have to be more cons than that."

"I won't say he's the perfect guy because no one is perfect, but maybe he's perfect for *you*. You have enough in common, but you're different, and those differences balance you out." Becka fixes me with an imploring stare. "I'm not saying it'll be easy. You'll annoy each other, you'll disagree, but you could also complement each other in a way that no one else can. You have to decide if you can look past his age."

CHAPTER 21

Ethan

WHEN I ENTER THE APARTMENT, I can hear Bridget speaking. She must still be in work meetings. It takes me a few minutes to put away the leftovers I brought over from the restaurant, and I'm desperate to get a shower after a small incident in the kitchen left me feeling rank.

Knocking quietly, I gingerly poke my head around the door and make eye contact with Bridget as she waves me in, keeping her arm off camera. She's sitting on the bed wearing a blazer on top and her silky sleep shorts on bottom. Her hair is pinned up in a neat bun, and she speaks about finances with stoic professionalism. This has been her work-from-home wardrobe since she started back a few weeks ago, and it makes me grin every time I see her in it. She's so fucking beautiful, and sometimes she has no idea how she affects me.

"Thank you, gentlemen. I'll get those projections to you by the end of day, but I think this will be a fruitful partnership."

Fuck, work boss Bridget is hot. She closes her laptop and flashes me a small smile. "I take it everything went well?" I ask as she pats the spot next to her.

I'm beside the bed in a few strides before her nose wrinkles. "Why do you smell like that?"

"Sorry, I wanted to hop in the shower first, but I didn't want to interrupt your meeting. Nyomi thought it would be funny to fill my water bottle with pickle juice, but she must have been in a hurry not to get caught because she didn't screw the lid on all the way, and when I threw my head back to rehydrate, I got a pickle juice shower. It was right before rush hit, and I couldn't change."

"Oh fuck, that's hilarious."

"Glad you find my misfortune so amusing." I roll my eyes. "Do you have more meetings? Cool if I take a quick shower?"

"I'm good. I was going to grab some water before I send over those projections and then log off for the day."

"I can grab it for you," I offer.

She shoots me a look, and I can't help but stare at her bottom lip. When she's annoyed, her bottom lip juts out a little more than normal, and it looks so fucking kissable.

"It's been like five weeks since I had surgery. I'm completely fine at this point. You don't need to keep waiting on me hand and foot."

My chest tightens whenever she reminds me that our living situation is temporary. What happens after my time here is up? What will I do if I can't see her every day, or if she starts pulling back or pushing me away?

Sensing my mood, she shifts tactics. "Water would be great, thanks."

Leaning down, I kiss her head before making my way to the kitchen. After grabbing her water, I rifle through the pantry, deciding what to make for dinner. When I complete the mental checklist of everything I need, I return to her bedroom, cup in hand.

I set it down with a flourish as I say, "Your water, m'lady," before bowing to the side of the bed.

The laughter that follows warms a place in me nothing else has touched. I live to make this woman laugh, to see her happy.

"Get up," she giggles at my antics.

"Yes, my queen," I tease as I stand. "Now, if you don't require anything else, I shall retire to the washing closet to scrub the smell of brine from my skin."

"You're ridiculous."

"But you like it."

The sound of her laughter follows me as I walk to the bathroom and disrobe. Once the water temperature is perfect, I step into the shower, letting the cascading warmth ease the tension from my muscles as I wash my hair and body. As I scrub away the stench of my day, my hand wanders lower, fisting my cock that's been hard since the sound of Bridget's laugh awakened it.

I brace a hand against the tile as I pump my hand up and down in hard strokes. Gathering the pre-cum at the tip, I rub it over the head of my cock as I lean my forehead against the shower wall and let out a small groan.

"Mind if I join you?"

I'm startled at the sound of Bridget's voice and the rush of cool air that hits me as she enters the shower, closing the glass door behind her.

Her naked body is a fucking masterpiece, and I reach out to run my hand over the curves of her waist and breasts.

"What is happening right now?" I grit out as her hand closes around my length and squeezes in long, twisting strokes.

She drops to her knees, but my hand catches her arm, pulling her up before she can continue. "We can't... not cleared... six weeks..." I rasp as her hand continues pumping my length.

"My hospital paperwork didn't mention anything about not sucking dick," she retorts. "And besides, how else am I supposed to repay my loyal subject?"

I'm going to worship this woman the minute I'm allowed.

She steps closer, walking me back until my calves hit the

tiled bench, then pushes my chest, forcing me to sit before dropping to her knees between my open thighs.

Taking my dick in her hand, she palms my length, licking from the root to the tip while cradling my balls in her other hand.

My head falls back and a growly "Fuck" escapes my throat as she places the tip of my cock against her lips and licks around the crown in a circular motion. A second later, her mouth is filled with my cock, taking me in as far as she can before my length hits the back of her throat.

I grab her hair, fisting it as her mouth works up and down, sucking me in hard as her cheeks hollow. She tries to take all of me, and when it's clear she can't, her hand pumps the base of my shaft, twisting and pulling as her saliva drips down, coating me.

"That's it, you can take it," I encourage, holding her head in place as I thrust my hips up into her mouth, her gagging noises echoing off the shower walls. She moans, and the vibrations feel like heaven on my dick, tickling the nerve endings until I'm about to explode.

"Fuck, sweetheart, I'm gonna come. Be a good girl and swallow every drop." I'm barely able to bark out my command before I'm spilling into her mouth. She laps it up like a kitten starved for milk.

Her finger swipes around her mouth, then dips between her lips as she sucks it clean, before releasing it with a gentle pop. My dick likes that a whole fucking lot as it starts to harden again, thinking there's going to be a round two.

"I'm going to go finish the projections I was working on. Are we on for dinner?"

"Going out tonight?" I excitedly ask.

I deflate a little when she says, "I thought we'd stay in. Didn't you say you wanted to teach me?" The thought of her in nothing but an apron briefly flashes in my mind, and I'm excited all over again.

"Embarrassed to be seen out with me, Hellcat?" I joke, but a pained look crosses her face briefly. Fuck, maybe she's ashamed of me.

"I'd rather not deal with the stares and judgment," she counters quietly, toweling off as she puts her robe on and exits the bathroom, leaving me to deal with the aftermath of the small emotional bomb she just detonated.

I decide on chicken parmigiana and gather the ingredients when she emerges from her room.

"First, I'm going to show you how to make the chicken," I explain, pulling the package out of the fridge and placing it on the counter.

"What about the sauce? Can I use the premade stuff from the jar at the store?"

"I mean, you could, but it'd be shit. True marinara sauce needs all day to marinate and soak up the flavors. I make it in large batches and can it so I always have it on hand. We'll use the jar I brought. But one day, I'll teach you how to make gravy the right way. Now, are you ready to get dirty?"

"Yes, chef," she replies with a wink.

And now my cock is hard, pressing against the seam of my pants as I pause my movements, setting down the ingredients I was gathering.

"That got you hard already, Pup? I just sucked your cock in the shower."

"That's not helping," I warn, blowing out a breath as I continue organizing my cooking space.

I spend the next several minutes teaching Bridget how to butterfly and bread the chicken, dipping it in the dry mixture, then the egg wash, and the dry mixture again.

Her chicken is butterflied unevenly in spots, and I show her how to use the knife to perfect the cut as we repeat the process with more breasts. We make enough for our meal, left-overs, and sandwiches. I want to make sure she has something to eat when I'm at the restaurant and can't cook for her.

Feeding people is my passion, but feeding Bridget is my calling. That this woman allows me to take care of something so sacred, fills me with a joy nothing else ever has. My one hope is that she'll still need me once these six weeks are over.

CHAPTER 22

Bridget

I'M CLOSING my laptop when Ethan emerges from the bathroom. He's fully dressed, his hair still damp from the shower, the ends curling around his ears, framing the handsome features of his face as he joins me, sitting on the edge of the bed as I set my laptop on the nightstand.

"I missed you," he admits as he leans in for a quick kiss. "The restaurant was crazy today. I'm starting to miss the dinner rush. It's constant and predictable, but lunch is utter chaos. Right when you think the rush is over, you get another wave of people. And whoever prepped this morning did a shit job. We had to eighty-six like half of the menu. Servers were pissed because customers were pissed. It was a total shit show."

"Mmm, you smell like Italian food," I moan into his skin because I didn't follow half of what he said.

He pulls the front of his shirt to his nose and inhales. "Fuck, do I? I showered, but it's hard to scrub off the smell of garlic."

Hooking my leg over his thigh, I inch closer to him, pulling the shirt out of his pinched fingers and against me as our bodies crash together. His hand grabs my jaw as his lips move over mine. I'm not sure if it's the all-clear I got from my doctor today, how fucking edible he smells right now, or the six tortuous weeks of emotional and sexual foreplay, but my libido is out of control, and I need this man more than I need air.

"Bridget, we can't," he says between kisses.

I rear back and look at him. He's being sincere, a look of concern etching his features. The rejection stings, and I sit back.

"What? What is it?" he asks.

"Nothing. I'm fine."

"Bullshit."

"Don't you want to…" I trail off, unable to form the words at how his rejection hurts more than I expected.

I see the moment it clicks for him. "I want to fuck you so bad, but we can't."

"Why not?"

"It hasn't been…" He starts to open his mouth in response but stops, seeming to do the calculations in his brain. "Has it been six weeks already?"

"It has," I purr, the sound a velvety rumble in my throat.

"Hell fucking yeah, come here." He grabs my thigh and pulls me onto his lap so I'm straddling him. The surprise on my face hits him as I see the concern in his eyes. "Fuck, did you think I was turning you down because you thought I didn't want to be with you?"

"Maybe," I say quietly.

"Hellcat, I'll fuck the fire out of you, you just have to say the word. I got so used to stopping things during your recovery that I lost track of how long it's been. The number of times I've had to shut this down only to take a cold shower is unbelievable." He grabs me hard, one arm wrapping around my waist as his right hand clasps the back of my neck, pulling me against him in a feverish kiss.

Suddenly, he pulls back to stare at me, our heavy breaths

creating a cacophonic rush in my ears as my wildly beating heart adds to the noise. "Wait, is it six weeks today? Exactly?"

"Does that matter right now?" I question, my hips still grinding against him, seeking friction against his thick length. He grabs my hips, and I look into his eyes and see the concern there.

"Truth or dare. Is this my last night here?"

I forgot I'd agreed to let him stay only until the six weeks was up. Suddenly, the thought of him leaving fills me with sadness. I've gotten used to him being here, gotten comfortable.

"Do you want it to be your last night?" I question hesitantly as my hands still their movements on his chest.

"Fuck no. But I know you need your space and you like being alone. I'll respect that if it's what you want."

I take a deep breath and stare into his eyes, wrapping my arms around his neck. "I know I put up a front that I crave chaos, but being alone is peaceful to me. I don't have to deal with people and their messy emotions. With my messy emotions. I'm okay with being on my own. I've never felt lonely while alone. Until I met you. Now my peace isn't peaceful. It's like I can't relax until I'm near you and I don't know how to feel about that."

"I know how *I* feel about that. I feel fucking amazing when I'm with you. I grew up in chaos. Our house was never quiet. Not with that many kids. I loved it, but I never felt at peace. You bring me peace. You feel like home. I like what we've created here these past six weeks. I want to keep going." The hand on the back of my neck tightens as he pulls me into him, our foreheads pressed together, our noses touching. "You keep trying to fight it. But I'll scale every wall you put up if it means that I get to bring you peace. Let me do that for you, be that for you. Fuck, sweetheart, please. *Non hai ancora capito quanto ci tengo a te.*"

It's the begging that undoes me. Or the Italian. Fuck, it's

hot when he casually slips that in. I have no idea what he said, but it feels like an important confession.

"Stay." I barely get the word out before his lips are on mine, tugging and devouring. Our tongues dance to a rhythm I can feel deep in my soul, as if the music was written just for us.

He tears his lips from mine and reaches into the cup on the nightstand, fishing out an ice cube. "Lie back and take these off. I've been dying to devour this pretty cunt," he commands as he puts the cube in his mouth. "I want you to drench my face and make this ice melt."

Fuck, I love the mouth on this man. He teases me with the ice, moving it up and down my inner thigh, his hot breath melting my resolve as my thighs drop further open. Pulling the cube from his mouth, he trails it along the apex of my thighs, chasing each cold swipe with a hot lick as I squirm against his hold.

Each lick moves closer to my aching core, and the juxtaposition of hot and cold lights up my skin. His tongue laps at my pussy, hot and aching, before he trails the ice behind it. He continues stroking me with the warmth of his tongue until the ice melts, and I'm left panting, needing more to ease the ache in my core.

He rewards me by pushing a finger into my pussy, working it open by making slow circles around my inner walls.

"What do you want, sweetheart?"

"I want you to make me come," I breathe out, barely able to focus as he slips a second finger inside, stroking them against my G-spot. His thumb starts rubbing small circles over my clit as his fingers continue teasing me.

"Try again. Tell me exactly what you want. Use your words."

"I want you to be a good boy and lick my pussy until I squirt all over your face, screaming your name. And then I want you to lick me clean."

"Fuck yes, my queen," he growls, lowering his head

between my legs and flattening his tongue, licking from my center all the way to my clit before removing his thumb and pulling my swollen bud into his mouth. The rapid flicks of his tongue make me feel like a storm cloud about to unleash a downpour during a summer thunderstorm.

His fingers continue stroking my inner walls, and I can feel my orgasm building quickly as he rests his free hand on my lower torso, holding me in place. The carnal need I have for this man is etched into my bones. I've never wanted anyone as much as I want Ethan right now.

"Yes, I'm so close, please, faster, fuck."

The trill of his tongue dances against my clit like the flutter of a hummingbird's wings, its rapid movements vibrating against me until I feel the explosion deep in my core, and I fall over the edge into the strongest, messiest orgasm of my life.

"Fuck, Ethan, yes, fuck," I cry out as my hands grip the sheets, desperate to hold on to this feeling like a musician savoring the final moments of a beautiful song.

I can feel his moans deep in my pussy as he continues licking and sucking, determined to get every drop he can as he extends my orgasm while his strong forearms hold me in place.

Suddenly, he flips me over, hips in the air, and yanks my thighs toward the edge of the bed. The sound of his hand hitting the flesh of my ass fills the room as he delivers several quick, hard strikes to each of my cheeks before his hand rubs gently, smoothing the sting. I squirm against him, the pain giving way to pleasure as I feel my arousal dripping down my thigh.

"You like that?" he asks.

I nod into the mattress and let out a small, muffled moan of agreement.

"I've wanted to light this ass up so many times over the past few weeks. Every time you said something negative about yourself, about us, my need to spank this ass grew." He smacks my ass again, hard. My head tilts forward as I moan and bite the blanket. The pain is intense, but the pleasure after is worth it.

"If you want me to stop, say 'red,' understand?"

I nod against the bed.

"I need your verbal confirmation, Bridget," he commands.

Tilting my head to the side, I'm overcome with desire. I want this man to punish me. I need it. "I understand," I breathe out as I bury my head back into the mattress.

"You're fucking beautiful, Bridget." *Smack.* "Exactly like you are right now." *Smack.* "It pains me that you don't know how incredibly beautiful you are." *Smack.* "This ass is fucking exquisite." *Smack.* "Are you going to talk shit about how you look again?" *Smack.*

I can barely get the word out. "No."

"That's my good girl," he praises as his hands palm both of my ass cheeks, rubbing and kneading them until his hands are replaced with his tongue licking streaks up each side of my ass.

"Oh shit, that's... that's so good," I whine.

"Whose ass is this?" he demands, and when I don't answer fast enough, his teeth sink into the flesh, nipping and sucking.

The sensation is too much as warmth builds in my core. "Fuck!"

He pulls back and smacks my left cheek. "I said, who does this ass belong to?"

"You," I breathe out, almost a whisper. I can't think straight with the way he's playing my body. He must approve of my answer because he continues rewarding me with slaps. Each one is intense, but the pain barely registers anymore as he continues peppering my ass and thighs with spankings.

I feel vulnerable and open, but instead of the anxiety that normally comes with those emotions, a deep sense of peace and joy washes over me. He's taken care of me in my most vulnerable state. *I'm safe with him,* my brain repeats with each blow to my backside.

My thighs squeeze together, seeking friction as an intense feeling builds in my core.

"Are you going to come for me, sweetheart?"

I have trouble forming words. All that comes out are some low moans and a nod.

"Spread your legs."

Obeying his command, I open my legs wider, and his palm smacks against my pussy.

"Your perfect cunt is so wet for me." His praise lights me up as his hand slaps against me again, harder and against my clit. That's all it takes for me to fall over the edge, exploding like a firework, each pulse and flutter a different color illuminating the night sky in my brain.

My mouth fails to form the words that are beating wildly in my chest. *Yes. This feels right. You feel like you're made for me. I want you. I might be falling for you.*

"Fuck, I need to be inside of you right now." His confession feels as urgent as the emotions swirling around my chest. The sound of his clothing hitting the floor is followed by the ripping of foil as he rolls on the condom.

Pulling my hips up and toward him, he thrusts into me in one quick movement.

"Fuuuck," he groans as he starts pulsing slowly inside of me. "I forgot how good your pussy feels squeezing my cock. Fucking made for me."

The stretch is as intense as the first time we were together, and I grip the blanket for leverage as my teeth bite the balled-up fabric, breathing through the delicious pain as it quickly morphs into an intense ecstasy.

His left hand digs into the flesh of my hip as he brings his right down over my ass, smacking it every time he pulls back.

For once, my mind is at ease and quiet. All thoughts and

anxiety spirals are silent as Ethan continues moving over me, the slapping of his hips against my ass getting more intense.

"I need to fuck you hard," he pants, no apology in his tone.

My response is a long moan of "Yyyeeeeeeee," incapable of forming the "S" sound due to the hard pounding of the huge cock inside me fucking with my ability to form words and finish thoughts. I can only focus on Ethan and the immense pleasure he's giving me.

Hands grab at my hips, and I'm turned on my side as he straddles my bottom leg, extending my top leg out at a right angle. His fingers push into the meat of my thigh, holding me in place, thrusting his hips up each time he's fully seated. His movements are slower and more controlled but no less intense as another orgasm builds in my core.

Coming is my only focus as my eyes close and stars dot my vision. I topple over the precipice of pleasure, my release bursting through me like a river breaking through a dam.

"This. Cunt. Is. Fucking. Mine," Ethan grunts out, thrusting on each word before he stills with a guttural groan, his release filling the condom. He collapses onto the bed next to me, twisting as he falls, pulling my leg onto him. Before I realize it, I'm on his chest, our heavy breaths syncing in a rhythm as we come down from the high of our simultaneous releases.

Neither one of us says anything for several minutes as we lie here holding each other. What we shared was intense, raw, emotional. His hands stroke up and down my back, lightly grazing the skin as goosebumps prickle my flesh. I feel the bed jostle briefly as he gets up to remove the condom before he returns and snuggles me in close.

The silence stretches between us, and my mind starts unraveling, trying to analyze what just happened and what it means.

Ethan must sense the shift in me, and his hands move up, stroking my hair as he whispers in my ear, "You did so fucking good, sweetheart."

My brain is having trouble processing, still coming down from the high as he rolls me over, the side of my head landing on his bicep. He leans into me, placing gentle kisses on my lips, cheeks, and neck, while his reassuring words wash over me.

"You're so goddamn incredible." *Kiss.*

"So fucking strong, sweetheart." *Kiss.*

"I'm so proud of you." *Kiss.*

He continues his soft kisses before stilling and rubbing my cheek with his thumb as he holds my face in his hands. Gradually, my breathing evens out, and my thoughts become lucid again.

"Welcome back, Hellcat. How are you feeling?"

"What just happened?" I croak, trying to process my feelings.

"You entered subspace. Have you ever engaged in a dom/sub dynamic before?"

"No. I've been spanked before, but that's never happened."

"Sometimes, your mind can disassociate from the pain your body feels. Your senses might feel heightened. Time might appear to slow down. Or speed up. You might feel extremely relaxed or blissed out." He runs his fingers down my back and along the back of my thigh. "Does this hurt?"

"It feels a little tender."

"Your skin is a little pink. I got pretty rough with you near the end. It might hurt a little to sit tomorrow. I'll have to pick up some arnica cream for you."

"I have some, actually."

The smirk on his face is playful. "You do?"

"Yeah, Becka made me a sex kit for the holidays this past year. She intended it to be a gag gift, but it has some useful items. I remember seeing arnica cream in it. I have no idea what it's for, though."

"It's to soothe your skin after impact play, spanking, flogging, whipping, caning, that sort of thing."

"How do you know so much about this?" I question, as a small streak of jealousy courses through me at the thought of him experiencing what we just did with anyone else.

"Jealous?"

"Maybe," I admit. Shit, what is happening to me?

"I dated a girl who was into BDSM about a year ago, and I learned a lot about the lifestyle. We weren't serious, but I was fascinated by the culture and deep in the throes of grief over losing Nonna. There's a lot of research about its ability to help people process trauma and emotions. It helped me back then, and part of me wondered if it might help you get out of your head and be with me in the moment."

His words should enrage me, but they don't. Instead, there's a dull throb in my chest as his admission pierces the pieces of my heart that are broken and scattered. Why does it feel as though he's picking them up and exposing them back to me, handling them with much more care than they deserve?

It's taken my brain a long time to warm up to the idea of letting someone in, but after tonight, it's clear that has already happened. Ethan has laid claim to a piece of me that I've never shared with anyone else, and the revelation is both thrilling and unsettling.

CHAPTER 23

Ethan

ALYX

Bro

You ever coming home?

I thought you were staying for six weeks.

Change of plans.

Why? Missing me already?

Fuck you and your pickle. I get enough of that
shit at the restaurant.

I'm going to come by later and grab some
clothes.

Moving in?

If she'd agree to it, yes.

Just squatting for now.

At least we're not roommates anymore.

Happy for you, bro

I'm gonna think of it as my own personal fuck
pad. At least rent is cheap.

Don't you mean free?

I'd feel bad about stiffing you with rent, but
you don't pay it.

It's the only decent thing my deadbeat sperm
donor did

Fuck, really? You never told me that.

Shit, don't tell my moms. Or Nyomi. They
don't know.

They wouldn't be cool with it?

Fuck no, they'd think it was a handout or him
buying me off.

So I take it they don't know that he paid for
your year in Italy?

Nope, and we're gonna keep it that way.

Feel free to stop by whenever. I'm working a
double today. The moms and Nyomi wanted
a spa day.

Shit, if I had known that I'd have come in to
help with lunch too.

It's a Wednesday, it'll be slow. Finishing prep
now. I'm glad you're doing more dinner
services again.

The dynamic duo is back, baby!

Hell yeah!

See you tonight

THE THOUGHT of picking up more dinner services should sound appealing. Cooking is all I've ever wanted to do, but lately, there's only one person I'm interested in feeding.

With Bridget's regular nine-to-five hours and my usual late-night shifts, seeing each other has become increasingly difficult. While I'm grateful that Mina and Dre were so accommodating during her recovery, it's been two months, and I don't want to make life difficult and fuck up everyone's schedule more than I have.

It makes me wonder if Bridget knew we'd see so little of each other after things went back to normal, and that's why she's been so agreeable to me staying with her. I'm lucky to see her on my way out the door to the restaurant. Though she's come in to eat a few times when I've led service, we don't get to eat together.

The restaurant is busiest on the weekends, so we don't get a whole day off together; we usually only get Monday and Tuesday nights to ourselves.

Most nights, she's asleep when I get home, shower, and crawl into bed with her. Occasionally, it wakes her and we fuck, and more than once, I've woken up to her mouth or pussy on my cock. It's starting to feel like my dick is just another way for her to work out her frustrations, though my dick is the only one she's doing that with, so I'll take it. And sometimes, after a middle-of-the-night fuck, she lets me hold her until she falls back asleep. While I may have gotten out of the friend zone for now, the emotional intimacy we built over the past two months is hard to maintain when we don't spend as much time together.

Glancing at the time on my phone, I text Bridget to see what her lunch plans are.

Lunch? My place?

I'll cook your favorite.

BRIDGET

How close is it to my office?

I only get an hour.

Why your place?

> It's about a 10 min drive.
>
> I need to grab a few things.
>
> Don't worry, I'm not moving in.

Three dots appear and disappear. I was going for playful, but now I'm worried I triggered her anxiety into thinking that I'm trying to move in with her permanently.

> I plan to make you come at least twice before we eat lunch.

Text me the address.

When I get to my apartment, I'm pleasantly surprised that it isn't a disaster. After I tidy up the living room and clean all of Alyx's dishes, I head to my room to fill my bag with more clothes. I throw in a few sweaters, hoping I'll still be at her place once the weather starts cooling down.

Things are great between us now. We've come a long way from me begging for a second date. Bridget has opened up to me in ways I never expected. But it often feels like one step forward and two back with her.

I choose to focus on the positive, on the things I can control. I cannot control her decisions, emotions, or how she reacts to me, but I can be there for her and support her through it. I can control the way I react to it.

Bridget shows up exactly ten minutes after she left work. Lunch is warming in the oven when I hear her soft knock on the door.

"Hey, gorg—"

Her mouth is on me before I can finish my thought. She loops her arms around my neck and jumps into my arms, wrapping her legs around my waist as I back into the apartment, kicking the door closed. Her firm grip on me tightens as she grinds her pussy against me while her tongue pushes into my mouth, dancing with mine in a way that feels wicked yet divine. The intensity matches one of our middle-of-the-night fucks, quick and hard.

"Fuck me against the door," she orders as her hand reaches down to free my cock from my pants. While I was not expecting her to jump me this quick, I'm not complaining.

I back her up against the door as she licks a trail from my collarbone to my ear before pulling the lobe into her mouth and nibbling. One-handed, I pull a condom out of my wallet and reach between us to maneuver it on. Thank fuck she's wearing a skirt. I pull her thong to the side and guide my cock to her entrance when she thrusts onto me and sinks down on my length.

"Oh fuck, that's good. You're such a good boy for me. I love it when you do what you're told."

Fuck, I love bossy work Bridget. I don't know what pissed her off in the office, but she can happily take it out on me if it means I get to enjoy this perfect cunt.

"You want me to pound this pretty pussy?" I thrust harder, banging her body against the door with each push of my hips.

"Holy shit, yes. Oh fuck, don't stop, I'm so close," she begs as I continue rutting into her. I don't even care what my neighbors will think if they hear us. Hell, they're probably used to the noises coming out of here because of Alyx.

Her grip on my shoulders tightens as her cunt flutters around my cock, squeezing out her release, holding me in place. The noises she makes have my balls tightening, threatening my orgasm.

I slow down my thrusts, wrap my arms around her, and walk to the couch. As I set her down on the cushion, I nip at her lips, teasing and playing until she's wriggling against me.

"Not like this." Her voice is raspy as she stands, walking around the couch as I follow her. She flips her black skirt up over her ass, pulls her thong aside, and leans over the back of the couch. Her ass is perfectly displayed for me, and I can't help kneeling in front of her as I lick up the seam, swirling my tongue over her puckered hole.

"Oh fuck… fuck… yes," she chants as I lick around her opening before pulling back and spitting. There's no way I can claim this ass without lube and then send her back to work. I'm not an asshole.

My saliva drips down her cheeks as I plunge my thumb into her cunt, coating it in her arousal. Once I'm satisfied with the makeshift lubrication, I push my thumb into her tight hole as I thrust into her pussy with my cock.

She lets out a loud moan and a string of curses.

"If you can't handle my thumb in here," I start, pushing the digit in and out, "then how are you going to handle my cock when I claim this hole?"

Never one to back down from a challenge, my hellcat pushes back against me as she looks over her shoulder. "Is that all you got?"

I answer her with a series of brutal thrusts as I circle my thumb in her ass, opening her up further. Pushing the top half of her body down into the cushions, I grip her hip with my other hand as I continue pounding into her. The cushions muffle her screams as she topples over the precipice, her pussy squeezing me like a vise grip.

I thrust in hard as my release barrels through me, right as the apartment door flies open. My body goes into protector mode as I fling myself over Bridget's naked body, trying to cover her up as my head twists, expecting to see Alyx.

"Frick!" my sister Emma screams as she slaps her hands over her face. "I'm sorry. Cheese and rice. Your whole butt is out. Oh my gosh, I think I saw your jewels dangling too. Shoot, sorry, can you pull your pants up?" she rattles on. Emma tends to ramble when she's flustered, and she was clearly not expecting to see the sight of her bare-assed brother balls-deep in someone. But what is she doing here?

"Why the fuck are you just walking into my apartment, Emma?" I grit out as I pull up my pants and cover Bridget's ass with her skirt. "You could use the goddamn doorbell or knock, for fuck's sake." My tone is firm, laced with anger, and for a moment, I regret how much of an asshole I sound like.

"Alyx and I hang out sometimes, but I knew he'd be at work today. I didn't know you'd be here. He said you haven't been around much," she says while I head to the bathroom to dispose of the condom and wash my hands.

I reemerge ready to demand answers. "Do you have someone out in the hall? Were you using my place as a fuck pad? Is that some kind of arrangement you two have?"

Her arms shoot up in defense. "Cheese and rice, no."

There's a look on her face that I can't quite place. Guilt? Regret? It's gone before I can decipher it. "Aren't you supposed to be in class?"

Bridget steps forward, clearing her throat. "Hi, I'm Bridget," she offers, reaching around me to extend her hand to Emma.

"I didn't see anything, okay. I might have seen more of him than I cared to, but you were covered. I didn't peep any of your jibbly bits," Emma stammers as she awkwardly laughs and her cheeks pinken.

Snaking an arm around Bridget's shoulder, I tug her from behind me and notice the flush on her face. It could be from the fucking or her embarrassment. Looking down at her beautiful face, I gently kiss her forehead and brush back a few stray hairs plastered to her forehead. "What she means to say is, 'Hi, I'm Emma, Ethan's sister. It's nice to meet you,'" I explain, shooting Emma a warning look.

"What he said."

"Cheese and rice?" Bridget questions.

"I don't curse. Our youngest sister is five, so I tend to get creative with my word choices," she explains as she nervously rubs her hands, her movements resembling those of a shy church mouse. It's ironic because she's nothing like the meek and mild religious students who attend her school.

"Now, will you tell me what you're doing here?" I question.

"Do you have any food?"

"Emma," I warn.

"Fine. I was skipping class. Please don't tell Mom and Dad."

Emma is a straight A student. She got into Faith Union College on a full academic scholarship. It's not like her to skip class.

"I'm not going to say shit. You're nineteen and can make your own decisions, but what's going on?"

"Nothing."

"Emma," I repeat.

"Fine. I have this professor that's riding me really hard."

My eyebrows shoot up to my hairline, but she interjects before I can ask. "Not like that. Biscuits!"

Bridget laughs beside me. "Are all your non-curses food-related?"

Emma smiles and looks at me. "I like her."

"So, the professor?" I prompt.

"Professor A-hole. He's just so… so… *difficult*. Nothing I do is ever good enough. I was top of my class in high school, and suddenly I feel like I can't do anything right. The semester just started, and we had to turn in our first paper, and when he handed them back, I got a C. I've never gotten a C in my entire fricking life! He's so mean. I want to punch him in his stupid, handsome face," she blurts out before slapping her hands over her mouth.

"I had a couple of professors like that in college," Bridget says sympathetically. "It was hard for me too. I was always so strong academically. But I came up with some tools that helped me."

"The worst part is I have him for the whole year because he's the only one who teaches this class, and it's a required class for me. I was coming here to kill time and study."

Bridget pulls her phone out of her pocket, unlocks it, and hands it to Emma. "Here, put in your number. I only have about twenty minutes left on my lunch break, but I'd be happy to connect and share some of my study tips from one valedictorian to another."

"That would be forking amazing!" Emma beams as she punches her number into Bridget's contacts, and I turn, heading into the kitchen.

"Follow me if you want to eat," I call out behind me.

Ten minutes later, Bridget gives me a quick peck and heads to the door.

"See you at home," she starts, then corrects herself. "I mean, see you later?"

"See you at your place," I reassure her, even though it kills me inside.

The door shuts behind her and Emma turns to me.

"Okay, I need details. Now," she demands while still chewing. Scooping another helping into her mouth, she mumbles, "Good gravy, this is delicious."

"Can you at least chew before you try to speak? But yeah, she's really fucking great, Em."

She giggles as she finishes her mouthful. "Sorry, this is really good."

"It's my signature dish at Mangia Bene. You should stop by more. I'd be happy to feed you and your friends."

"I might take you up on that, especially if Alyx is around too."

"There something I need to know about?"

"Nope, he's just become a friend I can count on. He offered to let me hang out here if I needed a break from class. Nothing is going on," she promises, but something tells me that's not the whole story. "And I'm so taking Bridget up on the offer. This professor is nonstop. I feel like he's constantly over my shoulder, picking my work apart. Putting me on the spot by calling on me first. It's a lot, and I don't know how to get off his radar."

"Anything you need a big brother to help with when it comes to Professor Asshole?"

"A-hole, and gosh, no," she says, looking a bit flustered.

Something more is going on there too, but I've learned it's best not to push my sister. She'll share it with me when she's ready.

"I'm here if you need me."

"Thanks, Ethan. And I really like Bridget. I can tell she's into you—I mean, aside from the humping. It's obvious by the way she looks at you. There's a connection there."

"I'm pretty sure I'm in love with her."

"Oh my gosh, that's so exciting! Have you told her?"

"I can't. I don't think she's there yet, and I don't want to scare her off."

"Oh, she's there, even if she doesn't tell you. Like I said, it's the way she looks at you. Has she met Mom and Dad yet?"

"She's not ready for all that yet. Baby steps."

I'm returning to Bridget's place an hour later with a bag full of clothes. Just as I enter the place, my phone buzzes with a text.

ALYX

When you said you were going to come by, I thought you meant you were going to stop by the apt, not cum.

How the fuck do you know that?

Also, you're welcome for doing your dishes.

Emma texted me that she walked in on you two.

Good for you, by the way.

You guys text? 😕

Chill, bro

It's not like that.

Just friends

Even though Emma is my stepsister, she's still family, blood or not, and I'm not excited at the thought of Alyx being interested in any of my sisters. But if he says they're just friends, then I believe him.

Alyx is a great friend and a great person, but he's a bit of a fuckboy. And while that works for him, I know that Emma is a relationship person, and a fuckboy is not something she's looking for or needs.

You're like family, but don't fuck with my sisters.

Respectfully

Pickle, I'm not fucking with Emma, I can promise you that.

I know you wouldn't. It was weird seeing her there when I knew she wasn't there to see me. Kinda sure she's crushing on her professor tho.

Professor A-hole?

Totally

Keep an eye on her for me?

Anything for you, bro.

CHAPTER 24

Bridget

THERE'S a slight chill in the breeze as the sun sets and night falls around me. We're almost halfway through September, and the evenings are starting to cool.

A night alone was exactly what I needed after a long day in the office. Every single person I interacted with today needed something from me, and I want an evening to recharge my social battery.

Ethan worked the lunch shift today, but he said he might stay through the dinner rush, so I don't have to worry about bailing on him since we don't have plans.

The sidewalks are somewhat deserted, and the city is winding down from the hustle of the workday as most rush hour traffic has died down. I've walked a good bit from home when I realize my stomach is growling, and I look around for a place to grab a bite. Sweet Serenity Café is about a block from here, and I get excited at the idea of eating alone.

Entering the restaurant, I let the hostess know that I'd like to sit on the patio. It's gorgeous, surrounded by a tall white fence; it blocks the view of the street, creating a cozy feel. The outside of the fence is adorned with painted flowers, and a beautiful mural done by a local artist. Inside, wrought-iron tables dot the area, each situated over the brick paver-covered ground. In the spring and summertime, the patio is covered in vibrant flowers and plants, and a wisteria-covered entrance makes you feel like you've stumbled into a secret garden.

The normal floral backdrop has been replaced with fall décor. Corn stalks, mums, and pumpkins atop bales of hay fill the space. A small scarecrow perches in the corner as fairy lights illuminate the area from overhead.

Normally, I pick up food from a restaurant and take it home. This is one of the few places I actually enjoy dining in. Well, here and Ethan's restaurant since I have a reason to go inside now. And I do enjoy the view over there as well. My cheeks flush as thoughts of Chef Ethan invade my thoughts.

I look up and swear my mind is playing tricks on me, conjuring a mirage of Ethan just as I was thinking about him. But holy fuck, it actually is Ethan. He's clearly not working. And he's with a woman. A beautiful woman who appears to be older than him, maybe even close to my age. They're standing next to a table, arms around each other in what feels like a longer-than-normal embrace. He knows this woman intimately. What the fuck?

Is he cheating on me? We've never even defined what we're doing, so would it technically be cheating? What if he's been seeing her this whole time? Am I the other woman, or is she?

Does he have a thing for older women? Is that why he's never been bothered by my age? Maybe he only dates older women. When I asked about past relationships, he never mentioned their ages. What if that's what he's into?

Suddenly, every moment we've shared feels cheap. Everything I once thought was special is tainted with these new thoughts that he's done this before, that I'm not the only older woman he's been with. I'm not special, just one of many.

I stand there at the patio entrance frozen, as though I'm trapped in place by vines that are holding me hostage.

The patio that's normally a fantastical dreamscape has

become my literal nightmare as I watch Ethan hold her in his arms, his fucking dimple on full display, face beaming with joy —that until now I thought he'd only felt with me—as he lowers his lips and kisses the woman's forehead in a way that's way too intimate for my comfort.

The gate snaps shut behind me, breaking me from my doomsday reverie. Slowly, Ethan's head turns toward the sound, briefly making eye contact with me, the mystery woman still wrapped in his arms.

No. Nope, I cannot be here. I cannot do this. This is why I don't do relationships. Every intrusive thought imaginable shouts in my brain, the noise an overwhelming rush of anxiety as I turn and run through the gate. I can hear shuffling behind me as I run down the street, dodging people as I get the hell out of there.

"Bridget!" Ethan calls out, but I keep running, determined to escape the hell I'm living. "Will you stop running?" he pants.

And give you the chance to lie to my face about what that was back there? No, asshole, I won't stop running.

Pain lances my chest, and I slow briefly to get my bearings. We're a few blocks from the restaurant and still too far from my apartment to outrun him. Fuck, I forgot he runs every day. How am I going to get out of this?

I'm turning down a side street when his hand grabs mine, pulling me back.

"Will you stop for one goddamn second?" His voice is gruff and demanding as he pulls on my arm, forcing me to turn toward him. "What was that back there? Why did you run? I was calling your name—"

A bitter laugh escapes me, interrupting his excuses. "You know exactly what that was, exactly what I walked in on." I stop myself before I say more. I'm not going to be that woman. I'm not going to give him the satisfaction.

The look of confusion on his face almost convinces me that

I'm wrong, but I press on. "I can't do this. You've made your bed. Don't make this a bigger mess than it needs to be." I start to turn, but his hand grips me tighter, holding me in place as a look of understanding crosses his features.

"Instead of talking to me, you've let your mind spiral into possibilities, none of which are true. Can you listen to me for a goddamn minute?" he angrily snaps before adding, "Please?"

Fuck, he's right. That's exactly what I'm doing. I have no idea who that woman is, and I haven't even given him a chance to explain before I've written him off. My heart beats wildly in my chest, adrenaline still coursing through me as I inhale a shaky breath, images of my high school ex, me alone in the hallway feeling humiliated and alone, flash through my mind. *They aren't the same person*, I tell myself.

"That was my mom, Ashley," he tells me. "She surprised me at the restaurant today and wanted to take me out for dinner. I didn't know she was coming by. Mina had dinner covered, so I left early."

Shit. I really did jump to conclusions.

"I'm an asshole," I groan as I cover my face with my hands.

"You're not an asshole," he says as he pulls me into a hug. "I don't know what you've gone through in past relationships that would make you so quickly jump to the worst possible conclusion, but I'm not and have never been, never will be, a cheater."

His arms leave my waist and cup my cheeks, and the voices screaming at me to run start to quiet in my head. But I won't give him this piece of my past. I can't. My pain is my baggage to carry, my cross to bear.

"It's clear you've been through some shit, and I'm not going to force you to talk about it. I get how that looked back there, and I can see it clearly triggered a trauma response in you. Your flight response kicked in so quickly that I almost didn't catch you. And I'm sorry that I raised my voice, but I didn't know how else to get you to stop."

My cheeks burn as his words pierce me. How does he see me? How is he able to read me so clearly? Why did my brain spiral to the worst possible conclusion without even giving him a chance to explain?

How the fuck did he get past all my walls and implant himself in my heart?

We stand there for several awkward minutes, him still holding me, his hand firmly clasped around my back as I listen to the rapid beating of his heart against his chest. I can't even remember if I responded to him, but relief fills me when it's clear he won't force me to share anything more with him than I'm willing to right now.

When my breathing returns to normal, and my heartbeat finally starts to even out, matching his rhythm, I look up into his eyes.

"Hey, Hellcat." He smiles down at me, his dimple popping as he leans down to press a kiss to my forehead.

"I'm sorry. I couldn't stop my spiraling thoughts."

"You don't owe me an explanation, but I'd love to know more if you're ever willing to share." He pulls me against him as we walk back the way we came.

"Wh-where are we going?" I stutter out.

"Back to the restaurant. I kind of left quickly, and I need to get back before my mom thinks I skipped out on her."

My legs lock, and I stop walking. "I can't go back there. This is so embarrassing. What is she going to think of me?"

"Nothing. She didn't see you, and I highly doubt her brain went where yours did because those thoughts didn't cross my mind either."

"I don't know."

He steps in close, his cool, crisp scent enveloping me. "If you're up for it, I'd love for you to meet my mom."

"What would we even tell her? You ran off chasing after me. She'll think I've lost my mind."

"We can say you didn't hear me because you had your

earbuds in. You traveled quite a distance, and it's unlikely she knows what's happening, only that I ran after someone I knew."

"What about the fact that she and I look to be similar in age?"

"She already knows how old you are."

"How does she know that?"

"Because I told her. Months ago."

"What? Why? We weren't even dating then."

"We talk once a week, at least, and she stops by the restaurant when she's in the area. Since I took time off to help you, I let her know why I wouldn't be at the restaurant as much. And your age doesn't matter to her. She's just thrilled that I'm happy. And you make me happy."

"Oh."

"Also, can we circle back to that dating comment?" He flashes me a boyish grin.

I playfully shove his side, but he pulls me in closer, kissing my temple.

"It's ok. I won't tell anyone you like me," he says as he squeezes my shoulder. "Seriously, though, I'd love for you to meet my mom. She's kind of been dying to meet you. I didn't want to overwhelm you if you weren't ready."

Am I ready? That's kind of a big step in a relationship. One I've only done one other time. But high school boyfriends don't count, right? I mean, I had to meet his parents since they drove us around on our dates before we got our licenses.

His green eyes pierce me with a look full of hope and awe. His face is so handsome that it's hard for me to say no. Reluctantly, I agree, and together we head back to the restaurant hand in hand, my eyes fixed on him as we walk, for once not giving a fuck what anyone walking by might think.

"Bridget, it's so nice to meet you." Ashley smiles warmly at me as she extends her hand. "Please, sit down and join us. Ethan has told me so much about you."

I sit next to Ethan and smile awkwardly, unsure what to say.

"Mom, please don't embarrass me," he pleads.

"What? I'm just so thrilled to meet her. You've told me how beautiful and smart she is, and I can tell that she keeps you on your toes. I'm thrilled there's someone out there giving you shit and keeping you honest."

"It's a full-time job keeping Ethan in check, so it's nice to see I'm not the only one who gets to have a little fun with him. Right, Pup?" I tease.

"There's my favorite hellcat." He squeezes my thigh under the table.

"Oh, I need to hear more about these nicknames." Ashley laughs as she sips her drink.

"He tends to follow me around—"

"Like a puppy?" She cackles, and it sends us all into a fit of laughter. "I'm sure he prefers Pup to Pickle."

"Hell yeah, I do," Ethan chimes in. "And I call her hellcat because she gives me hell."

"You like it."

"I really do." He beams at me.

"Gah, you two are so cute," Ashley exclaims, and I shift a little in my seat, needing to address the elephant in the room before the pressure in my chest gets worse.

"And you don't think it's weird that we're about the same age and I'm dating your son...well, stepson?"

"Honestly, if you're both happy, I don't care how old either of you are. You're consenting adults, and my opinion has no place in your relationship. As women, we're so hard on ourselves, let alone each other, and that saddens me. Don't we get enough of that from the patriarchy? You wouldn't believe how many people judge me because I was so young when I started having kids. Or because I'm divorced. Or because I'm almost forty and have a five-year-old, and honestly, I kind of want to have another baby before I'm too old to do so."

"Really, Mom?" Ethan laughs. "I'm not changing any more diapers. You guys are on your own."

"We'll cross that bridge when we get there. But I'm having fun trying." She winks.

"Jesus Christ!" Ethan wails, and I can't help laughing at his unease.

Ashley makes a "See what I'm talking about" gesture towards Ethan as if to prove her point before turning to him. "And she was worried about being judged. Look at you."

He throws his hands up in defense, realizing the error he made. "I'm not judging. I just don't want to hear about you and Dad bumping uglies."

"That's fair," Ashley concedes. "So, how'd you two meet?"

"Mom."

"What? I want to hear her tell it."

Shit. Telling his mom we had a one-night stand that turned into a Nurse Nightingale situation is not exactly how I planned to spend my evening.

"We, uh, we met at a club," I answer, shoving several fries into my mouth to avoid any follow-up questions.

Ethan makes a "See, I told you so" movement with his head, and I laugh at how he and his mom think their silent conversations aren't obvious. I guess he's able to read more than just me.

CHAPTER 25

Ethan

THE PAST FEW weeks have been amazing. I've never been happier. Bridget and I have spent almost every night together, and it feels like I'm finally making progress with her. Ever since she met my mom, something has shifted, and she's more open to the idea of us.

Most nights, we order in, or I cook at her place, and we watch movies or read together. I love our quiet nights and the quality time we spend together. But I'm starting to feel like her dirty little secret, because other than her apartment, the only place we go out in public together is Mangia Bene.

When I suggest other places to try or that we go out to a movie, she always has an excuse for why we can't go. We've encountered a few awkward interactions over the past few months, but nothing as bad as that nurse thinking I was her son while she was prepping for surgery.

There are the occasional stares from people the few times we're out, and I know Bridget notices them, but I'm proud to be seen with such a strong, beautiful woman, and I'm convinced those stares have more to do with how fucking hot she is.

———

Dinner rush is finally over, and I toss my apron in the linen hamper at the back of the kitchen.

"Fuck, bro, if I never see another black truffle risotto, I'll die a happy man." Alyx complains.

Laughing, I ask, "What did you do to piss off Dre? She knows you hate that station."

"I told her Nyomi couldn't move in with me," he admits, and guilt washes over me like cold rain soaking through my clothes.

"Shit, that because of me?"

"Yes and no. She knows you're spending a lot of time at Bridget's, but they don't know you've all but moved out. If she moves in and sees you're never there, she's gonna be pissed sleeping on the couch. Plus, I kind of like having the place to myself. I don't wanna be cockblocked by my sister."

"That makes me feel a little better. It's nice having a place to crash if Bridget needs her space, but I can't bring up moving in. It might spook her. But I feel bad putting Nyomi out."

"Don't. Honestly, I think it's my moms that don't want Nyomi pussy-blocking them. You coming by anytime soon to grab more clothes? Or are you still living out of that duffle bag? She let you have some closet space yet?"

"Mostly out of the bag. I've got a drawer, and a few things hung up in her closet, and all my shit was on her bathroom counter before she organized it in a neat little tote for me. I don't want to rush her."

"I get that. You work tomorrow?" he asks as he heads for the door.

I take a step closer to him. "Actually, I wanted to ask you about something. I kind of need your advice."

"If you use two fingers, they usually come faster," he jokes.

"Jesus fuck," I groan, dropping my head in my hands.

"Look, if you don't know how to make her come by now—"

"I know how to make her come. Fucking hell, keep your voice down," I warn, glancing around us to make sure no one is listening. "This isn't about that."

"Only fucking with you, bro. What's up?"

"Things are really good between us right now, but Bridget is still stressing about the difference in our ages."

"For real? She's hot, what's she worried about?"

"Some nurse mistook me for her son back when she had her surgery. It's still fucking with her to the point that we spend most of our nights in. I don't want to push her to go out somewhere if she's not ready, but I need her to see that she's the only one hung up on our ages. Plus, I want to go out for my birthday somewhere other than my place of employment."

"You could take her to a Cobras game," he suggests. "She is a fan, right? If she's a Pythons fan, you may need to dump her."

Our local hockey team, the Columbus Cobras, have a long-standing rivalry with the Pittsburgh Pythons. You can't go anywhere in this city without hearing jokes about which city has the bigger snake.

"She likes the Cobras," I assure him. "But that's way too public. She'd never be okay with that."

"I have an idea. You know about Pulse?"

"The sex club?"

"Yeah, it might be the perfect place to take her. Ain't no one there giving a fuck about how old either of you are. In fact, that might be a turn-on if you want to add to your party of two. Think she might be down?"

"I doubt she's looking to add a third, but she might be open to checking out the club," I say slowly, and the more I think about it, the more perfect it sounds. It would be a great way to take her out in public while being free from judgment.

Alyx pulls out his wallet and hands me a black plastic card

with the club's logo on the front. Flipping it over in my hands, I see his name embossed on the back and what looks like a membership ID number. "Show them this, and they'll let you in. It shows I'm vouching for you. You just gotta follow the club rules, cool?"

"Cool. Thanks, bro."

"No problem, I got you."

CHAPTER 26

Ethan

WE WALK INTO THE CLUB, Bridget nervously clutching my arm as we approach security. It took a little convincing to get her on board, but a few pops of my dimple, followed by multiple orgasms and some last resort begging about it being my birthday, and here we are.

"Relax, this'll be fun. I've got you, Hellcat, promise," I whisper into her ear. She nods and swallows, my eyes tracking the way her throat bobs.

"Welcome to Pulse," the hostess greets us. "Are you members?"

"No, but I have this," I say as I hand her Alyx's card. Bridget looks at me quizzically. I lean down into her ear. "It's Alyx's. He won't tell anyone we're here, if that's what you're worried about."

"Is he here tonight?"

"Nah, he's at the restaurant," I reassure her as I reach down and squeeze her ass. I can feel the way her body shivers at my touch.

"I'll need both of your IDs and phones. We have a strict no-phone policy in the club. For the privacy of our guests, we don't allow videos or photos to be taken inside. We'll hold on to your phones and IDs until you leave. You can retrieve them here on your way out. Are you familiar with the club's rules and bracelet system?"

We shake our heads, and she continues, "Here at Pulse, your safety is our primary concern. Our members are thoroughly vetted with extensive background checks. All members pay a yearly fee and must produce regular STI tests for full access to the club. Failure to do so will limit access to parts and perks of the club. Members are awarded two guest passes a year, and guests using those passes have limited access to the club and its members. As Alyx's guests, you have access to the main room of the club and the private rooms. However, you're not allowed to invite anyone in the club to join you in any activities without a clean STI test on file. You can only partake in consensual play between the two of you. Normally, a guest pass would only give you access to the main room, but since Alyx is also an employee, we can make an exception for you."

My eyebrows shoot up, and I try to hide the look of surprise on my face. He's also an employee? Why the fuck would he keep that secret from me? Finding out he also works at a sex club would be less shocking than the sight I have burned into my brain of walking in on him balls-deep inside multiple partners. I'm not yucking his yum, but I'd just prefer a warning so I don't have to see my friend in compromising positions.

"Alyx works here too? Did you know?" Bridget whispers in my ear while the hostess's back is turned.

"I had no clue," I whisper back. "But I'm not surprised. I'm pretty sure that's not something he advertises at the restaurant in front of Mina and Dre."

Our hostess continues, "We have a full bar with a two-drink maximum for the safety of all patrons and employees. No drug use is permitted in the club. And we have a zero-tolerance policy regarding hate speech, bullying, and violence.

There's no warnings for that, you'll just be immediately removed from the club and banned."

Pointing to a sign on the wall, she recites the color-coding from memory as we follow along.

"Black means only watching."

"Blue means open to men joining."

"Pink means open to women joining."

"Green means open for anyone to join."

"Yellow means here with someone, not open to adding anyone."

"Red means looking for a sub."

"White means looking for a dom."

I glance at Bridget to see her reaction. Her eyes darken as she looks at me, and her earlier fears are nowhere to be seen.

The hostess's voice breaks our focus as she asks, "Do you know what color bracelet you'd like? Without an STI test on file, you won't be able to seek out other partners in the club, so black and yellow are your only options for now."

Confident in my choice based on our earlier conversation, I say, "Black."

"Yellow," Bridget says at the same time as me.

We're handed two bracelets each, one black and one yellow.

"Is this your way of telling me that you're *with* me?" I ask with a hint of a smirk on my face.

"If you play your cards right," she purrs while slipping on her bracelets and sauntering over to the black velvet-curtained entrance of the club.

Sensual music plays throughout the club as the sounds of moans punctuate the steady beats. At first, I assume the moans are coming from the music, but looking around, I realize they're live. The club's main room has a stage in the corner with a short catwalk that juts out from it. Several booths line the wall. There's a bar on the opposite corner from the stage, while the middle of the room has small round tables scattered throughout. The lower tables include chairs, while the taller ones have people gathered around them.

We make our way over to a booth, and I pull Bridget in close to me, practically forcing her to sit on my lap as I glance around. There are people coupled up, engaging in different acts all over the room. Some are observing like us, while others explore their sexuality uninhibited. Near the bar, a bouncer is standing in front of an opening that leads to the private rooms.

Someone comes by to take our drink order, and Bridget orders a bourbon neat. I have a feeling she'll need it to loosen her up for what I have planned.

As Bridget sips on her drink, her hand snakes up my thigh, and my cock jumps at her touch. Most days, all it takes is a look from her, and I'm at full mast, ready to go. She's incredibly sexy, and it baffles me that she doesn't see that. That past boyfriends have made her question herself and her worth pisses me off to no end. She comes across as a confident, powerful woman, but the more I've gotten to know her, the more I've seen the woman who is a powerhouse in the office but is broken emotionally. The masks she wears fool most, but not me, and peeling them back has allowed me to see all her beautifully broken pieces. I want to be there for her as she puts them back together. Hell, I'd put them together for her if she'd let me, but even though we've made a lot of progress in the past few weeks, we still have a long way to go before she fully trusts me. And I'm hoping tonight is another step towards that.

Looking around the room, I notice several couples and point them out to Bridget. With my hand holding her neck, I pull her face close to my lips, whispering in her ear, "Do you see that couple onstage?"

Her eyes track the couple; a man, probably in his late twenties, has a petite blonde woman, who's easily in her late forties, tied up and bound on a bed. Her arms secured above her head, she lies there bared to him as he feasts on her.

"Fuck, that's hot," she starts as I feel her shift in her seat. "Look at how he's devouring her."

"That's what you look like when I do that to you. See how he looks at her, licking and sucking, and then looking at her with adoration. That's how you make me feel."

Bridget's focus shifts to a couple at one of the low-top tables in the middle of the room. They appear to be in their thirties, both wearing green bracelets that broadcast that they're open to anyone joining them. An older man, maybe mid-fifties, approaches and pulls up a chair to join them. The men take turns kissing the woman before leaning forward and kissing each other as the woman watches. I notice Bridget rubbing her thighs together at the sight. "You might have a little voyeur in you. Is watching them turning you on?"

"It kind of is. He walked right up and they let him join them even though he's..."

"Even though he's what? Older than them?"

"I wasn't going to say that. It's just that the couple is hot, like an eight or nine, and the guy that joined them is like a five at best."

"Based on the way they're all sucking face, I'm guessing that couple doesn't agree with your assessment. And really, it's up to them, isn't it?"

"Sorry, that was a shitty thing to say. Sometimes I have difficulty turning off that voice in my head, and it comes out of my mouth unfiltered."

"Is that the same voice that says all the shitty things about my age versus yours?" I prod gently. "The same voice that convinces you that you aren't attractive without makeup? Because I think that voice is full of shit."

She looks at me with shock on her face that quickly morphs to confusion, like she's thinking over the truth in my words.

"How do you do that? It's like you're in my head. It feels like you know me better than anyone else."

She's easy to read, yet she acts like no one else ever has. But the more I think about what she's shared with me, the more I'm convinced that no one's ever paid close enough attention to her micro-expressions to decipher what she's saying without words.

How her eyebrows furrow when she's working through a problem, and she's stalling to practice reciting an answer in her head, careful to weigh out her words before she speaks.

How she chews on the bottom right part of her lip, moving it back and forth in her teeth when she's trying to hide something.

How she plays with her left earlobe when she's nervous, tucking it in and letting it pop back into place, only to repeat the gesture until her anxiety abates.

It blows my mind that no one in her life has taken the time to understand her, but I'll gladly be the first.

With my hand under her chin, I angle her face toward mine as I press our foreheads together. "You make it easy for me to know you. All it requires is attention, and if you haven't noticed, I have difficulty keeping my eyes off you."

Her hand is still on my leg, squeezing and groping as I move mine under her arm and onto her leg. I slowly make a path up her thigh and under the hem of her dress until I'm grazing the fabric of her panties.

"Keep looking. Tell me what you see," I say, distracting her as I draw her focus back to the club.

Her head swivels as she looks around the room, and I continue dragging my fingers up and down her panties, reveling in how they dampen the more I stroke.

"I... uh..." She struggles with words as I continue my movements. "There's a couple over by the bar. The younger guy with the man-bun..."

While she speaks, I remove a small vibrator from my pocket and pull aside her panties as I push the tip of the toy into her pussy.

"What are you—oh fuck," she cries as her head falls back against my arm around her shoulders.

"It's a little gift I got you," I say seductively.

"What if someone sees us?" she rasps, her breath picking up as I move the toy in and out, adding my fingers in, teasing her.

"Do you think anyone in this room gives a fuck what I'm doing to you right now? Look around. No one cares who we are to each other, how old we are, or that your cunt is stuffed full of my fingers." I remove my hand from between her thighs and bring it to my mouth. Her eyes track the movement as I suck her juices off my fingers. "Fucking delicious."

"Are you just going to leave it there and tease me?" she asks with fire in her eyes.

I pull the remote from my pocket and hold it in front of her face. "As long as you worry about what other people think, this stays off. I'll turn this up for every fuck you don't give."

Her brows knit together. "That doesn't make sense. How can I show you when I don't give a fuck?"

I turn the remote on and click the plus sign, setting it at the lowest vibration. Her eyes widen the slightest amount. "You let me put this in you in front of everyone. That gets you two clicks." I hit the button again. "But then you got mouthy, so I'm going to take one away." I hit the minus sign on the device.

"Oh shit," she moans as her ass wiggles against the seat. I pull her lips to mine, juggling the remote control so it's in my hand around her shoulder, freeing up my other to cup her breast. She thrusts her tongue against mine, pulling my lips into her mouth before she sucks hard on my bottom lip. I hit the plus button two more times.

"One for kissing me in public like that for the first time. And one for not giving a fuck who sees me touch your breast."

She grabs my hand and moves it under her dress. Her skin feels warm and soft as my palm caresses her nipple through the fabric of her bra. "Good girl," I groan as I turn up the vibration.

Her tits heave against my hand. I feel her wiggling in the booth and notice that she's reached around and unhooked her bra. The fabric falls limp on her chest as I pull it down and tweak her nipple, rolling it between my fingers. "Yes, just like that," she moans as I hit the plus button twice.

"Keep this up, and I'm going to want to spread you out on this table and fuck you in front of this whole club."

Her head shoots up. "I don't..." she objects as I hit the minus button.

"All you have to do is not give a fuck. I won't do anything you don't consent to. You can stop this at any time. You can take my words as promises you want me to fulfill, or sexy, empty threats that make you wet but go no further. I've gotten you off with only my words before. Eyes on me, no one else. Can you do that for me, Hellcat?"

Her eyes widen as my words sink in, nodding her head before resting it against my arm.

My finger presses the plus sign again as I whisper against her ear, "You can do it, sweetheart, focus." She squirms in her seat as she begins stroking my length. "Fuck, that's it," I say, pushing against her hand as I hit the plus sign two more times on the remote.

"Holy shit," she cries out. "I need..."

"What do you need?" I ask, still thrusting against her hand under the table.

Bridget climbs onto my lap, straddling me in the booth. I grip her hips, remote still in hand, and start gliding her pussy against my cock. Her head falls back as I tap the remote, cranking it up as high as it goes. I'm going to reward my little hellcat for this, knowing how huge a step this is.

"So fucking needy for this cock. Are you gonna use it till you come with everyone watching?"

"Oh, yes, Ethan, fuck," she moans against my ear, her face buried against my neck as she continues to dry hump me. Her arms are wrapped around my neck as they squeeze tighter. "I'm going to... fuck, oh fuck, I'm coming!" Her hips slow as she rides out her release. I turn off the remote and pocket it. Grabbing her face, I pull it into mine, kissing her lips, her cheeks, her chin, and her neck.

"I'm so fucking proud of you, my perfect fucking queen," I say between kisses.

The little noises and moans of appreciation she makes send a bolt of lust straight to my cock, making it ache to be free of its restraints.

"Did you?" she asks, looking down at my lap before looking up at me again.

"No, sweetheart, this was about you," I assure her as my hand smooths between her legs, pulling out the toy before slipping it into my pocket.

Suddenly, her body stiffens as she drops her forehead to my shoulder, cursing under her breath. "What's wrong?"

"I see someone I work with. Shit. Shit. Shit."

Fuck, that reaction stings. She was making big steps toward being proud to be seen out with me. "Are you embarrassed to be seen here with me?"

She shakes her head against me, her face still planted firmly against my chest. "It's not that. There's a man a few booths behind you with black hair and a nice suit. He's the CEO of my company. I don't care if he sees us together, but I don't want him to see me in a sex club. Oh shit, I'll never be able to show my face at work again."

Craning my neck, I twist to find the man she's describing. He's sitting a few booths away, sipping a drink while a young woman plants kisses on his neck. "The guy with the blonde?" I clarify.

"That's him, his name is Mark. Please get me out of here before he sees me."

"I've never seen you cower from anyone like this before."

"He's practically my boss and someone I've spent years cultivating a persona for so he would see me as an equal he could respect and promote. I worked too damn hard impressing that man to lose it in an instant because he saw me *here*."

"I got you. I'm taking you to a private room. Wrap your legs around my waist, and keep your head on my shoulder."

I move to the end of the booth and stand, holding her in my arms with a hand under her ass, doing my best to cover anything peeking out of her short dress. The bouncer waves us through the rope, and I head down the hallway, looking for an unoccupied room. Sounds of pleasure surround us as people moan and cry out from the rooms we pass. Near the end of the hall, I see that room ten is free, and I close the door behind us as we enter.

The space is simple. There's a king-sized bed in the middle of one wall, and the opposite wall is made entirely of mirrors. There's a dresser next to the door and a sink on the other side of that. Bridget still clings to me as I soothe her, body trembling uncontrollably. "Are you okay? You're breathing awfully fast."

"I... I... I th-think... I ca–I c-can't... b-breathe," she stutters out, clutching at her chest with one hand. I cross to the bed, holding her as I sit on the edge.

"Bridget, breathe. You're having a panic attack. It's okay." I rub my hands up and down her back in a soothing motion. "Look at me. I know what you're feeling is scary, but it's not dangerous. I'm going to keep you safe, I promise. Can you take a deep breath and hold it for five seconds?"

Her pupils are dilated, and she's having trouble focusing as she sucks in a shaky breath. I take a deep breath too and hold it, nodding at her to do the same. She takes a measured breath, making several attempts to hold it before she's successful.

"That's my good girl. Focus on my eyes. Now exhale. Good, I'm so proud of you. Take another deep breath and hold it for six seconds." I continue making slow strokes on her back with my knuckles. "Now focus on my dimple. I know how much you love it."

"I do n-not," she protests through shuddering breaths. I move a hand to her wrist, feeling for her pulse point as I glance at the clock on the wall behind her.

"Keep holding that breath," I say as I count her heartbeats. I've got to get her to calm down. "It's okay. I've caught you staring at this dimple a lot. I know you like it." I wink at her as the tension eases from her shoulders. "Good, now exhale. That's it. Keep listening to my voice. Nod if you can do that."

Giving the slightest nod, she lets out a breath, and I resume making circles and light strokes on her back as I try to relax her.

"Take another deep breath and hold it. You're doing amazing. Keep listening to my voice and focusing on the way I'm stroking your back. Exhale and nod if you can feel my hands on your back." She slowly nods as her eyes focus on mine.

"Good, we're going to play a little counting game. Can you tell me five things you can see in this room?"

Her eyes dart around, and I can tell she's having difficulty focusing. It's as though I'm giving her a test she didn't study for. "B-bed... mirror... uhhh... light fix–fixture ...p–pillows... red walls."

"That's so good. Can you tell me four things you can touch?" I implore, moving my hands to her hips, lightly squeezing them.

She looks down at my chest as her hand reaches up to play with the fabric on my shirt, "Your body. This bed. The floor. Um... your legs." She squeezes me with her thighs as she straddles me, and I can feel the tension starting to leave her body as her breathing becomes less chaotic.

"That's it. You're doing so well. Focus on one of those things as you continue taking deep breaths," I coax as I dig my fingertips into her hips, squeezing and massaging before moving up to rest them on her waist. We sit there for several minutes, her hands palming my shoulders, her thighs squeezing mine, and I continue to model breathing for her. "Three things you can hear."

"Your voice... music..." She trails off as she concentrates, closing her eyes to listen to the noises in the club. "I think someone's moaning?" She lets out the tiniest laugh as her eyes open and flit up to meet mine.

"Tell me two things you can smell."

"Your cologne. It's sea salt, bergamot, and maybe citrus?" She stares into my eyes, baring her soul for me. She knows the individual notes of my cologne as though she's memorized it. Fuck, that's hot.

"You're right. Now tell me something you can taste."

She thinks for a second, a little more color returning to her cheeks. "Bourbon."

I can feel the tension easing out of her body as we sit there, her breathing slowly returning to normal as I grab her wrist again, checking her pulse. It's down but still high. "This is not the kind of pulse I thought I'd encounter in a club named Pulse."

She lightly chuckles as she releases another breath. Returning my hand to her waist, we stare at each other for a few beats as I continue miming for her to copy my deep breaths. She lowers her forehead to my chest as she wraps her arms around my neck. My arms band around her back as I pull her into an embrace. We sit on the bed, inhaling deeply as we cling to each other. Her nose rubs along the column of my neck. It brings me immeasurable joy to know that my smell calms her.

The room is silent except for our breathing when my voice pierces through the stillness, "I've got you, sweetheart. Keep breathing for me so I can get your heart rate back to normal, okay?"

She nods against my neck as I kiss along her hairline. Once I feel her arms start to relax their hold, I reach for her face and hold her cheeks in my palms. "How are you feeling? How can I help you?"

Blinking up at me, her pupils have returned to their normal size as she appears to be coming down from the rush of adrenaline that flooded her system. Her mouth opens and closes several times before she speaks, "How did you do that? How did you know I was having a panic attack and know what to do?"

"Lizzy has a lot of panic attacks," I say, stroking my thumb along the apple of her cheek.

"And you researched everything about them so you could help her?"

"I did. She had them quite frequently for many years. The breathing helps her the most, and so does grounding, but since she's nonverbal, I have to describe things for her to see, feel, smell, touch, and taste. Kind of like when I had you look at my eyes and dimple."

"I don't know what came over me."

"Do you have panic attacks often?"

"Not normally, but I've had a few. Most of them seem to be work-related. Seeing Mark must've triggered it. Thinking about losing everything I've worked so hard for scares me. I've spent my entire life trying to impress men like him so I could get ahead. If he sees me here, I'll be reduced to a sexual creature. I'll no longer be 'one of the guys.' If he doesn't respect me, I'll have given up everything for nothing. I can't..." Her breathing starts to pick up again.

"Shhh, just breathe," I soothe as I move one hand behind her neck and the other around her shoulders, pulling her into me. "You're safe with me. He's not here. He didn't see you," I say softly against her skin as I hold her tightly to me.

"Why are you holding on so hard?" she asks so quietly I almost miss it.

"Sorry." I loosen my grip on her.

She lets out a deep breath as she locks eyes with me. "I didn't mean that. I'm a mess. You deserve so much more than this, so much more than I can give you. You deserve someone who doesn't make you sneak around, someone who isn't worried what others think. Why are you holding on so hard to me?"

My heart stutters in my chest as the meaning of her words sinks in. "I'm holding on so hard because everything good in my life leaves, and you're the best thing that's ever happened to me. My bio mom split to chase her next high because I wasn't enough, my dad works all the time and there are too many of us fighting for his attention and I'm not enough to capture it, and while my Nonna didn't choose to leave, she was taken away from me and nothing I did for her was enough. Every adult in my life has left me because I wasn't enough. But with you, I feel like I'm enough. I've always felt like my purpose was to help others, but I've never felt more important than when I'm with you. If someone as beautiful and strong as you needed me? Fuck, I could do anything."

We sit there in silence, and I hope that the weight of my confession sinks into the depths of her heart. Several minutes pass before she speaks.

"I do need you. I didn't know how much I needed you until now, but it's more than that, Ethan. I want you. And that terrifies me. I've only ever wanted one person before, and when that ended, it fucked with me."

"I will do everything in my power to be everything you want, and I'm not going anywhere. I mean it when I say you're it for me," I say as I hold her face in my hands and kiss her forehead. "What do you need right now? I can go check to see if your boss is gone, and we can sneak out."

"No, it's fine. I just need to sit for a minute. Can you hold me?"

"I'll always do anything you ask of me."

We sit there in a private room of a sex club, her straddling my lap, while I hug her tightly, one hand around her waist while the other tangles in her hair at the nape of her neck. And there is nothing I'd rather be doing.

CHAPTER 27
Bridget

"SURE YOU'RE ready to meet my parents?" Ethan asks.

"I've already met your mom, and I really liked her."

"Yeah, she's great. The girls are excited to meet you, and I think you'll like my dad too. That's assuming he even makes it. There are always a lot of plumbing emergencies around Thanksgiving. One year, he got called out on a job that kept him out most of the day. Apparently, a toddler tried to flush half the turkey down the toilet and ended up clogging it so badly they needed a plumber to snake it, which led to a bigger issue they uncovered."

My eyes shoot to him in surprise. "Please, do tell me more about this disgusting toilet discovery while we prepare a lovely meal for your family," I say sarcastically.

"Suffice it to say, those flushable wipes aren't actually flushable, despite what the package may say. It was a costly repair involving digging up pipes in their front yard."

"Lovely. What is it with you and poop?"

"I only asked you once, and it was a valid part of your post-op care."

I can't help the laugh that pops out of me as he darts

around the island and grabs me from behind, lifting me in the air. "You enjoy fucking with me, don't you?"

"I can think of something I enjoy more, Pup."

He sets me down and slaps my ass, leaving an impressive sting before he rubs it in soothing circles. "First we cook, then we fuck." He reaches around me and pulls two aprons out of the drawer. He loops the strap around my neck before tying the strings around my waist and kissing my neck.

The kitchen feels warm and inviting when he's in it with me, and I've grown to love our time cooking together over the past few months. Ethan walks to his overnight bag and pulls out a small green plastic box. It looks worn and resembles something I'd once used in grade school to organize notecards for studying before I came up with my study guides.

"What's that?"

"This is probably the most valuable thing I own." He sets the box in front of me and gestures with his hands for me to open it. My hands glide along the cool granite of the island before clasping the box, its texture slightly bumpy in my hands. Small pieces of dried food and flour dot the surface of the box.

"For a chef, I figured this would be cleaner."

"That's part of the magic of what's inside."

Popping the lid open, my fingers trace over the rough edges of multiple note cards before settling on a random card near the middle of the box and pulling it out. "Peach cobbler," I announce.

"Number thirty-seven. That's a good one. It tastes better when you use fresh peaches. I prefer Red Haven, a variety of peach from Michigan. It's a sweet peach with very little fuzz. Nonna and I tried numerous other varieties, but Red Havens always made the best cobbler."

I glance at him in confusion, but he nods his head toward the card. I turn it over to see a small "37" written on the top left of the card. With the way I was holding it, there's no way he would've seen the number on the back. "Do you have all of these memorized?"

"I do. My Nonna is the one who taught me how to cook and encouraged me to go to culinary school, much to my dad's disapproval." I look at him curiously. "He didn't go to college, and I think he was hoping I would, but my dreams were elsewhere. Ever since Ashley brought Nonna into my life, cooking became my passion. We'd spend weekends making almost every recipe in that box, perfecting each one. For my eighteenth birthday, Nonna gave me her recipe box with every meal we'd ever prepared and a few more we'd never tried. She's the one who supported my cooking more than anyone else."

"That's incredible. It kind of feels serendipitous, in a way, to be standing here with this." I say, gesturing to the recipe box.

"How so?"

"Well, you do make my favorite meal, and I assume that's because of her."

His dimple is out on full display as his emerald eyes bore into mine. "It is."

"And now we're going to pick something from here to make together."

I continue flipping through the cards, struggling to find a rhyme or reason for how they are arranged. "Is there an organizational system here? My left brain is freaking out because there are desserts next to appetizers. I think my eye is starting to twitch."

The sound of Ethan's low laugh fills the room. It's deep and booming, small crinkles appearing around his eyes as he throws his head back, tremors rocking his body, shoulders heaving. "Fuck, I love—" Another laugh escapes his body, cutting him off.

For a second, I wonder if he's about to make a declaration, and in this moment, I decide that the way he could finish that sentence doesn't scare me. I try to maintain my composure. "I don't understand what's so funny."

Strong hands wipe at his eyes, the tears gathering on the pads of his fingers. "I just love how your mind works. How you're unabashedly... well, you." He sobers a bit as he stares at the box. "A part of my heart breaks every time I look at one of these notecards. Seeing Nonna's handwriting and smelling the weathered cards always gets to me. I'm half convinced that my tears are a secret ingredient at this point because it's hard not to be overwhelmed with grief when I use these cards. I usually don't have to pull them out that often since I have them all memorized now."

"Bullshit."

"Try me. Give me any number, one through two hundred eighty-six."

"One hundred ninety-one."

He lets out a small chuckle. "That one is a crockpot lasagna. She was so pissed at me. I think I was around fourteen, and I had so much going on with school. I was helping watch the girls in the afternoon, so I didn't have much time to cook and finish my homework by the time track practice was over. Ella was around eight, I think, and was super picky. All she wanted to eat was lasagna, but I didn't have time to make it, and she wouldn't eat it if it was frozen. Said that she could 'taste the ice crystals' or something, and I needed a lasagna recipe that wouldn't take me a lot of time. Nonna was born in Italy and thought cooking lasagna in a crockpot was a sin, especially because you could throw the uncooked boxed noodles in. She gave me so much shit."

He smiles briefly before clearing his throat and continuing, "It's the only Italian meal we ever prepared where she allowed me to use premade boxed noodles. Normally, we made our own from scratch. It wasn't half bad. I mean, nothing compares to her actual lasagna—number forty-three, in case you're wondering." I flip through the cards and grab number forty-three and blink, stunned that he can remember that. "But it was good, and Ella liked it. I'd throw everything in the crockpot before school, set it to low, and it'd be ready by dinner."

The shock on my face must be evident, so he nods to the box, and it feels like he's daring me to pick another one. "Number two hundred sixty-one."

"Oh, that's a good one. My buddy Maddox had invited me to a cookout, and I had the best potato salad I'd ever tasted. I came home and told Nonna all about it, and we tried so many variations to replicate it. Turns out it was an Amish potato salad that was sweet and tangy."

"That sounds delicious."

"It is." He grins at me, his dimple on full display. "Satisfied?" I nod slowly, in awe of this amazing man. "So, like I was saying, I usually can't look at these recipe cards without breaking down at some point because each one is a memory of a time with her that I'll never get back. But you healed me by simply being you, pulling me out of my head before I could spiral."

"How'd I do that?"

"Your fucking left brain. Of all the things you could've said or asked. You couldn't get over the lack of organization. I bet you want to go through this box and organize them, don't you?"

I can feel my face flush at his suggestion as I nod in agreement. That's exactly what I want to do, and it's bothering me that there isn't a system in place to organize them. How do you find what you need quickly? It doesn't seem efficient. His hand glides up my cheek, gently squeezing my face and pulling me out of my thoughts.

"They are organized chronologically based on when we first made each dish. She numbered each one on the back."

I flip the card in my hand, staring again at the small number before returning it to the box. My fingers move to the back of the box and pull out a card with the number three hundred on it. Holding it up to him, I ask, "I thought you said there were two hundred and eighty-six?"

"I told you to pick a number up to that. There are three hundred cards in there. We had planned to make the last fourteen recipes but never got the chance. Her cancer spread quicker than we'd anticipated, and she was bedridden the last several months of her life."

I place a hand on his chest, gaze into his eyes, and whisper, "I'm so sorry." I return the card to the box and withdraw another. Flipping it in my hand, I notice several marks on the back. "What are all the little tick marks?"

"That's how many times we made each recipe."

"And the stars on some of these?" I pull out another card, examining it closely.

"Those are secret recipes that only the two of us know. Each one of those has an ingredient missing from the instructions. Only she and I know what's missing and how to incorporate it."

"This is incredible. It's like a timeline of your relationship."

"It is. It's why I tear up when I see them, and all those memories come flooding back. It's also why I'm so grateful for the way your brain works and the levity you provide. The joy you bring to my life calms me. It provides a balance I never knew I needed, so thank you." He wraps me in his arms, kissing the top of my head as we stand there holding each other, our breathing becoming synchronized. And in this moment, it truly feels like he's part of me, that we are part of each other. Two souls destined to find one another despite our ages or backgrounds.

"Thank you for sharing this with me, for letting me be a part of this."

His hand snakes along my neck and fists my hair, touching me and holding me in place as his eyes bore into mine. His nose trails along my jaw, and I can feel his deep inhale as he murmurs in my ear. "Berries and vanilla, so fucking good."

Pulling back slightly, he guides my mouth to his in a bruising kiss. His tongue licks at the seam of my lips, and I open for him. Warmth pools in my core as he fills me with passion, his mouth taking while his tongue teases, giving me the pleasure I crave that only he can provide. Breaking the kiss, his other hand grabs my waist, squeezing and tickling as a loud laugh spills out of me.

"Ethan," I cry between laughs. "What are you doing?"

"Making a core memory by engaging every one of my senses. I want to burn this into my brain, this moment here with you. This is something I want to remember every fucking day for the rest of my life. The way you feel in my hands. The way your eyes light up. The incredible way you smell. The way you taste sweet and sensual. And the melodic way you laugh. Fuck, I can't get enough of you."

He presses his lips to mine again, and I can feel his hunger for me grow. His arms pull me in tighter as his hips start rocking against me, his erection becoming hard to ignore.

"I want you so bad right now," he growls in my ear as his tongue licks down my neck before stopping on that sweet spot where it meets my shoulder.

"First, we cook, then we fuck. Those were your words, were they not?" I practically moan as he sucks on that spot on my neck, pulling the sensitive flesh into his mouth hard before soothing it with a kiss. I pull back, giving him a playful swat on the chest. "You're not giving me a hickey the day before we see your family. I'm already freaking out about meeting them."

That fucking dimple has me backing down as he places tender kisses on my swollen lips. The way he smiles at me makes my chest tighten. "Mom can't stop talking about how great you are. She's been begging to meet us for lunch again. And my sisters are all going to love you. You have nothing to worry about."

"And your dad? Jesus Christ, he's going to think I'm some kind of cougar. Or sugar mama."

"I don't give a fuck if he does. I've made my way despite him. Hell, I've had to bail his ass out financially several times, and I've also watched the girls so he could pick up extra shifts. He knows I'm fully capable of taking care of myself financially. And the fact that I spend more nights over here than I do at my place has nothing to do with how much you make and more to do with privacy. Unless you prefer to go to my place where we can listen to Alyx have loud group sex through the thin apartment walls?"

"That might be kind of hot, actually."

"Does my hellcat need to go back to the sex club?"

"Maybe there's another one we can try? I'm not too keen on running into my CEO again. Thankfully, he didn't see me, or I don't think he did anyway. He hasn't acted any differently toward me at work."

"I can ask Alyx if he knows of any other clubs. But right now, I need you to decide what dish we're bringing tomorrow. And choose wisely. Whether or not they accept you hinges on what dish you pick."

Rolling my eyes, I pin him with a look.

"I'm only fucking with you. Seriously, they are going to love you. Lizzy's already made you a bracelet."

"She did?"

"Yup. She sent me a pic last night. You're one of us now." He winks.

The recipe box feels heavy in my hands, the decision weighing on me. I carefully flip through the cards as I read over each one, before stopping on the perfect dish. Pulling the card out, I proudly hold it up as I declare, "This one."

If I wasn't looking at him, I'd miss the way his forehead crinkles in worry. The movement is so brief, but I catch it, and it fills me with doubt. "Do you think someone else will be bringing sweet potato casserole?"

"No one else will be bringing that," he replies, his voice so low I almost don't hear him.

"What's wrong?" The despondent look on his face gives me pause.

"Nothing, I just haven't made that one in a long time."

"Aren't up to the challenge?" I try to shake him out of his sudden melancholy as he chews on his lips, a small furrow returning to his brow.

He straightens and blows out a long breath before turning to the oven to preset. Before I can say anything else, he's returning from the small pantry, his arms full of ingredients as he sets them down on the counter. The fact that he won't look at me and hasn't said anything has anxiety bubbling up in my chest, causing me to worry I've said the wrong thing. He just said he liked my teasing, but he's not bantering back now.

"Ethan, it's okay. We can make something else."

His movements still as he looks over at me. "Sorry, I…" His words trail off as his head drops, his arms leaning against the island for support. A smaller shudder racks his body before he straightens up and wipes his cheeks.

"Really, I can pick another one," I insist.

"I told you I would do anything you asked of me, and I want to do this with you, I promise. That one holds extra memories, and I just—fuck, I just need a minute. I promise you, I'm okay."

I grab his cheek and pull his head down to mine, gently kissing his forehead.

The warmth I felt against him fades as I move to the other end of the island, giving him space as I examine the card. It's card number five, one of the first, so it must be important to him if they've been making it that long. Based on the number of tick marks on the back, twenty-two, it must be a favorite. There's no star on this card, so it doesn't hold any secrets, but it's obvious it's well-loved by the way the ink is smeared and the edges of the card are bent. Flipping the card over, I examine the ingredients and start matching them up with what Ethan's piled onto the counter, but he interrupts me before I can finish.

"If you're looking for marshmallows, you aren't going to find them. Nonna didn't think marshmallows were fancy enough for the type of gourmet dishes she preferred. 'Marshmallows only belong in hot chocolate, s'mores, and Rice Krispie treats, and heaven help you if you need a recipe for any of those things,' she'd say."

I can't help but chuckle every time he does an impression of his Nonna. "You realize that you hunch your shoulders when you quote her? It's kind of adorable."

His cheeks turn pink, and he shakes his head, smiling to himself as if recalling a favorite memory.

"What can I do?" I ask, placing the card back in the box so it won't get dirty.

"First, we need to wash, peel, and cut the sweet potatoes," he says as he fills a pot with water and places it on the stove.

I move to the sink, bag in hand, and pull out a sweet potato to begin scrubbing. Ethan comes up behind me, setting a bowl to my left before he covers my hands with his, helping me wash the potato.

"This reminds me of that scene in *Ghost* when they make the pottery," I tell him. "Except we're washing potatoes, not making art."

"Some would argue that a good meal is art," he murmurs against my ear, nipping on the lobe before he turns away and melts butter in a pan on the stove.

"Your cooking is art, and I'll happily indulge in every creation," I promise as I continue scrubbing.

We finish our parts, me scrubbing, peeling, and chopping as Ethan completes the topping for the dish. It's a streusel-like concoction, and I lean over to smell it. "What's in this?"

"Butter, brown sugar, cinnamon, nutmeg, and flour. Then I

add chopped pecans," he explains as he turns to check the boiling potatoes. "Want to stir that for me?"

"Did you add bourbon to this? It has a little bit of a smoky flavor," I ask as my finger swipes the side of the bowl.

"I added a little in when melting the butter. Nonna swore it was for flavoring, but I'm convinced she liked to drink while we cooked. She would always sample the booze we added." He smiles to himself, reliving the memory in his head.

After draining the water, he dumps the potatoes into a bowl and mashes them with a fork. I'm mesmerized by his movements, his biceps and forearms flexing with each stroke of his hand.

"Eyes up here, Hellcat," he teases as he mixes the butter, brown sugar, nutmeg, and salt until they are fully incorporated before he folds in two eggs. "I also like to sprinkle a little cinnamon in to intensify the nutmeg. And then I add a little maple syrup to give it a warm, caramel flavor," he explains before turning to the counter and grabbing an orange. "But the real trick is a little orange zest to brighten up the flavor profile. The citrus flavor complements the sweetness of the potatoes." He shaves off the outer rind of the orange and stirs it in before scraping it into the pan and adding the topping.

"I feel like I was privy to some trade secrets here. Is that it?"

"Now it bakes for forty minutes."

"I don't have the card memorized like you, but I can check to see if you forgot any steps."

"No need, it's all up here." He taps the side of his head, flashing his dimple at me in a big grin as he gathers all the bowls and spoons to wash in the sink.

Together, we clean up our mess, him scrubbing and washing, me drying.

"There's something I want to prepare you for tomorrow," he begins, handing me a pot to dry.

Toweling the dish off, I set it on the counter. "What is it?"

"I told you Lizzy is autistic and nonverbal."

"Yes."

"I just want you to be prepared in case she doesn't react to you the way you're expecting."

"I appreciate that. I've been around children before, but I don't have a lot of experience with anyone on the spectrum. Is there anything I should know?" I ask, understanding how important this is to him.

"She has sensory issues, especially with loud noises. They tend to overwhelm her and can send her into a panic attack. While Lizzy prefers to spend a lot of time in her room, we're careful not to yell too much in the house so we don't trigger her. It's hard with that many people, especially when emotions run high, but she does have a pair of noise-canceling headphones that help."

"Good to know."

"Also, she has difficulty making and maintaining eye contact. I don't want you to think she's rude if she doesn't look at you or speak to you. It doesn't mean she doesn't like you."

"Got it. Is there anything I can do to make her comfortable?"

"Just be yourself around her. I've already told her a lot about you and shown her your picture, so she'll be prepared."

He leans in and kisses my temple as he hands me the last utensil to dry. Fuck, it's getting harder to keep these feelings for him inside, and I wonder if he knows already. His ability to read me is so profound it's as though he's deciphering a language only we understand.

CHAPTER 28

Ethan

THE CASEROLE IS COOLING on the counter, and all the dishes are put away in their designated places. The chaos of cooking is now contained, like a painter's studio after a masterpiece is finished.

"Are you saying I can call you my girlfriend?"

"Jesus Christ. You're exhausting."

"Yeah, but you like it when I wear you out." I notice how she shivers at my words and touch.

"We're not doing the girlfriend/boyfriend thing. It's juvenile. And despite your age, this is anything but juvenile."

I'm going to ignore that comment about my age. "What can I call you?"

"I'm yours. Does it need a title?"

"How is that going to work? 'Hi, Mom, Dad, I'd like you to meet Bridget. She's mine.'"

Her head falls back, a throaty laugh bubbling out of her. "Fuck no. That's ridiculous. It sounds like you're a dog pissing all over his property. Claiming me in the bedroom with a 'mine' is one thing. Saying it out loud to another adult sounds ludicrous."

"C'mon, Bridge, just say you'll be my girlfriend."

Immediately, her body tenses.

"I told you not to call me that."

"I'm sorry, I forgot about that. What is it about that nickname that shuts you down like this?" I reach down and tilt her chin up with my finger. Pushing the hair out of her face, I tenderly kiss her forehead, letting her know that she can trust me with all her broken pieces.

"I dated someone who called me that. That name reminds me of him, and I don't want to think about him or who I was back then."

"Can I ask what happened?" She shifts uncomfortably. My hands slide up to cup her cheeks, and I look into her eyes, deciding to take a different approach. "You don't have to tell me anything you don't want to, but you're amazing, you know that?"

The look in her eyes breaks me. I've never seen this woman cry, and I swear she's as close as she gets to it right now. "You've been so patient with me." I give her a moment to collect herself, knowing that this is important for her to get through.

"I haven't spoken his name in years. I fell in love with the boy I gave my virginity to in high school. He cheated on me, and the worst part is how I found out, from whispers in the hallway, people staring at me as I walked to class, and rumors circulating throughout the whole school. It was humiliating. I know why he chose her over me. I don't blame him for that. No one ever chooses me. But I couldn't stay there, so I transferred schools, and I vowed not to let relationships distract me from the goals I wanted to accomplish. He made me feel worthless, so I spent my life proving my value and I never wanted to let anyone in, only to have them strip me of my worth again."

"Is he the reason for all these walls?"

"Yes."

"I'm sorry, sweetheart. I'm sorry that my words reminded

you of that pain. I won't call you that again." I kiss the top of her head as my arms encircle her. She clings to me, and that embrace gives me life. Having this strong woman lean on me and share her pain with me, it's everything. "Thank you."

"For what?"

"I know you don't trust easily, and it means everything to me that you trust me with your pain. Your heartache. Your broken pieces don't scare me, and I'll collect them all if you allow me into your heart, because I know your worth. You're priceless, worth more to me than the most precious gemstone, and I promise I'll take better care of your heart than any man could."

"What makes you think that?" I see a hint of a smile curl on her lips. There she is. My feisty queen.

"Because I've already tamed the most carnal part of you. Now I want the rest of you. I want to be your calm in the storm, like you are for me. You're my shelter, my safe place, my home."

"Are you sure you're only twenty-two? You're wiser than most people I know who are twice your age."

"Keep deflecting with humor, and your ass will be sore tomorrow." I think about turning her cheeks pink with my hand. My cock twitches at the images it conjures in my head.

Her hands move down my back and grip my ass. "Is that a promise?"

"It is, sweetheart."

"How do you do that? How do you get me to open up? You make me feel things I've never felt with anyone before, and I can't wrap my head around it. You're so young. I shouldn't want you like this. I'm old enough to—"

"Fuck that noise. Seriously, fuck whoever told you that. I don't care how old you are. This thing between us is real. What I feel for you is real. Okay?"

"I think that I might..." she trails off, and my heart leaps out of my chest. We stand there holding each other for several minutes. Her mouth opens and shuts multiple times as if she's struggling to find the right words for her confession.

"You might what?"

Be cool, man. Don't push her too hard on this. Several beats of silence pass between us, and it feels like an eternity as I wait for her confession. Her words linger in the silence between us. I cup her cheeks and stare into her eyes, silently urging her to continue. Letting her know with my eyes that she's safe.

"I… I think…" I wait several heartbeats to see if she'll finish her thought.

When it's clear she won't continue, I ask, "Do you want to know what I think?"

"What?" I see the brief look of relief in her eyes. This is hard for her.

"I think I'm in deeper than you realize. No, I *know* I am. Every day, I fall for you more and more. With each piece of you that you share with me, my attraction grows, my affection magnifies, and my intention intensifies."

I gauge her reaction to my words. She isn't pulling away. She isn't running. She's standing in front of me, arms around my neck, clinging to me and my words.

"And what are your intentions?"

"To love you more than any man has before. To treat you like a queen and fuck you like the hellcat you are. To help you as you heal, as you grow. To be here when you need me and respect your space when you need distance. I'm not going anywhere. And it's okay if you aren't there yet. I'll be here when you're ready. I'll stand in front of you and protect you while fighting your battles. I'll follow behind you as you kick ass and take names, providing you with the backup you deserve but will refuse."

She laughs as a tear streaks down her cheek. I move my thumb to swipe it. "Don't mind that," she says, tilting her eyes to my tear-soaked thumb. "It's just the abundance of strength my eyes can no longer contain."

I kiss her cheek softly. "I love your strength. And I'll stand beside you as a partner, as your equal, because I fucking love you, Bridget. You're my partner. In crime. In life. In peace. And I need you to know that."

More tears spill over her lashes, her blue eyes becoming more vibrant as my palms cup her cheeks.

"I don't think I've ever seen anyone or anything more beautiful than you are right now, your strength leaking all over my fingers, your eyes so blue and full of hope. You're exquisite, and I'll happily call you mine. Or whatever you allow me."

"I don't know when or how you got in. But you're here." She moves my hand from her cheek to cover her heart, which is beating wildly in her chest. "In my heart. I know you think I'm not there yet, and while it may have taken me longer to get here, I promise you I'm with you. While my speech may not be as good as yours, I fucking love you too, Ethan."

I cannot kiss her fast enough. Our mouths crash together, a frenzy of lips, teeth, and tongues. She nips on my lower lip, knowing what it does to me as I scoop her in my arms bridal-style and take her back to our bedroom.

"Now be my good girl, Hellcat, and strip down," I command as I set her down next to the bed. "I want to worship my queen."

She stands and slowly removes her clothes, teasing me with the pace as she walks to the other side of the bed. I tear off my clothes and wait for her to approach me. The physical distance between us is torture now that I've finally bridged the gap in her emotional distance. "Get on your hands and knees and crawl to me," I order as I follow the jiggle of her tits as she moves toward me on the bed. She stops at the edge and sits back on her knees, looking up at me as if waiting for further instruction.

The thought that I can tame this hellcat, that only I can

provide her with the kind of pleasure she needs, awakens something inside of me.

"Lie back and show me that beautiful cunt," I demand as I follow her movements. She lowers herself to the bed and spreads her legs. Her juices drip down her pussy as I pull her ass closer and drop to my knees.

"This." I lick up the center of her pussy and swirl my tongue around her clit before grazing it with my teeth and thrusting my finger in to stroke her G-spot. "Is mine."

"Yours." Her voice is raspy.

Yanking her up to sit, my hand covers her heart. "This is mine too," I promise, my tone brooking no argument as I move my thumb to her clit, my finger still slowly pumping in and out of her.

She nods as her breathing picks up, her chest rising and falling with each breath.

"I need to hear you say it, sweetheart."

"My heart is yours. All of it. Only yours," she says on a shaky breath.

My hand clasps her neck as I pull her mouth to mine. "This is mine." I let my words sink in as I kiss different parts of her body and whisper, "Mine." Her neck, jaw, ear, shoulder, breasts. I move down her arms, her stomach, and legs.

The whole time I whisper my claim over her, my hand continues working her perfect cunt. I can tell the moment she's close when her back arches off the bed, and her moaning grows louder and higher in pitch. "Every inch of this beautiful body is mine."

"Oh fuck, fuck, Ethan, yes, yours, fuck," she moans as she coats my hand, the rush of slickness making my cock harden further.

Removing my hand from her heat, I suck my fingers into my mouth as I savor the taste of them. "Perfect," I groan as her eyes follow my every movement.

Her body is pliant as I stand between her legs and pull her against me.

"I can't get enough of you." I pick her up, her legs wrapping around my waist as I turn and sit, my cock nestled against her heat as her legs tighten around me. We sit there clinging to each other, our eyes locked.

With one arm around her waist, the other grabs her neck, pulling her lips to mine. This kiss is sensual and consuming. It isn't urgent or frantic. With each thrust of her tongue against mine, I can feel her walls falling. Her hands are grasping at my neck. My face. Down my back. It's as though she can't get me close enough.

Unlike every other time we are together, there's nothing rushed about our movements. Something has shifted, and we both can feel it. This is different. This is real.

Her soft, wet center grinds against my hard cock. I love the way her soft parts meet my hard, like we were made for each other.

With each kiss and squeeze of her hand on my body, she's making a promise to me without words. She may have finally made the verbal declaration, but her body has been telling me she loves me for weeks. Maybe longer.

She breaks the kiss, her lips brushing mine as she whispers, "I need you." Her grinding gets faster as I pull a nipple into my mouth, my hands on her ass guiding her movement. The warm palm of her hand connects with my cock as she guides it into her pussy, easing onto my length.

"Fuuuck," I groan against her as the feel of her pussy envelops my senses. Nothing else exists but the feel of her in my arms, her cunt swallowing my cock. After a few moments of bliss, I pull away from her mouth. "Condom?"

"I started the pill again. I stopped after surgery. Wanted to feel you bare against me. I don't want anything in between us anymore," she stutters out as my thrusts punctuate her words.

"Fuck yeah," I rasp as I pound into her tight heat while her hips make slow, steady circles, her clit rubbing against my pelvis.

Nothing has ever felt more perfect than this moment, making love to this flawless fucking woman. I burn the image of her body bouncing in my lap into my brain. The way she smells of berries and vanilla. Her little perfect gasps each time my cock hits that spot deep inside her. The curves of her breasts, as they press against my chest, feel so soft, the warmth of her skin heating mine. Pressing my lips to hers, her tongue dances against mine as the sweet taste of her devours my senses. I never want to forget this night for the rest of my life.

"Made for me," I whisper against her lips.

Our rhythm is steady and sensual as my climax builds quickly, surprising me. "Fuck, you feel so good. I'm not going to last," I grit out, my hand moving between us to find her clit. I need her to come with me.

"I'm close… oh fuck… right there. Yes!" After a few more thrusts while pinching her clit, her arms clasp tighter around my neck as she chants, "Ethan, fuck, fuck, fuck."

A guttural roar escapes my throat as I come inside her. My cock swells as hot spurts of cum fill her wet heat. I collapse back on the bed with her body pressed against mine, my cock still inside her. After our breathing evens out, she slides off to one side, a leg still slung over me.

"Do you think, one day, you'll let me claim you here?" I ask, curious to see how much of herself she's willing to give, as my hand slides up her ass cheeks.

"I don't know," she says. "Your dick is big—"

"Can't hear that enough." I grin, chuckling, the movement from my chest jiggling her tits against me.

"I enjoyed your finger there before, and that time you ate me out while I sucked you off… Fuck, your tongue was everywhere. That felt good—"

"Shit, you're making me hard again," I warn as I grip her thigh.

"Down, boy." I grind my length against the thigh draped over it. "But your finger is not a dick, so maybe that's something we work up to... with practice and toys?"

That's fair, and I want her to be completely comfortable with what we're doing. But her question at the end has my cock painfully hard at the thought. My fingers stroke up the inside of her thigh until I connect with her pussy. "You want me to fill your ass with a plug while I fuck this perfect cunt?" I pull her leg over my hip and thrust into her.

"Shit! Ethan, oh fuck!" she moans as I hold her leg in place, rolling onto my side as I push my cum deeper with each thrust.

"I told you, sweetheart, I'll do anything you ask of me. I'll fuck you however you want, wherever you want," I promise her, rutting into her, holding her in place by gripping her ass.

"Oh fuck... I'm coming... Fuuuck," she moans.

Her pussy clenches around me, and I pull out as she squirts her cum all over, soaking both of us. "Fuck, sweetheart, that was so fucking hot," I groan as I move down her body, trailing my tongue to clean her before pushing it into her cunt, lapping up all her sweet wetness. Her hands thread into my hair as she guides me up to her clit that's still pulsing against me. The taste of us combined in her pussy sends a bolt of lust straight to my cock, and I move my hand to pump my length.

"Shit, I'm still... fuck... so good." She trembles against me as I lean over her, my hand still stroking hard, my pace quickening.

Her eyes finally flutter open, and I'm not sure if it's my movements shaking the bed or the high she's coming down from, but I see the minute they connect with my cock and dilate, the ring of blue a mere sliver around her pupils.

"Where?" is all I can grit out as I concentrate on holding back the release that's on the verge of overtaking me.

"My tits, mark me, claim me."

"Fuuuck." That's all it takes for me to explode, painting her perfect tits and nipples with my cum.

I collapse onto the bed, one of my legs over hers, mirroring her earlier position on me as I lick up her chest, cleaning her.

"Come here," she begs before pulling my face to hers and kissing me with passion. Her tongue pushes against mine, licking at the taste of us on my tongue as my body melts against her.

"Made for me," she whispers like an answer to my prayers.

CHAPTER 29
Bridget

I SET the dish on the warming plate on the dining room table as Ethan moves behind me and helps me take off my coat, hanging it in the closet by the door. He places my purse in one of the chairs, and it feels like he's saving my seat.

"Where is everyone?" I ask as I look around. The house is cozy and inviting, and it's obvious kids live here. Artwork is framed on every wall, and the girls' school photos are hung in collages.

"Expecting a bigger fanfare for your arrival, my queen?" he teases in a mock bow.

"Jesus, stop that," I laugh.

"Mom's probably in the kitchen, and the girls are probably scattered in the basement or their rooms. I think Emma's coming later, but the other four should be around here. Like I mentioned yesterday, Dad's probably out on a call. We'll see if he actually joins us."

"OMG, is this her?" a feminine voice squeals.

I turn, and a petite blonde child with beautiful blue eyes peers up at me. "Hello."

"Hi, I'm Erin. Oh my gosh, you're pretty. Do you want to

play My Little Pony with me and Evie? She's five, and she's super annoying."

"Erin, be nice," Ethan warns.

"But sometimes she can be super annoying! She wants to play it the wrong way, and she's so bossy."

Ethan kneels so he's eye level with her. "Erin, we've talked about this. It's not nice to call someone bossy just because they know what they want or because they disagree with you. How would you feel if someone did that to you?"

"I would be mad. I'm sorry." She hangs her head as she speaks and pushes her toe into the carpet.

"It's okay, squirt," he says as he ruffles her hair. "How about you and Evie go play ponies in the basement? I want to introduce Bridget to your sisters and show her around the house first."

"Okay. It was nice to meet you." She smiles and throws her arms around my waist in a quick hug before running off.

Ethan grins at me. "She likes you. Not everyone gets an invite to the Pony Palace on the first meeting."

His words are oddly comforting, and I smile in response as he leads me up the stairs and down a hallway before stopping in front of a room. He knocks on the door and waits. Two knocks sound faintly from inside, and he opens the door.

Inside, the blinds are open and every light in the room is on. A girl sits at a table near the window, hunched over, her fingers digging through a container of beads. This must be Lizzy.

"Hey, Lizzy girl. Can I introduce you to someone?" Ethan calls, his voice even, his volume low.

Lizzy nods quickly as she continues working, her focus unchanging.

Ethan guides me to the table and pulls out the chair for me on Lizzy's right. He crosses behind her while trailing his hand along her shoulders as he settles into the chair on her left.

"Lizzy, I brought Bridget here to meet you." She nods as she continues working on her bracelet.

"Hi, Lizzy, I've heard so much about you."

She reaches into her box of beads and pulls out a bracelet before balling it up in her fist and holding it out in front of me. I stare at her hand for several seconds, unsure what to do.

"She wants to give you something. Hold out your hand," Ethan clarifies.

With my hand palm up, I extend it out just as her hand opens, and the bracelet falls into it. She points her finger to her chest and then reaches out to tap against mine. She then points at Ethan, and his smile is warm and bright when I look at him.

"She's saying she made this for you and that she's thankful from the bottom of her heart."

"For what?" I ask, my attention directed at her.

Her eyes flick up and hold mine for a millisecond, and I'm struck by the beautiful blue hue before they look down at my hand, her finger urgently pointing to the bracelet. Holy shit, she looked at me. I glance over at Ethan, and he beams back at me.

"She likes you," he encourages, fully understanding the importance of this moment.

Turning the bracelet over in my hand, I examine it closely. It's beautiful. There are blues and purples, some glass are almost crystalline. And there are a series of numbers, each separated by a heart.

"This is gorgeous. What do the numbers mean?"

Lizzy points at Ethan and then me before clasping her hands together.

I read out the numbers. "Six, seventeen, fifteen."

"That's my birthday, the night we met, and your birthday," Ethan explains.

Something warms in my chest, and I swear I can feel the cracks in my heart heal from the love in this room, from these two souls that see value in me.

"This is incredible," I gush as I slip it on my wrist and look at Lizzy. "Thank you. I love it so much."

She lays her forearm in front of me, her palm up as she continues arranging beads with her left hand.

I look at Ethan in confusion, but he's already out of his seat and pulling something from her dresser. It resembles a sponge, and he reaches for Lizzy's hand. "Here, I've got it. Give me your arm," he gently commands, but she moves it from his reach, making several grunts as she thrusts it closer to me. He laughs and asks, "Are you sure?"

Her head nods enthusiastically as her left hand continues sorting beads.

"Here." He hands me the strange sponge, and I take it, unsure of what to do next. "It's a surgical brush. It's part of her sensory diet. When she gets overwhelmed emotionally, she likes physical touch to calm her down. It's called brushing therapy." He reaches across the table to offer me his arm. "You run the brush up and down her arm applying gentle pressure. Try it on me, and I'll let you know if it's too hard or soft."

The brush feels light in my hand as I run it up and down the corded muscle of his forearm.

"You can push a little harder," he coaxes as Lizzy grows impatient next to me, tapping her arm up and down as her leg bounces in a frantic rhythm. "You'll get your turn," he tells her as he runs his hand along her shoulder.

I run the brush up and down a little more as he gives me more direction. "That pressure is perfect. Now, you want to move it around in a random pattern, never rubbing one area too long. She likes it best when you change up the pattern."

Taking a few more practice swipes on him, I grow confident in my strokes before I turn to Lizzy and move the sponge along her skin. As I apply light pressure to my swirls and strokes, her leg slowly calms its manic bouncing and a small noise escapes her throat.

"She likes it. You're doing great," Ethan praises as I continue my movements.

There's a knock on the door, and Lizzy turns her head slightly before knocking twice on the table. My brows knit in question as I make eye contact with Ethan. "Two knocks mean 'come in,'" he says right as a tiny child bounds into the room. Lizzy pulls her arms back, and I set the brush on the table, turning my attention to the ball of energy that must be Ethan's youngest sister.

"Mom needs you in da kitchen, Finn."

"Finn?" I mouth at him.

"Tell her I'll be right there. Thanks, Evie."

"Is dis your girlfriend?" she asks, carefully sounding out the word, the Rs coming out more like Ws.

His bright green eyes look at me, and I wonder if this is why he mentioned titles last night.

Before he can answer, I stand and go over to her. "I'm his girlfriend. You must be Evie."

She beams. "Dat's me."

Before I can say another word, she tears out of the room, leaving the door open behind her, chanting, "Finn's got a girlfriend, Finn's got a girlfriend, Finn's got a girlfriend!"

He stands and walks to the dresser, pulling out a small timer with what looks like a clock face. "Lizzy, I'm going to set a twenty-minute timer for you. When it goes off, clean up your beads, wash your hands, and come down for dinner, okay?"

She grunts and points to her right at a pair of headphones on her bed. Ethan hands them to her before placing his hand on my back as he escorts me out of the room.

"Evie has trouble with some of her consonant sounds, and when she was a toddler, Ethan came out as 'Ee-fin.' I didn't want to correct her, so the nickname stuck," he explains as we walk down the stairs.

"That's adorable. You're so good with all of them," I say,

sounding positive, but deep down, my gut is churning with anxiety.

He's *too* good with them. He seems like he was born to be a father. How could he not want children of his own one day? What if he's telling me he doesn't want them because I don't? I know he said he doesn't want kids and he won't change his mind, but what if it all was a lie?

At the bottom of the stairs, he grabs my hand, turning me toward him. "I can feel your anxiety. I know this is new to you, not having a big family or siblings of your own, and they can be a lot. But I promise you, while I love them so much, I don't want any of my own." He pulls me into him and rubs my back.

"Stop reading my mind," I joke nervously.

"Did you notice I did the same with Lizzy? I've had a lot of practice reading thoughts," he says. "You start blinking more rapidly when you're having overwhelming thoughts. Your body also stiffens, and you're more tense under my touch. But I've found that touching you calms you down," he says, whispering the last part in my ear as he tilts my head, planting a soft kiss on my lips.

"Gross. No one wants to see you suck face, Ethan," a voice calls out from the living room, and I pull back from him, my cheeks pink with embarrassment.

"Leave them alone, Ella," Ashley calls out from the kitchen.

"Don't encourage them, Mom," Ella quips back.

"Yeah, definitely could do without this. No kids, I promise," he mutters in my ear as he clasps my hand and leads me to the living room to introduce me to another sister.

"Bridget, this is Ella, my extremely opinionated teenage sister," he says in a way only a brother can.

"Nice to meet you. Ooh, you do have great skin," she blurts before turning on her big brother. "Look, bro, I'll cockblock you all I want after you ran Chad off the other night." She looks back at me and offers a quick "No offense."

"None taken. Sorry about Chad, but based on the name alone, I'd say he did you a favor."

Ethan lets out a laugh that rolls through his body, like a ripple spreading across a calm lake.

"I like her." She grins at me. "I take back the cockblock, but if you're gonna make out, don't do it around me," she adds, making a gagging face.

"Ella, can you let Erin and Evie know that we're going to eat soon and to start cleaning up?" Ashley calls.

"Ugh, they're not going to listen to me, but I'll try," she agrees as she stomps off toward the basement muttering, "This will be minutes of my life that I'll never get back."

"Ethan, come here!" Ashley exclaims from the dining room, and we walk over as she points to our casserole on the table. "Is this what I think it is?"

"It is." I can feel Ethan's gaze as he wraps his arm around me and pulls me against him. "Bridget helped me make it," he tells her as he kisses the side of my head.

I blush as my eyes connect with Ashley's.

"Ethan makes the best sweet potato casserole." Ashley has tears in her eyes. "He hasn't made it since he graduated from high school, and then my mom passed last year and I figured the dish died with her. No one makes it better than him, aside from my mom, and only the two of them know the secret recipe. The girls and I have never been able to replicate it. And he's refused to make it since she's been gone. I wasn't sure if he would ever make it again."

I turn to stare at him. He did this for me. He put aside his grief and shared a sacred ritual with me. One he never intended to repeat. One he only shared with his family. "But that card didn't have a star on it. You said the ones with stars had secret ingredients." I turn to examine his face, confusion marring my features. He shrugs nonchalantly, stuffing his hands in his pockets like it's not a big deal. But it's a huge fucking deal. It's everything. "Thank you."

MYA MORE

I throw myself into his arms, not caring who's watching. This man has let me all the way in, given me every piece of himself. I'm not sure what I did to deserve it, but I'll do everything in my power to return that love and trust.

"I love you," he says as he presses a kiss atop my head, his arms wrapping around me.

"I love you too," I reply, looking up into his deep green eyes.

I hear a door open and shut from somewhere in the direction of the kitchen. "Ethan! You made it!" a deep voice booms.

The blood freezes in my body. No, it can't be.

I know that voice.

I turn in Ethan's arms as I come face to face with his father.

Ashley starts with introductions. "Hank, this is…"

"Bridge." An uncomfortable silence permeates the air.

Ethan stiffens behind me as he growls an almost inaudible "Mine." In any other situation, I would laugh at the absurdity of it, but at this moment, all humor has left me as I stare into the blue eyes of the man who took my virginity and broke my heart.

The reason I moved schools.

The reason I don't date.

The reason I don't trust men.

Ethan's arms tighten around my waist. He knows I'm going to run. His ability to read my intentions now feels like a lead weight holding me down. "It was him?" I can feel his hot breath against my ear. "My father?" His voice cracks, and I can hear the hurt, feel it to the depths of my soul.

"Henry." His name is a full sentence on my tongue. A lifetime of running. Of brokenness. Of hiding emotions.

"Fuck, no one's called me that since high school." He laughs, the sound foreign in my ears as my heart hammers in my chest. "I go by Hank now. What are you doing here?" His eyes flick down to Ethan's arms around my waist, and I see the realization hit him.

"Have you two already met?" Ashley asks, confusion all over her face as her eyes dart between me and Henry.

"You could say that," Ethan mutters behind me.

"Oh shit!" My hands fly to my mouth as it suddenly hits me who Ethan is. I was so blinded by seeing my cheating ex. Floored that he's the father of the man I love. And now devastated at the realization that Ethan is the product of the affair that destroyed me.

Bile rises in my throat as I attempt to pry myself out of Ethan's embrace. I can't be here. "I need some air. Excuse me," I choke out as I grab my purse from the chair and stumble toward the door. Throwing it open, I sprint outside, not caring that I left my jacket. My entire world is crashing around me, like an avalanche burying everything in its path.

Faintly, I can hear someone, probably Ethan, shouting my name. My feet can't move fast enough as I run down the sidewalk while digging in my purse for my phone. I need to get away from here. From him, from them, from everyone. Away from the man I am hopelessly and foolishly in love with—my ex's son.

CHAPTER 30

Ethan

"FUCK!" I shout, as my mom and dad join me on the porch as Bridget's silhouette vanishes from sight.

"Can someone please explain to me what is going on? Is Bridget okay?" my stepmom yells, but all I can see is red as I spin around and stare down my father.

"Ashley, honey, Bridge is—"

"Don't!" I yell at my father, my volume louder than intended, as I cross to him in three steps. Getting close to his face, I jab my finger into his chest. "Don't you dare call her 'Bridge' or say her name to me. She told me what you did. Do you know how much you fucked with her emotionally? She had to change schools because of what you and Monica did. Am I the reason you broke up? Am I the reason she lost all her friends?"

"Ethan, calm down. Let me explain."

"What is there to explain? You cheated on her with Monica. And guess what happened after that? Me! Nine months later, you paid for those choices."

"Is that what you think I did?"

"I know that's what you did. She told me. She fell for you, and you cheated on her. And now I'm in love with her, and somehow you've fucked that up too." I spit the words like venom, and my aim hits its mark as his face appears crestfallen.

"Oh my gosh!" My stepmom takes a step toward me and places her hand on my shoulder. "Ethan, are you saying that—"

"Dad and I fell in love with the same girl? You're goddamn right I am."

I don't care if I've made this awkward for him. But the second I see the hurt on my stepmom's face, I falter. "Mom, I'm sorry. Shit, I didn't think about how this would affect you." I cover her hand on my shoulder with mine and squeeze it.

"Honey, it's okay. I know your dad dated women before me. I know he's been in love before. I'm okay with that." Her eyes soften as her words wash over me, and her eyes dart between us. "What I'm not okay with is you letting this come between you two."

"How can it not? You saw her! She couldn't get out of here fast enough once she realized who he was." I turn toward my father. "Do you know that I can't even call her Bridge without her flinching? You did that. You." My finger presses into his chest again as he stumbles slightly, caught off guard by my outburst.

My stepmom cups my cheek, redirecting my attention back to her. "I wasn't talking about this coming between you and Bridget. I knew you were meant for each other the minute I saw that casserole. I'm talking about you and your father. He was your age once. He made some dumb decisions, we all have at some point, but you were never one of them." She looks between us and gestures to the kitchen. "You boys better work this out before we eat. I have some things to finish in the kitchen, and I'm not spending the rest of this holiday in awkward silence." She turns and walks into the house, closing the door behind her.

"I'm not staying." My tone is final, my words bitter as I spit them at my father.

"Son," he warns, shifting his weight while crossing his arms over his chest.

"Don't. I've spent the last few months, hell, the entire time I've known her, jumping over the walls you created around her heart. Do you know how hard that was? How much it took to break through her hurt and get her to trust me? And it's all because of you."

"You're right."

"And another thing, I... What?"

"You're right. I did hurt her. Deeply. And I've never gotten over how I treated her. I didn't intend to hurt her. But, fuck, I was a teenage boy. I spent more time than I care to admit letting my dick make decisions for me."

I shoot him a look. "If you think I want to hear about you fucking my girl, you're seriously delusional."

"Jesus, no. All I'm saying is that in my youth, I let the wrong head guide me more than I'd like to admit. I'm not trying to justify my actions or make excuses, but I did a lot of dumb shit I'm not proud of. But the minute I got Monica pregnant, my priorities changed. I was scared shitless. I was already a fuck-up in life, and I honestly have no idea why Bridget was with me. She deserved better. But I didn't want to fuck up being a father because one of those shitty choices I made gave me you. And I don't regret that."

A bit of the tightness in my chest eases at the sincerity of his words. "That's a shit apology."

"It's not an apology. I certainly owe Bridget one, and I'll own that. She didn't deserve that. But I wouldn't change my choices back then. I've never regretted having you."

His words sink in, and a bit of my anger lessens right as the front door swings open, and the sounds of Lizzy's meltdown reach us. Ella pokes her head out of the door and meets my gaze.

"Sorry to interrupt, but I think the yelling triggered Lizzy. She wasn't wearing her headphones when she came down."

Shit, I forgot about the timer I set.

"Ethan, can you help? You're always able to calm her down the quickest."

"Yeah, I'll be there in a minute," I promise as she slips inside. Of course she asked me. Dad has no clue how to help Lizzy and often upsets her more. I'm the one with all the fucking patience, but in this moment, it's dangerously thin.

Dad's stern gaze meets mine. "This isn't over, but we can talk later. Go help your sister."

"Yes, sir." I mockingly salute. I'm not one to let my anger get the best of me; I can normally rein it in, but I've never been more angry or panic-stricken in my life.

I can't fucking lose Bridget.

She's going to run. She literally just did. But if I don't get out of here soon, she may not be at the apartment when I get back.

I slide my phone out of my pocket and send her a text.

Sweetheart, I love you.

Please stay at the apartment.

I'll be there as soon as I can get out of here,
but Lizzy is having a meltdown.

Wait for me

Please

There's no reply and no dots bouncing. I pray that she hasn't already run, leaving my broken pieces behind.

CHAPTER 31

Bridget

ONCE THE CAR pulls up outside my apartment, I thank the driver and hurry inside like someone is chasing me. There's no telling what happened after I left. If Ethan ran out behind me, he could be minutes from showing up. Or maybe he chose to stay behind and be with his family.

The thought of him choosing them over me causes a tightness in my chest as my breathing picks up. I wouldn't be surprised if he stayed behind; it is Thanksgiving, after all. He should be with his family, and despite our recent confessions, I can never be family to him. He should choose them.

Besides, no one chooses me. His father didn't, so why would Ethan?

I can't fucking do this.

Tears start welling in my eyes as I enter my apartment, set my purse on the kitchen island, and stand there paralyzed, trying to calm my rising panic attack. There's a faint vibration from my purse, and I reach in to fumble around for the power button, not even looking at the screen as I shut it off. I throw my head back and let out one guttural scream, then swipe the tears from my face and try to compose myself. This is all I'll allow myself to feel as I shove these emotions into a neat little box in my heart. I can do this. I will do this.

How did I not see this? How did I not know they were related?

They have the same last name, but Black is a fairly common last name, like Jones or Smith. It didn't even occur to me. I know several people with that last name, and I didn't assume they were all related to Henry.

Hank.

Whatever the fuck he wants to be called now. Did Ethan ever call him by his first name to me, or just refer to him as 'Dad'?

Now that I know they're related, I guess I can see some small resemblances. But Ethan's eyes are nothing like Henry's, not in shape nor in the stunning green color. His perfect fucking mouth is uniquely his own, and Henry doesn't have that delicious dimple.

Thinking back to high school, I have little to no recollection of that time in my life after I found out he cheated. My brain went into self-preservation mode, saving me from the emotional trauma I endured. Not a single image of Monica, the other woman, Ethan's biological mother, comes to mind. He must share her features, but I have no clue. I can't remember if we'd ever met in high school.

I look around the apartment, unsure of what to do next. I can't stay here. There's nothing to stop him from showing up. He has a key that I gave him when he helped after my surgery, and even if I used the chain on the door, I'm not sure I'd be strong enough to turn him away if I saw him.

I move to the window and stare down at the street. After several minutes, I decide it's safe to take a shower. The need to rinse the day off me is too strong. There's not a door between me and the shower that isn't locked. I need to be sure that if he does come over, he can't find me when I'm the most vulnerable and naked.

Once the water heats up, I slip in and let it wash everything off my body.

My anger.

My heartache.

My grief.

All my fucking emotions.

I collapse onto the shower floor, crying until the water is cool on my skin and a shiver wracks my body. Peeling myself off the tile, I shut off the water. The apartment is silent as I carefully slip out, wrap a towel around myself, and walk to the sink.

The mirror taunts me with my reflection as I reach for my cleanser to finish the half-assed job I started in the shower. But my hand freezes as a pang of sadness stabs my chest. I can't even wash my face without thinking about him.

I hurry through my routine, giving thoroughness a big fuck you, before slipping into pajamas. According to the clock on my nightstand, it's been two hours since I got home. His parents live an hour outside the city, and I worry that he could show up soon.

Emerging from the cocoon of my bedroom, I'm no fucking butterfly. I feel like shit, and I look it too. I grab my phone from my purse, turn it on, and set it face down until the notifications stop buzzing. My thumb swipes up to clear everything, so I don't have to see what Ethan's texts say.

Scrolling until I find Becka, I decide it's time to fill her in on the shitshow that is my Thanksgiving.

> Turns out Ethan and I have more in common than orgasms.

BECKA

> Didn't we already establish this?

> Ethan is my ex's son. The one in high school who cheated on me.

And got someone pregnant?

Wait...

Holy shit!

Ethan is Henry's child?

> Yes, Ethan is Henry's son.
>
> He goes by Hank now.
>
> I guess it makes him feel like more of an adult than being called Henry.

Idgaf what he likes being called.

WTF?!?!

How are you handling this?

Where are you?

I assume you left his parents' house?

> You assumed correctly.

Come over. I have wine. And leftovers.

> I can't.

Oh no, you don't. If you aren't coming here, I'm coming to you.

You're not shutting me out. I know you.

> I can't do this, Becka.

Can't do what?

Talk to me?

Be with Ethan?

> All of it.
>
> It's too much.
>
> I'm not fine.

Babe, I get it. I mean, I don't, but I do.

I can't imagine how you feel right now.

But you're not alone.

I'm coming over.

With wine and ice cream.

> Don't.

He could show up any minute. I need to deal with him, and I need time to process. Raincheck?

Anything you need, babe.

I'm here for you.

I set my phone on the counter right as a knock sounds at the door. It's soft and timid, nothing like Becka's greetings, so it must be Ethan.

"Bridget, please, can we talk?" he speaks quietly through the door. I unfasten all the locks and open the door, his handsome face now holding a hollowed expression etched with despair. His green eyes are bloodshot and puffy, a stark contrast to their normally vibrant hue.

His features are drawn and slack, lacking the usual dimpled smile, and his once neatly styled hair now falls in disheveled tufts as though he's been tugging on it. The weight of his emotional turmoil is evident in every tremor of his voice and the slumped posture that makes him seem smaller than before.

The heartbreak on his face is too much to bear so I turn to the kitchen determined to busy my hands with a meaningless task so I don't have to face his hurt. I hear the door click behind him as he follows me.

"You've got to believe me, if I knew he was your ex, I wouldn't have brought you there. I wouldn't have put you through all of that." I see his hand reach out in my peripheral, so I move quickly around the counter to put distance between us.

There is truth in his words, but a thought nags me, and I blurt it out before I can stop myself. "But you wouldn't have kept dating me." Even though my back is turned, I can feel the wound I inflict on him.

"Hell yes, I would have stayed with you. I know this is a fucked-up situation, but it doesn't change how I feel about you," he vows, grabbing my hand and forcing me to face him.

He takes a step toward me, so I step back to keep distance between us as I pull my hand from his grasp.

"For fuck's sake, I lost my virginity to your dad. How is this *our* story? How do I explain that to people?" I shout, pulling at the strands of my damp hair, desperate to say anything that will create distance between us.

"Who says you have to? And who cares what other people think?"

"I do! I care!"

"I don't. I don't care who you lost your virginity to. I don't care about all the other men you've been with before me. Those experiences shaped you into who you are, and I love who you are. If everything hadn't happened the way it did, we might not be the people we are now. You might not have become the amazingly strong, independent woman I fell in love with, or maybe we'd never have crossed paths at all. I believe everything has to happen the way it did to make us who we are at this exact moment. And I don't give a fuck what anyone else thinks about that. It's just me and you."

287

Despite the sincerity in his eyes, I flinch. How can he not understand?

"As a woman, I don't have the luxury of not giving a fuck. I've tried, I really have, but I'm constantly reminded that everything I do is wrong or not enough. I have to put on a mask at work to be someone I'm not because if I show my true self, I'll never be enough. Even Becka only gets pieces of the real me.

"I'm so tired of being a version of myself to please someone else. Be the perfect daughter, the perfect student, the perfect friend, the perfect employee. Be the perfect girlfriend so he'll fall in love with you. I was so young when I lost my virginity, and it felt like I gave him every part of me, and he didn't want it. So I made sure that every guy who came after him only got the pieces of me that I was willing to give. That's why I don't do relationships. Because this is how they end. I break, and I get hurt." I will the welling tears to remain at bay. Crossing my arms over my chest, I stare him down, determination on my face. There's no way I'll give in.

"You don't think it kills me to see you hurt?" His deep voice is soft and soothing as he takes a step closer to me, his hands balling into fists at his side.

"The only person who has ever seen the real me is you. You came barging into my life demanding pieces of me. You said you'd never hurt me. And you didn't. But I am hurt. It feels like life has erected this unscalable wall between us, keeping us apart. This isn't love. It can't be. I can't be in love with my ex's son. I can't."

"But you are. And I'm in love with you. You don't get to choose who you love, and believe me, I get that this situation sucks. But even if I knew about your past with my dad, I'd still choose you. That first night with you, I knew. I knew there was something special between us, that there was something special about you. I'm not saying it was love at first sight, but I did fall in love with you quickly."

"But is it love? It can't be if it hurts like this." My arms squeeze tighter under my chest as I draw my body in on itself, trying to protect my heart from his declarations.

"I know it's real because of that pain," he says as he soothes a hand down my arm while crooking the other under my chin, forcing me to look up at him. Looking at him is too difficult. I'm not ready to face the truth in his words or the emotions he wears so openly.

My back hits the wall as I take another step out of his reach, throwing my hands out to ward him off. "It's not real. We were forced to be around each other when you stayed here for six weeks. Anyone would develop feelings in that situation. I feel affection for you because you took care of me when no one else could. I didn't fall in love with Henry's son. I didn't. That would be... messed up."

"It's so much fucking more than that for me. You need to know that." He steps into me, his hand on my hip, grounding me and forcing me to connect with him.

"I don't know that," I say as I push his hand off me and walk to the living room. "You're twenty-three. You don't know what you want. You don't know what love is. You're too young." The words feel hollow and wrong as they leave my mouth, but it's the only thing I can say to push him away and put that wall back up around my heart.

"Ahhh." He throws his head back and growls. "Enough with that shit. We both know that I have the emotional maturity of someone well beyond twenty-three. I had to learn to process my emotions in a healthier way because I had little sisters looking up to me who needed a parental figure since my dad was never around to do it his own goddamn self. But I'm a man with real emotions, and I've had enough of you throwing my age in my face as justification for what you think is your poor decision-making."

"Fuck you." I'm grasping at straws. I don't know how to

make him see that we can't do this. I cannot allow Henry, Hank, whatever the fuck his name is back into my life.

"We both know I'm good for you. We are good for each other. If we were the same age, you'd have no argument, so cut that shit out right now and fight with me like an adult who owns their shit. You chose to be with me. We've had months together, and I fall harder and deeper every day."

"Fuck—"

"You, yeah, you said that. You hide behind all these walls, but I know the real you, so stop yielding to the pressures of society. I don't give a fuck what my dad thinks about us. I don't give a fuck what other people think about us being together. I only care about how you feel, about us, about me. You're my best friend, my home, the love of my fucking life, and I'm not throwing that away because you slept with my dad in high school. He's not part of this relationship. I'll fight for you every day to prove that this is real. That what I feel for you *is* real."

With every word, he steps closer to me, closing the distance I put between us until he's inches from me, his hand cupping my cheek as he rests his forehead against mine.

"I can't do this with you," I rasp.

"What are you saying?"

Something cracks in my chest as I push him away, taking another step back until I collide with one of the floor-to-ceiling windows. "I need time to process this. I need time to decide if this is what I want. I don't know if I can handle being with you if he's part of it."

"He's not part of this," he insists as he closes the distance between us and cages me against the window. "Please don't run. Don't shut me out." His pleas ghost against my skin as his face dips down, and his stubble grazes my cheek and neck. He kisses the spot where my neck meets my shoulder. "I love you."

His mouth hovers over my skin for several heartbeats,

waiting for me to return the words, but I can't. I can't say the words he needs, but I also can't watch his heart shatter from my silence. My lips press together as I close my eyes and turn away from him. "I think you should go back to your place for a while."

He tenses around me. "How long is a while?" His voice cracks with emotion.

"I don't know," I admit, still unable to look at him.

He places a gentle kiss on my exposed neck as he pushes back from the window and makes his way down the hall to my bedroom.

There's no light in his eyes when he emerges a few minutes later, bag in hand. "This isn't over," he states, but even he doesn't believe it. "I packed what I could, but I will be back when you're ready to talk again."

As he slips through the front door and the snick of it closing echoes through the space, I collapse onto the floor and release every emotion I've been holding in. My neat little box is broken, and not even I can fix it.

CHAPTER 32

Bridget

EXACTLY ONE WEEK LATER, I hug the throw pillow against my chest as Becka settles in next to me on the couch, spoon in hand.

"Here, try this." She shoves her spoon in my mouth quicker than I can consent to the frozen dairy being forced upon me.

"What the fuck?" I complain through a mouthful of ice cream.

"It's delicious, isn't it?"

"It's actually really good, but I would've liked a choice in the consumption. I can't place the flavor. What is it?" I question as I reach for the container to look at the label.

"It's my own concoction. I mix some peach Moscato into my vanilla for a boozy milkshake."

"Why the fuck do we keep meeting for coffee to chat when this is an option?"

"Fuck if I know." She shovels another spoonful into her mouth. "Oh, that's right, you're a workaholic with a busy schedule, and until recently, your nights were booked with a certain sous chef."

"Fuck. Hand it over. I'm going to need more if we're jumping into this."

"Can I tell you a story?"

"Anything to take my mind off of the shitshow that is my life."

"Robert is the only man I've ever been with. He was my college sweetheart, and we were young when we got married. I'm not the same person I was back then. I've changed, and so has he. I had to learn how to grow as a person while I was with someone else, and along with that came the very real possibility that while I was growing, we could grow apart. He's the only person I truly trust with my heart and my body, but lately I worry that I'm not enough for him."

I touch her shoulder in comfort as confusion etches her features. "This is new," she says.

"What is?" I ask curiously.

"You're touching me. Normally, I'm the one hugging you against your will."

Shit, she's right. I start to pull my hand back when hers covers it before I can retreat. "I like Ethan for you, Bridget. I've seen a transformation in you. You seem happier, more at ease, more yourself. I'm glad you let someone in."

"Fuck all good it did me when we can't be together."

"Who says you can't? As awkward as I'm sure this situation is, I doubt Ethan would walk away. But lemme guess, you did."

"I literally ran away from the house. I may have left my jacket there."

"Which one?"

"The black suede one."

"The biker one, with the belt?"

"Yeah."

"Fuck you, that's my jacket!"

"Oh shit, I forgot you let me borrow that."

"Yeah, well, it was like three years ago, and it looked better on you anyway. Now I guess it's Ashley's turn to enjoy it." She pushes my shoulder playfully, and I'm thankful for her ability to bring levity to any situation. "I got that jacket at a point in my life when I was still figuring out who I was as a wife and a mother. Maybe it came to you at a time when you needed it most, and now it can move on to bless some other broken individual."

"It's not a magical pair of pants that bonds us into a sisterhood, it's a jacket. And I doubt Ashley needs it. She's happily married to Hank," I say with an eye roll as I shove another serving of boozy ice cream into my mouth.

"Okay, tell me more about that."

"There's not much to tell. I've met her before, and she's lovely. Does it make me an asshole to say that she deserves better? They seem happy, but Henry—I mean, Hank—doesn't deserve someone as wonderful as her."

"Maybe that's your hurt talking?"

"Maybe. But how is it fair? Where the fuck is karma in all this? That asshole cheated on me, and yet he ends up with a wonderful wife, a bunch of kids, and a happy life. Why does he get happily ever after when I've been miserable because of him my whole life?"

Becka puts her ice cream down and looks me straight in the eye. "This might not be what you want to hear, but I think it's what you *need* to hear. Bridget, you aren't miserable because Hank cheated on you and broke your heart. You're miserable because you've held on to that hurt your entire life. You've let that hurt make decisions that it had no right making for you."

A sob bursts from my throat. "I don't know how to let it go," I cry. "How do I let it go?"

Becka wraps me up in a hug as I sob into the fabric of her shirt, staining it with my tears. "You choose yourself. Every day. All that hurt you feel means you lived. That you loved. But you have to learn from that pain and use it to help you grow. You experienced some traumatic shit in high school, finding out your ex cheated, knocked someone up, and none of your friends supported you. It's no wonder you have trust issues. But you used that pain as a weapon to keep others away, thinking it would protect you from any future pain. And the thing is, we weren't meant to live life alone. Why do you think I tried so hard to be your friend?"

I can't help but lash out. "So, you took pity on me because you saw I was alone and had no one else?"

"I'm gonna let that one go since I know you're hurting," she chides as her hand rubs up and down my back as if to soothe the monster my emotions have become. "I chose you because I could tell you needed a friend, and I wanted to be that for you. You make me laugh. You make me think. You're so fucking smart, and deep down, I knew you had a beautiful soul. Plus, you do my taxes," she says, making me laugh. "I always felt like we were soulmates. And before you get all weird on me thinking I'm about to profess romantic feelings for you, I believe that someone can have multiple soulmates, but not all soulmates are romantic types of love. And you're one of mine."

"I kind of like that," I say, pulling back and wiping my face.

"Of course you do. We're soulmates. And I also think that Ethan's soul is perfectly matched to yours in ways mine can't be. I hope you can talk this through with him. But no matter what happens, please don't shut the world out. I know you may not feel like it, but there are people in this world who love you and need you. Like me. I love you."

Her words remind me of something Ethan told me when he was staying with me after surgery, how he needed to tell the people in his life that they were loved. It feels like the universe sent me two souls to heal my broken pieces. Two reminders that I'm loved.

"I love you too," I whisper against her.

"Don't worry, I won't tell anyone." She chuckles into my hair. "Also, how long is this hug? Ready for me to let go?"

"No, but I need to." I release her.

"I do have one question for you that's been eating away at me since you texted."

Unsure where she's going with this, I take a shaky breath. "Okay?"

"How did you never put it together? You've been intimate with both of them. You're telling me there were no similarities?"

"I'm not comparing their dicks and bedroom moves with you. That's weird as fuck."

"Jeez, I'm not asking you to do that! But they have to look alike. That's all I'm saying. You never looked at Ethan and thought he looked familiar?"

"Honestly, no. Ethan must take after his biological mother. Hank has blue eyes and blond hair. It must be where all Ethan's sisters get their hair and eye color, but I'd never met them until that night. Now that I know who their dad is, I could see him in them, but not in Ethan. I'm sure I could find some similarities if I put them next to each other, but the thought of that..." I don't even want to try to compare the amazing man I'm in love with to the asshole that created him.

Becka nods in understanding. "So, what are you going to do?"

"I don't know. I don't see a way that we could be together. I can't let Hank back into my life. He's a reminder of my past—"

"He's a reminder of who you *were*, not who you *are*. You've grown so much since he last knew you. Hell, you've grown so much just since you met Ethan."

"But how would this even work? I'm not spending holidays around that man. I'm not sure if I'll ever be comfortable being around him, and even though he hasn't had the best relationship with his dad, Ethan shouldn't have to choose between us."

"For what it's worth, he'd choose you. I've seen the way he looks at you. Ethan loves you more than anything."

"But what if it's not enough?"

"The way he loves you is more than enough. How did you leave things with him?"

"He came by after I ran out, but I made him leave. He packed a bag, and I haven't talked to him since. He texts me every day, but I don't reply. I told him I needed some time, but I'm struggling to see a way past this."

"Take the time you need, but you should talk to him. Soon."

I sigh and lean back against the couch. My body aches, and my exhaustion threatens to consume me. It's amazing how deep emotions can wreak havoc on your body. It feels like I've had a hangover for a week straight.

Ethan's face appears when I close my eyes, and it comforts me more than it should.

CHAPTER 33
Ethan

Bridget, I love you and I'm gonna text you every day until you believe me. I know you need space, but I know we can get thru this.

Good morning, sweetheart. I miss waking up next to you.

Told my dad to fuck off today. I'm so fucking mad at him for the shit he did to you. I'm sorry. I wish I could be there holding you right now.

Got some cleanser and cream for my face today, couldn't remember the brand you use, but this shit isn't as good.

[selfie of my face with a puppy mask and pouty lips.] Your pup misses you.

Please, can we talk?

Let me know when you're ready to talk. I'm not going anywhere, you're it for me.

I love you so fucking much, Hellcat.

Gonna stop by your apartment tomorrow and pick up a few things. Be there around noon. Hope I see your gorgeous face.

Hey sweetheart, just left your place. I left your favorite in the fridge. I hope you're eating. The fridge looked pretty empty and Dre said you haven't been by the restaurant. Love you.

Not sure if you're getting these messages or not since they're not marked read. Please give me something to let me know you're okay. Bouncing dots, leave me on read, something please, sweetheart.

It's snowing and all I want to do is hold you on the couch and watch the Cobras game with you and feel you against me. Not cuddling, of course cuz you don't do that.

I miss you giving me shit, Hellcat. I love your confidence. Strong women are hot as fuck and you're the strongest woman I know.

Hope you're giving someone hell today, gorgeous, since it can't be me. I'm here when you're ready to talk. I love you.

CHAPTER 34

Bridget

IT'S BEEN two weeks since I asked Ethan for space, and my apartment doesn't feel the same since he left. Work has been a welcome distraction, and I've been pouring myself into end-of-year income and cash flow statements. It could be the stress, but I've been craving salty snacks like crazy, and I'm bloated from all the extra salt intake.

My emotions are all over the place. One minute I'm sobbing uncontrollably, and the next I'm ready to break shit, mad at the world for everything it's thrown at me. Why does he have to be related to that man? The one that broke me and changed the way I look at men.

Fuck, I need another snack. Padding into the kitchen, I rifle through the pantry like a rabid raccoon only to come up empty-handed. I slip on my winter boots and dig my keys out of my purse, but I can't find them. Emptying out the contents onto the counter, I scan the items for my keys when my eyes lock on something that makes bile rise in my stomach.

Fuck.

Doing some quick mental math, I come up short. No, no, no. This can't be right. The plastic crinkles between my fingers as I grip it tighter in my hand.

I can't do this. I don't want this. I just need some fucking pretzels, not an existential crisis as the world continues to fuck me over.

"Ahhh!" I angrily scream as I hurl the tampon across the room. It lands with a pathetic thump against the window before bouncing onto the floor.

I count to ten, focusing on my breathing, using all my senses like Ethan taught me. Fuck. Ethan. I could be carrying his child. A child he says he doesn't want but definitely deserves. And in this moment, I realize that if I am pregnant, I can't have an abortion; I couldn't do that to him. But could I keep a baby? No, that's not a life I want—but the thought of being tied to Ethan in a permanent way sparks hope in my chest.

I definitely don't want to be a mother, but imagining Ethan being forever connected to me because of another person fills me with more emotion than I know how to handle as tears slip down my cheeks.

"Ethan's soul is perfectly matched to yours in ways mine can't be."

Could Becka be right? Is that why the thought of keeping him overpowers my fear of potential motherhood?

I throw on my coat and wrap a scarf around my neck as I hurry out of my apartment and down to the street. The drug store is a few blocks away, and I need answers before I spiral out of control.

The cold December air nips at my exposed cheeks as I tug my scarf tighter. I'm so engrossed in my mission that I don't hear the person behind me.

"Bridge."

I spin around and come face to face with Henry. Hank. Whatever. "You don't get to call me that. You burned this bridge, Hank." I spit his name like venom. "You broke me. You don't get to use pet names with me anymore."

He throws his hands up in defense. "I'm sorry. I didn't mean anything by it."

"Fuck you. What are you even doing here?" I look around, trying to spot Ethan, because that can be the only reason Hank's here. "How do you know where I live?"

"I didn't."

"Did Ethan tell you?"

"He would never betray your trust like that. That one is as loyal as they come."

"Good to know the apple fell far from your tree," I retort as I absentmindedly rub my stomach.

"I deserve that."

"You didn't tell me how you got my address," I demand, unwilling to spend one more minute of my life catering to this man.

"I overheard Ethan talking to Ashley back when he was helping you after surgery. He said the girl he was seeing lived a block from his restaurant. I tried to google you, but I didn't find anything, so I figured I'd walk the blocks around his restaurant."

"You've been walking around his work, hoping to run into me?" I don't know whether I should feel flattered or stalked.

"He doesn't know I'm here."

"Why *are* you here?" I question, my eyes narrowing.

"I know I hurt you..." he begins.

"I gave you everything. Every piece of me. And you didn't deserve it."

"I didn't."

"And now I'm broken, feeling like I can't let anyone in, like I can't trust anyone. Because of you, I closed myself off so no one else could take from me what I wasn't willing to give."

He looks down for a moment before speaking again. "I'm so sorry I hurt you, that my choices caused you so much pain. I didn't think about how it would affect you, and I should have. I made a lot of shitty decisions in my life, and hurting you was one of them."

"I'm who I am despite what I went through, despite what you did to me. I gave you several firsts that you didn't deserve. But all Ethan did was give. His time. His understanding. His love. And somehow, you're still fucking with my love life over twenty years later."

"The bad decisions I made in my youth shouldn't steal your future joy. Despite how he came about, Ethan is one of the best decisions I've ever made, and I'm so incredibly proud of the man he's become. He deserves to be happy. At times, I feel like he raised me. I was a kid having a kid, and I had no clue what the fuck I was doing. But despite my shortcomings, he was a good kid and an even better man."

"How are you not bothered by all of this? I'm in love with your son, for fuck's sake."

"I'm not the same man since I fell in love with Ashley. She brings peace to my life. She grounds me and brings me joy in a way I've never known, even after all these years together. Everyone deserves a love like we have, especially you and Ethan. I've seen him grow since meeting you, and you pulled him out of his grief when none of us could. I'm not justifying my actions, but you and I weren't a good match for each other. We were kids with a lot of growing up to do. Even at twenty-three, Ethan is a better man than I was at that age."

"I can't believe you're standing here trying to convince me to stay with your son."

He laughs ruefully. "It's not my job to tell you what to do or how to feel, but he loves you. He doesn't deserve to pay for the sins of my youth. And neither do you. Maybe we were meant to go through what we did so I could raise the perfect man for you, even if I couldn't be it. Maybe that's how I atone. You don't have to trust me, just him. Don't punish him for the sins of his father."

The wind picks up, whipping my scarf around me as I stare

at him. His words cut me but have landed their mark. But I'll be damned if I ever give him credit for any of that.

"Just think about it. He loves you." He clamps a hand on my shoulder and squeezes it once before he walks away.

Since I'm also headed in that direction but don't want to walk after him, I stand there a minute and let his words sink in. I need to respond to Ethan. I can't go on ignoring him forever.

I blow out a breath, a cloud of water vapor rushing out of my mouth in the cold air as I turn and head to the drugstore.

The journey back to my apartment is a blur. I've never been more excited to take a test, and that's saying something since I was an excellent student.

Tapping my fingers on the counter, I lean over my vanity and stare at my reflection in the mirror. While I don't notice any changes in my appearance, it's obvious that the past couple of weeks have been weighing on me. There are bags under my eyes, and they're puffy from crying. The timer on my phone dings and I turn it off, bracing myself as I flip over the stick.

Negative.

When my period starts a few days later, I'm relieved, but also overcome with a feeling of melancholy when I realize I'm truly alone. There's nothing tying me to Ethan. No reason to reach out to him.

Fuck.

Lying on my bed with the heating pad pressed to my abdomen, I bury my face in my pillow and scream as I unleash every emotion I've contained over the past few weeks. Hell, over the past twenty years. A lifetime of hurtful words that nicked me come flooding through my thoughts, smashing all the pieces left of my heart.

"You're not good enough for a guy like Henry."

"He's having her baby, and you expect him to choose you? Why would he ever pick you over her?"

"Honey, you're too pretty to be a secretary."

"You'll never get ahead with an attitude like that, but I can make an exception for a body like yours."

"How can you not want kids?"

"You'd make a terrible mother anyway."

"Your son can take your personal belongings and wait for you in the waiting area."

"Aren't you too old for him?"

The only person who has ever quieted these thoughts in my head and soothed my rough edges is Ethan. I sob, afraid I may have fucked this up forever.

My phone screen lights up the room, and I lean over to read it, swiping at my face so I can make out the words through the bleariness. It's Ethan's daily text. I've yet to open the thread and read all his messages, but I've read most of each one as the notification appeared on my phone. I scroll through until I reach the last one.

PUP

Please talk to me, sweetheart. I love you.

How does he always know what I need, even when he can't see me? His ability to read me was always unnerving, but for once, it's the most comforting feeling in the world. The dots start bouncing, and I crack a smile for the first time in weeks.

Are you there? I can see you've read my messages now. Thank fuck. Are you okay? Can we talk?

Okay

My screen lights up with an incoming call, and I put it on speakerphone, since I don't have the strength to hold it to my ear.

"Bridget? Sweetheart, are you okay? Fuck, I've missed you

so much." His voice floods my senses, bringing up every emotion I've felt over the past few days.

"It's good to hear your voice," I croak out between sobs.

"Shit, are you crying? Are you at home? Can I come see you?" he says frantically, as if I'm something ephemeral he's trying desperately to hold on to.

"Tomorrow at two. We can talk then," I say before ending the call.

CHAPTER 35

Bridget

I HOLD the apartment door open as Ethan walks in. His gait doesn't have the confident swagger it used to, and it hurts wondering if it's because of me.

"We need to talk," I start as I motion for the couch.

"Fuck, that's never a good start," he says as he sits on the couch next to me. It isn't lost on me that he's sitting as close to me as he can without touching me.

"There's no easy way to say this—"

"Just rip the fucking Band-Aid off," he pleads.

Shit, he thinks I'm breaking up with him. I place a hand on his thigh. "A few days ago, I realized that I hadn't gotten my period and that I was a week late." His eyes connect with mine, and I don't see the emotions I expected to see there. I know he said he didn't want kids, but part of me was sure that the thought of me pregnant would make him happy—yet he's not smiling.

"The night before Thanksgiving," he says quietly. "But you were on birth control. Fuck!" he yells, anger lacing his words as he stands. I remain still, giving him space to process his feelings, completely understanding where he's coming from since I felt the same way when I found out.

"Shit, okay, we'll figure this out." He sits and turns to me with a look of determination as he squeezes my hand. "I'll support you, whatever you want to do."

"I'm not pregnant. It was a false alarm. Probably residual hormone issues from my remaining ovary or the hormones in the pill fucking with my system."

A look of relief washes over his face. "Thank fuck. Sorry, that sounds awful, but like I told you, I am not interested in having kids. We'd figure it out if you were pregnant, but I'm so thankful you're not."

"You really don't want to be a father?"

"I honestly don't. I kind of feel like an asshole for my reaction to the idea that you might be pregnant, though."

"You're not an asshole for not wanting kids." I laugh at the irony of my words.

"What's so funny?"

"I've never wanted kids, and I'm always made to feel like an asshole because of it. I never thought I'd be convincing you of the same thing I have difficulty believing for myself. Because everyone expects me to want to be a mom, but I absolutely don't want that."

"You're not an asshole."

"But I kind of am. Not because of the not wanting to be a mom thing, but because of how I've treated you. When I thought I was pregnant, I wasn't initially as terrified as I thought I would be. Since the day I met you, I've felt wanted and cherished. The more time we spent together, the more you made me feel loved and cared for, even when I didn't want it. Even when I felt I didn't deserve it."

"You deserve to be loved, Bridget. I'm sorry that you felt rejected by past boyfriends and friends. That was their problem, their insecurities. It was not a reflection of what you deserved. And I hate that you spent most of your life convincing yourself that you were the problem, that you didn't deserve happiness. Because the right person for you is worth the drama."

A tear trickles down my cheek as Ethan's thumb swipes it away. "It's still weird that the past boyfriend you're referring to is your father."

"Yeah, it didn't feel right to say 'I'm sorry my dad cheated on you and made you feel unworthy.' I'm still pissed at him. He fucked up, and you deserve better than how he treated you."

I blow out a deep breath, overwhelmed by my emotions and the weight of my confession. "I've never opened up like this to anyone before. It feels like my thoughts are scattered, and I'm all over the place, talking in circles, but bear with me while I get this all out.

"I spent a lot of time on my own trying to move past those feelings, thinking I could use men for sex and skip the relationship part. It served me for a while, but deep down, I was never truly happy. But you made me happy—you *make* me happy. And while I'm thankful I'm not pregnant, part of me was devastated. Because if I was pregnant, it meant that I'd be bound to you in an unbreakable way. It forced me to think about the future, and the thought of being tied to you forever gave me hope. And when I realized I might have lost that permanent connection to you, it hurt more than anything has.

"My love for you is bigger than my anger with him. Greater than my fear. Larger than my loneliness. It's crazy when you think about it. The way he hurt me and the way he raised you shaped us into the people we are. The pain he caused me could only be healed by you, and you never would've been able to do that if he hadn't raised you the way he did. It's as if you were made for me."

He moves his hand to my thigh, making small circles with his thumb as I continue, "I don't want to have a baby, but I want to be tied to you. I want you in my life like that. After Thanksgiving, I was in shock. I couldn't believe you were Henry's son and that I'd fallen in love with you. And then I was angry, feeling like I could never be with you because it meant having Henry in my life too, and I don't know if I can do that. And I won't ask you to break ties with him. All of that made me feel helpless. Mad that I couldn't have you, and looking for any way I could bargain with the universe so that we could be together. And after I missed my period, I felt depressed. I finally had to accept that I'd have to learn how to be happy without you."

Ethan leans in closer, and the scent of his cologne floods my senses, creating a visceral feeling in my brain. Sea salt, bergamot, citrus—it smells like him, like home.

"Fuck that. Why can't you have me? I want to be tied to you like that too. I've wanted that since the first night I met you. I know this stuff with my dad is complicated, but *he's* the complication. Not me. Not you. You and I are easy. We fit. We can figure out everything else together." His hands cup the sides of my face, pulling me into him as my arms wrap around his shoulders. "I love you more than anything in this world, Bridget. I'd choose you over anything else. Over anyone else. We can get through this. Please, sweetheart, say you'll try, please," he begs as he presses his forehead against mine.

I pull back and stare into his eyes, ready to bare my soul to another person. To *my* person. "You're my first. Not my first kiss or my first fuck, and not the first to utter those words. You're the first man in my life to show me what 'I love you' actually means. The first to make me feel like I am enough.

"You're the only person who has ever truly chosen me. And I pushed you away. I'm sorry it took me this long to see it. No one's ever put me first. Cared about me more than others, than themselves. The attention you gave me because of that was overwhelming. I didn't know what to do with it." His eyes fill with concern, and he releases his hold on my cheeks before I clasp his wrists, holding them in place to let him know that I need his soothing touch.

"Your father hurt me deeply. We were children, young and selfish. You said he'd always wanted a big family, which makes sense. He was following his heart."

"And his dick," Ethan interjects through clenched teeth. I smooth a hand on his cheek and continue.

"True, but I was selfish too. I had goals for my life, and I wasn't willing to put anyone ahead of them, not Henry, not anyone. Until you. I held on to that hurt and turned it into a shield to protect myself, but somewhere along the way, I was also using it as a weapon, pushing away person after person. I isolated myself, never truly letting anyone in for fear of getting hurt. And it wasn't just romantically. The number of friendships I have held at arm's length is larger than I care to admit. And I probably would've done it to Becka too, if she hadn't been so persistent. It's hard for me not to be that way.

"The first time I let someone into my heart, they betrayed me. And it wasn't just him. I lost so many friends after he cheated on me. No one wanted to be associated with me, and my friends picked his side which made me feel selfish for being upset. They said I should have been more understanding because they were having a baby together. As if creating a child justified him leaving me. It's another reason why I never wanted to have kids."

He kisses my forehead. "I'm not my father. It'll be a while before I can be around him. And it kills me that my existence changed the course of your life. That it made you never want to have children of your own. But in some fucked up way, it feels like it was supposed to happen this way. There is too much about us that just makes sense, too much that fits together so perfectly. Women my age can't accept that I don't want kids, but you accept it, even if you fought it at first. I came from a loud, big family, but I crave the kind of quiet life that you have. And if your quiet is ever too much, a quick visit with my family or friends will scratch that itch."

I pin him with a stern look. "It may be a long time before I feel comfortable around parts of your family. But I'm willing to try. I might need a free pass to escape if it's too much."

"You know I'd do anything for you, Hellcat. You're it for me. And never has anyone been a more perfect match for me sexually."

"No one's ever cared about all the little things that make me happy. You care about what kind of ice I like, and you not only listened to how I take my coffee, but you applied that knowledge to make it better. You went through my whole nighttime skincare routine, and you watched videos to pick up pointers to improve it because you knew it was important to me.

"You've shared parts of yourself with me that you've never given to anyone else. And you never tried to change me. Never made me feel like I wasn't good enough. You pay attention to all the little things that make me happy. You've put my happiness over your own like it was nothing. And it didn't hurt you. Didn't even break you. How do you do that? I'm willing to learn. Because over the past few weeks, I've figured out some things. I'm lonely when I'm not with you. I've never felt lonely when alone, until you. And I honestly care about your happiness. I want to know what kind of ice you prefer. What are all the little things that make you happy?"

"You make me happy," he says sporting a huge grin, his dimple making me smile.

"I don't want to be without you. I know I've done nothing but push you away. But you never flinched. You waited. You were patient and kind. I don't scare you, even though everything about this, everything about loving another person this much scares me. Being this vulnerable and open terrifies me. Being without you these past few weeks hurt more than anything I've ever experienced. It hurt more than losing any other relationship."

"You don't know how much I appreciate you sharing that with me, for letting me in and trusting me with your heart. I promise I'll take care of it because I choose you. Not the life you think I want. That's not what I want. I want you. All of you. All your broken pieces that you've hidden from the world. The parts of you that only I get to see. I'm more than happy with the life I've chosen. The life you've chosen. It's ours. I helped raise five sisters, and I'm sure my siblings will have more kids than that between them. I'm content only being an uncle. What I'm not okay with is not being your partner. You're my home, and I'm more than content with you as my family. You're everything I need. Just you. Your happiness is my happiness."

"I love you so fucking much, and I'm sorry it took me this long to let you in. Now shut the fuck up and kiss me. I'm done talking."

He pulls me in for a bruising kiss. It's passionate and desperate, both of us clawing at each other like we can't get close enough to each other as he pulls me to straddle his lap.

I don't know how we'll navigate everything, but I know we're better together.

Epilogue

One Month Later
Bridget

"ARE you ever going to fuck me in the kitchen?"

"I know you want me to say yes, but that's a hard pass for me, sweetheart."

"Why not?" I pout, sticking my lower lip out, knowing he can't resist it.

His eyes lock on my mouth as he slowly stalks over to where I'm leaning on the counter. Bracing an arm on either side of me, he licks at the seam of my mouth before sucking on my lower lip, and my panties instantly flood. This man has total control of my body.

"You know why. But I'll gladly fuck you on any other surface of this apartment."

"I thought dating a chef would mean endless banging on kitchen counters."

"Dating a chef isn't like what you read in romance books. I'm not going to risk you getting salmonella because I can't walk ten steps to the couch to fuck you. Plus, the cleanup required to make the surface fuckable is kind of a boner killer."

"Yes, chef," I say with a dejected sigh.

"Now *that*. That makes me fucking feral for you," he groans, licking a trail up my neck.

"Not feral enough to fuck me on the granite island," I pout as I playfully push him away and walk to the pantry to grab something.

"Sounds like someone needs to be tied down and spanked tonight."

"That can be arranged," I say as I return with his Nonna's recipe box. "But first, I have a surprise." I set the box on the counter.

Ethan hugs me from behind, his thick forearms encompassing my waist as he squeezes me, pressing soft kisses to my neck. "What's this?"

I turn in his embrace and look directly into his deep green eyes. "I want to cook the rest of your Nonna's recipes. With you. I figured we could do one a week?"

"Sweetheart, I would love that." He grabs my face in his hands and kisses me fiercely. When he pulls back, there's a hint of mischief in his eyes. "Let's do one a month. You know, really draw it out."

Prior to last month, the thought of that kind of commitment would've sent me running faster than a cheetah at top speed. But now? Now I feel at home for the first time in my life.

"Deal," I agree as he slants his lips over mine. The kiss is deep and passionate, filled with the promise of so much more.

"First we cook," he starts.

"Then we fuck," I finish as he kisses my forehead.

"I'm going to warn you, there's a reason why teenage Ethan skipped some of these, though my palate has changed so this might not be so bad. Which one should we start with?" he asks with an eagerness I haven't seen in months.

"Do we have ingredients for any of them? I'm not keen on trudging through the frozen tundra at the moment."

He opens the box, flipping through the cards quickly. "This zuppa toscana could work. We have everything for this one."

After our reunion, we spent most of the holiday season at my apartment. There was no way either of us were ready to be around his dad. Ethan still found ways to spend time with his sisters when his dad was working and was able to trade shifts at the restaurant so he could work lunch shifts and have his evenings off with me.

We had a small get-together at Becka and Robert's but mostly holed up at my place for the holidays. Fuck it—our place. Ethan's practically moved in, and we haven't spent a night apart in over a month.

A hand grips my waist, pulling me from my thoughts. "You wanna chop up the onions while I brown the sausage?"

"Is that a euphemism for anal?" I ask as I burst into laughter.

"I figured you'd make a dick joke, but I didn't expect you to go there." He barks out a laugh as we both dissolve into a fit of laughter.

Two hours later we've finished our meal and are side by side at the sink washing and drying our dishes in what has become an almost nightly routine.

"I'm really glad you suggested this. It means a lot to me that you want to cook with me, and Nonna, in a way. I think she would've liked you. It almost feels like she's here giving her blessing when we cook." He leans in and nips at my neck before kissing it.

"Maybe she is. It's nice to have someone's blessing from your family."

Ethan's hands still in the water and then he reaches over me to grab a towel. "You have the full blessing of my entire family. My mom loves you, and my sisters all think the world of you, especially Lizzy."

Blowing out a breath, I turn to face him. "I know. Ashley is great. We text every week. And I love your sisters."

"But?"

"But what happens when they find out about my past with Hank?"

"Who's going to tell them? And that was so long ago, it doesn't matter anymore. The only role he plays in your life is your partner's father. They don't have to know any specifics."

"What about Monica? Don't you think it'll be weird when she finds out her baby daddy's ex is dating her son?"

"I haven't spoken to her in years, and neither has my dad. I give no fucks about her opinion."

"What about aunts, uncles, cousins? I know your family is a big part of your life. And I..." I trail off as my breathing increases. I'm spiraling, I can feel it. What we have feels right, and I am terrified of losing it. Those few weeks I spent without Ethan were miserable, and the thought of a random family member's opinion undoing everything we've built is sending me into a panic attack.

"Breathe, sweetheart," he says, pulling me into him and wrapping me in his arms. "I would walk away from those relationships, family or not, before I would ever let that happen. You have me."

I blow out a breath and press my ear against his chest, letting the rhythm of his beating heart calm my nerves as my mind quiets, my brain finally catching up with the truths my heart realized months ago. I am exactly where I'm supposed to be.

Four months later
Bridget

The instructor says something to us in Italian, and it's a struggle to follow her directions. Ethan surprised me with a trip to Italy for my birthday and arranged a private cooking class with a teacher from his culinary school.

It's also been a year since we met, and I'm worried that

Ethan plans to propose to me on this trip. Every time he kneels or squats, I wander off or find something to distract myself. I love this man, but I'm not in a hurry to get married. He either thinks I'm neurotic or nuts at this point.

Ethan moves behind me and takes my hands in his helping me knead the dough. "Like this, Hellcat," he whispers into my ear as a bolt of arousal zips through me. There is nothing sexier than when he takes charge and bosses me around in the kitchen.

My hands are clammy, and I struggle to use the right amount of pressure. "Are you sure this counts as this month's recipe card? This doesn't feel like it has enough veggies to count."

"It's close enough. I remember skipping that card despite Nonna pushing it on me several times because I didn't like all the veggies on the pizza and Nonna insisted we had to make the card exactly like it said. She didn't do that with other recipes—we'd add shit all the time making up secret recipes— so I was convinced this recipe was her way of getting me to eat more veggies. Italians don't put a lot of toppings on their pizza, but I didn't find that out until I got to culinary school."

"But the card said veggie pizza, and this is orzo–"

"Pizza Ortolana. I'm counting it. We make our own rules," he says, kissing my neck before moving away to stretch his dough.

It's the last day of our trip and I'm enjoying my doppio on the balcony. We've spent the last several days relaxing by the pool or the beach, strolling the streets, or fucking. He gave me the exact vacation I mentioned during truth or dare.

"Mmm, I want more of this," Ethan says, coming up behind me as I lean against the rail of the balcony overlooking the water.

"More of what?"

"Days like this. Me and you, the views, no agenda."

"Me too," I agree, looking up at him and kissing his cheek.

"I have a surprise for you," Ethan says as he pulls me into the villa.

Fuck, this is it, he's going to propose.

Picking me up, he walks us into the kitchen and sets me down on the island, then drops onto his knees.

"What are you doing?" I ask with a tremble in my voice.

"Something you've wanted for a while now," he says as he lifts my shirt and spreads my legs. Pulling my thong to the side, he licks along my inner thigh up to my now-drenched pussy.

Pausing over my clit, his breath tickles me as he says, "You wanted me to fuck you in a kitchen. We aren't making any more meals in here before we leave, and we already paid a cleaning deposit for this place."

His words are music to my ears, and I let out a sigh of relief when I realize he isn't proposing but is finally giving me kitchen sex.

"Now be my good girl—"

"In Italian," I beg.

"Cazzo, donna," he says before descending on my pussy, holding me to the counter, and eating me with a fervor he's never shown, and this man has eaten me out a lot. My orgasm is all-consuming and hits quickly, drenching us both as I moan a string of curses.

"Hai un sapore così buono. Ora prendi il mio cazzo."

The intensity in his eyes is overwhelming as slips down his shorts and pulls out his cock. He rips off my panties and pushes into me, his thick cock filling me almost to the point of pain, a good pain that quickly morphs into pleasure. "Fuck, Ethan. Yes. So good," I moan.

"Fanculo, tesoro, ti amo così tanto."

"I love you," I moan, pulling him into a passionate kiss as

319

my pussy tightens around him, squeezing him as his movements turn erratic and he clings to me, whispering in Italian.

This is exactly what I want, a lifetime of passionate moments with this man.

One month later
Ethan

"Where are all the peas?" Bridget shouts from the kitchen.

"On my dick," I croak back with my legs propped up on the couch, frozen peas pressed against my crotch as I try to get comfortable.

It's been a month since we got back from Italy. While we had an amazing trip, I noticed Bridget's anxiety spiking quite a bit and realized she must have been worried I was going to propose. I know she loves me, but she is not the kind to rush into marriage, so I know I need to give her more time to come around to the idea. However, it was important to me that she knew how serious I was about her and our child-free life, so I got a vasectomy.

"Oh shit, was your appointment today?"

With Bridget preoccupied by another merger at work, I figured this was the perfect time to have it done since I wouldn't see much of her and wouldn't be distracted by thoughts of her perfect ass during recovery.

"Yup. Alyx took me. Gave me shit the whole time too."

"Lemme guess, endless jokes about you being neutered?"

"It doesn't help that you call me pup. I did flash him my balls after just to prove that they were still there. He did not appreciate that, but he shut up real quick."

"You two are too much." She laughs as she walks toward me, eyeing my makeshift ice pack. "We have many different options for ice, Pup, you didn't have to use all the peas." She leans over me, her head upside down, as she kisses my forehead.

"But this doesn't melt and make a mess," I say, readjusting it on my junk.

"When can we…" she trails off, her voice a little breathy.

"Don't, Hellcat. Don't use that voice on me right now," I warn.

"I don't know what you're talking about." She knows exactly what she's doing. "Just let me know if you've pooped yet," she jokes.

"You're never going to let me live that down, are you?" I groan. "I'm out of commission for about a week, which is why I planned this when you had a lot going on at work. Please don't give me a boner right now, I'm a little afraid of what might happen," I beg just as the doorbell rings.

"Saved by the bell." She moves to answer it, swaying her hips as she goes. I have to look away and push the peas tighter against the ache in my groin.

"Emma! It's so good to see you. Were we expecting you?" Bridget says as she pulls my oldest sibling into a quick hug, and then helps carry her bags into the kitchen.

"Ethan texted me saying he needed groceries," she offers, but there's a hint of sadness in my sister's normally chipper tone and my hackles rise.

"I'm the worst girlfriend ever," Bridget says as she moves around the kitchen putting items away. "I've been so consumed at work, I totally forgot his procedure was today."

A sob bursts from Emma's throat as she braces herself on the counter. I'm frustrated that moving is so uncomfortable right now and that I can't get to her, when I see Bridget pull her into a hug. Bridget is not very affectionate with anyone other than me, and it tugs at my heart to see how much she's grown since I first met her. I love this woman so goddamn much.

"Shhh, it's okay," Bridget soothes as Emma's grip tightens on her. "I promise I'll be a better girlfriend," she teases as her fingers comb through Emma's dirty blonde locks.

Emma's shoulders shake, and I can tell that Bridget's joke has eased some tension in her.

"What's going on, Emma?" I ask, wincing as I push myself to sitting and swing my legs to the floor, attempting to stand.

"Let's sit so he doesn't try to hurt himself," Bridget says as she ushers Emma onto the loveseat across from me.

"It's nothing. Shoot, I'm sorry," Emma sobs, wiping at her tears.

Bridget's eyes connect with mine in a knowing look. "How about you hang with us tonight? We're making migas from Nonna's recipe cards. I'd never heard of it before, but Ethan showed me the ingredients, and it sounded delicious, like a Tex-Mex scramble. I'm assuming those groceries are the ingredients Ethan asked you to pick up for him?"

Emma nods as she continues swiping at her face.

"Then it's settled. You and I will cook while Ethan bosses us around."

"He's good at being bossy," Emma says as a hint of a smile crosses her lips.

"And maybe after we can pop on some face masks and watch a movie?" Bridget offers.

"Only if Ethan wears one too," my sister agrees, smirking at me.

"Oh, he always wears one," Bridget assures her.

"I do. We have a whole get-unready-with-me routine. I'll even let you film me doing it if you want."

It's clear something is going on with my sister, and while she might not be ready to share, she knows we'll be here when she's ready to talk.

Five Months Later
Bridget

"Such a good fucking girl," he whisper-growls as he pushes his cock deeper into my throat.

After a year and a half of blow jobs, and a lot of practice, I'm finally able to take almost all of Ethan's cock, and I enjoy every second of turning him into a whimpering, whispering mess of a man.

It's actually adorable to see the way his eyes light up then immediately roll back in his head as soon as my lips touch his skin, like he almost can't believe this is real, that I'm real. And let me tell you what it does to my ego. I've always been a very sexual person, and after years of no-strings sex with men, I'm aware of the control I have over them when I'm between their knees. But Ethan is the first man to look at me with a reverent appreciation when I go down on him.

There's a knock on the door, and I pause my movements and let Ethan answer since I have a mouthful.

"Occupied," he grits out before cupping my cheek and tucking a loose strand of hair behind my ears.

"Hurry the fuck up, *son*," the voice bellows back as my eyes get wide and I look up at Ethan.

He cups my neck and pushes his cock deeper into my mouth as drool dribbles down my chin and tears prick my eyes.

"I'm coming, I'm coming," Ethan manages to say with a somewhat normal tone, but he grabs the sink behind me as I tug on his balls and run my finger further back. His breaths get shallow and quick before he is exploding in my mouth as I eagerly work to swallow every drop.

Ethan stuffs himself back in his pants and flushes the toilet, presumably to make it sound like he was using it, while I wash my hands. He nods to signal that he's going to leave first and I stand behind the door to wait for the all-clear.

"Hey, Dad. It's about time you showed up. We were supposed to meet thirty minutes ago," he says as he closes the door behind him. Hank reached out a few days ago to meet up with us.

"Bridget, you can come out too."

Shit. Is it possible to crawl into a hole and die of embarrassment? I thought I was too old to worry about getting caught by my boyfriend's parents. It's doubly worse that said parent is also my ex.

I slowly emerge into the hallway, and I can feel the blush heating my cheeks, but I refuse to speak first as Ethan wraps an arm around my waist and kisses my cheek.

"I'm not going to say anything about whatever you two were doing in there because you are two consenting adults," Hank starts before Ethan interjects.

"Damn right you're not. It's none of your business."

"Be that as it may, you are in my house."

"Waiting over thirty minutes for you. I was beginning to think you weren't going to show, and considering the way you treated my queen in the past, I'll be damned if I let her wait around only to be disappointed by you again, so I took matters into my own hands. I don't waste her time because it's precious to me. She's precious to me."

The flush on my cheeks deepens as my heart melts at his words. This man has proven that he will choose me time and time again. He has protected me while still letting me stand up for myself. But the fact that he's willing to call his dad out has my heart swelling in my chest.

The three of us stand there in awkward silence for a few beats as Ethan pulls me further into his side, his scent enveloping me and calming me.

"That's fair. I'm sorry," Hank says, breaking the silence. "Have you two eaten?"

"We had a pork roast earlier," Ethan says, flashing me a dimple as I remember the sweet moments we shared making Nonna's latest recipe card and the even steamier moments we shared after. "I think Bridget is more than satisfied."

"Ethan!" I bury my face in his chest as he wraps his arm around me, holding me in place. While I am aware that Ethan is making this into a pissing contest, there is something oddly sweet about the way he is letting his father know where he stands with me every chance he gets.

Hank clears his throat, and I can hear him shift, obviously uncomfortable. "I called you here tonight because I need your help."

Ethan's muscles stiffen under my touch. "What's going on? Is it serious? One of the girls?"

"No, it has nothing to do with them, or Ashley. Can we sit down and discuss this?"

"You're scaring me," Ethan says as he grips me tighter.

"No one is sick or dying. Jesus, I'm not good at this." Hank sighs as he runs a hand through his hair and grips the back of his neck, as we follow him to the living room. He has a laptop set up on the coffee table, and Ethan and I take a seat on the couch opposite him.

The tapping of keys fills the silence as we wait for Hank to explain himself. There's a look of desperation in his eyes as he turns the laptop around and gestures at it.

"What am I looking at?" Ethan asks, but as I stare at the screen, I immediately know where this is going.

"It's a P&L," I say, but Ethan's brows knit, his confusion evident. "Profit and loss statement," I elaborate.

"Luther is selling the business, and I want to buy him out, but I can't make sense of any of this. I want to know if I'm making a good financial decision."

"No, absolutely not. She's not doing this for you. She doesn't owe you anything," Ethan barks as he stands and points a finger at Hank.

I should be angry and tell him to fuck off. But his decision impacts several little girls I have grown to adore, and advising him would benefit them. I would never forgive myself if I could've helped him make a better decision that would set his daughters up with a more promising financial future. This is what I do; acquisitions are a considerable part of my job, and helping him would cost me very little, but the payout it would afford his family would be worth it.

"I'll help," I croak out, my voice barely above a whisper as Ethan turns to me and cradles my face in his hands.

"Are you sure, sweetheart? You don't have to do this."

"Helping with this is about more than him. He could spend more time with your sisters and set them up with a better financial future," I explain before turning to Hank. "That is, if Luther knew what he was doing with his books. I'll need more than just a P&L. Do you have tax returns, a cash flow statement, and a balance sheet? What about debts the company might have?"

He turns the computer around and clicks the mouse, pulling up the requested items as he motions me over.

"Did Luther say why he wanted to sell?" I ask as I sit next to him and scroll through the documents.

"Just that he had another opportunity come along, and he wanted to pursue that."

I click through all the financial documents and do some quick analysis. "Everything looks good. Expenses are low and the business is profitable, but there are a few debts to consider. You could mention those in negotiations. Based on his asking price, you could structure this as an asset sale, which would transfer everything over to you."

"Would you be willing to help me through this process as an advisor? I would pay you, of course."

I blow out a deep breath as I lock eyes with Ethan, and the warmth and love I see there encourages me. "I would be willing to discuss a business arrangement with you."

We spend the next few minutes mapping out a plan for the buyout, and while it's just a baby step, my chest warms at the thought that this is progress toward healing my hurt, and I'm optimistic about the implications for how this will impact my future with Ethan.

Three Months Later
Ethan

"I can't believe this is our last recipe card," Bridget sighs as she leans over to pop the chicken in the oven.

We've spent the last fourteen months cooking what's left of Nonna's recipe cards and in those months, Bridget's flourished and grown, finally letting all her walls down. We've never been closer, and I've never been happier. This woman pulled me out of my grief, and together we've healed ourselves and each other. And I don't want it to end.

"Actually, it's not," I retort as I swat her ass.

"Yes, it is, this is the last one," she says, flipping through Nonna's box until she pulls out the final card. Her brows furrow as she studies the ingredients on the card, and I see the confusion on her face when she realizes it's not the same chicken dish we made.

She follows my lead when cooking like a perfect sous chef, so I'm not surprised she hasn't looked at the recipe until now when she's used to me bossing her around.

I reach into my back pocket and pull out the new recipe card and hand it to her face down. As she brings it close to her face, I pull the box out of my pocket and drop to my knee right as she reads the name of the dish we've prepared.

"Marry me chicken?" she asks, and then her eyes lock with mine as she drops the card and covers her mouth with her hands.

"I want a lifetime of recipe cards with you, Hellcat," I tell her, taking her hand in mine. "Tonight's recipe was the first in a long list of new recipes I want to make with you."

"Ethan," she whispers as a tear caresses her cheek.

"You're my favorite book. Every chapter, every page, every fucking word of your story is a goddamn masterpiece, and I would be honored to be your person among the pages."

"The king to my queen," she offers.

"You're it for me, Bridget. There's not a chapter of my life that will ever feel complete if you're not in it. Our story was meant to be written together, and I would be the luckiest man alive if you agreed to be my wife. Will you marry me?"

"Hell yeah, Pup, I'll marry you," she says as I slip the ring on her finger and stand, pulling her into me before sealing my mouth over hers.

Two years ago, I was lost, not sure where my life was headed. I never would have imagined myself finding my soulmate in a dance club. Together, we've learned a lot about ourselves and each other, and I am thankful to have found my strength in Bridget. She is my home, my soulmate, and I can't wait to see what life has in store for us. Together.

Want to read more about what Bridget and Ethan were up to during those fourteen months?
https://dl.bookfunnel.com/px4znqiqbv

Acknowledgments

There are so many people that helped make this possible.

To my amazing editor, Sarah, at Lopt and Cropt! Thank you for your patience, encouragement, and feedback as I navigate this new and exciting journey! You turned my story into reality, and I will forever be grateful for your guidance!

Cass and Kelli, I couldn't have done this without you two. You believed in me and begged me to tell this story once I shared the idea. Thank you for your friendship and all the bracelets.

To all my beta readers, thank you for taking a chance on me. Your feedback was helpful and encouraging, and I appreciate you all so very much! And thank you, Chiara, for your help with the Italian.

To my romance-era ladies, Amanda, Bianca, and Layla, I am so thankful that fictional peens brought us together. Thank you for the laughs, encouragement, videos, and millions of voice memos. Your excitement for this story and these characters means more to me than you know! You have been my biggest cheerleaders and I will forever be thankful for you all. And Layla, if you've made it this far…Yay! You finally read my book!

To my work wife, Misty, I forgive you for skipping out on our mountain getaway because it allowed me to get the bulk of this book done. Thank you for your support, heifer! Next time, you're coming with me, and we will see bears!

Kerri, congrats! It's a book, and it's spelled K-E-R-R-I. You can keep the dreams coming if it means I get more ideas and not babies.

Heather, thank you for diving headfirst into this magical reading journey with me. Now hurry up and catch up to my chapter so we can talk all the theories, preferably kid-free, at a cabin in the mountains!

Tony, thank you for your unwavering interest in my story and for encouraging me to tell it. Everyone needs a Party Ken in their life, and I am so glad to have you in ours! I will look at cover models with you anytime!

Dave, I had to add a little mansplaining to bust your balls. Seriously, thank you for building us a beautiful deck full of big deck energy. It's become a place for me to write and find inspiration. I can't wait for my proper library!

KT, thank you for putting up with me and understanding that while we may have grown a lot since sixth grade, my perverted sense of humor has remained that of a thirteen-year-old boy. I find comfort in your friendship, the lugubriousness, and the jubilation. I'll never let go, Jack.

Chris, thank you for answering my never ending technical questions. I can feel your British eye roll from miles away, and it brings me joy.

Ashli, I love you, mama! Thank you for your encouragement and friendship. I will always want to play mermaids with you, even when I ghost you to write a book. Let's celebrate with tangy, fermented cream!

Thank you to all my work friends who encouraged me this past year when I said I wanted to write a book one day and listened to me talk about it nonstop. Darren, Brenton, Michael, Zach, Matt, Paula, Jessica, Britney, Envy, Jason, Albert, Kim, David, Danielle, and Blakely.

Shelly beans, seeeeeeeeeester, I love you. Thank you for letting me talk your ear off about romance books, even though I know you hate talking on the phone.

Jen, my Aries bestie, thank you for always keeping it real. I know this book is long. I hope you enjoy it anyway. Thank you for supporting me through this crazy dream!

To Sissy and Mimi, thank you for being part of my village! I could not function without you two. Love you!

Althea, we need to go to the park and let the children run around so I can tell you about my next book. I miss my PTO buddy. I need to hear all of your reactions to what happens next.

Katie, my favorite everything and nothing friend. We need to go shopping soon. Or to a craft fair. Or get lunch. Or have one of our late night talks where you try to stay awake on me and fail. Thank you for being a huge support and a great listener.

Aunt Sandy, thank you for encouraging me with my writing. Sorry, there are no dragons in this one!

To Adrian, Abby, Jenni, and Liz, thank you for letting me pick your author brains about indie publishing. I appreciate your patience with me and thank you for answering all my questions!

I'm sorry I skipped karaoke to write more chapters again, Anna! We will sing again soon and this time we'll nail the ending, for good.

Mom, I miss you every day. I wish you were here. You would be so proud, even if this isn't how a lady would behave. Surprise! I'm not a lady, but you knew that and you loved me anyway. Thank you for always choosing me and being my cheerleader. You are the wind beneath my wings.

To my husband, the love of my life, and my real-life forever book boyfriend. None of this would be possible without you. I'm thankful for this life we've built together, the family we've created, and the future still to come. Thank you for all the meals you make while I type away. Thank you for corralling the chaos so I can escape to my writing cave and create the stories in my mind. I love you 3000.

About the Author

Mya has always had a passion for storytelling and has a background in theatre, film, and education. She lives in the Midwest with her husband and children, working a nonromantic job by day while writing romance at night. Her books are contemporary romance with more love, more spice, and more HEAs. When she's not writing, she enjoys reading, singing karaoke, playing mermaids in the pool, and doing puzzles.

I love hearing from readers! Check out my socials below or email me at myamorewrites@gmail.com

www.authormyamore.com